W9-CEW-142

TIME FOR KIDS

ALMANAC 2007

with

FACT MONSTER™

Beth Rowen
EDITOR

Curtis Slepian
MANAGING EDITOR

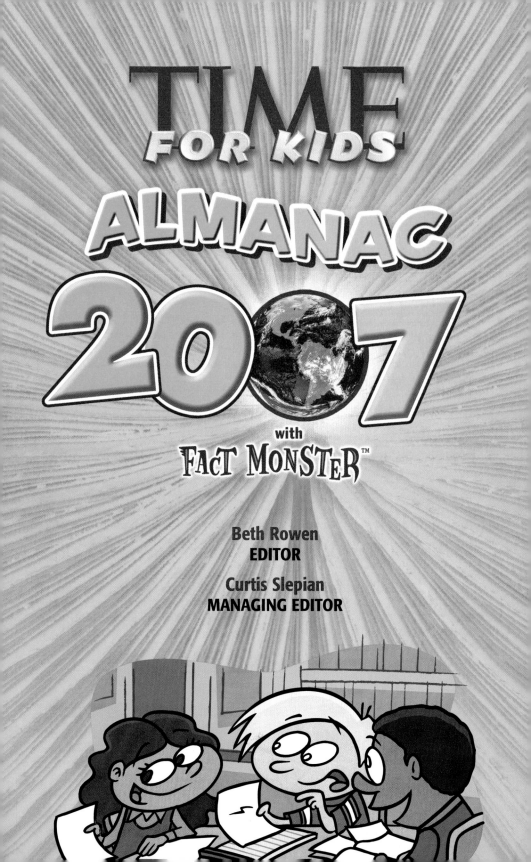

TIME FOR KIDS ALMANAC 2007
with FACT MONSTER

FACT MONSTER
EDITOR: **Beth Rowen**
CONTRIBUTORS: **Borgna Brunner, Christine Frantz, Holly Hartman, Shmuel Ross**
FACT-CHECKING AND PROOFREADING: **Christine Frantz, Shmuel Ross**
DESIGNER: **Sean Dessureau**
INDEXING: **Marilyn Rowland**
EDITORIAL DIRECTOR: **Borgna Brunner**

TIME FOR KIDS ALMANAC
MANAGING EDITOR: **Curtis Slepian**
COPY EDITOR: **Peter McGullam**
PHOTOGRAPHY EDITOR: **Bettina Stammen**
MAPS: **Joe Lertola**
ART DIRECTION AND DESIGN: **Georgia Rucker**
COVER DESIGN: **Rachel Smith/Georgia Rucker**

TIME INC. HOME ENTERTAINMENT
PUBLISHER: **Richard Fraiman**
EXECUTIVE DIRECTOR, MARKETING SERVICES: **Carol Pittard**
DIRECTOR, RETAIL & SPECIAL SALES: **Tom Mifsud**
MARKETING DIRECTOR, BRANDED BUSINESSES: **Swati Rao**
DIRECTOR, NEW PRODUCT DEVELOPMENT: **Peter Harper**
FINANCIAL DIRECTOR: **Steven Sandonato**
ASSISTANT GENERAL COUNSEL: **Dasha Smith Dwin**
PREPRESS MANAGER: **Emily Rabin**
BOOK PRODUCTION MANAGER: **Jonathan Polsky**
MARKETING MANAGER: **Kristin Treadway**
RETAIL MANAGER: **Bozena Bannett**
SPECIAL SALES MANAGER: **Ilene Schreider**
ASSOCIATE PREPRESS MANAGER: **Anne-Michelle Gallero**
ASSOCIATE MARKETING MANAGER: **Danielle Radano**

SPECIAL THANKS: **Alexandra Bliss, Glenn Buonocore, Suzanne Janso, Robert Marasco, Brooke McGuire, Chavaughn Raines, Adriana Tierno, Britney Williams**

SPECIAL THANKS TO IMAGING: **Patrick Dugan, Eddie Matros**

Published by TIME For Kids Books
Time Inc.
1271 Avenue of the Americas
New York, New York 10020

ISSN: 1534-5718
ISBN 10: 1-933405-33-3
ISBN 13: 978-1-933405-33-9

We welcome your comments and suggestions about TIME For Kids Books. Please write to us at:
TIME For Kids Books
Attention: Book Editors
P.O. Box 11016
Des Moines, IA 50336-1016

CONTENTS

Contents

5

WHO'S NEWS

Olympic Dreams

Courageous athletes, unexpected heroes and come-from-behind victories are hallmarks of the Olympics. The Winter Games in Turin, Italy, were no exception. Japan's Shizuka Arakawa skated flawlessly to win gold in figure skating, outperforming America's Sasha Cohen and Russia's Irina Slutskaya. It was Japan's first-ever Olympic figure-skating gold medal. Italy's Enrico Fabris also surprised people. The 24-year-old speedskating policeman won two gold medals and one bronze and captured the hearts of his countrymen.

Shizuka Arakawa

The Swedish men's and women's hockey teams did better than expected. The women won a silver medal, losing in the finals to the Canadian team. The men's team won the gold medal, beating Finland.

Hannah Teter

U.S. speedskater Shani Davis also made the Games special. In winning the 1,000-meter race, he broke barriers by becoming the first black athlete in Winter Olympics history to win an individual gold medal.

The performance of the American ski team was a surprise. American alpine racer Bode Miller was a pre-Olympic favorite, but he failed to win a medal in his five races. The one bright spot for the U.S. ski team was Ted Ligety's win in the combined slalom-downhill event.

Shani Davis

On the other hand, American snowboarders ruled. Hannah Teter, Seth Wescott and Shaun White nabbed gold in their events. White wowed spectators with consecutive 1,080s—three complete rotations in the air. Awesome, dude!

Who's News

go See photos from the Games and take our trivia challenge at timeforkids.com/olympics

Iraq's Woes Increase

U.S. and allied troops remained in Iraq in 2006, trying to prevent the country from slipping into full-scale civil war. In February insurgents bombed the golden dome atop the Shiites' most revered shrine in Iraq, the Askariya in Samarra. The bombings sparked deadly attacks between Shiites and Sunnis. More than a thousand people were killed in the violence. The fighting occurred while Iraqi leaders were struggling to form a coalition government.

As the situation grew worse in Iraq, support of the war and for President Bush's handling of the conflict decreased in the U.S. Politicians and citizens debated if, how and when the U.S. should withdraw from Iraq.

A bomb damaged the Golden Dome.

Nuclear Power Play

Over the past year, the war of words between the United States and Iran has heated up. "We will not allow Iran to have a nuclear weapon," said U.S. Vice President Dick Cheney.

President Mahmoud Ahmadinejad of Iran

develop nuclear energy for peaceful purposes only.

Iran's President Mahmoud Ahmadinejad insists that his country has the right to create nuclear energy

Nuclear energy is at the heart of the conflict with Iran, an oil-rich country in the Middle East. Nuclear energy can be used as a fuel source or can be turned into a powerful weapon. The Nuclear Nonproliferation Treaty of 1968 limits production of destructive atom bombs. By 2006, 187 countries, including Iran, had signed the treaty and vowed to

using enriched uranium. Although that does not violate the 1968 treaty, enriched uranium is a key ingredient of nuclear weapons.

The U.S. believes that Iran cannot be trusted and has urged the United Nations to review the case against Iran. The U.N. Security Council has the power to impose sanctions, or punishments.

A Civil Rights Champion Dies

Coretta Scott King, the widow of civil rights activist Martin Luther King Jr., died on January 31, 2006. She was 78 years old.

After her husband was assassinated in 1968, King dedicated her life to pursuing his dream of ending racism and poverty in America. Shortly after he died, she created the King Center, in Atlanta, Georgia, to promote her husband's vision of peace and justice for all people. King also led the effort to establish a national holiday in her husband's name.

The Reverend Jesse Jackson said this of King: "Like all great champions, she learned to function with pain and keep serving."

Coretta Scott King

go Hear Martin Luther King Jr.'s famous *I Have a Dream* speech at timeforkids.com/csking

President Bush watches Alito being sworn in as a Supreme Court Justice.

A New Justice Joins the Court

In 2006 Samuel A. Alito Jr. was sworn in as the 110th Justice of the U.S. Supreme Court. "He will make all Americans proud as a Justice on our highest court," said President George W. Bush.

Bush nominated Alito, 55, to succeed retiring Justice Sandra Day O'Connor. Alito joined the bench just months after the confirmation of a new Chief Justice, John G. Roberts Jr.

Alito was ready to take on the role of the nation's newest Justice. "I will do everything in my power to live up to the trust that has been placed in me," he said. Politicians as well as the public will be closely following the decisions made by the new Justices.

Rebuilding New Orleans

Parade floats and happy crowds filled the streets of New Orleans in March 2006. Six months after Hurricane Katrina devastated the city, partygoers were celebrating Mardi Gras. The yearly carnival gave the struggling city a rare chance to celebrate.

A construction crew repairs a levee.

But even as people danced in the streets, there was evidence of hardship around the city. Hundreds of thousands of people had lost their homes in the storm. Many of the city's neighborhoods were still empty. The population was only a third of the size of

O.P. Walker High is open.

New Orleans before the big storm.

Planners are hard at work trying to rebuild the city. Construction crews are working to make the levees, or floodwalls, stronger. The New Orleans school system must also be rebuilt. The State of Louisiana hopes to open schools that are much better than they were before Katrina. The people of New Orleans want the same for the rest of their city.

A Baseball Breakthrough

Effa Manley

Effa Manley made baseball history in 2006. For the first time, a woman was elected to the National Baseball Hall of Fame in Cooperstown, New York. Manley co-owned the Newark Eagles, a team in the Negro Leagues. The team from New Jersey won the Negro Leagues World Series in 1946. The Negro Leagues was formed because African American players were not allowed to play on the same field as white players. In 1947, Jackie Robinson broke baseball's color barrier. Robinson was the first African American to play in the Major Leagues.

Manley owned the Eagles with her husband, Abe. For more than 10 years, she ran the team's business operations. Manley was also a civil rights activist. She died in 1981 at the age of 84.

Tomb Raiders

In 2006 a major mummy discovery was made in Egypt. Archaeologists uncovered an ancient tomb in the Valley of the Kings outside Luxor, Egypt, at the bottom of a 33-foot-deep pit. A narrow shaft leads down to a tomb door made of stone blocks. Inside the tomb are five sarcophagi, or stone coffins, with mummies. One sarcophagus (sar-KA-fah-gus) has fallen and another is partly open, showing the brown cloth that covers the mummy inside. The sarcophagi have colorful funeral masks.

Archaeologists think the tomb is about 3,000 years old. They say it is the most important discovery of its kind since King Tutankhamen's tomb was unearthed in 1922!

At the bottom of the shaft, archaeologists found the lost tomb.

Icy material extends above Enceladus.

Water Wonderland

In 2006 spacecraft *Cassini* made what appears to be a major discovery. The spacecraft snapped pictures of what look like water geysers on one of Saturn's moons, Enceladus (en-SELL-ah-dus).

The source of Enceladus's water is thought to be underground, in reservoirs that are under extreme pressure. This pressure forces the water up through cracks in the moon's surface. Researchers say the erupting geysers are made of ice particles and water vapor.

NASA scientists say the geysers offer the best evidence yet that liquid water exists close to the surface of a world other than Earth. They also think the discovery of water indicates that the icy moon could have supported life at one time—or may still be able to.

Cassini may have found liquid water on Saturn's moon.

Who's News

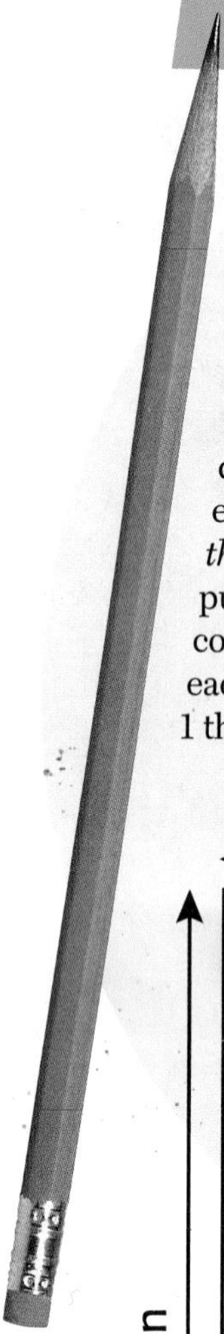

Do You Sudoku?

Sudoku is the number game that is sweeping the United States in books, magazines and newspapers. The object of the puzzle is to fill in all of the missing numbers in a grid. Each row has nine squares, each column has nine squares and each box has nine squares (*see the diagram below*). When the puzzle is complete, every row, column and box must contain each of the numbers from 1 through 9, but only once. In every Sudoku puzzle, some of the numbers in the grid have already been filled in. You have to figure out the number that goes into each empty square.

Even teachers are getting in on the craze. Some schools are using the puzzles to show kids that numbers are fun. Sarah Leventhal, a seventh-grade student at Murray Avenue Middle School, in Huntingdon Valley, Pennsylvania, agrees. "I like Sudoku because it challenges your mind and makes you think a lot," Sarah told TFK. Try it yourself. You can find the answer at *timeforkids.com/sudoku*.

Row

6	8	3	7	4	5	1	2	9
1	5	4	3	2	9	6	7	8
7	2	9	8	6	1	3	4	5
8	4	7	2	3	6	9	5	1
3	6	5	1	9	7	4	8	2
2	9	1	5	8	4	7	6	3
9	1	6	4	5	2	8	3	7
4	3	2	9	7	8	5	1	6
5	7	8	6	1	3	2	9	4

Column

↑ Square

Box

Junk Those Ads!

A 2005 government study found that kids' food choices are swayed by ads, especially when the ads use cartoon or movie characters. Unfortunately, most foods marketed to kids are fast foods, candy and sugary breakfast cereals. The study calls for companies to market only healthful foods to kids. SpongeBob can already be found on packages of carrots. Maybe Jimmy Neutron can sell Brussels sprouts!

Armpit Is Back

When he was a college student in 1976, Louis Sachar helped out at an elementary school. Sachar enjoyed spending time with the kids so much that he decided to try writing a children's book. That book, *Sideways Stories from Wayside School*, became the first of more than 20 books he has written for children.

Sachar's latest, *Small Steps*, hit bookstores in 2006. It features some of the same characters that readers met in his 1999 best-selling book, *Holes*, which won a National Book Award as well as a Newbery Medal. Four years later, *Holes* was made into a popular movie. "It's a fun, exciting story with characters that you really care about," Sachar said of *Small Steps*.

Sachar hopes his book will foster children's love of reading. "A good book becomes a part of you," he says.

Author of the *New York Times* #1 bestseller **HOLES**

LOUIS SACHAR

SMALL STEPS

Louis Sachar writes about kids who are underdogs.

Brown Delivers

Chris Brown

Watch out, Usher! The R&B sensation Chris Brown is giving off the same sparks Usher did when he hit the scene. The teen singer, songwriter and dancer is a small-town boy—he comes from Tappahannock, Virginia (population: 1,900). But Brown has enjoyed big-time success with his self-titled debut disc and No. 1 single, "Run It." "I want to give all those people in small towns hope," he says. "You don't have to be from New York or L.A. to make it in music or follow your dream."

An Idol to Americans?

Kelly Clarkson

Kelly Clarkson didn't know she wanted to be a singer until junior high. Fast-forward to 2002: that year Kelly won the first-ever *American Idol* contest. Since then, Kelly has released two albums, featuring hits like "Breakaway" and "Since U Been Gone." In 2006 her career reached new heights when she won a Grammy Award for Best Female Pop Vocal Performance and sang "All of You" onstage during the Grammy show.

What's her advice for people who want to follow their dream? "The thing is that a lot of people love the entertainment world, so you've really got to have a lot of drive and you really have to want it and go for it and be able to sacrifice things."

Cars

Screen Gems

For lovers of animation and sequels, 2006 is a great year. From Pixar, the animation wizards of *The Incredibles*, comes *Cars*. In this funny feature, the stars are, well, cars. It's the story of a race car that learns lessons about life while sharing the road with some talkative autos.

Another cool animated film, *Over the Hedge,* tells of a wise-guy raccoon named JR and his buddy Vern, a turtle, who live with a group of animals in a forest. JR and his friends must somehow adjust to the encroaching world of humans.

Maybe the year's hottest live-action movie is *Superman Returns*. In this sequel

to *Superman II*, the Man of Steel, played by newcomer Brandon Routh, has his work cut out for him as he tries to save the Earth from total destruction.

Superman is not the only character making a comeback. Captain Jack Sparrow, played by Johnny Depp, also returns in *Pirates of the Caribbean: Dead Man's Chest*. Sparrow squares off with the supernatural again in the form of Davey Jones, captain of *Flying Dutchman*, the legendary ghost ship. Sparrow must also deal with the marriage of Will Turner (Orlando Bloom) and Elizabeth Swann (Keira Knightley).

Superman Returns

Over the Hedge

ANIMALS

ZOO

Turning the Tide for Sea Turtles

Biologists and governments fight to save the sea creatures

Olive ridleys leave the water by the thousands to lay eggs on La Escobilla Beach in southern Mexico.

As evening falls, thousands of sea turtles emerge from the waves pounding La Escobilla (es-koh-*bee*-yah) Beach in Mexico. They crawl across the sand on unsteady flippers. Each is returning to the beach where it was born. They are back to lay their eggs.

La Escobilla Beach is in Oaxaca (wah-*hah*-kah), Mexico. Every year from June to December, olive ridley sea turtles come ashore to build their nests and lay their eggs. Then they cover the eggs with sand and return to the ocean. In 45 days, the babies hatch and scamper into the ocean.

Turtles have been around longer than dinosaurs, but they're no match for modern predators. Many turtles are victims of illegal hunters who kill them for their meat and shells and raid nests for eggs. Sea turtles face many other dangers. Some get caught in fishing nets or fall victim to the effects of pollution.

Today, the world's population of sea turtles has become dangerously small. Scientists warn that without action, two of the species that live in the Pacific Ocean, the loggerhead and the leatherback, will be extinct in 30 years.

But the success of a program in Mexico shows that turtle survival is possible. There are now about 1 million olive ridley nests at La Escobilla. That's four times as many as there were in 1990, when sea turtle hunting was banned in Mexico.

What has helped to turn the tide besides the hunting ban is community education and tough tactics. Federal agents patrol area beaches, guarding nesting turtles and their eggs.

Scientists hope to hatch similar success stories elsewhere. Biologist Wallace J. Nichols has studied the sea turtle populations of Mexico. He told TFK, "Seeing the success at La Escobilla inspires people working at other projects."
—By Kathryn Satterfield

The world's seven species of sea turtles are all on the endangered list. Five of the species can be found along North America's Pacific Coast. Four species, below, have been slower than olive ridleys to recover in the Pacific region.

- The number of nesting GREEN TURTLES has dropped from 25,000 to 500.
- Only a few dozen HAWKSBILLS nest in the region.
- Fewer than 1,000 LOGGERHEADS nest on Japan's beaches.
- The number of nesting LEATHERBACKS dropped from 91,000 in 1980 to fewer than 5,000 in 2002.

Mexican agents patrolling La Escobilla ask children to be careful around the sea turtle eggs.

Animals

19

Extinct, Endangered and Threatened Species

Many species are disappearing from our planet. Sadly, by 2025, as much as one-fifth of the world's species may be gone. **Extinct** means that the entire species has died out and can never return. **Endangered** animals are those in immediate danger of becoming extinct.

Threatened species are likely to become endangered in the future.

Humans are largely responsible for animals becoming extinct, endangered or threatened. Here are some of the things that can lead animals to become endangered.

Jaguar

Mission blue butterfly

Destruction of Habitat
Humans destroy precious habitat—the natural environment of a living thing—when they fill swamps and marshes, dam rivers and cut down trees to build homes, roads and other structures or developments.

Pollution
Oil spills, acid rain and water pollution have been devastating for many species of fish and birds.

Hunting and Fishing
Many animals are overhunted because their meat, fur and other parts are very valuable.

Houston toad

Introduction of Exotic Species
When foreign animals or plants are introduced into a new habitat, they sometimes bring diseases that the native species can't fight. Exotic species, although able to prey on native species, often have no natural enemies.

There are 1,078 endangered and threatened species of animals in the world. The list includes:

- 349 species of mammals, such as the red wolf, the sperm whale and the jaguar.

- 271 species of birds, such as the California condor, the whooping crane and the northern spotted owl.
- 126 species of fish, such as coho salmon.
- 116 species of reptiles, such as the green sea turtle.

- 48 species of insects, including the mission blue butterfly.
- 30 species of amphibians, including the Houston toad.

Classifying Animals

There are billions of different kinds of living things (organisms) on Earth. To help study them, biologists have created ways of naming and classifying them according to their similarities and differences. The system most scientists use puts each living thing into seven groups, organized from most general to most specific. Therefore, each kingdom is composed of phylums, each phylum is composed of classes, each class is composed of orders, and so on.

Kingdoms are huge groups, with millions of kinds of organisms in each. All animals are in one kingdom (called Kingdom Animalia); all plants are in another (Kingdom Plantae). It is generally agreed that there are five kingdoms: Animalia, Plantae, Fungi, Prokarya (bacteria) and Protoctista (organisms that don't fit into the four other kingdoms, including many microscopic creatures).

Species are the smallest groups. In the animal kingdom, a species consists of all the animals of a type that are able to breed and produce young of the same kind.

From **largest** to smallest, the groups are

Kingdom
Phylum
Class
Order
Family
Genus
Species

TIP
To remember the sequence for classification, keep this sentence in mind:

King Philip came over from great Spain.

A SAMPLE CLASSIFICATION:
Humpback Whale

KINGDOM: Animalia **includes all animals**

PHYLUM: Chordata **includes all vertebrates, or backboned, animals**

CLASS: Mammalia **includes all mammals**

ORDER: Cetacea **includes all whales, porpoises and dolphins**

FAMILY: Balaenopteridae **includes six species of whales**

GENUS: Megaptera **the humpback whale is the only species in this genus**

SPECIES: Megaptera novaeangliae **the humpback whale**

Did You Know?
Taxonomy is the science of classifying organisms, such as animals.

For a look at how animals communicate:
www.factmonster.com/animalcommunication

Animals

Animal Groups

Penguins are birds.

Almost all animals belong to one of two groups, **vertebrates** or **invertebrates**. Adult vertebrates have a spinal column, or backbone, running the length of their body; invertebrates do not. Vertebrates are often larger and have more complex bodies than invertebrates. However, there are many more invertebrates than vertebrates.

Vertebrates

Reptiles are cold-blooded and breathe with lungs. They have thick, scaly skin, and most lay eggs. Reptiles include turtles and tortoises, crocodiles and alligators, snakes and lizards.

Fish breathe through gills and live in water. Most are cold-blooded and lay eggs (although sharks give birth to live young). Fish eggs, however, don't have shells. Most fish are covered with scales.

Mammals are warm-blooded and are nourished by their mothers' milk. Most live on land, but whales and dolphins, which breathe with lungs, live in water. Most mammals are born live, but the platypus and echidna are hatched from eggs. Most mammals also have body hair.

Dinosaurs were reptiles, although some scientists believe that some dinosaurs were warm-blooded.

Birds are warm-blooded animals with feathers, wings and lightweight bones. They lay eggs, and most birds can fly. Some, including penguins and ostriches, cannot fly. All birds breathe with lungs.

Amphibians are cold-blooded and live both on land (breathing with lungs) and in water (breathing through gills) at different times of their lives. Three types of amphibians are caecilians, salamanders, and frogs and toads. Caecilians are primitive amphibians that resemble earthworms. They are found in the tropics.

Dolphins are mammals.

Tortoises are reptiles.

Spider

Octopus

Invertebrates

Sponges are the most primitive of animal groups. They live in water, are sessile (do not move from place to place) and filter tiny organisms out of the water for food.

Echinoderms, including starfish, sea urchins and sea cucumbers, live in seawater and have external skeletons.

Worms come in many varieties and live in all sorts of habitats—from the bottom of the ocean to the insides of other animals. They include flatworms (flukes), roundworms (hookworms), segmented worms (earthworms) and rotifers (philodina).

Earthworm

Mollusks are soft-bodied animals, some of which live in hard shells. They include snails, slugs, octopuses, squid, mussels, oysters, clams, scallops and cuttlefish.

Arthropods are the largest and most diverse of all animal groups. They have segmented bodies supported by a hard external skeleton (or exoskeleton). Arthropods include insects, arachnids (spiders and their relatives) and crustaceans (such as shrimp and crabs).

Coelenterates are also very primitive. Their mouths, which take in food and get rid of waste, are surrounded by stinging tentacles. Jellyfish, corals and sea anemones are coelenterates.

Did You Know?

No one knows for sure how many species of animals there are on Earth. Most scientists agree there are about 1 million species of animals and at least 20,000 species of fish. More than 10,000 new animal species are discovered each year.

TFK

Top 5

Snow geese

Most Common U.S. Birds

Every year, thousands of people take part in the Great Backyard Bird Count. They count the number of each species of bird they spot in their area. The list helps scientists who study U.S. bird populations. These are the five most common birds in the U.S., according to a recent count.

1.	Snow goose	835,369 individuals
2.	Canada goose	688,715
3.	Red-winged blackbird	480,989
4.	European starling	342,047
5.	American crow	282,991

Source: Great Backyard Bird Count

Animals

23

Animals on the Job

People and animals have worked together for thousands of years. Some dogs have been taught to guard against enemies and others to herd cattle. Cats have been used to hunt mice and other rodents to prevent them from stealing food and spreading disease. Some animals are trained to help people in other ways.

- **Seeing-eye dogs** help blind people to get around safely, and hearing dogs help the deaf by alerting their owners to doorbells, alarms, sirens and people calling them.

- Specially trained **capuchin monkeys** can help quadriplegics—people who can't use their arms or legs. The monkeys can change CDs, scratch itches, fetch food and even comb hair.

- **Female pigs** use their ample snouts to find truffles—a tasty and pricey fungus that grows underground.

- **Homing pigeons**, who return to their nests from wherever they're released, have been used to carry messages for thousands of years.

- **Dogs in K-9 units** (the name comes from *canine*, which means *dog*) help police officers by chasing and holding criminals. Some are trained to sniff out drugs or explosives or to find missing people.

Warm-Blooded and Cold-Blooded Animals

Warm-blooded animals regulate their own body temperature; their bodies use energy to maintain a constant temperature. Cold-blooded animals depend on their surroundings to establish their body temperature.

Snakes are cold-blooded.

Fascinating Animal Facts

African elephant

Chameleon

Cats have about 250 muscles in each ear.

African elephants are the largest and heaviest mammals on land. They weigh up to 14,000 pounds, and can eat as much as 600 pounds of food a day.

The inland Taipan is considered the most poisonous snake on the planet. One bite from this shy reptile, which is native to Australia, contains enough toxin to kill about 100 people.

The blue whale is the world's biggest animal, even larger than any dinosaur. An average-size adult is 80 feet long and weighs about 120 tons. This giant is also the loudest animal on Earth. Its call, which is louder than a jet plane, can be heard for hundreds of miles.

The smallest fish in the world is believed to be the *Paedocypris progenetica*, which was recently discovered in Indonesia. It measures just over one-third of an inch long and has a see-through body.

Sea horses are the only fish whose eggs are carried by the father, not the mother.

Giraffes not only have long necks, they also have enormous tongues, which can be 18 inches long.

Kangaroos can jump as far as 30 feet in one leap.

Hippopotamuses are quick-footed giants. They can weigh up to 9,000 pounds and run as fast as 20 miles per hour.

The anopheles mosquito is the deadliest creature on Earth. It's responsible for more than 300 million cases of malaria each year and causes between 1 million and 3 million deaths.

A cockroach can live as long as a week without a head.

Sharks continually replace lost teeth. A shark may grow 24,000 teeth in a lifetime.

Shark

For frequently asked animal questions:
www.factmonster.com/animalfaqs

Animals

25

Zooming in on Zoos

The first zoo (short for "zoological garden") in the U.S. opened in Philadelphia in 1859. Today, there are more than 200 zoos in the U.S., far more than in any other country. Here are some top American and foreign zoos.

San Diego Zoo
San Diego, California

Started in 1916, this was one of the first zoos that put animals in natural habitats instead of behind bars. Visitors stroll through its 1,800 acres, past lush greenery (6,500 types of plants) to see 4,000 animals of about 850 species. **Animal Attractions:** Monkey Trails and Forest Tales is a mini tropical forest that holds more than 30 species of African and Asian animals, including such endangered monkeys as Schmidt's guenons and mandrills. Also worth a look is the Lion Camp, home to six lion cubs.

Smithsonian National Zoo
Washington, D.C.

The zoo is known for its programs to reintroduce captive animals to the wild and for its fight for conservation. But it's also a lot of fun to visit. Founded in 1889, it has about 2,700 animals representing 435 species spread over 163 acres. **Animal Attractions:** Amazonia is a re-creation of a section of a rain forest, complete with a tropical river, where sloths, hummingbirds, titi monkeys and other animals hang out. The zoo's most famous residents are Mei Xiang and Tian Tian, giant pandas from China, and their cute cub, Tai Shan.

Bronx Zoo
The Bronx, New York

It is one of the largest city zoos, containing more than 4,000 animals, including rare snow leopards. Real plants, trees and rocks added to artificial ones make exhibits look like part of the natural world. The Bronx Zoo is famous for conservation work that helps save wildlife around the globe. **Animal Attractions:** Congo Gorilla Forest, where two troops of lowland gorillas interact over a large territory. The Butterfly Garden is a giant greenhouse holding more than 1,000 North American butterflies that flutter around visitors.

London Zoo
London, England

Britain's most famous zoo, it houses more than 650 species of animals, including more than 100 that are threatened. It was founded in 1828 as the world's first zoo created for scientists like Charles Darwin to study animals. **Animal Attractions:** Among the zoo's 7,000 animals are such rare ones as the wombat devil, the four-eyed opossum and the bell bird, which makes the loudest noise of any bird. The biggest attraction may be the koalas, which eat only eucalyptus leaves placed on their perches by zookeepers.

Berlin Zoo
Berlin, Germany

One of Europe's biggest zoos, it is also one of the most popular. More than 3 million people visit the zoo and its aquarium each year. One reason is the park's wide walkways, artificial ponds and beautiful fountains. But the main draw is the nearly 14,000 animals representing nearly 1,500 species—the most species in any zoo. **Animal Attractions:** Miniature hippos frolic in a glass pool. The zoo is filled with familiar favorites, such as apes, monkeys, giraffes, African wild dogs and storks, most in large, open spaces.

Taronga Zoo
Sydney, Australia

Overlooking Sydney harbor, it has amazing views of downtown Sydney. What's in the zoo is also eye opening: About 340 different species of animals and more than 2,600 individual critters. **Animal Attractions:** Most interesting is the collection of Aussie animals, including wombats, koalas, kangaroos, platypuses and rare bridled nail-tailed wallabys. Other unique sights are leopard seals (an Antarctic animal that attacks other seals), Australian pelicans and the deadly inland Taipan snake.

Toronto Zoo
Toronto, Canada

Put on your walking shoes— there are about 6 miles of paths leading through the 710-acre park, making it one of the biggest zoos in the world. That's a lot of room for its 5,000 animals, which are grouped by geographical region. **Animal Attractions:** In the Malayan Woods Pavilion, artificial rain sprays free-flying birds, butterflies and humans alike. The Grizzly Bear Trail and the Lion Trail are great, as are amazing animals such as the naked mole-rat, blue poison dart frog, cheetah, electric eel and Przewalski's horse.

Odd Animals

Take a look at some of the world's most bewildering beasts.

Bongo The bongo, found in Africa, is known for its graceful, spiraled horns and beautiful striped hide. Timid, well camouflaged and mostly nocturnal, it is one of Africa's most mysterious animals.

Capybara At 4½ feet long and weighing as much as 140 pounds, this short-tailed, sleepy-eyed beast from South America is the world's largest rodent. Its semi-webbed feet help make it a good swimmer, and it spends much of its time around water or wallowing in mud.

Civet This silky cat-shaped mammal, found in Africa and Asia, is remarkable for its beautiful spots, raccoon-like face and unusual scent, which was once used in making perfumes. Civets grow 2 to 3 feet long (not including the long tail). They will eat almost anything, from meat to fruit.

Echidna The spiny echidna is one of only two monotremes, or egg-laying mammals. It spends most of its time alone, burrowing in the ground and catching insects with its long, sticky tongue. It is found in Australia, New Guinea and Tasmania.

Jerboa Its long, powerful back legs make this mouse-size rodent a jumping wonder—it can leap 10 feet in a single bound. The jerboa, found in Africa and Asia, never drinks, getting liquid only from the bugs and plants that it eats.

Kiwi Looking at the rounded brownish body of this flightless bird from New Zealand, it's easy to see where the kiwi fruit got its name.

Pangolin This scaly mammal of Africa and Asia comes out at night to search for bugs. It has no teeth, but its sticky tongue can stretch out 2 feet. Shy and quiet, the pangolin curls into a ball when frightened.

Tarsier This squirrel-size primate from Southeast Asia has huge eyes to let it see in the dark. It can also turn its head nearly all the way around.

Animals

27

Top 10 DOG Breeds

1. Labrador retriever
2. Golden retriever
3. German shepherd
4. Beagle
5. Dachshund
6. Yorkshire terrier
7. Boxer
8. Poodle
9. Chihuahua
10. Shih tzu

Source: The American Kennel Club

Top 10 CAT Breeds

1. Persian
2. Maine coon
3. Exotic
4. Siamese
5. Abyssinian
6. Oriental
7. Birman
8. American shorthair
9. Tonkinese
10. Burmese

Source: Cat Fanciers' Association

Pet Ownership

Pet ownership reached its highest point in 2004, with 63% of U.S. households owning a furry—or scaly—friend. Here's a look at the most popular pets in America.

ANIMAL	% OF U.S. HOUSEHOLDS OWNING PET	NUMBER OF PETS IN U.S.
DOG	39%	73.9 million
CAT	34	90.5 million
FRESHWATER FISH	13	139 million
BIRD	6	16.6 million
SMALL ANIMAL	5	18.2 million
REPTILE	4	11 million

Source: American Pet Products Manufacturers Association

4%

34%

Top Pet Names

Did you know your furry friend was destined to be a "Smokey" the moment you looked at her? You're not alone. The American Society for the Prevention of Cruelty to Animals (ASPCA) conducted a survey to find out which pet names are most popular in the U.S. Here are the top 10.

1. Max
2. Sam
3. Lady
4. Bear
5. Smokey
6. Shadow
7. Kitty
8. Molly
9. Buddy
10. Brandy

Animal Names

ANIMAL	MALE	FEMALE	YOUNG	GROUP NAME
bear	boar	sow	cub	sleuth, sloth
cat	tom	queen	kitten	clutter, clowder
cattle	bull	cow	calf	drove
chicken	rooster	hen	chick	brood, clutch
deer	buck	doe	fawn	herd, leash
dog	dog	bitch	pup	litter, pack
duck	drake	duck	duckling	brace, team
elephant	bull	cow	calf	herd
fox	dog	vixen	cub	leash, skulk
goose	gander	goose	gosling	flock, gaggle, skein
horse	stallion	mare	foal	pair, team
lion	lion	lioness	cub	pride
pig	boar	sow	piglet	litter
sheep	ram	ewe	lamb	drove, flock
swan	cob	pen	cygnet	bevy, wedge

Fast Tracks

Forget about challenging a cheetah to a race. The fastest human sprinter only reaches a speed of about 28 m.p.h.

ANIMAL	SPEED (M.P.H.)
PEREGRINE FALCON	200+
CHEETAH	70
LION	50
ZEBRA	40
GREYHOUND	39
DRAGONFLY	36
RABBIT	35
GIRAFFE	32
GRIZZLY BEAR	30
CAT	30
ELEPHANT	25
SQUIRREL	12
MOUSE	8
SPIDER	1
GARDEN SNAIL	0.03

Source: James G. Doherty, general curator, Wildlife Conservation Society

A sow with her piglets

Animal Gestation & Longevity

Here's a look at the average gestation (the time an animal spends inside its mother) and longevity (life span) of certain animals.

ANIMAL	GESTATION (DAYS)	LONGEVITY (YEARS)
CAT	52–69	10–12
COW	280	9–12
DOG	53–71	10–12
HAMSTER	15–17	2
HORSE	329–345	20–25
KANGAROO	32–39	4–6
LION	105–113	10
PIG	101–130	10
PIGEON	11–19	10–12
RABBIT	30–35	6–8
WOLF	60–63	10–12

Source: James G. Doherty, general curator, Wildlife Conservation Society

Animals

ART

This Monkey's Business Was Art

American art collector Howard Hong was not monkeying around when he paid $26,352 for three paintings created by a chimpanzee. The three brightly colored abstract pieces were painted by Congo, a chimpanzee artist. They were created during the 1950s, when Congo was just 3 years old!

The paintings were sold at an auction in London, England. "We had no idea what these things were worth," said Howard Rutkowski, a director at the auction house. "We just put them in for our own amusement."

Born in 1954, Congo created about 400 drawings and paintings between the ages of 2 and 4. Congo died in 1964.

Congo was discovered as an artist in 1957. That's when animal behaviorist and painter Desmond Morris first held an art exhibition with chimpanzee art. Morris wanted to understand

A painting created by Congo the chimpanzee

chimps' ability to create and explore in an artistic way. He said that studying the animals could help us understand why humans express themselves through art.
—*By Jill Egan*

MAGNIFICENT MUSEUMS

Take a quick tour of some of the best art collections in the world.

METROPOLITAN MUSEUM OF ART; NEW YORK CITY

Founded in 1870, the "Met" holds the nation's greatest art collection. It displays American and European paintings, medieval art and armor, masks from Africa, mummies from Egypt and Aztec gold sculpture, as well as rare treasures from Asia, the Middle East and ancient Greece, Crete and Rome.

TOP ART: *Self Portrait* (Rembrandt), *Cypresses* (Vincent van Gogh), *The Harvesters* (Peter Brueghel the Elder), *Young Woman with a Water Jug* (Jan Vermeer), **Midnight Ride of Paul Revere** (Grant Wood)

Art © Estate of Grant Wood/
Licensed by VAGA, New York, NY

PRADO; MADRID, SPAIN

Completed in 1819, the Prado originally held paintings owned by the royal family. In 1868, it became a national museum. It is famous for its collection of Spanish, Flemish and Venetian paintings.

TOP ART: *Naked Maja* (Goya), **Burial of the Count of Orgaz (El Greco)**, *Adam and Eve* (Albrecht Dürer), *Garden of Earthly Delights* (Hieronymus Bosch)

LOUVRE; PARIS, FRANCE

Once one of the world's largest palaces, it is now one of the world's largest art museums—and maybe the most famous one. Since 1793 the Louvre has been gathering an incredible collection of ancient and Western art, including 6,000 European paintings dating from the 13th century to the middle of the 19th century. It could take days for visitors to explore the museum's many long halls.

TOP ART: *Mona Lisa* (Leonardo da Vinci), *The Lacemaker* (Jan Vermeer), *Embarkation for Cythera* (Jean-Antoine Watteau), **Venus of Milo,** *The Raft of the Medusa* (Théodore Géricault)

UFFIZI GALLERY; FLORENCE, ITALY

This museum was originally a palace built in the 16th century for Cosimo I de' Medici. In 1591, the public was allowed to view the artwork inside, making the Uffizi the first public art museum in the world. Today, the Uffizi holds the world's best collection of Renaissance art.

TOP ART: *Primavera* and *Birth of Venus* (Sandro Botticelli), *Annunciation* (Leonardo da Vinci), *Holy Family* (Michelangelo), *Venus of Urbino* (Titian)

TATE GALLERY AND TATE MODERN; LONDON, ENGLAND

When it opened in 1897, the Tate Gallery had only 65 works. The national collection of Britain now includes more than 65,000 pieces of British artwork from the early 16th century to the 20th century. A separate, newer museum, called the **Tate Modern,** holds the national collection of modern art from all over the world.

TOP ART: *Marilyn Diptych* (Andy Warhol), *God Judging Adam* (William Blake), *The Opening of Waterloo Bridge* (John Constable), *Nocturne: Blue and Gold* (James Whistler), *Red on Maroon* (Mark Rothko), *The Kiss* (Auguste Rodin)

For a look at other museums, go to:
factmonster.com/greatmuseums

Art

GREAT ARTISTS

1. CHRISTO (BORN 1935) Bulgarian-born modern artist who wraps buildings and other objects in different types of colorful, flowing fabric. In 2005, Christo and his wife, Jeanne-Claude, installed "The Gates," 7,500 panels of orange nylon suspended between 16-foot-tall painted steel posts, in New York City's Central Park.

2. JACOB LAWRENCE (1917-2000) American artist best known for his brilliant depiction of the African American experience. His greatest work was a series of paintings called *The Migration of the Negro*.

CLAUDE MONET (1840-1926) French painter who was a founding father of Impressionism, a style of painting that used color and light rather than lines to portray a scene. His many famous paintings include series of water lilies and haystacks.

3. MICHELANGELO (1475-1564) Renaissance sculptor, painter, architect and poet. He created some of the world's most famous works of art, including the sculpture *David* and his painting on the ceiling of the Sistine Chapel.

4. LOUISE NEVELSON (1900-1988) American sculptor who used pieces of wood, metal and other materials to create huge walls and abstract arrangements.

GEORGIA O'KEEFFE (1887-1986) American painter whose work was inspired by deserts in the Southwest. She also painted flowers, such as calla lilies, orchids and hollyhocks.

5. PABLO PICASSO (1881-1973) Spanish artist considered by many to be the greatest 20th century painter. His amazingly original and innovative style can be seen in such works as *Guernica* and *Les Demoiselles d'Avignon*.

REMBRANDT (1606-1669) Dutch Baroque artist whose hundreds of richly ornate paintings depict historical and biblical scenes. He also painted many portraits.

6. ANDY WARHOL (1928-1987) An American artist who made the Pop Art movement famous. By creating images of ordinary objects like soup cans, he redefined the meaning of art.

 See kids' reviews of best art websites at timeforkids.com/arts

The Color Wheel

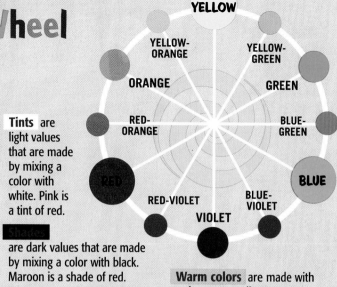

A color wheel shows how colors are related.

- Red, yellow and blue are the **primary** colors. Primary colors are the most basic colors.
- Orange, green and violet are the **secondary** colors. A secondary color is made by mixing two primary colors.
- **Intermediate,** or tertiary colors, are between primary and secondary colors. They are made by mixing a primary and a secondary color.

VALUE The lightness or darkness of a color is called its **value.** You can find the values of a color by making its tints and shades.

Tints are light values that are made by mixing a color with white. Pink is a tint of red.

Shades are dark values that are made by mixing a color with black. Maroon is a shade of red.

Analogous colors sit next to each other on the color wheel. The colors tend to look pleasant together because they are closely related.

Warm colors are made with red, orange, yellow or some combination of these.

Cool colors are made with blue, green, purple or some combination of these.

TFK Top 5

Most Expensive Paintings Ever Sold

Price	Painting
1. $104 million	*Boy with a Pipe* by Pablo Picasso
2. $82.5 million	*Portrait of Dr. Gachet* by Vincent van Gogh
3. $78.1 million	*Au Moulin de la Galette* by Pierre-Auguste Renoir
4. $76.7 million	*The Massacre of the Innocents* by Peter Paul Rubens
5. $71.5 million	*Portrait de l'artiste sans barbe* by Vincent van Gogh

---

TFK Mystery Person

CLUE 1: One of the 20th century's greatest artists, I was born in a small town in Mexico in 1907.

CLUE 2: I suffered from polio and was hurt in a bus accident. I expressed my pain in my paintings, especially my many self-portraits. My work also highlighted Mexican culture and history.

CLUE 3: Because of my intense life and work, I am often viewed as an icon of feminism.

WHO AM I?

(See Answer Key that begins on page 342.)

Art

33

BOOKS

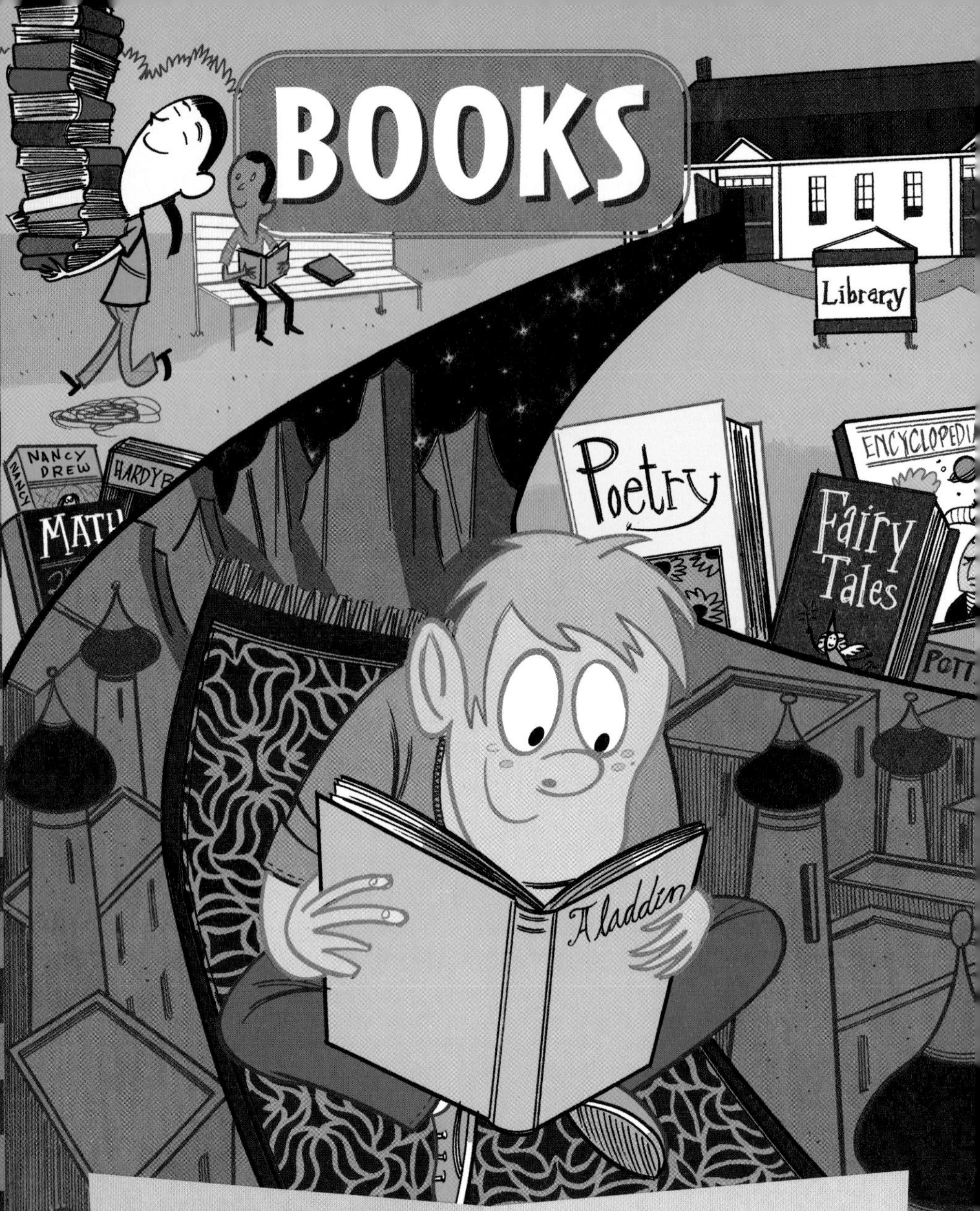

Harry-a-Like Books

If you love the Harry Potter books, check out these series that are recommended by the American Library Association.

The Chronicles of Prydain, Lloyd Alexander

The Oz Series, L. Frank Baum

The Spiderwick Chronicles, Holly Black

Dark Is Rising Sequence, Susan Cooper

Young Wizard Series, Diane Duane

Chrestomanci Books, Diana Wynne Jones

Keys to the Kingdom, Garth Nix

A Series of Unfortunate Events, Lemony Snicket

The Bartimaeus Trilogy, Jonathan Stroud

The Enchanted Forest Chronicles, Patricia Wrede

go Check out Potter trivia, games, photos and more at timeforkids.com/potter

Harry Potter Timeline

1965 Joanne Rowling is born on July 31 in the British town of Chipping Sodbury.

1990 While stuck on a delayed train between Manchester and London, Rowling gets the idea for Harry Potter. She begins writing his story that night.

1995 Rowling finishes her first book, *Harry Potter and the Philosopher's Stone*.

1996 British publisher Bloomsbury Press accepts the book.

1997 **SPRING:** Scholastic Books wins the rights to publish the series in the U.S. Rowling quits her teaching job to devote her time to writing.

JUNE 26: The first book in the series—*Harry Potter and the Philosopher's Stone*—is published in the United Kingdom (U.K.). Because Bloomsbury is afraid that young boys won't want to read a book by a woman, they suggest she use her initials. Joanne adds her grandmother's name, Kathleen, to her own, producing J.K. Rowling.

1998 **JULY 2:** The second book, *Harry Potter and the Chamber of Secrets*, is published in the U.K.

SEPTEMBER 1: Scholastic publishes the first book, renamed *Harry Potter and the Sorcerer's Stone*, in the U.S. British spelling, punctuation, grammar and vocabulary are translated into American English.

1999 **JUNE 2:** *Harry Potter and the Chamber of Secrets* is published in the U.S. It shoots to the top of the best-seller lists.

JULY 8: The third book, *Harry Potter and the Prisoner of Azkaban*, is published in the U.K.

SEPTEMBER 8: *Harry Potter and the Prisoner of Azkaban* is published in the U.S. The Harry Potter books hold the top three positions on the New York *Times* best-seller list.

2000 **AUGUST 21:** After a long search, Daniel Radcliffe, Emma Watson and Rupert Grint are chosen to play Harry, Hermione and Ron on film.

JULY 8: The fourth book, *Harry Potter and the Goblet of Fire*, is published in both the U.K. and the U.S. More than 5 million copies of the book are printed. This is the first time the book is released at the same time in both countries. It's also the first time it's released on Saturday, so children can buy and read the book without skipping school. Both these practices are followed for the rest of the series.

2001 **NOVEMBER 16:** The first film is released and earns a record-setting $90 million in its opening weekend.

2002 **OCTOBER 25:** Actor Richard Harris, who played Dumbledore in the movies, dies.

NOVEMBER 15: The second film opens. On opening weekend, this movie makes $88 million in America.

2003 **JUNE 21:** The fifth book, *Harry Potter and the Order of the Phoenix*, is released. The first printing is 6.4 million copies in the U.S. alone—the most of any book ever. At 870 pages, it's the longest book in the series.

2004 **JUNE 4:** The third film, *Harry Potter and the Prisoner of Azkaban*, opens in the U.S. and grosses $93.7 million in its first weekend of release. Michael Gambon takes over the role of Dumbledore.

2005 **JULY 16:** The sixth book, *Harry Potter and the Half-Blood Prince*, is released. The U.S. first printing is a record-shattering 10.8 million copies. In another first, Braille and large-print editions are released on the same day as the other editions.

NOVEMBER 18: The fourth film, *Harry Potter and the Goblet of Fire*, is released. It earns $102 million in the U.S. in its opening weekend.

For Harry Potter quizzes, reviews and more: www.factmonster.com/harrypage

Books

How a Book Is Made

It usually takes at least two years for an idea to go from an author's head to a published book. Rachel Orr, an editor at HarperCollins, tells you how it's done.

1. After an author writes a story, he or she sends the manuscript to an editor at a publishing house. If the editor likes it, the author is given a contract.

2. Next, the editor and designer search for an illustrator who is perfect for the story. Usually the author and the illustrator never even meet!

3. Whether a manuscript is three pages or 203 pages, it takes a lot of time to edit. The author and editor work to make sure every word is right.

4. Editors help with the main concepts, while copy editors catch spelling and usage mistakes—ones even your computer will miss.

5. Meanwhile, the illustrator has been working hard on the sketches. Sometimes many pictures are revised. It's exciting when the final art arrives!

6. The designer scans the art onto the pages and places the text. These unbound pages are called galleys. The author, editor and designer make corrections and changes on galleys.

7. The corrected galleys, in the form of computer files, go to the printer. The printer makes a version of the book called proofs. These pages are checked to see that the printed colors match the original art.

8. The last chance to make changes in the book is in blues. These pages are like blueprints—they show how the book will look when it's printed.

9. Once the blues are approved, the proofs are folded together into unfinished books. The publicity department uses them to spread the word about the book.

10. Last, the finished books are bound and shipped to the warehouse. From there, they are sent to stores and libraries across the country.

Did You Know?

Since at least the 4th century B.C., some people have tried to ban or destroy books for moral, political or religious reasons. *Blubber*, by Judy Blume, *Harriet the Spy*, by Louise Fitzhugh, and *Sylvester and the Magic Pebble*, by William Steig, are a few examples of books that have been banned.

For summaries of favorite kids' books:
www.factmonster.com/bigread

Boys Book Club

A new page-turning program aims to get good books into guys' hands

Jon Scieszka is looking to inspire boys everywhere to become big readers.

Author Jon Scieszka (shes-ka) taught elementary school for 10 years. During that time, he learned a valuable lesson: too many boys struggle with reading. So he wrote *The Stinky Cheese Man*, The Time Warp Trio series and other books that he thought would appeal to boys who otherwise don't like to read. Part of what's missing for boys, Scieszka told TFK, "is that motivation to want to be readers."

The U.S. Department of Education's reading tests show that boys have scored lower than girls in every age group every year for the last 30 years. Scieszka thinks the low scores

have to do with different learning styles and interests. "It's not to say that boys are worse at reading," he says. "They just need things structured differently."

In general, boys are more likely than girls to read how-to manuals, comic books and sports news instead of fiction. Nonfiction articles and humor pieces are not always seen as acceptable book-club material. "We have to expand what we call reading," Scieszka says.

Scieszka recently started a nonprofit literacy effort called Guys Read that aims to connect boys with books they will enjoy. It includes a website,

Guysread.com, and a new book, *Guys Write for Guys Read*.

The book is a collection of illustrations and essays created by—you guessed it—guys. Scieszka edited the book. Contributors include the authors Gary Paulsen and Daniel Handler, as well as the artists Matt Groening and Mo Willems. They share their own important, funny or embarrassing experiences as guys.

Scieszka says he chose only male contributors because they could serve as role models: "I thought the boys could see themselves in all these different guys."

—*By Kathryn R. Satterfield*

go Read TFK's entire interview with Jon Scieszka at timeforkids.com/jon

Types of Poems

HMMM... **WHAT** RHYMES WITH TREE...?

BALLAD A poem that tells a story similar to a folk tale or legend and often has a repeated refrain

ELEGY A poem that mourns the death of a person, or one that is simply sad and thoughtful

EPIC A long, serious poem that tells the story of a heroic figure

EPIGRAM A very short, witty poem: "Sir, I admit your general rule,/That every poet is a fool,/ But you yourself may serve to show it,/That every fool is not a poet." (Samuel Taylor Coleridge)

HAIKU A Japanese poem that is composed of three unrhymed lines of five, seven and five syllables. Haiku often reflect on some aspect of nature.

IDYLL Either a short poem depicting a peaceful country scene, or a long poem that tells a story about heroic deeds or extraordinary events set in the distant past

LIMERICK A light, humorous poem of five lines

LYRIC A poem, such as a sonnet or an ode, that expresses the thoughts and feelings of the poet. A lyric poem may resemble a song in form or style.

ODE A lyric poem that is serious and thoughtful in tone and has a very precise, formal structure

PASTORAL A poem that describes life in the country as calm and peaceful

SONNET A lyric poem that is 14 lines long

Books

37

Types of Literature

Here are examples of different styles of fiction (made-up stories) and nonfiction (books about real-life events and people).

An **autobiography** or a **memoir** is the story of a person's life written or told by that person.
EXAMPLE:
26 Fairmount Avenue by Tomie dePaola

A **biography** is the story of a person's life written or told by another person.
EXAMPLE:
Traitor: The Case of Benedict Arnold by Jean Fritz

A **fable** is a story that teaches a moral or a lesson. It often has animal characters.
EXAMPLE:
"The Country Mouse and the City Mouse"

A **folktale** is a story that has been passed down, usually orally, within a culture. It may be based on superstition and may feature supernatural characters.
EXAMPLE: The story of Paul Bunyan

A **legend** is a story that has been handed down over generations and is believed to be based on history, though it typically mixes fact and fiction.
EXAMPLE:
The legend of John Henry

A **myth** is a traditional story that a particular culture or group once accepted as sacred and true. It may center on a god or supernatural being and typically explains how something came to be.
EXAMPLE: The story of the 12 labors of Hercules

Fantasy novels are often set in worlds much different from our own, and they usually include magic, sorcery and mythical creatures.
EXAMPLE: *The Lion, the Witch and the Wardrobe* by C.S. Lewis

Science fiction stories examine how science and technology affect the world. The books often involve fantastic inventions that someday may be a reality.
EXAMPLE:
A Wrinkle in Time by Madeleine L'Engle

Puzzles & Games

Anagram Anxiety

A playful publisher turned the titles of some famous kids' novels into anagrams. (An anagram is a word or phrase made by switching around the letters of another word or phrase.) Can you unscramble the anagrams to come up with the correct titles? Hints: the names of the authors are correct, and you can ignore the punctuation.

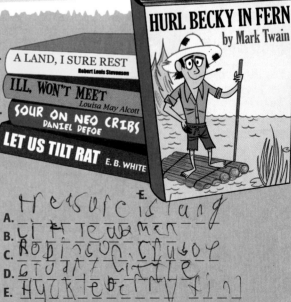

A. A LAND, I SURE REST
Robert Louis Stevenson

B. ILL, WON'T MEET
Louisa May Alcott

C. SOUR ON NEO CRIBS
DANIEL DEFOE

D. LET US TILT RAT E. B. WHITE

HURL BECKY IN FERN
by Mark Twain

A. Treasure Island
B. Little Women
C. Robinson Crusoe
D. Stuart Little
E. Huckleberry Finn

(See Answer Key that begins on page 342.)

Top 5

Largest Libraries in the U.S.

You may think your school library has lots of books, but check out how many titles these libraries hold.

INSTITUTION	NUMBER OF VOLUMES HELD
1. Library of Congress	29,550,914
2. Harvard University	15,181,349
3. Boston Public Library	14,933,349
4. Yale University	11,114,308
5. Chicago Public Library	10,745,608

Source: American Library Association

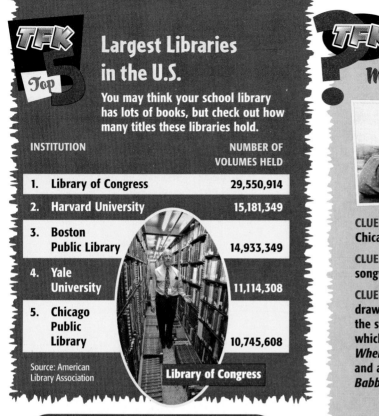

Library of Congress

TFK Mystery Person

CLUE 1: I was born in Chicago, Illinois, in 1930.

CLUE 2: I was an author, a songwriter and an artist.

CLUE 3: My simple line drawings illustrate many of the silly rhymes in my books, which include *Falling Up*, *Where the Sidewalk Ends* and a new one, *Runny Babbit*.

WHO AM I?

(See Answer Key that begins on page 342.)

---

go Read TFK's interview with Lynne Rae Perkins at timeforkids.com/perkins

---

BOOK AWARDS

The **CALDECOTT MEDAL** honors an outstanding American picture book.
2006 winner:
The Hello, Goodbye Window, Chris Raschka (illustrator); Norton Juster (writer)

The **NEWBERY MEDAL** honors an outstanding example of children's literature. The Newbery winner is not a picture book.
2006 winner:
Criss Cross, Lynne Rae Perkins

NATIONAL BOOK AWARD FOR YOUNG PEOPLE'S LITERATURE
2005 winner:
The Penderwicks, Jeanne Birdsall

The **CORETTA SCOTT KING AWARDS** recognize black authors and illustrators whose works have promoted an understanding and appreciation of all cultures.
2006 winners:
Writer: Julius Lester, *Day of Tears: A Novel in Dialogue*
Illustrator: Bryan Collier, *Rosa*

BOSTON GLOBE HORN BOOK AWARD
2005 winners:
Nonfiction: *The Race to Save the Lord God Bird*, Phillip Hoose
Picture Book: *Traction Man Is Here!*, Mini Grey
Fiction and Poetry: *The Schwa Was Here*, Neal Shusterman

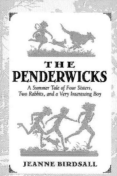

THE PENDERWICKS
A Summer Tale of Four Sisters, Two Rabbits, and a Very Interesting Boy

JEANNE BIRDSALL

Books

BUILDINGS & LANDMARKS

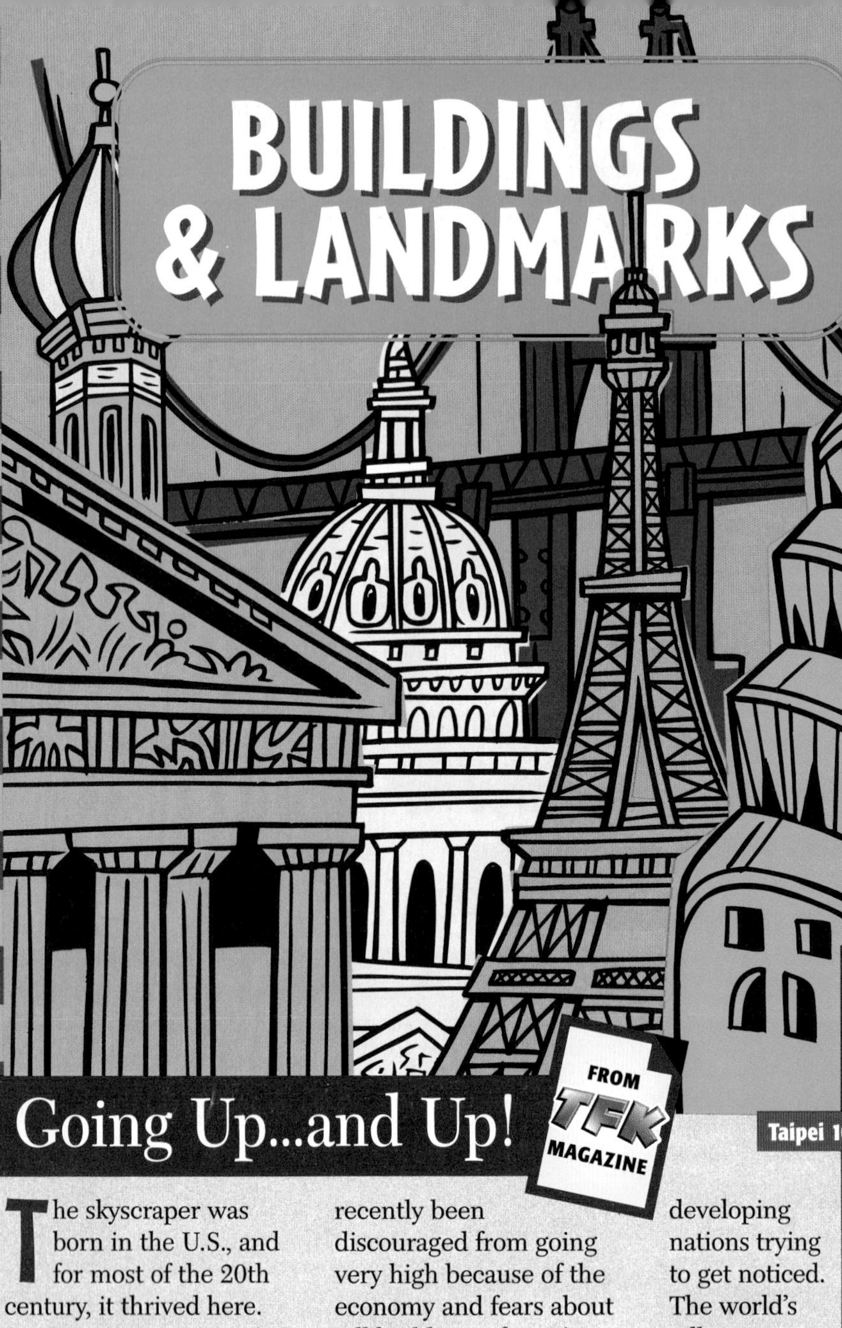

Going Up...and Up!

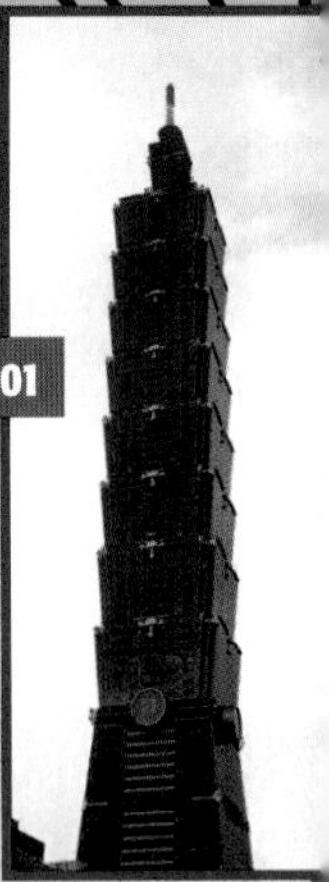

Taipei 101

The skyscraper was born in the U.S., and for most of the 20th century, it thrived here. Seventeen years ago, nine of the world's ten tallest buildings were in the U.S. (The 10th tallest was in Toronto.) Now just two are in the U.S.: the Sears Tower in Chicago and the Empire State Building in New York City. All the rest are in Asia. American developers have recently been discouraged from going very high because of the economy and fears about tall buildings after 9/11.

Even before the attacks of September 11, the tall building had been losing ground as a symbol of power, wealth and importance, at least in Western countries. But elsewhere in the world, extreme verticals are still in fashion, especially for developing nations trying to get noticed. The world's tallest building is the 1,670-foot-tall Taipei 101 in Taiwan. After it was completed in 2004, Taiwan's neighbor China decided to make its own giant building, the Shanghai World Financial Center, even taller. The building's architects

THE SKY'S THE LIMIT!

See how some of the world's tallest towers stack up against each other.

1. **BURJ DUBAI**
Dubai, U.A.E. (2008–under construction)
More than **2,000 feet**
Eventual height is secret.

2. **FREEDOM TOWER**
New York City (2009–under construction)
1,776 feet
Plans call for windmills to provide 20% of the building's power.

3. **TAIPEI 101**
Taipei, Taiwan (2004)
1,670 feet
The world's tallest building as of 2006

4. **SHANGHAI WORLD FINANCE CENTER**
Shanghai, China (2007–under construction)
1,614 feet
It will have the highest outdoor observation deck in the world.

5. **PETRONAS TOWERS**
Kuala Lumpur, Malaysia (1998) **1,483 feet**
Both of the towers have 32,000 windows and are 88 stories high.

6. **SEARS TOWER**
Chicago (1974) **1,450 feet**
The tallest building in the U.S. (spires count; antennas do not)

7. **JIN MAO TOWER**
Shanghai, China (1999)
1,381 feet
Has the world's highest hotel rooms

8. **WORLD TRADE CENTER**
New York City (1972, 1973)
1,368 feet and **1,362 feet**
Both towers were destroyed on Sept. 11, 2001.

9. **TWO INTERNATIONAL FINANCE CENTER**
Hong Kong (2003)
1,362 feet One of the few buildings in the world that has double-decker elevators

10. **EMPIRE STATE BUILDING**
New York City (1931)
1,250 feet
The world's ninth tallest building as of 2006 (it was the tallest for 41 years)

changed their designs so it would have more floors that are occupied by people than the tower in Taiwan.

Asia isn't the only place where the new "supertalls" are going up. Coming soon is the Burj Dubai, in Dubai, one of the United Arab Emirates in the Middle East.

When completed in 2008, it will supposedly rise to a height of more than 2,000 feet. The exact height is a secret so other builders who have projects in the planning stages won't pump up their towers a few feet higher. Experts agree that it won't be long before a tower rises to

3,000 feet—more than twice the height of either tower of the World Trade Center.

However the competition for tallest building ends, one thing is sure—skyscrapers are reaching new heights.
—*By Richard Lacayo*

Buildings & Landmarks

For a list of the world's tallest buildings:
www.factmonster.com/tallestbuildlings

41

SEVEN WONDERS OF **THE ANCIENT WORLD**

Since ancient times, people have put together many "seven wonders" lists. Below are the structures that were probably on the original list.

1. PYRAMIDS OF EGYPT

A group of three pyramids located at Giza, Egypt, was built around 2680 B.C. Of all the ancient wonders, only the pyramids still stand.

2. HANGING GARDENS OF BABYLON

These terraced gardens were located in what is now Iraq. They are said to have been built by Nebuchadnezzar II around 600 B.C. to please his queen.

3. STATUE OF ZEUS (Jupiter) AT OLYMPIA

The sculptor Phidias (fifth century B.C.) built this 40-foot-high statue of gold and ivory. It was located in Olympia, Greece.

4. TEMPLE OF ARTEMIS (Diana) AT EPHESUS

This beautiful marble structure, begun about 350 B.C. in honor of the goddess Artemis, was located in Ephesus, Turkey.

5. MAUSOLEUM AT HALICARNASSUS

This huge above-ground tomb was erected in Bodrum, Turkey, by Queen Artemisia in memory of her husband, who died in 353 B.C.

6. COLOSSUS AT RHODES

This bronze statue of Helios (Apollo) was about 105 feet high. It was the work of the sculptor Chares. Rhodes is a Greek island in the Aegean Sea.

7. PHAROS OF ALEXANDRIA

The Pharos (lighthouse) of Alexandria was built during the third century B.C. off the coast of Egypt. It stood about 450 feet high.

For more about famous structures around the world:
www.factmonster.com/structures

SEVEN WONDERS OF THE MODERN WORLD

This "seven wonders" list celebrates monumental engineering and construction feats of the 20th century. It was put together by the American Society of Civil Engineers.

1. EMPIRE STATE BUILDING

Finished in 1931, it towers 1,250 feet over New York City. Until the first tower of the World Trade Center was finished in 1972, it was the world's tallest building.

2. ITAIPÚ DAM

Built by Brazil and Paraguay on the Paraná River, it is the world's largest hydroelectric power plant. Completed in 1991, it took 16 years to build this series of dams whose length totals 25,406 feet.

Itaipú Dam

3. CN TOWER

In 1976 it became the world's tallest freestanding structure. It soars about one-third of a mile (1,815 feet) above Toronto, Canada.

CN Tower

4. PANAMA CANAL

It took 34 years to create this 50-mile-long canal across the Isthmus of Panama. Its huge locks connect the Atlantic and Pacific Oceans.

5. CHANNEL TUNNEL

Known as the Chunnel, it links France and England. It is 31 miles long, and 23 of those miles are 150 feet below the seabed of the English Channel. High-speed trains whiz through its side-by-side tubes.

6. NORTH SEA PROTECTION WORKS

The Netherlands is below sea level, so a series of dams, floodgates and surge barriers have been built to keep the sea from flooding the country during storms. The biggest part of the project, which some compare in scale to the Great Wall of China, was a 2-mile-long surge barrier across an estuary.

7. GOLDEN GATE BRIDGE

For many years, this suspension bridge that connects San Francisco and Marin County was the longest in the world. Begun in 1933, it took about four years—and 80,000 miles of steel wire—to complete the graceful 1.2-mile-long bridge.

TFK Puzzles & Games

High, There!

Something's wrong with these landmarks! Can you put them in their correct size order, from tallest to shortest?

- A. Clock Tower of Big Ben
- B. Eiffel Tower
- C. Great Pyramid of Cheops
- D. St. Louis Arch
- E. Statue of Liberty
- F. Washington Monument

(See Answer Key that begins on page 342.)

Buildings & Landmarks

43

FAMOUS STRUCTURES

- The **Akashi Kaikyo Bridge** in Japan, also known as the Pearl Bridge, is the world's longest suspension bridge. It has a main span of 6,529 feet. It cost $3.6 billion to build and was completed in 1998. The bridge was designed to withstand a magnitude 8.5 earthquake.

- The 12th century temples at **Angkor Wat** in Cambodia are surrounded by a moat and have walls decorated with sculpture.

- The **Brooklyn Bridge,** built between 1869 and 1883, was the achievement of engineer John Roebling. It was the first steel-wire suspension bridge in the world.

- The **Colosseum of Rome,** the largest and most famous of the Roman amphitheaters, was opened for use in A.D. 80.

- The **Dome of the Rock** dominates the skyline in the Old City of Jerusalem. Completed in A.D. 691, this Islamic shrine is decorated with intricate mosaics. It is located on a site that is important to Muslims, Christians and Jews. Its gold-plated dome was replaced in 1993.

Great Wall of China

- The **Eiffel Tower** in Paris was built in 1889. It is 984 feet high (1,056 feet tall including the television tower).

- The **Great Wall of China** (begun 228 B.C.), designed as a defense against nomadic tribes, is so big and long that it can be seen from orbit!

- **Machu Picchu** is an Inca fortress in the Andes Mountains of Peru. It is believed to have been built in the mid-15th century.

- The **Palace of Versailles** in France was built during the reign of Louis XIV in the 17th century and served as the royal palace until 1793.

- The **Pantheon** at Rome was begun in 27 B.C. It has served for 20 centuries as a place of worship.

- The **Parthenon of Greece,** built on the Acropolis in Athens, was the chief temple to the goddess Athena. It is believed to have been completed by 438 B.C.

Dome of the Rock

- The white marble **Taj Mahal**, built 1632–1650 at Agra, India, was a tomb for Shah Jahan's wife.

- The **Tower of London** is a group of buildings covering 13 acres. The central White Tower was begun in 1078. It was once a royal residence.

- The **Vatican** is a group of buildings in Rome that includes the residence of the Pope. The Basilica of St. Peter, the largest church in the Christian world, was begun in 1450.

- London's **Westminster Abbey** has been the coronation site of almost every British king and queen since William the Conqueror in 1066. It is also the burial site of many kings, queens and other famous people, including Isaac Newton, Charles Darwin and Charles Dickens.

Pantheon

Homework Tip!

If your home is noisy, use your school or local library to complete assignments.

Sea Lights

For centuries, lighthouses helped keep sailors safe at sea. They guided ships and alerted sailors to dangerous areas. Most boats today, however, are equipped with specialized navigation equipment, making many of the lighthouses that dot U.S. coastlines unnecessary. But these towers, full of history, still stand tall.

Lighthouses were made from stone, brick, concrete, wood, steel and cast iron. They were built in many shapes and sizes. They may be tall (where the land is flat) or short and squat (on a high cliff) and can be shaped like a square, an octagon, a cone or a cylinder.

Each lighthouse flashed a unique pattern of light. This helped sailors figure out their location. For example, a light might have a 12-second period of darkness and a 3-second period of brightness. A chart told sailors what lighthouse flashed which pattern, helping them to figure out their position at sea.

Groups and organizations throughout the country have raised money to restore and preserve these national treasures.

Cape Hatteras lighthouse

LIGHTHOUSE FACTS

- **First lighthouse in the U.S.: Boston Light, Massachusetts (1716). It remains the only lighthouse with lighthouse keepers.**

- **Oldest original lighthouse in service: Sandy Hook, New Jersey (1764)**

- **Tallest lighthouse: Cape Hatteras, North Carolina (191 feet)**

- **First lighthouse to use electricity: Statue of Liberty, New York (1886)**

- **Only lighthouse with an elevator: Charleston, South Carolina (1962)**

Buildings & Landmarks

For profile of famous architects and their work:
www.factmonster.com/famousarchitects

CALENDARS & HOLIDAYS

BANG!

NEW YEAR

Federal Holidays

NEW YEAR'S DAY
January 1
New Year's Day has its origin in ancient Roman times, when sacrifices were offered to Janus. This two-faced Roman god looked back on the past and forward to the future.

MARTIN LUTHER KING JR. DAY
Third Monday in January
Honors the civil rights leader

WASHINGTON'S BIRTHDAY
Third Monday in February
Sometimes called President's Day to honor both George Washington and Abraham Lincoln, it is officially called Washington's Birthday.

MEMORIAL DAY
Last Monday in May
A holiday dedicated to the memory of all war dead

INDEPENDENCE DAY
July 4
It celebrates the Declaration of Independence, which was adopted on July 4, 1776. The Declaration stated that the 13 colonies were independent from Britain.

go Check out holiday trivia at timeforkids.com/holiday trivia

2007

JANUARY
S	M	T	W	T	F	S
	1	2	3	4	5	6
7	8	9	10	11	12	13
14	15	16	17	18	19	20
21	22	23	24	25	26	27
28	29	30	31			

1 New Year's Day
15 Martin Luther King Jr.'s Birthday

FEBRUARY
S	M	T	W	T	F	S
				1	2	3
4	5	6	7	8	9	10
11	12	13	14	15	16	17
18	19	20	21	22	23	24
25	26	27	28			

14 Valentine's Day
18 Chinese New Year
19 Washington's Birthday observed

MARCH
S	M	T	W	T	F	S
				1	2	3
4	5	6	7	8	9	10
11	12	13	14	15	16	17
18	19	20	21	22	23	24
25	26	27	28	29	30	31

11 Daylight Saving Time begins
17 St. Patrick's Day
20 Spring begins

APRIL
S	M	T	W	T	F	S
1	2	3	4	5	6	7
8	9	10	11	12	13	14
15	16	17	18	19	20	21
22	23	24	25	26	27	28
29	30					

1 April Fool's Day
22 Earth Day

MAY
S	M	T	W	T	F	S
		1	2	3	4	5
6	7	8	9	10	11	12
13	14	15	16	17	18	19
20	22	23	23	24	25	26
27	28	29	30	31		

13 Mother's Day
28 Memorial Day

JUNE
S	M	T	W	T	F	S
					1	2
3	4	5	6	7	8	9
10	11	12	13	14	15	16
17	18	19	20	21	22	23
24	25	26	27	28	29	30

17 Father's Day
21 Summer begins

JULY
S	M	T	W	T	F	S
1	2	3	4	5	6	7
8	9	10	11	12	13	14
15	16	17	18	19	20	21
22	23	24	25	26	27	28
29	30	31				

4 Independence Day

AUGUST
S	M	T	W	T	F	S
			1	2	3	4
5	6	7	8	9	10	11
12	13	14	15	16	17	18
19	20	21	22	23	24	25
26	27	28	29	30	31	

SEPTEMBER
S	M	T	W	T	F	S
						1
2	3	4	5	6	7	8
9	10	11	12	13	14	15
16	17	18	19	20	21	22
23	24	25	26	27	28	29
30						

3 Labor Day
22 Fall begins

OCTOBER
S	M	T	W	T	F	S
	1	2	3	4	5	6
7	8	9	10	11	12	13
14	15	16	17	18	19	20
21	22	23	24	25	26	27
28	29	30	31			

8 Columbus Day
31 Halloween

NOVEMBER
S	M	T	W	T	F	S
				1	2	3
4	5	6	7	8	9	10
11	12	13	14	15	16	17
18	19	20	21	22	23	24
25	26	27	28	29	30	

4 Daylight Saving Time ends
11 Veterans Day
22 Thanksgiving

DECEMBER
S	M	T	W	T	F	S
						1
2	3	4	5	6	7	8
9	10	11	12	13	14	15
16	17	18	19	20	21	22
23	24	25	26	27	28	29
30	31					

20 Winter begins
25 Christmas
26 Kwanzaa begins

FOR A DESCRIPTION OF THE RELIGIOUS HOLIDAYS, SEE PAGE 201.

LABOR DAY
First Monday in September
A day set aside in honor of workers, it was first celebrated in New York City in 1882.

COLUMBUS DAY
Second Monday in October
This holiday honors Christopher Columbus's landing in the New World in 1492.

VETERANS DAY
November 11
Honors all men and women who have served America in its armed forces

THANKSGIVING
Fourth Thursday in November
First took place in 1621 to celebrate the harvest reaped by the Plymouth Colony after it survived a harsh winter

CHRISTMAS DAY
December 25
Celebrates the birth of Jesus

Calendars & Holidays

47

Other Fun Holidays

GROUNDHOG DAY
February 2
Legend has it that on this morning if a groundhog sees its shadow, there will be six more weeks of winter.

MARDI GRAS
Last day before Lent
Mardi Gras, or "Fat Tuesday," is a time of carnivals and parades before Ash Wednesday starts the penitent Christian season of Lent.

VALENTINE'S DAY
February 14
Named for the third-century martyr St. Valentine, this day is celebrated with candy, cards and other tokens of love.

MOTHER'S DAY
Second Sunday in May
Having a day to honor mothers goes back at least as far as 17th century England, when Mothering Sunday began.

FATHER'S DAY
Third Sunday in June
This U.S. holiday honoring fathers began in 1910 in Spokane, Washington.

HALLOWEEN
October 31
Halloween is celebrated with jack-o-lanterns, costumes, trick-or-treating and the telling of spooky stories.

KWANZAA
December 26 through January 1
Kwanzaa, an African American holiday, honors the values of ancient African culture.

TFK
Puzzles & Games

A Kooky Classroom

It's April Fool's Day. Ms. Reynolds's students have noticed that their classroom looks a little weirder than usual. Circle 10 things in the picture that are not right.

(See Answer Key that begins on page 342.)

For national holidays around the world:
www.factmonster.com/holidays

A WORLD OF FUN

CHINESE NEW YEAR

Chinese New Year is the longest and most important celebration in the Chinese calendar. The new year begins on the first day of the Chinese calendar, which usually falls in February, and the festivities continue for 15 days.

At Chinese New Year celebrations, people wear red clothes, give children "lucky money" in red envelopes and set off firecrackers. Red symbolizes fire, which the Chinese believe drives away bad luck. Family members gather at each other's homes for big meals. Chinese New Year ends with a lantern festival. People hang decorated lanterns in temples and carry lanterns to an evening parade under the light of the full moon. The highlight of the lantern festival is often the dragon dance. The dragon, which can stretch to 100 feet, is usually made of silk, paper, bamboo—and people!

MAY DAY

Children in England celebrate the end of winter and the arrival of spring on May 1 each year. The festivities center around a huge striped maypole that's decorated with flowers and streamers. Children hold the streamers as they dance around the pole, weaving intricate patterns as they pass each other. Adults also join in on the fun. A group of six or eight dancers arrange themselves in two lines and wave handkerchiefs or sticks as they dance by each other. A May Queen is crowned each year to preside over the celebration. May Day dates back to ancient times, when Romans honored Flora, the goddess of spring.

RAKSHA BANDHAN

Every August, brothers and sisters in northern India show their love for each other by celebrating Raksha Bandhan. This tradition dates back more than 500 years. The girls tie a bracelet of silk threads, called a *rakhi*, around their brothers' wrists. The boys then promise to protect their sisters. The siblings also give each other a piece of Indian candy, called *laddu*. At the end of the ceremony, the children exchange gifts.

DAY OF THE DEAD

Day of the Dead is celebrated on November 1 in Mexico, Ecuador, Guatemala and other parts of Central and South America. Families gather to pray to the souls of dead relatives, asking them to return for just one night. People decorate altars in their homes and gravesites with food, candles, candy skulls and marigolds to welcome the souls back to Earth. Skeletons are displayed throughout cities, and people dressed as skeletons parade through the streets. *Pan de los muertos* (bread of the dead) is baked in the shape of a skull and crossbones, and a toy is hidden inside each loaf. The person who bites into the toy is said to have good luck. Day of the Dead sounds like a grim event, but it's really a time to celebrate and remember the lives of dead family members.

For more international festivals:
www.factmonster.com/festivals

Calendars & Holidays

Days

A day is measured by how long it takes Earth to rotate on its axis once—24 hours. The names of the days are based on seven celestial bodies—the Sun (Sunday), the Moon (Monday), Mars (Tuesday), Mercury (Wednesday), Jupiter (Thursday), Venus (Friday) and Saturn (Saturday). The ancient Romans believed these bodies revolved around Earth and influenced its events.

Months

Months are based roughly on the cycles of the Moon. A lunar (Moon) month is 29½ days, or the time from one new Moon to the next.

But 12 lunar months add up to just 354 days—11 days fewer than are in our calendar year. To even things out, these 11 days are added to months during the year. As a result, most months have 30 or 31 days.

Years

The calendar most Americans use is called the Gregorian calendar. In an ordinary year this calendar has 365 days, which is about the amount of time it takes the Earth to make one trip around the Sun.

Earth's journey actually takes slightly more than a year. It takes 365 days, 5 hours, 48 minutes and 46 seconds. Every fourth year these extra hours, minutes and seconds are added up to make another day. When this happens, the year has 366 days and is called a leap year.

Groups of Years

Olympiad:	4 years
Decade:	10 years
Century:	100 years
Millennium:	1,000 years

Did You Know?

To help you remember how many days are in each month, say: "30 days has September, April, June and November. All the rest have 31, except February, which has 28."

Seasons

In the Northern Hemisphere, the year is divided into four seasons. **Each season begins at a solstice or an equinox.**

In the Southern Hemisphere, the dates (and the seasons) are reversed. The summer solstice (still the longest day of the year) falls around December 21, and the winter solstice is around June 21. So when it's summer in North America, it's winter in South America (and vice versa).

> **The spring equinox brings the start of spring, around March 21. At the equinox, day and night are about equal in length.**

> **The summer solstice, which happens around June 21, has the longest daylight time. It's also the first day of summer.**

> **Fall begins at the autumn equinox, around September 21. Day and night are about equal in length.**

> **The winter solstice, around December 21, has the shortest daylight time and officially kicks off winter.**

Spring to Summer

Every spring, we "spring forward," or move our clocks ahead one hour to gain extra daylight during the early evening. This makes the days seem longer, giving us more daylight for play—and for work. The practice is called Daylight Saving Time (DST), or "summer time." It evens out in the fall, when we "fall back" an hour, and the days seem much shorter.

The law that established daylight time does not insist that all states observe DST. In fact, Arizona and Hawaii receive so much sun throughout the year that gaining another hour of sunlight in the summertime is not considered necessary.

In August 2005, in an attempt to conserve oil, Congress passed a bill that extended Daylight Saving Time by a month. Beginning in 2007, DST will start the second Sunday of March and end on the first Sunday of November.

TFK Mystery Person

CLUE 1: I was born in New York City in 1889.

CLUE 2: When I was 8 years old, I wrote a letter to the New York *Sun* asking if Santa Claus exists. The newspaper's response is now one of the most famous editorials of all time.

CLUE 3: I later became a teacher and a principal in New York City.

WHO AM I?

(See Answer Key that begins on page 342.)

Birthstones

MONTH	STONE	MONTH	STONE
January	Garnet	July	Ruby or star ruby
February	Amethyst	August	Peridot or sardonyx
March	Aquamarine or bloodstone	September	Sapphire or star sapphire
April	Diamond	October	Opal or tourmaline
May	Emerald	November	Topaz or citrine
June	Pearl, alexandrite or moonstone	December	Turquoise, lapis lazuli, blue zircon or blue topaz

COMPUTERS & THE INTERNET

Internet Safety Rules and Tips

It seems as if there are rules and tips for everything, from crossing the street to spelling a word. The Internet is no different. Here are some things to remember to make sure you have a safe, enjoyable experience online.

- Don't give out your real last name, address, phone number, password or school name to any website unless you check with your parents first.

- Treat everyone that you meet online as a stranger, and use the same rules for dealing with strangers online as you would for strangers you see on the street.

- Don't agree to meet face-to-face with a person you've met online unless you first get permission from your parents. If your parents allow you to meet this person, you should take them with you and meet in a public place.

- Don't send people pictures of yourself unless you have permission from your parents.

- Tell your parents or teacher if you get an e-mail that makes you feel uncomfortable. Don't respond to it.

- If you're at a site and see or read something that makes you feel uncomfortable, let your parents or teacher know.

- As in the real world, treat others online the way you would like to be treated.

- Don't download any software or pictures without first asking a parent or teacher.

Mean Messages

Bullies have entered cyberspace.
What can kids do to stop them?

Jessica felt that she could not escape. "I was in tears every day when I went to the computer," she says. What was making her life so miserable? A girl who had been picking on her at school started attacking her online.

Jessica, 12, is not alone. Many kids are feeling the sting of online teasing. Bullying has moved beyond school and into cyberspace, the world of computer networks. The problem is growing.

Parry Aftab heads an organization that teaches kids how to deal with cyberbullies. Aftab has found that 55% of kids ages 9 to 14 have experienced some form of online bullying. "Cyberbullying is any way of using interactive technology to humiliate, frighten or target another child," she says.

Computers, cellphones, pagers and interactive games are the weapons that cyberbullies use. Bullies send hateful e-mails and instant messages. They create websites with mean words and embarrassing pictures. They steal passwords and spread rumors. Cyberbullying may not inflict physical pain, but it causes emotional hurt.

The issue is now being addressed by schools, communities, parents and kids themselves. The nation's first cyberbullying summit was held in 2005 in White Plains, New York. More than 500 people attended. Kieran Halloran, 12, came with a group from his middle school. Kieran learned that if no one tries to stop online bullying, "the problem can grow."

One solution to cyberbullying is education—teaching kids and adults how to deal with online attacks. Aftab's group trains students to become TeenAngels, who pass on anti-bullying advice to others. Mary Lou Handy, a teacher in New Jersey, advises a chapter of Teen Angels. "It's influential when it comes from one child to another," Handy says. "Kids [learn to] think on their feet."

—By Nicole Iorio

Stop a Cyberbully

Parry Aftab, the executive director of WiredSafety.org, offers tips on dealing with troubling messages.

- **BE PRIVATE.** Keep passwords, pictures and secrets to yourself.

- **TAKE FIVE.** Instead of replying to a message that upsets you, step away and do something you enjoy for five minutes.

- **STOP, BLOCK AND TELL.** Stop before you reply. This way you won't do anything that you will regret. Block the sender. Tell someone you trust about the message.

- **SAVE THE EVIDENCE.** Save mean messages on your computer or use monitoring software.

- **GOOGLE YOURSELF.** Check to make sure that your name isn't in any unwanted places. Tell an adult if it is. Your parents can help you take action.

Cyberspace expert Parry Aftab talks with a group of New Jersey TeenAngels about how bullies threaten kids online.

Computers & the Internet

53

Internet Stats and Facts

Top Things Kids Do on the Internet

Here's a look at what kids ages 12 to 17 do online.

ACTIVITY	% OF KIDS ONLINE
Send or read e-mail	89%
Play online games	81
Go online to get news or information about current events	76
Send or receive instant messages	75
Buy things online, such as books, clothing or music	43
Send or receive text messages using a cellphone	38

Source: Pew Internet Project

Cyberkids

This table shows the percentage of U.S. kids who surf the web.

AGE	% OF AMERICAN KIDS WHO USE THE INTERNET
3–4	19.9%
5–9	42.0
10–13	67.3
14–17	78.8

Source: U.S. Dept. of Commerce

Wired World

These are the countries with the most Internet users.

COUNTRY	NUMBER OF USERS
1. U.S.	185,550,000
2. China	99,800,000
3. Japan	78,050,000
4. Germany	41,880,000
5. India	36,970,000
6. United Kingdom	33,110,000
7. South Korea	31,670,000
8. Italy	25,530,000
9. France	25,470,000
10. Brazil	22,320,000

Source: Computer Industry Almanac, Inc.

Did You Know?

Blogging is the hottest new Internet trend since instant messaging. A blog, a contraction of the words of *web* and *log*, is an online diary that people post for others to read. About 32 million Americans read blogs.

For a history of the Internet:
www.factmonster.com/Internet

Internet Research Guide

The Internet has become a convenient tool for finding information on just about anything. Here are some important things to keep in mind when you're doing research on the Internet.

>> Be as specific as possible with search terms.
If, for example, you heard scientists have discovered that Jupiter has more moons than previously thought, include all the information you know when doing your search. If you simply search for *Jupiter*, you'll get too much general information. But if you type in *Jupiter*, *moon* and *new*, chances are you'll find out what you want much more quickly.

>> If you're searching for a specific phrase, put the words in quotes. The search engine will only look for the exact term that's inside the quotes. For example, if you want information on the Vietnam War, type *"Vietnam War"*.

>> Use the word AND (in uppercase letters) to indicate that you want two or more terms to appear in the search results. For example, if you're looking for hurricanes that occurred in Bermuda, you'd type *Bermuda AND hurricanes*.

Similarly, you can use the word *NOT* (in uppercase letters) to eliminate a term from the search. For instance, by typing *Bermuda NOT shorts*, you are telling the search engine that you are not interested in Bermuda shorts. You can also use the plus sign (+) and minus sign (-) in place of *AND* and *NOT*. Don't put a space between the sign and the words in the search term.

>> If you're not having luck with your search term, try using a synonym. Instead of typing *Revolutionary War*, try *American Revolution*. Or instead of *9/11*, try *September 11*.

>> When searching for a biography, it helps to type the word *biography* after the person's name in the search engine. That weeds out some irrelevant search results. Biographies on the web are sometimes unreliable, so it's very important to check dates and other facts against other biographies—in books, say—to make sure they are accurate.

>> Go directly to a site if you know it will help you. For example, if you're looking for information on Saturn, you might try NASA's site first. You can type the URL directly in the address bar of your web browser. If you don't know the URL, you can search for the site using a search engine.

>> Try different search engines if one isn't producing results. Google, Ask Jeeves and Yahoo are some reputable search engines.

>> Know your source! Anybody can put up information on the Internet and claim to be an expert. The information you read on someone's home page may be incorrect. The websites of government sources, schools and publishers of magazines and newspapers are more accurate. If you use other sources, verify the information in a book or on another website.

Computers & the Internet

To learn how a computer works:
www.factmonster.com/computers

Video Game Timeline

1972 The era of video games begins: Pong is invented.

Magnavox's Odyssey, the first home video-game system, is released.

1977 The Atari 2600 game system sells millions of units.

1978 Space Invaders blips its way into arcades everywhere.

1980 Pac-Man is released.

1981 The first video-game magazine, *Electronic Games,* debuts.

1982 The first hit song based on a video game, "Pac-Man Fever," is released.

Tron, the first movie about video games, hits theaters.

1986 The Nintendo Entertainment System (NES) is released in the U.S. To compete with the NES, Sega introduces the Sega Master System (SMS).

1989 Nintendo releases the handheld Game Boy.

1993 The Senate investigates video-game violence.

Myst is released.

1994 The Entertainment Software Rating Board is created. Ratings on the games' packaging indicate the suggested age of players.

1995 Sony releases the PlayStation in the U.S.

1997 Kids go crazy for Tamagotchi, a virtual pet.

2000 The Sims sells millions of copies.

2001 Microsoft and Nintendo introduce their next-generation systems within days of each other: the Xbox and Nintendo's GameCube.

2002 The Sims surpasses Myst as the best-selling PC game ever.

2005 Sony releases the PSP, a portable system.

Top-Selling Video Games of 2005

RANK	TITLE	PLATFORM
1.	Madden NFL 2006	PlayStation 2
2.	Pokemon Emerald	Game Boy Advance
3.	Gran Turismo 4	PlayStation 2
4.	Madden NFL 2006	XBox
5.	NCAA Football 2006	PlayStation 2
6.	Star Wars: Battlefront II	PlayStation 2
7.	MVP Baseball 2005	PlayStation 2
8.	Star Wars Episode III: Revenge of the Sith	PlayStation 2
9.	NBA Live 2006	PlayStation 2
10.	LEGO Star Wars	PlayStation 2

Source: The NPD Group

Quality Control

This computer factory has a lot of bugs in it. In each row, only one of the computer parts (A through D) matches the correctly made part shown in the first column. Can you find the perfectly made computer part in each row? The rest go in the junk heap!

(See Answer Key that begins on page 342.)

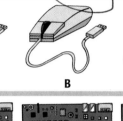

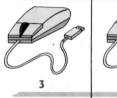

Did You Know?

About 71% of all kids ages 3 to 8 use computers, and more than 92% of kids ages 9 to 17 use them, according to the U.S. Census Bureau. In addition, nearly 60% of all U.S. homes have at least one computer.

Mystery Person

CLUE 1: I was born in London, England, in 1791. From an early age, I was interested in math.

CLUE 2: Around 1830, I designed the Difference Engine, a machine that performed simple mathematical calculations. Next, I tried to make a device that used cards with holes to quickly compute complicated functions. I called it the Analytical Engine.

CLUE 3: My advanced ideas earned me the title "Father of the modern computer."

WHO AM I?

(See Answer Key that begins on page 342.)

Computers & the Internet

57

DINOSAURS

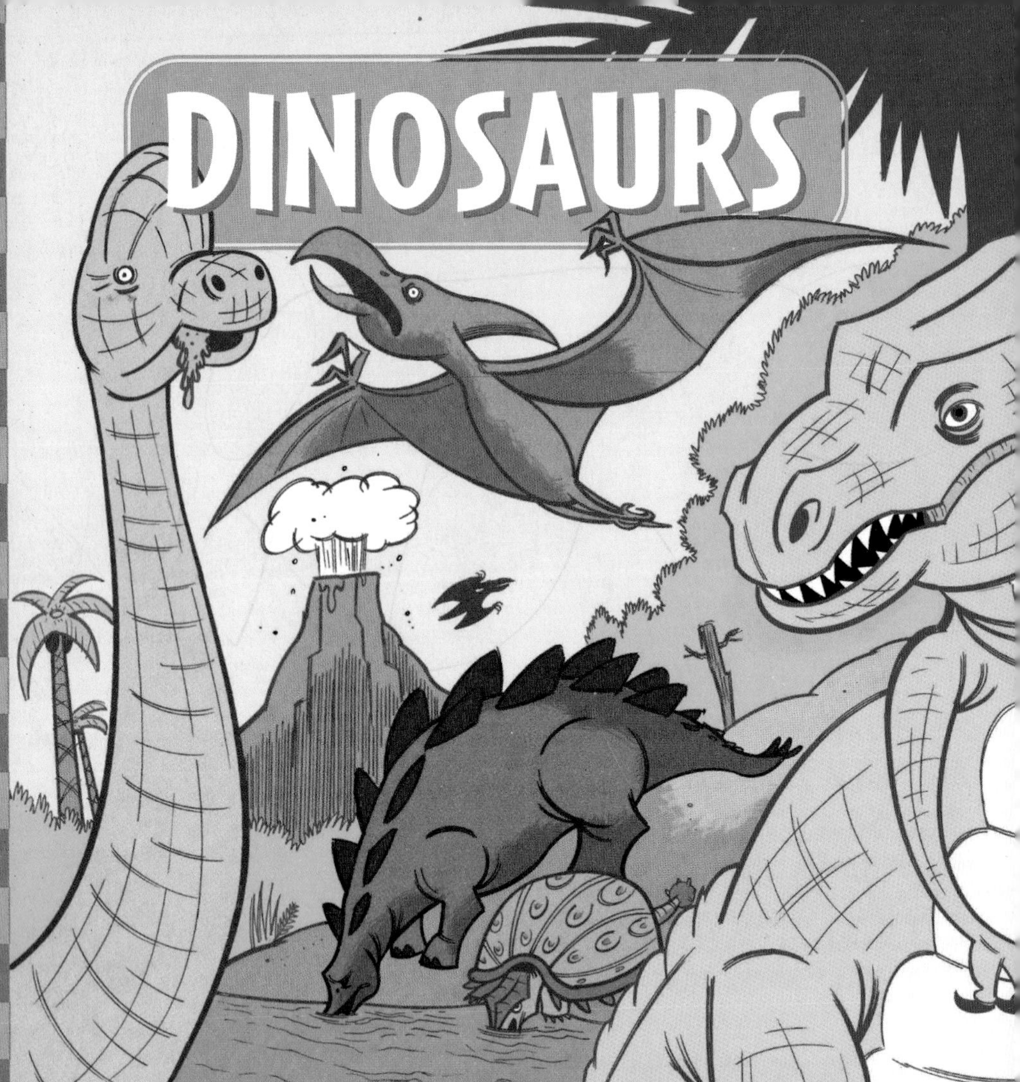

1. TRIASSIC 245 MILLION TO 208 MILLION YEARS AGO

- During the Triassic Period, all land on Earth existed as one enormous mass. It was called Pangaea. The supercontinent slowly began to break up during the Triassic Period.

- Some reptiles, frogs, turtles and crocodiles existed earlier, but dinosaurs didn't appear until late in the Triassic Period.

- The period marked the rise of small, lightly built dinosaurs.

- The first mammals evolved during the Triassic Period.

- Most of the plants that existed were evergreens.

- The period ended with a mass extinction that wiped out most animals. The dinosaurs that survived flourished in the Jurassic Period.

Eoraptor

Triassic dinosaurs include:

Coelophysis "hollow form"

Desmatosuchus "link crocodile"

Eoraptor "dawn thief"

Ichthyosaurus "fish lizard"

Iguanodon "iguana teeth"

Plateosaurus "flat lizard"

Saltopus "leaping foot"

Ichthyosaurus

DAYS OF THE DINOSAURS

Dinosaurs lived throughout the **Mesozoic Era,** which began 245 million years ago and lasted for 180 million years. It is sometimes called the Age of Reptiles. The era is divided into **three periods,** shown here: the Triassic, the Jurassic and the Cretaceous.

Allosaurus

2. JURASSIC 208 MILLION TO 146 MILLION YEARS AGO

- The supercontinent Pangaea continued to break apart.
- Dinosaurs ruled the land during the period.
- Herbivores and carnivores increased in size; some of the largest dinosaurs emerged during the Jurassic Period.
- Birdlike dinosaurs first appeared.
- Flowering plants began to appear late in the period.
- The Jurassic Period also ended with an extinction, but only a few types of dinosaurs died out.

Jurassic dinosaurs include:

Allosaurus "different lizard"
Apatosaurus "deceptive lizard"
Archaeopteryx "ancient wing"
Brachiosaurus "armed lizard"
Compsognathus "pretty jaw"
Diplodocus "double-beamed"
Mamenchisaurus "Mamenchin lizard"
Stegosaurus "plated lizard"

Brachiosaurus

3. CRETACEOUS 146 MILLION TO 65 MILLION YEARS AGO

- Pangaea continued to separate into smaller continents.
- A wide variety of dinosaurs roamed the land.
- Birds flourished and spread all over the globe.
- Flowering plants developed.
- Mammals thrived.
- Dinosaurs became extinct by the end of the period. The extinction marked the end of the Age of Reptiles and the beginning of the Age of Mammals.

Cretaceous dinosaurs include:

Ankylosaurus "crooked lizard"
Velociraptor "speedy thief"
Megaraptor "huge robber"
Pteranodon "winged and toothless"
Seismosaurus "quake lizard"
Triceratops "three-horned face"
Troödon "wounding tooth"
Tyrannosaurus rex "tyrant lizard"

Triceratops

Velociraptor

Ankylosaurus

A Dino Bone Breakthrough

Areas of the bone have bundled strands of tissue, a trait never before seen in a fossil so old.

In 2005, scientists at North Carolina State University, in Raleigh, announced a thrilling discovery. The 70 million-year-old fossil of a *Tyrannosaurus rex* contained blood vessels and other soft tissues. Such tissues had never been recovered in a dinosaur bone.

The fossil was found in Montana. Scientists believe that this *T. rex* weighed 5 tons and was 40 feet tall.

In the lab, dinosaur experts, or paleontologists, noticed unusual tissue fragments lining the walls of the bone's marrow cavity. Normally, after a few million years, soft tissues are replaced by mineral deposits.

A microscope revealed that the tissues contained tiny blood vessels and reddish-brown dots that are thought to be cells' nuclei, or central structures. Some researchers hope to recover dinosaur DNA—the chemical that makes up genes—from the tissues.

Could dinosaurs be cloned from the DNA, as they were in the *Jurassic Park* movies? Scientists think not, but they hope the tissues will provide clues to the biological makeup of the animals.

—*By Joe McGowan*

How Fossils Form

Fossils are the remains or imprints of prehistoric plants or animals. They are found in sedimentary rock (formed from sand and mud), coal, tar, volcanic ash or hardened tree sap. Usually only the hard parts of plants and animals, such as their bones and teeth, become fossils.

Most animals that became fossils either lived in water or were washed into a body of water. After an animal died, its soft parts, such as its fur, skin, muscles and organs, decomposed. The hard parts that remained were buried under moist layers of mud or sand, where there was no oxygen or bacteria to cause them to decay. Over time, many of these bodies of water dried up. The sediment that covered the bones eventually turned into solid rock. Over millions of years, minerals in the surrounding rock replaced the original animal tissue and formed a fossil.

Sometimes water seeped into the rocks and dissolved the animal tissue. When this happened, the outline of the animal remained intact between the layers of rock, leaving a fossil in the form of a natural mold.

Paleontologists, or scientists who study dinosaurs, use fossils to learn about the creatures who roamed Earth millions of years ago.

Extreme Dinos

LARGEST
Seismosaurus
"quake lizard"
- Cretaceous Period
- It measured about 120 feet from head to tail and stood about 18 feet tall.

SMALLEST
Compsognathus
"delicate jaw"
- Jurassic Period
- This tiny creature was about the size of a chicken and weighed about 6.5 pounds.

FASTEST
Ornithomimus
"bird mimic"
- Cretaceous Period
- This dinosaur, which looked like an ostrich, could run about 40 to 50 m.p.h.

SMARTEST
Troödon
"wounding tooth"
- Cretaceous Period
- Troödon had the largest brain size to body size ratio of all known dinosaurs. It's believed to have been as smart as modern-day birds.

MOST FAMOUS
Tyrannosaurus rex
"tyrant lizard"
- Cretaceous Period
- T. rex ran the show during the Cretaceous Period and still dominates the popular imagination.

OLDEST
Eoraptor lunensis
"dawn plunderer"
- Triassic Period
- Eoraptor lunensis lived about 227 million years ago.

DUMBEST
Stegosaurus
"plated lizard"
- Jurassic Period
- This giant's brain was the size of a walnut. If the ratio of brain size to body size indicates intelligence (or lack of it!), then this 3-ton herbivore was certainly not a mental giant.

MOST TEETH
Hadrosaurs
"duck-billed lizards"
- Cretaceous Period
- Several of these plant eaters had about 960 cheek teeth.

TFK Mystery Person

CLUE 1: I am one of the best-known dinosaur experts in America. I found my first fossil when I was 8 years old.

CLUE 2: One of my many major discoveries about dinos is that some dinosaurs may have laid their eggs in nests and taken care of their babies.

CLUE 3: I was the science adviser for the *Jurassic Park* movies.

WHO AM I?
(See Answer Key that begins on page 342.)

Did You Know?

A male dinosaur is called a bull; a female is called a cow; a young dinosaur is referred to as either a hatchling or a juvenile. A group of dinosaurs is called a herd (for plant eaters) or a pack (for meat eaters).

For dinosaur FAQs:
www.factmonster.com/dinofaqs

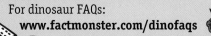

Dinosaurs

ENVIRONMENT & ENERGY

SUGAR CA
$0.2

GALLONS   19.

COST $5.5

The Future of Energy

FROM TFK MAGAZINE

Here are some cool new ideas for renewable energy sources

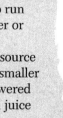

Americans consume 21 million barrels of oil every day to fuel our cars, heat our homes and power our farms, factories and cities. But as the price of oil goes up, many experts worry that it will become more difficult and expensive to tap the world's underground oil supplies. That is why scientists are searching for other ways to meet the nation's energy needs. Here are some creative ways that humans can use nature's power.

Catch a Wave

Dams are used around the world to channel rivers in order to produce electricity. But the future of water power may lie in harnessing the motion of ocean waves and the rise and fall of tides along the shore.

Tom Denniss and his company, Energetech, are trying to figure out the best ways to do this. One of their projects in Australia uses a four-story-high floating power plant that turns the motion of waves into electricity. "Wave energy," Denniss told TIME, is "more consistent, predictable and concentrated than wind. It's also inexhaustible."

A Sweet Ride

Drivers in Brazil are filling up with fuel that comes from sugarcane. A new kind of car, called a Flex car, runs on either regular gasoline or ethanol, a kind of alcohol that can be produced from sugarcane. Sugarcane is a crop that is grown all over Brazil.

The sales of those cars, which look and work like regular vehicles, out-number sales of gasoline models in Brazil. "People see Flex cars as the car of the future," sugarcane-fuel booster Alfred Szwarc told TIME.

Pigpen Power

Machines called biogas digesters can turn poop into a power supply. The smelly waste is put into a tank where tiny bacteria break it down into simpler substances, including methane gas. The gases that are produced can be burned to heat homes and generate electricity. The technology has been used for many years in places such as Nepal, China and India.

Digesters keep getting easier to use and less expensive. One at-home system that produces gas for cooking as well as for fertilizer costs only $180.

Soaking Up the Sun

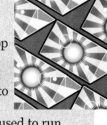

For years, large, rooftop solar panels have turned sunshine into electricity that can be used to run factories, heat water or cool homes. This alternative energy source is being used on a smaller scale too. Solar-powered backpacks that can juice up cellphones and iPods are on the market. Also in the works is clothing that could one day keep a laptop computer humming anywhere that the Sun shines.
—*By Andrea Delbanco*

Environment & Energy

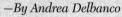
go

Test how much you know about protecting the environment at timeforkids.com/eq

ENERGY AND THE EARTH

Energy is the power we use for transportation, to heat and light our homes and to manufacture all kinds of products. Energy sources come in two types: nonrenewable and renewable.

NONRENEWABLE SOURCES OF ENERGY

Most of the energy we use comes from fossil fuels such as coal, natural gas and petroleum. Once these natural resources are used up, they are gone forever. Uranium, a metallic chemical element, is another nonrenewable source, but it is not a fossil fuel. Uranium is converted to a fuel and used in nuclear power plants.

The process of gathering these fuels can be harmful to the environment. In addition, to produce energy, fossil fuels are put through a process called combustion. Combustion releases pollution, such as carbon monoxide and sulfur dioxide, and may contribute to acid rain and global warming.

Did You Know?

Fossil fuels are called that because over many millions of years, heat from the Earth's core and pressure from rock and soil have reacted with the fossils (or remains) of dead plants and animals to form fuel.

RENEWABLE SOURCES OF ENERGY

Renewable sources of energy can be used over and over again. Renewable resources include solar energy, wind, geothermal energy, biomass and hydropower. They generate much less pollution—in both their gathering and in production—than do nonrenewable sources.

- **Solar energy** comes from the Sun. Some people use solar panels on their homes to convert sunlight into electricity.
- **Wind turbines,** which look like giant windmills, generate electricity.
- **Geothermal energy** comes from the Earth's core. Engineers extract steam or very hot water from the Earth's crust and use the steam to produce electricity.
- **Biomass** includes natural products such as wood, manure and corn. These materials are burned and used for heat.
- Dams and rivers generate **hydropower.** When water flows through a dam, it activates a turbine, which runs an electric generator.

Top Energy Producers and Consumers

The United States produces the most energy in the world, and it also uses the most—more than double the amount used by China, the world's second largest energy consumer. Here's a look at the world's top energy consumers and producers.

PRODUCERS

In 2003, total world energy production was 419 quadrillion Btus. *Btu* is the abbreviation for British thermal unit. One Btu is nearly equal to the amount of energy released when a wooden match is burned.

	COUNTRY	BTUS PRODUCED
1.	United States	70.5 quadrillion
2.	Russia	49.2 quadrillion
3.	China	44.1 quadrillion
4.	Saudi Arabia	23.2 quadrillion
5.	Canada	18.4 quadrillion
6.	Iran	11.3 quadrillion

Source: U.S. Department of Energy

CONSUMERS

	COUNTRY	% OF WORLD ENERGY CONSUMED
1.	United States	23%
2.	China	11
3.	Russia	7
4.	Japan	5
5.	Germany	3
6.	India	3

Source: U.S. Department of Energy

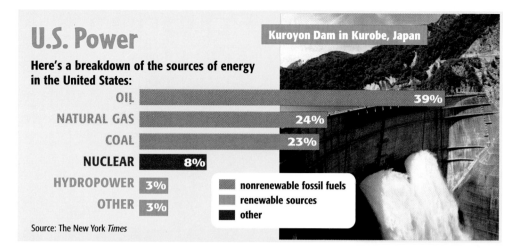

U.S. Power

Here's a breakdown of the sources of energy in the United States:

Kuroyon Dam in Kurobe, Japan

OIL	39%
NATURAL GAS	24%
COAL	23%
NUCLEAR	8%
HYDROPOWER	3%
OTHER	3%

- nonrenewable fossil fuels
- renewable sources
- other

Source: The New York *Times*

Oil Reliance

Each day, the United States uses about 21 million barrels of oil—more than any other country in the world. It imports about 58% of it. Here's where we get the oil.

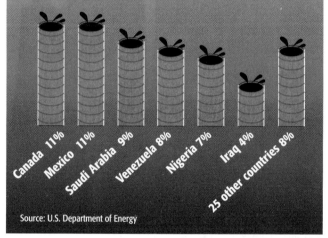

Canada 11% Mexico 11% Saudi Arabia 9% Venezuela 8% Nigeria 7% Iraq 4% 25 other countries 8%

Source: U.S. Department of Energy

Oil Reserves by Country

These are the countries with the greatest oil reserves—oil that can be taken from the ground with current technology.

RANK	COUNTRY
1.	Saudi Arabia
2.	Canada
3.	Iran
4.	Iraq
5.	Kuwait

Source: U.S. Energy Information Administration

Did You Know?

Crude oil is used to make not only gasoline, diesel fuel and heating oil, but also such products as plastic, fertilizer, pesticides, crayons, detergents, polyester and deodorant.

For an environment glossary:
www.factmonster.com/envterms

An oil rig in the United Arab Emirates

Environment & Energy

65

Perils of Pollution

Human-caused pollution may be making the world a warmer place, a process called **global warming.** Scientists think pollution could contribute to a rise in the Earth's surface temperature over the next 100 years. A warmer world could mean big trouble. Hotter temperatures are causing some ice at the North and South Poles to melt and the oceans to rise. The warmer climate is changing our weather patterns and could result in dangerous tornadoes and droughts.

Acid rain occurs when rainwater is contaminated with pollutants like nitrogen oxide and sulfur dioxide. These gases come from fuels being burned at high temperatures, as in car exhausts. When acid rain falls, it can damage wildlife and erode buildings.

The **ozone layer,** a thin sheet of an invisible gas called ozone, surrounds Earth about 15 miles above its surface. Ozone protects us from the Sun's harmful rays. In recent years, the amount of ozone in the atmosphere has decreased, probably due to human-made gases called chlorofluorocarbons (CFCs). As the ozone level decreases, the Sun's rays become more dangerous to humans.

The Earth stays warm the same way a greenhouse does. Gases in the atmosphere, such as carbon dioxide, methane and nitrogen, act like the glass of a greenhouse: they let in the Sun's light and warmth, but they keep the Earth's heat from escaping. This is known as the **greenhouse effect.** Scientists think that if too many of these greenhouse gases are released into the atmosphere, from pollution, for example, the gases can trap too much heat, causing temperatures to rise.

Pollution is the contamination of air or water by harmful substances. One source of pollution is **hazardous waste**—anything thrown away that could be dangerous to the environment, such as paint and pesticides. These materials can seep into water supplies and contaminate them.

Dirty Water

In 2004, people removed eight million pounds of garbage from our oceans. Here are the top 10 types of debris they found.

RANK	DEBRIS
1.	Cigarettes and cigarette filters
2.	Food wrappers and containers
3.	Caps and lids
4.	Plastic drink bottles
5.	Bags
6.	Glass drink bottles
7.	Cups, plates, forks, knives and spoons
8.	Drink cans
9.	Straws and stirrers
10.	Tobacco packaging and wrappers

Source: The Ocean Conservancy

Did You Know?

Every year, Americans throw away 50 billion food and drink cans, 27 billion glass bottles and jars and 65 million plastic and metal jar and can covers. More than 30% of our waste is packaging materials.

For a list of pollutants:
www.factmonster.com/pollutants

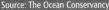

Earth-Altering Accidents

Three Mile Island

Accidents that destroy the delicate balance of nature or cause a large number of people to suffer are known as disasters. Here are some of the most famous environmental disasters to have been caused by human activity.

LOVE CANAL

Love Canal, a small town in upstate New York, was contaminated by waste from chemical plants. Beginning in 1947, chemical companies could legally dump their waste products into the town's canal. In the 1950s, families began to settle in the area without being told about the waste and the health problems it might cause. A foul smell developed, trees lost their bark and leaves fell throughout the year. In the 1970s, scientists found that the drinking water contained high levels of 82 industrial chemicals; seven of them were thought to cause cancer. The people of Love Canal had an unusually high rate of cancer and birth defects. Many of the houses had to be abandoned. By the 1990s, the town had been cleaned up, and families began moving back to the area.

THREE MILE ISLAND

On March 28, 1979, the worst accident in U.S. nuclear reactor history took place at the Three Mile Island power station, near Harrisburg, Pennsylvania. Coolant (the fluid that keeps a machine cool) escaped from the reactor core. The leak was caused by a combination of mechanical failure and human error. Luckily no one died, and very little radioactivity was released into the air.

BHOPAL CHEMICAL LEAK

An explosion in the Union Carbide chemical plant in Bhopal, India, in December 1984 released a deadly gas that is used to make pesticide. The gas formed a cloud that killed 2,500 people and caused another 50,000 to 100,000 to become ill. Trees and plants in the area became yellow and brittle. The explosion was caused by a mechanical failure.

CHERNOBYL

At 1:23 A.M. on Saturday, April 26, 1986, the reactor blew at the nuclear power plant in Chernobyl, Ukraine (then part of the Soviet Union). The explosion ripped open the core, blew the roof off the building, started more than 30 fires and allowed radioactive material to leak into the air. About 30 people were killed, and nearly 300 others were treated for radiation poisoning. Violations of safety rules were at the bottom of this tragic event.

Exxon Valdez oil spill

EXXON VALDEZ OIL SPILL

On March 24, 1989, 11.2 million gallons of crude oil spilled from the tanker Exxon Valdez into Alaska's Prince William Sound when the ship's hull hit a reef and tore open. The spill cost billions of dollars to clean up and killed millions of birds, fish and other wildlife. The tragedy was caused by human error and could have been avoided.

Did You Know?

The United States first celebrated Earth Day on April 22, 1970. More than 20 million people marched in parades, sang songs and attended teach-ins on the environment.

For a look at how people have affected the environment:
www.factmonster.com/environhistory

Environment & Energy

The Three Rs

Recycling is a great way to conserve resources and help the environment. Remember the three Rs:

1. REDUCE Reducing waste is the best way to help the environment. Buy large containers of food whenever possible. For example, buy one 32-ounce container of yogurt rather than four 8-ounce cups.

2. REUSE Rather than throw things away, find ways to use them again. Use food containers for paint cups or for storing toys or art supplies. Cut old clothes into pieces and use them as rags.

3. RECYCLE Recycled items are new products made out of the materials from old ones. Recycle all of your used paper and your aluminum, plastic and glass containers.

Change Those Wasteful Ways

Do you ever take a really long shower on a cold morning? Or turn up the heat rather than put on a sweater? If you do, you're wasting precious resources. Follow these guidelines to conserve our natural resources. Every bit counts!

- Turn off the lights and television when you leave a room.

- Set your computer to sleep mode. It darkens the screen when not in use.

- Turn off or turn down the heat or air conditioner when you go to bed or when you leave your home for a long time.

- Turn off the water while brushing your teeth and lathering up.

- Run dishwashers only when they are fully loaded. The light-wash feature uses less water.

- Dripping faucets need to be fixed. One drop per second wastes 540 gallons of water a year!

- Don't use water toys that require a constant flow of water.

- Don't water your lawn too often. Grass only needs to be watered about once a week in the summer. Lawns can go two weeks without water after a heavy rain.

- Ask your parents to fix drafty windows and doors.

- Encourage your parents to buy appliances that have an Energy Star label. The label has the word *energy* and a picture of a star with a rainbow.

- Walk or ride your bike rather than have your parents drive you places.

- Use both sides of paper when you draw or write.

- See if your favorite newspaper or magazine is available on the Internet before you buy a copy. Print only the pages you need.

- Use plastic containers for snacks and sandwiches rather than plastic bags.

go Learn how to help the environment at timeforkids.com/house

What Americans Throw Away

	% OF ALL TRASH
Paper products and cardboard	36%
Yard waste	20%
Food waste	9%
Metals	9%
Glass	8%
Plastics	7%
Rubber and leather goods	3%
Other	8%

Dirty Cities

Are you breathing dirty air? Below are lists of the dirtiest cities in the United States and the world.

RANK		METROPOLITAN AREA
U.S.	1.	Los Angeles–Long Beach–Riverside, California
	2.	Bakersfield, California
	3.	Fresno-Madera, California
	4.	Visalia-Porterville, California
	5.	Merced, California

Los Angeles

Source: American Lung Association

WORLD	1.	Mexico City, Mexico
	2.	São Paulo, Brazil
	3.	Cairo, Egypt
	4.	New Delhi, India
	5.	Shanghai, China

Source: World Health Organization

Mexico City

TFK Top 5

Largest National Forests in the U.S.

Tongass National Forest

There are 155 national forests in the U.S. The two largest are located in the biggest state, Alaska. Tongass National Forest is about the size of West Virginia. Here are the largest forests.

1. Tongass National Forest, Sitka, Alaska
   25,913 square miles

2. Chugach National Forest Anchorage, Alaska
   8,433 square miles

3. Toiyabe National Forest Sparks, Nevada
   5,051 square miles

4. Tonto National Forest Phoenix, Arizona
   4,489 square miles

5. Gila National Forest Silver City, New Mexico
   4,232 square miles

Source: Land Areas of the National Forest System

Did You Know?

Recycling one ton of paper saves 17 trees and 17,000 gallons of water. More than 30 million trees are cut down to produce a year's supply of newspapers.

Environment & Energy

69

MAJOR BIOMES OF THE WORLD

Have you visited any biomes lately? A biome is a large community of plants and animals that is supported by a certain type of climate.

Polar bear

Raccoon

Deciduous Forest

WHERE: This biome is in the mild-temperate zone of the Northern Hemisphere. Major regions are found in eastern North America, Europe and eastern Asia.

SPECIAL FEATURES: Deciduous trees lose their leaves in fall. The natural decaying of the fallen leaves enriches the soil and supports plant and animal life.

WHAT LIVES THERE? Oak, beech, ash and maple trees are typical, and many types of insect and animal life abound. In the U.S., the deciduous forest is home to many animals including deer, American gray squirrels, rabbits, raccoons and woodpeckers.

Arctic Tundra

WHERE: The Arctic tundra is a cold, treeless area of low, swampy plains in the far north around the Arctic Ocean.

SPECIAL FEATURES: This is Earth's coldest biome. The Arctic tundra's frozen subsoil, called permafrost, makes it impossible for trees to grow.

WHAT LIVES THERE? Animals that live in this biome include polar bears, Arctic foxes, caribou and gray wolves. Plants that you might find include small shrubs and the lichen that covers the tundra's many rocks.

Arctic fox

Zebras

Coniferous Forest

WHERE: The coniferous-forest biome is south of the Arctic tundra. It stretches from Alaska across North America and across Europe and Asia.

SPECIAL FEATURES: These forests consist mainly of cone-bearing trees such as spruce, hemlock and fir. The soil is not very fertile, because there are no leaves to decompose and enrich it.

WHAT LIVES THERE? Some animals that thrive in this biome are ermine, moose, red fox, snowshoe rabbits and great horned owls.

Grasslands

WHERE: Grasslands are known throughout the world by different names. In the U.S. they are called prairies. In tropical areas they are called savannas.

SPECIAL FEATURES: Grasslands are places with hot, dry climates that are perfect for growing food. This inland biome includes vast areas of grassy fields. It receives so little rain that very few trees can grow here.

WHAT LIVES THERE? The U.S. prairies are used to graze cattle and to raise cereal crops. There is little variety of animal life. Today, common grassland animals include the prairie dog in North America, the giraffe and the zebra in Africa and the lion in Africa and Asia.

70

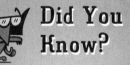

Did You Know?

An ecosystem is a community of plants and animals in an environment that supplies them with the raw materials they need, such as nutrients and water. An ecosystem may be as small as a puddle or as large as a forest.

Bighorn sheep

Mountains

WHERE: Mountains exist on all the continents. Many of the world's mountains lie in two great belts. The Circum-Pacific chain runs from the West Coast of the Americas through New Zealand and Australia, and through the Philippines to Japan. The Alpine-Himalayan system stretches from the Pyrenees in Spain and France through the Alps, and on to the Himalayas before ending in Indonesia.

SPECIAL FEATURES: A mountain biome is very cold and windy. The higher the mountain, the colder and windier the environment. There is also less oxygen at high elevations.

WHAT LIVES THERE? Mountain animals that have adapted to the cold, the lack of oxygen and the rugged landscape include the mountain goat, bighorn sheep and puma. Lower elevations are often covered by forests, while very high elevations are usually treeless.

Rain Forest

WHERE: Tropical rain forests are found in Asia, Africa, South America, Central America and on many Pacific islands. Brazil has the largest area of rain forest in the world—almost a billion acres.

SPECIAL FEATURES: Tropical rain forests receive at least 70 inches of rain each year and have more species of plants and animals than any other biome. The thick vegetation absorbs moisture, which then evaporates and falls as rain.

Toucan

A rain forest grows in three levels. The canopy, or tallest level, has trees between 100 and 200 feet tall. The second level, or understory, contains a mix of small trees, vines and palms, as well as shrubs and ferns. The third and lowest level is the forest floor, where herbs, mosses and fungi grow.

WHAT LIVES THERE? The combination of heat and moisture makes the tropical rain forest the perfect environment for more than 15 million plants and animals. Some of the animals of the tropical rain forest are the jaguar, orangutan, sloth and toucan. Among the many plant species are bamboo, banana trees and rubber trees.

TFK

Mystery Person

CLUE 1: In 1940 I was born in Nyeri, Kenya, where I have spent much of my life working to protect the environment.

CLUE 2: I founded the Green Belt Movement, a group that plants trees across Kenya and at least 15 other nations in Africa.

CLUE 3: In 2004, I was awarded the Nobel Peace Prize, the first environmentalist and the first African woman to win it.

WHO AM I?
(See Answer Key that begins on page 342.)

For a glossary of environmental terms:
www.factmonster.com/envterms

Environment & Energy

71

FOOD

TRY THIS AT HOME

Do you get tired of having cereal for breakfast every morning? Dazzle your mom with an offer to serve up some fruity French toast. Be sure to ask a parent to help you use the stove.

INGREDIENTS
- 3 eggs
- 3/4 cup of milk
- 1 teaspoon of vanilla extract
- 2 tablespoons of butter or margarine
- 6 slices of bread
- powdered sugar
- about 2 cups of fresh or frozen berries

OTHER THINGS YOU'LL NEED
- medium-size mixing bowl
- small mixing bowl
- mixing spoon
- 2 forks
- frying pan
- spatula
- plate
- measuring cups and spoons

DIRECTIONS
1. Slice the berries into small pieces and put them in the small mixing bowl.
2. Mash them with a fork. Set them aside.

Farmers Serve Up School Lunch

Fresh-picked fruits and vegetables get straight A's on kids' lunch trays

Students at Washington Elementary School in Fayetteville, Arkansas, can't wait to eat their vegetables and fruits. One Wednesday, Washington's cafeteria buzzed with excitement as kids enjoyed sweet cherry tomatoes and slices of juicy watermelon.

The school is taste-testing a farm-to-school program that brings fresh, locally grown fruits and vegetables to the cafeteria. It is the first of its kind in the state. Leigh Anne Robinson, 9, likes the fresh take on lunch. "When I bought lunch at school before, I just picked at the vegetables," she told TFK. "Who knows how long they'd been sitting at the store." If students continue to eat it up, the program will spread throughout the district.

The National Farm-to-School program says that at least 400 school districts in 23 states are serving farm-fresh foods for lunch. The movement sprouted in Florida and California in the late 1990s. Since then, farm-fresh programs have cropped up in schools across the country. Not only is this approach good for kids, but buying from area farmers also helps keep the local economy healthy too.

Doug Davis, the food-service director for schools in Burlington, Vermont, launched the city's program in 2003.

Students in Albuquerque, New Mexico, eat locally grown watermelon.

Burlington's students now eat 10% to 20% more vegetables than they did when the program began.

Part of his success, Davis says, is bringing farmers into the class-room and getting kids to help with recipes. After a while, the taste of fresher produce sells itself. "Yes, it's good for you," he says. "But a tomato picked this morning will taste better than a tomato picked [far away] and put on a truck."

—By Kathryn R. Satterfield

---

3. Crack the eggs and drop them into the other mixing bowl. Beat them with a fork until the yolks are mixed in with the whites.

4. Add the milk and vanilla extract to the eggs, and mix well.

5. Heat the frying pan over medium heat.

6. While the pan's heating up, place a slice of bread in the egg and milk mixture. Cover it completely, and let the bread absorb some of the liquid.

7. Put the butter or margarine on the pan, and let it melt. Turn the heat to low.

8. Place the soaked bread in the frying pan, and cook until the bottom of the bread is light brown. Use the spatula to check the bread. While it's cooking, put another slice of bread into the egg and milk mixture.

9. Flip the bread, and cook the other side for about 2 to 3 minutes.

10. Put the French toast on the plate. Spoon some of the berries on top, and sprinkle with powdered sugar.

11. Repeat steps 8 through 10 until the bread is gone. You may have to add more butter to the pan.

Food

73

Trouble on the Table

For thousands of years, farmers have improved their crops by crossbreeding plants that have good traits. They take pollen from one plant and add it to the flowers of another plant to produce a plant with the traits they want. But crossbreeding is slow and unreliable.

Now, there are amazing shortcuts. Scientists can take a gene from one living thing and put it directly into another plant or animal. That way, the changes can be made more precisely in a much shorter time period.

Scientists say the new techniques have created crops that are pest-proof, disease resistant and more nutritious. For example, a rice has been modified so it gets an extra boost of vitamin A from a daffodil gene. The rice was made for those who don't get enough vitamin A in their diet.

Not everybody thinks bioengineering is a good idea. Many people say these genetically modified, or GM, foods may end up harming the environment and humans. They fear that plants with new genes forced into them will accidentally crossbreed with wild plants and create pesticide-resistant superweeds. They also say GM foods could carry genes that trigger allergies or other side effects.

So far, GM foods haven't harmed anyone. Most genetic researchers believe that if troubles do crop up, they will be manageable.

Some corn in the U.S. has been genetically modified.

Stuffed!

Hall-of-Fame chowhounds set these records during food-eating contests. We raise our forks–and barf bags–in salute!

Butter Don Lerman ate seven quarter-pound sticks of salted butter in 5 minutes.

Candy bars Eric Booker devoured two pounds of chocolate candy bars in 6 minutes.

Doughnuts Eric Booker ate 49 glazed in 8 minutes.

Eggs Sonya Thomas swallowed 65 hard-boiled eggs in 6 minutes, 40 seconds.

Grilled-cheese sandwiches Timothy Janus scarfed down 31 sandwiches in 10 minutes.

Hamburgers Don Lerman (again!) ate 11¼ burgers, each one a quarter pounder, in 10 minutes.

Mayonnaise Oleg Zhornitskiy swallowed four 32-ounce bowls in 8 minutes.

Pizza Richard LeFevre wolfed down 7½ extra-large pizza slices in 15 minutes.

Watermelon Jim Reeves ate 13 pounds in 15 minutes.

Source: International Federation of Competitive Eating

Going Organic

Some people don't want to eat food that has been sprayed with pesticides. Nor do they want genetically modified food (see the article above). What's the alternative? Organic food. For a food to be certified as organic by the government, it must be grown without artificial pesticides and fertilizers. Milk, meat, poultry and eggs are designated as organic if they are not treated with hormones or antibiotics. (Hormones make animals larger; antibiotics keep them disease-free.) In addition, food can't be labeled organic if it is genetically altered or irradiated (processed with radiation to kill harmful germs). Organic foods are often more expensive than regular foods, but some people think the more natural products are worth the extra money.

For superstitions about food:
www.factmonster.com/foodsuperstitions

What's Cooking?

CHECK OUT HOW SOME FAVORITE FOODS WERE FIRST COOKED UP.

POTATO CHIPS

In 1853 a diner at a restaurant in Saratoga Springs complained that the French fries were too thick. So the chef made the potatoes paper thin and deep fried them. The diner loved these crisp potato chips, but they didn't become popular until the 1920's, when Herman Lay began to sell them nationally.

CHOCOLATE CHIP COOKIES

In 1930 Ruth Wakefield was baking chocolate cookies at the Toll House Inn restaurant in Whitman, Massachusetts, when she ran out of baking chocolate. Thinking fast, she broke up chunks of a chocolate bar and added them to the dough. After baking the cookies, Wakefield discovered that the chips in the cookie hadn't melted but were scattered throughout the cookie. It turned out to be a tasty discovery!

CORN FLAKES

In 1894 Will Keith Kellogg was trying to come up with a vegetarian food that could be served to hospital patients. Kellogg tried boiling wheat. When he accidentally left the pot out, the wheat became very soft.

Kellogg rolled the wheat and let it dry. The result? Thin, delicious flakes of wheat. Later, he did the same with corn to produce Cornflakes, which became a popular breakfast cereal.

ICE-CREAM CONES

In 1904 an ice-cream vendor at the St. Louis World's Fair ran out of dishes. Ernest Hamwai, a nearby pastry salesman, helped him out. He rolled pastry into a cone so the ice cream could fit inside–a very cool invention.

SANDWICH

In the 1700's a hungry Earl of Sandwich was gambling in a London club when he asked that roast beef be placed between two slices of bread. Why? He didn't want to get his hands–and cards–greasy. Thus the sandwich was born.

POPSICLES

In 1905 an 11-year-old named Frank Epperson was trying to make soda pop by mixing powdered soda and water. When he left the mixture outside overnight, it froze, with the mixing stick standing upright. Frank sold his frozen pops as Epperson icicles, which later became known as Popsicles.

TFK Mystery Person

CLUE 1: I started cooking with my mom when I was 7.

CLUE 2: I became a professional chef and have opened several successful restaurants around the country.

CLUE 3: I have a hit TV cooking show on the Food Network where I "kick it up a notch." Bam!

WHO AM I?

(See Answer Key that begins on page 342.)

TFK Top 5 Ice-Cream Flavors

The United States produces more than 900 million gallons of ice cream and frozen desserts each year. That's more than any other country. Here are the flavors supermarket shoppers buy most.

	Flavor	%
1.	Vanilla	33% of sales
2.	Chocolate flavors	19%
3.	Nut/caramel flavors	7%
4.	Neapolitan	5%
5.	Strawberry	4%

Source: The NPD Group

Food

75

GEOGRAPHY

29,035 FEET

MANTLE

PLATE

OUTER CORE

INNER CORE

AMERICAS

Exploring Volcanoes

Here's a hot scoop from a volcano expert

TFK talked to Donna O'Meara, a volcano researcher. There are more than 1,500 active volcanoes on Earth. O'Meara and her husband have visited about 100 of them.

TFK: How did you become interested in volcanoes?

O'Meara: I was always interested in science and nature. But I was not encouraged to pursue a career in science. Then I met Stephen O'Meara, a planetary geologist who needed a field assistant and introduced me to my first volcano—Kilauea volcano, in Hawaii. From then on, I have combined my love of scientific research, photography and writing with researching active volcanoes and educating children and adults about them. Now I love my job!

TFK: Could you describe a typical day in your life as a volcano researcher?

O'Meara: Once we arrive at an active volcano, we try to get a local guide or geologist to give us some background about the volcano. Then, we pick a site to set up camp. We don our gas masks, hard hats and fire-retardant suits and monitor each eruption. In notebooks, we record the height of the eruption, the type and time of eruption and any other descriptive factors that we see.

TFK: What is the greatest challenge about your job?

O'Meara: Staying alive! A person can be killed at an erupting volcano. It is important to use your natural given senses at an active volcano. Do you smell methane? Get out of there fast. Feel the ground shake? Run!

Donna and Steve O'Meara at White Island volcano in New Zealand. The O'Mearas were married at Kilauea volcano in Hawaii. It is pictured here giving off a nice display of lava.

The Soufriere Hills volcano in Montserrat, West Indies, is just one of the volcanoes Donna O'Meara has studied.

TFK: What has been your scariest experience in researching volcanoes?

O'Meara: My worst experience was being trapped one entire night on the lip of Stromboli volcano in Italy. It was too dangerous to get down the mountain after dark. A 1,500-foot explosion went off about every half hour, yards from my head. I thought I'd never make it through that night, but I did.

—By Brenda Iasevoli

Deadliest Volcanoes in History

VOLCANO	COUNTRY	YEAR	NUMBER OF DEATHS
Mount Tambora	Indonesia	1815	92,000
Krakatoa	Indonesia	1883	36,417
Mount Pelée	Martinique	1902	29,025
Nevada del Ruiz	Colombia	1985	25,000

Did You Know?

Many of the world's volcanoes are lined up along the Ring of Fire, a belt that encircles the Pacific Ocean. This region experiences frequent earthquakes and volcanic activity. Mount Saint Helens is located in the ring. So are about 75% of the world's volcanoes!

Geography

EARTH ON THE MOVE

If you look at a map of the world, you'll see that the continents look as if they are pieces of a big puzzle. For example, if you pushed South America and Africa into each other, they would fit together as one land mass.

Many scientists believe that until about 200 million years ago, the world was made up of a single supercontinent called Pangaea. It eventually separated and drifted apart into the seven continents we have today. This movement is called continental drift.

According to the theory of plate tectonics, the Earth's lithosphere—the crust and the outer part of the mantle—is not one giant piece of rock. Instead, it's broken into several moving slabs, or plates. These plates slide above a hot layer of the mantle. The plates move as much as a few inches every year. The oceans and the continents sit on top of the plates and move with them.

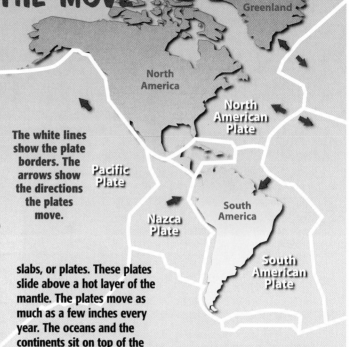

The white lines show the plate borders. The arrows show the directions the plates move.

Greenland

North America

North American Plate

Pacific Plate

Nazca Plate

South America

South American Plate

Earthquakes

There are millions of earthquakes each year, ranging on average from 18 major quakes annually to more than 2 million minor ones that are barely felt. We can usually expect one exceptionally large earthquake per year.

An earthquake is a trembling movement of Earth's rocky outer layer, called the crust. The crust is divided into several plates that are slowly and continuously shifting. Most earthquakes occur along a fault—a crack in the crust between two plates—when two plates crash together or move in opposite directions. A quake begins at a point called the focus.

Although "on the Richter Scale" is still a common expression, the scale developed by Charles Richter in 1935, is no longer the most widely used magnitude measurement. It was found to be imprecise in measuring the biggest earthquakes. *(See Did You Know? on page 79.)*

A tsunami is a series of giant sea waves that follows an earthquake or a volcanic eruption. The waves can be up to 50 feet tall and move at about 600 miles per hour. The waves can cause massive destruction when they break on land.

The 1989 Loma Prieta, California, earthquake caused this crack.

For the deadliest earthquakes:
www.factmonster.com/deadlyquakes

Major Quakes

The two deadliest earthquakes in history struck in China. In 1556, about 830,000 people were killed by an earthquake in Shaanxi (also spelled Shensi) province. As many as 650,000 died after a trembler in Tangshan, China, in 1976.

More recently, on December 26, 2004, a magnitude 9.0 earthquake occurred off the west coast of Sumatra, Indonesia. It caused a tremendously powerful tsunami in the Indian Ocean that hit 12 Asian countries. More than 225,000 people were killed, and millions more were left homeless. It was the deadliest tsunami in history.

The 2005 earthquake in Kashmir leveled this 10-story building.

In October 2005, an earthquake with a magnitude of 7.6 struck the Pakistani-controlled part of the Kashmir region. About half of the region's capital city, Muzaffarabad, was destroyed. More than 81,000 people died in the disaster, and about 3 million lost their homes.

Journey to the Center of the Earth

INNER CORE: The center of the Earth. About 800 miles thick, it is made of solid iron and nickel.

OUTER CORE: The outer core surrounds the inner core. It's composed mostly of liquid iron and nickel and is about 1,400 miles thick.

MANTLE: The mantle is about 1,800 miles thick and extends nearly to the surface of Earth. It's made up of rock.

CRUST: The outer layer of Earth, made up mostly of rock, the crust measures between 5 miles and 25 miles thick. It is thinnest under the oceans.

Did You Know?

The most widely used scale to measure the intensity of an earthquake is moment magnitude. It is based on the size of the fault on which an earthquake occurs and the amount of land that slips during an earthquake.

Geography

THE SEVEN CONTINENTS

CONTINENT	APPROXIMATE AREA	HIGHEST POINT	LOWEST POINT
1. AFRICA	11,608,000 square miles (30,065,000 sq km)	Mount Kilimanjaro, Tanzania: 19,340 feet (5,895 m)	Lake Assal, Djibouti: 512 feet (156 m) below sea level
2. ANTARCTICA	5,100,000 square miles (13,209,000 sq km)	Vinson Massif: 16,066 feet (4,897 m)	Ice covering: 8,327 feet (2,538 m) below sea level
3. ASIA (includes the Middle East)	17,212,000 square miles (44,579,000 sq km)	Mount Everest, bordering China and Nepal: 29,035 feet (8,850 m)	Dead Sea, bordering Israel and Jordan: 1,349 feet (411 m) below sea level
4. AUSTRALIA (includes Oceania)	3,132,000 square miles (8,112,000 sq km)	Mount Kosciusko, Australia: 7,316 feet (2,228 m)	Lake Eyre, Australia: 52 feet (16 m) below sea level
5. EUROPE (Ural Mountains divide Europe from Asia)	3,837,000 square miles (9,938,000 sq km)	Mount Elbrus, bordering Russia and Georgia: 18,510 feet (5,642 m)	Caspian Sea, bordering Russia and Kazakhstan: 92 feet (28 m) below sea level
6. NORTH AMERICA (includes Central America and the Caribbean)	9,449,000 square miles (24,474,000 sq km)	Mount McKinley, Alaska, U.S.: 20,320 feet (6,194 m)	Death Valley, California, U.S.: 282 feet (86 m) below sea level
7. SOUTH AMERICA	6,879,000 square miles (17,819,000 sq km)	Mount Aconcagua, Argentina: 22,834 feet (6,960 m)	Valdes Peninsula, Argentina: 131 feet (40 m) below sea level

Source: WorldAtlas.com

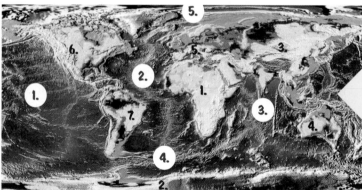

RED NUMBERS INDICATE CONTINENTS

BLUE NUMBERS INDICATE OCEANS

THE FIVE OCEANS

In 2000, the International Hydrographic Organization delimited (marked the boundaries of) a fifth ocean. The new ocean, called the Southern Ocean, surrounds Antarctica and extends north to 60 degrees south latitude. It is the fourth largest ocean, bigger only than the Arctic Ocean.

OCEAN	AREA	AVERAGE DEPTH
1. PACIFIC OCEAN	60,060,700 square miles (155,557,000 sq km)	13,215 feet (4,028 m)
2. ATLANTIC OCEAN	29,637,900 square miles (76,762,000 sq km)	12,880 feet (3,926 m)
3. INDIAN OCEAN	26,469,500 square miles (68,556,000 sq km)	13,002 feet (3,963 m)
4. SOUTHERN OCEAN	7,848,300 square miles (20,327,000 sq km)	13,100–16,400 feet* (4,000–5,000 m)
5. ARCTIC OCEAN	5,427,000 square miles (14,056,000 sq km)	3,953 feet (1,205 m)

*Official depths of the Southern Ocean are in dispute.

- Asia and Europe are not separate landmasses. They are divided by the Ural Mountains.

- Antarctica has no countries. The U.S. and other countries have science stations there, but no nation owns the land.

- Europe has no desert.

- Africa, the world's hottest landmass, has no cold climate.

- Australia has only one country, Australia.

Mount Everest, Himalayan Mountains

Record Breakers

LARGEST LAKE: CASPIAN SEA
152,239 square miles (394,299 sq km)

LONGEST RIVER: THE NILE
4,180 miles (6,690 km)

SHORTEST RIVER: THE ROE
Montana, U.S., 201 feet (61 m)

LARGEST ISLAND: GREENLAND
839,999 square miles (2,175,600 sq km)

LONGEST MOUNTAIN RANGE: THE ANDES
South America, more than 5,000 miles (8,000 km)

HIGHEST WATERFALL: ANGEL (SALTO ANGEL)
Venezuela, 3,212 feet (979 m) high

BIGGEST DESERT: SAHARA
3.5 million square miles (9.1 million sq km)

HIGHEST MOUNTAIN: MOUNT EVEREST, HIMALAYAN MOUNTAINS
Bordering Nepal and China, 29,035 feet (8,850 m) above sea level

LOWEST POINT ON LAND: THE DEAD SEA
Bordering Israel and Jordan, water surface 1,349 feet (411 meters) below sea level

LARGEST SEA: THE MEDITERRANEAN SEA
1,144,800 square miles (2,966,000 sq km)

LARGEST ARCHIPELAGO: INDONESIA
3,500-mile (5,632-km) stretch of 13,000 islands

DEEPEST LAKE: LAKE BAIKAL
Russia, 5,315 feet (1,620 m) deep

LARGEST GULF: GULF OF MEXICO
615,000 square miles (1,502,200 sq km)

LARGEST PENINSULA: ARABIA
1,250,000 square miles (3,237,500 sq km)

Did You Know?

About 97% of all water on Earth is saltwater, which humans can't use for drinking or household use. Nearly 2% of the world's freshwater is frozen in the ice caps of Antarctica and Greenland, and still more is deep in the ground. Only about one-third of 1% of all water on Earth is available for human use.

For a list of the largest lakes in the world:
www.factmonster.com/largelakes

Geography

IMPORTANT EXPLORERS

Ibn Batuta

1000
Leif Eriksson (Viking) explored Labrador and Newfoundland in Canada.

1271 Marco Polo (Italian) explored China.

1325–1349 Ibn Batuta (Arab) explored Africa, the Middle East, Europe, parts of Asia.

1488 Bartholomeu Dias (Portuguese) rounded South Africa's Cape of Good Hope.

1492 Christopher Columbus (Italian) arrived in the West Indies.

1498 Vasco da Gama (Portuguese) explored the coast of India.

1513 Ponce de León (Spanish) reached Florida.

1519–1521 Hernando Cortés (Spanish) conquered Mexico.

1519–1522 The expedition led by Ferdinand Magellan (Portuguese) circled the globe.

1532–1533 Francisco Pizarro (Spanish) conquered Peru.

1535–1536 Jacques Cartier (French) sailed up Canada's St. Lawrence River.

1539–1542 Hernando de Soto (Spanish) explored the southeastern U.S.

1607 John Smith (British) settled Jamestown, Virginia.

1609–1610 Henry Hudson (British) explored the river, strait and bay that bear his name.

1769 James Cook (British) explored New Zealand.

1804–1806 Meriwether Lewis and William Clark (American) explored the northwest U.S.

1909 Robert E. Peary (American) reached the North Pole.

1911 Roald Amundsen (Norwegian) reached the South Pole.

James Cook

Myths About Explorers

John Alcock and Arthur Brown, aviators

MOST PEOPLE THINK...

... Christopher Columbus discovered America.
The Vikings, led by Leif Eriksson, were the first Europeans to land on the coast of North America in the year 1000. Christopher Columbus landed on the Caribbean island of San Salvador in 1492, thinking he had reached the East Indies. He never set foot on what would eventually be known as the United States.

... Ferdinand Magellan was the first person to sail around the world.
He actually died before the voyage was over. Magellan set sail from Spain in 1519 with five ships and 270 men. He was killed in a fight with the natives of Mactan Island in the Philippines in 1521. In 1522, one of his ships, with 18 original crewmen, completed the journey.

... Charles Lindbergh was the first person to fly across the Atlantic Ocean.
In fact, he was the first to fly solo (alone) across the Atlantic in 1927. The first nonstop flight across the Atlantic was made by John Alcock and Arthur Brown, two British aviators, in 1919.

The Magnificent Seven

Can you identify the seven continents? To make things tougher, their relative sizes are wrong and we've turned them in different directions.

(See Answer Key that begins on page 342.)

1.

2.

3.

6.

7.

4.

5.

CLUE 1: I was born in Italy in 1914. As a child, I loved nature and learning about different cultures.

CLUE 2: To prove that ancient peoples could have traveled great distances over the oceans long before Christopher Columbus, I made a 101-day voyage from Peru to Polynesia on an ancient-style boat. The book I wrote about the trip, *Kon-Tiki*, became a worldwide best seller.

CLUE 3: To show that the ancient Egyptians could cross the ocean, I sailed in a boat made of reeds from Morocco to the Caribbean in 57 days.

WHO AM I?

(See Answer Key that begins on page 342.)

The Lines on a Map

The equator divides Earth into halves, or **hemispheres.** The Northern Hemisphere is the half of Earth between the North Pole and the equator. The Southern Hemisphere is the half between the South Pole and the equator.

Earth can also be divided into the Western Hemisphere, which includes North and South America, and the Eastern Hemisphere, which includes Asia, Africa, Australia and Europe.

Latitude measures distance from the equator. Latitude is measured in degrees and is shown on a map by lines (called parallels) that run east and west.

Longitude measures distance from the prime meridian, an imaginary line on a map that runs through Greenwich, England. It is measured in degrees and is shown on a map by lines (called meridians) that run north and south.

The **Tropic of Cancer** is a line of latitude that is a quarter of the way from the equator to the North Pole. During the summer solstice, the Sun is directly over this line. The **Tropic of Capricorn** is a line of latitude a quarter of the way from the equator to the South Pole. During the winter solstice, the Sun is directly over this line.

The **Antarctic Circle** lies three-quarters of the way between the equator and the South Pole. Three-quarters of the way between the equator and the North Pole lies the **Arctic Circle.** The Arctic is known as the Land of the Midnight Sun because in summer the Sun never sets.

Arctic Circle

Prime meridian

Equator

Line of latitude

Tropic of Cancer

Line of longitude

Tropic of Capricorn

Antarctic Circle

Geography

83

GOVERNMENT

THE CONSTITUTION

In 1787 leaders of the states gathered to write the Constitution—a set of principles that described how the new nation would be governed. The Constitution went into effect in 1789. The Constitution begins with a famous section called the **preamble.** The preamble says that the U.S. government was created by the people and for the benefit of the people:

We the people of the United States, in order to form a more perfect Union, establish justice, insure domestic tranquility, provide for the common defense, promote the general welfare and secure the blessings of liberty to ourselves and our posterity, do ordain and establish this Constitution for the United States of America.

The leaders of the states wanted a strong and fair national government. But they also wanted to protect individual freedoms and prevent the government from abusing its power. They believed they could do this by having three separate branches of government: the Executive, the Legislative and the Judicial. This separation is described in the first three articles, or sections, of the Constitution.

The Constitution was originally made up of seven articles.

ARTICLE I creates the Legislative Branch—the House of Representatives and the Senate—and describes its powers and responsibilities.

ARTICLE II creates the Executive Branch, which is led by the President, and describes its powers and responsibilities.

ARTICLE III creates the Judicial Branch, which is led by the Supreme Court, and describes its powers and responsibilities.

ARTICLE IV describes the rights and powers of the states.

ARTICLE V explains how amendments (changes or additions) can be made to the Constitution.

ARTICLE VI says the Constitution is "the supreme law of the land."

ARTICLE VII tells how the Constitution would be ratified (approved and made official) by the states.

As Article V shows, the authors of the Constitution expected from the beginning that amendments would be made to the document. There are now 27 Amendments.

The first 10 Amendments are known as the Bill of Rights. They list individual freedoms promised by the new government. The Bill of Rights was approved in 1791.

THE BILL OF RIGHTS

AMENDMENT I guarantees freedom of religion, speech and the press.

AMENDMENT II guarantees the right of the people to have firearms.

AMENDMENT III says that soldiers may not stay in a house without the owner's permission.

AMENDMENT IV says that the government cannot search people and their homes without a strong reason.

AMENDMENT V says that every person has the right to a trial and to protection of his or her rights while waiting for a trial. Also, private property cannot be taken without payment.

AMENDMENT VI says that every person shall have the right to "a speedy and public trial."

AMENDMENT VII guarantees the right to a trial in various types of legal cases.

AMENDMENT VIII outlaws all "cruel and unusual punishment."

AMENDMENT IX says that people have rights in addition to those listed in the Constitution.

AMENDMENT X says that the powers the Constitution does not give to the national government belong to the states and to the people.

Government

For the complete Constitution, including all the amendments:
www.factmonster.com/constitution

The **Legislative Branch** is made up of the two houses of Congress—the **Senate** and the **House of Representatives.** The most important duty of the Legislative Branch is to make laws. Laws are written, discussed and voted on in Congress.

There are **100 Senators** in the Senate, two from each state. Senators are elected by their states and serve six-year terms. The Vice President of the U.S. is considered the head of the Senate but does not vote in the Senate unless there is a tie. The President Pro Tempore of the Senate presides over the chamber in the absence of the Vice President. The Senator in the majority party who has served the longest is usually elected to the position.

The Senate approves nominations made by the President to the Cabinet, the Supreme Court, federal courts and other posts. The Senate must ratify all treaties by a two-thirds vote.

The House of Representatives has **435 Representatives.** The number of Representatives each state gets is based on its population. For example, California has many more Representatives than Montana has. When Census figures determine that the population of a state has changed significantly, the number of Representatives in that state may shift proportionately.

Representatives are elected by their states and serve two-year terms. The Speaker of the House, elected by the Representatives, is considered the head of the House.

Both parties in the Senate and the House of Representatives elect leaders. The leader of the party that controls the house is called the majority leader. The other party leader is called the minority leader.

Both houses of Congress elect whips. The whips keep track of votes on bills, try to persuade party members to vote along the party line and make sure lawmakers show up for votes.

"Whip" comes from the British word for the person who whips dogs to keep them running with the pack during a fox hunt.

CONGRESS

SENATE

100 members
6-year terms

President Pro Tempore	Senate Majority Leader	Senate Minority Leader
Ted Stevens (R)	Bill Frist (R)	Harry Reid (D)

HOUSE OF REPRESENTATIVES

435 members
2-year terms

Speaker of the House	House Majority Leader	House Minority Leader
Dennis Hastert (R)	John Boehner (R)	Nancy Pelosi (D)

go Go to Congress Connection and find out who represents you at timeforkids.com/cabinet

★ THE EXECUTIVE BRANCH ★

THE PRESIDENT

George W. Bush

THE VICE PRESIDENT

Richard Cheney

THE CABINET

The President is the head of the Executive Branch, which makes laws official. The President is elected by the entire country and serves a four-year term. The President cannot serve more than two four-year terms. He or she approves and carries out laws passed by the Legislative Branch, appoints or removes Cabinet members and officials, negotiates treaties and acts as head of state and Commander-in-Chief of the armed forces.

The Executive Branch also includes the **Vice President** and other officials, such as members of the **Cabinet.** The Cabinet is made up of the heads of the 15 major departments of the government.

The Cabinet gives advice to the President about important matters.

Secretary of Agriculture	Secretary of Commerce	Secretary of Defense	Secretary of Education	Secretary of Energy
Mike Johanns	Carlos Gutierrez	Donald Rumsfeld	Margaret Spellings	Samuel W. Bodman

Secretary of Health and Human Services	Secretary of Homeland Security	Secretary of Housing and Urban Development	Secretary of the Interior	Attorney General
Michael O. Leavitt	Michael Chertoff	Alphonso Jackson	Gale Norton	Alberto Gonzales

Secretary of Labor	Secretary of State	Secretary of Transportation	Secretary of the Treasury	Secretary of Veterans Affairs
Elaine Chao	Condoleezza Rice	Norman Mineta	John W. Snow	Jim Nicholson

For more information on the President's cabinet:
www.factmonster.com/cabinet

Government

THE JUDICIAL BRANCH ★

The **Judicial Branch** oversees the court system of the U.S. Through court cases, the Judicial Branch explains the meaning of the Constitution and laws passed by Congress. **The Supreme Court** is the head of the Judicial Branch. Unlike a criminal court, the Supreme Court rules whether something is constitutional or unconstitutional—that is, whether or not it is permitted under the Constitution.

On the Supreme Court there are **nine Justices,** or judges: eight associate Justices and one Chief Justice. The judges are nominated by the President and approved by the Senate. They have no term limits.

The Supreme Court is the highest court in the land. Its decisions are final, and no other court can overrule those decisions. Decisions of the Supreme Court set precedents—new ways of interpreting the law.

Justices of the Supreme Court, from left to right: Anthony M. Kennedy, Stephen G. Breyer, John Paul Stevens, Clarence Thomas, John Roberts, Ruth Bader Ginsburg, Antonin Scalia, Samuel A. Alito Jr.

Significant Supreme Court Decisions

1803 *Marbury v. Madison*
The first time a law passed by Congress was declared unconstitutional

1857 *Dred Scott v. Sanford*
Declared that a slave was not a citizen and that Congress could not outlaw slavery in U.S. territories

1896 *Plessy v. Ferguson*
Said that racial segregation was legal

1954 *Brown v. Board of Education*
Made racial segregation in schools illegal

1966 *Miranda v. Arizona*
Stated that criminal suspects must be informed of their rights before being questioned by police

2003 *Grutter v. Bollinger* and *Gratz v. Bollinger*
Ruled that colleges can, under certain conditions, consider race and ethnicity in admissions

For other Supreme Court cases:
www.factmonster.com/courtdecisions

The Road to the Bench

Selecting a Justice for the Supreme Court is a step-by-step process. Here's how it happens.

STEP 1: The President and close advisers meet with and interview several candidates.

STEP 2: The President officially nominates the top candidate.

STEP 3: The Senate Judiciary Committee holds confirmation hearings. The committee reviews and discusses the candidate's qualifications and experience during the hearings. It votes on whether or not to endorse the nominee.

STEP 4: The entire Senate votes, including the members of the Judiciary Committee.

STEP 5: If a majority of the 100 Senators vote in favor of the nominee, the candidate is confirmed and he or she takes the oath of office and joins the other Justices on the bench. If the Senate votes down the confirmation, the process starts again.

Supreme Court Fact File

YOUNGEST JUSTICE APPOINTED
Joseph Story—age 32

OLDEST JUSTICE APPOINTED
Horace Lurton—age 65

OLDEST JUSTICE TO SERVE
Oliver Wendell Holmes—retired at age 90

SHORTEST TERM
John Rutledge—4 months, 3 days as Chief Justice
Thomas Johnson—5 months, 10 days as associate Justice

LONGEST TERM
William O. Douglas—36 years, 209 days

FIRST AFRICAN AMERICAN JUSTICE
Thurgood Marshall

FIRST WOMAN JUSTICE
Sandra Day O'Connor

PRESIDENT TO APPOINT THE MOST JUSTICES
George Washington—11

ONLY PRESIDENT WHO DID NOT NOMINATE A JUSTICE
Jimmy Carter

ONLY JUSTICE TO APPEAR ON U.S. CURRENCY
Chief Justice Salmon P. Chase on the $10,000 bill, which is no longer printed

ONLY PRESIDENT TO SERVE AS A JUSTICE
William Taft

Did You Know?

The Supreme Court opens for business the first Monday of each October. The term ends in late June or early July, once the court has heard all the cases on its docket.

go Learn more about the nation's highest court at timeforkids.com/supremecourt

Government

The system of checks and balances is an important part of the Constitution. With checks and balances, each of the three branches of government can limit the powers of the others. This way, no one branch becomes too powerful. Each branch "checks" the power of the other branches to make sure that the power is balanced among them. How does this system of checks and balances work?

The process of making laws (see the following page) is a good example of checks and balances in action. First, the **Legislative Branch** introduces and votes on a bill. If the bill

passes, it then goes to the **Executive Branch,** where the President decides whether the bill is good for the country. If so, the bill is signed and becomes a law.

If the President does not believe the bill is good for the country, it does not get signed. This is called a veto. But the Legislative Branch gets another chance. With enough votes, the Legislative Branch can override the Executive Branch's veto, and the bill becomes a law.

Once a law is in place, the people of the country can test it through the court system, which is under the control of the

Judicial Branch. If someone believes a law is unfair, a lawsuit can be filed. Lawyers then make arguments for and against the case, and a judge decides which side has presented the most convincing arguments. The side that loses can choose to appeal to a higher court, and the case may eventually reach the highest court of all, the U.S. Supreme Court.

If the Legislative Branch does not agree with the way in which the Judicial Branch has interpreted the law, it can introduce a new piece of legislation, and the process starts all over again.

CONGRESS

PRESIDENT

SUPREME COURT

1. A MEMBER OF CONGRESS INTRODUCES THE BILL.

When a Senator or Representative introduces a bill, it is sent to the clerk of the Senate or House, who gives it a number and title. Next, the bill goes to the appropriate committee.

2. COMMITTEES REVIEW AND VOTE ON THE BILL.

Committees specialize in different areas, such as foreign relations or agriculture, and are made up of small groups of Senators or Representatives.

The committee may reject the bill and "table" it, meaning it is never discussed again. Or the committee may hold hearings to listen to facts and opinions, make changes in the bill and cast votes. If most committee members vote in favor of the bill, it is sent back to the Senate and the House for debate.

3. THE SENATE AND THE HOUSE DEBATE AND VOTE ON THE BILL.

Separately, the Senate and the House debate the bill, offer amendments and cast votes. If the bill is defeated in either the Senate or the House, the bill dies.

Sometimes, the House and the Senate pass the same bill, but with different amendments. In these cases, the bill goes to a conference committee made up of members of both houses of Congress. The conference committee works out differences between the two versions of the bill.

Then the bill goes before all of Congress for a vote. If a majority of both the Senate and the House votes for the bill, it goes to the President for approval.

4. THE PRESIDENT SIGNS THE BILL—OR NOT.

If the President approves the bill and signs it, the bill becomes a law. However, if the President disapproves, he or she can veto the bill by refusing to sign it.

Congress can try to overrule a veto. If both the Senate and the House pass the bill by a two-thirds majority, the President's veto is overruled and the bill becomes a law.

You're Out

The President, the Vice President and other U.S. officials can be impeached—that is, formally charged with "high crimes and misdemeanors," which include bribery, perjury, treason and abuse of power.

Under the Constitution, only the House of Representatives has the power to impeach a federal official. If a majority of the House votes for impeachment, then the Senate holds a trial and votes on whether to convict the official. If two-thirds of the Senate votes for conviction, the official will be removed from office.

Only two Presidents have been impeached: Andrew Johnson and Bill Clinton. However, neither was convicted by the Senate.

For a list of U.S. officials who have been impeached: www.factmonster.com/impeached

Government

HOW THE PRESIDENT GETS ELECTED

1. CANDIDATE ANNOUNCES PLAN TO RUN FOR OFFICE.

This announcement launches the candidate's official campaign. Speeches, debates and baby kissing begin.

2. CANDIDATE CAMPAIGNS TO WIN DELEGATE SUPPORT.

The first stage of a presidential campaign is the nomination campaign. At this time the candidate is competing with other candidates in the same party, hoping to get the party's nomination. The candidate works to win delegates—representatives who pledge to support the candidate's nomination at the national party convention—and to persuade potential voters in general.

3. CAUCUSES AND PRIMARY ELECTIONS TAKE PLACE IN THE STATES.

Caucuses and primaries are ways for the general public to take part in nominating presidential candidates.

At a caucus, local party members gather to nominate a candidate. A caucus is a lively event at which party leaders and activists debate issues and consider candidates. The rules governing caucus procedures vary by party and by state.

A primary is more like a general election. Voters go to the polls to cast their votes for a presidential candidate (or delegates who will represent that candidate at the party convention). A primary election is the main way voters choose a nominee.

4. NOMINEE FOR PRESIDENT IS ANNOUNCED AT NATIONAL PARTY CONVENTION.

There are two primary political parties in the U.S.—the Democratic Party and the Republican Party. The main goal of a national party convention is to unify party members. Thousands of delegates gather to rally support for the party's ideas and to formally nominate party candidates for President and Vice President.

After the convention, the second stage of the presidential campaign begins: the election campaign. In this stage, candidates from different parties compete against each other as they try to get elected President.

5. CITIZENS CAST THEIR VOTES.

Presidential elections are held every four years on the Tuesday after the first Monday of November.

Many Americans think that when they cast their ballot, they are voting for their chosen candidate. Actually, they are selecting groups of electors in the Electoral College.

6. THE ELECTORAL COLLEGE CASTS ITS VOTES.

Some Founding Fathers wanted Congress to elect the President. Others wanted the President to be elected by popular vote. The Electoral College represents a compromise between these ideas.

Every state has a number of electors equal to its number of Senators and Representatives. In addition, there are three electors for the District of Columbia. Laws vary by state, but electors are usually chosen by popular

go Follow the path from getting nominated to getting elected at timeforkids.com/presidency

vote. An elector may not be a Senator, Representative or other person holding a national office.

In most cases, the electoral votes from a particular state go to the candidate who leads the popular vote in that state. (Only Maine and Nebraska divide electoral votes among candidates.)

This "winner takes all" system can produce surprising results; in the elections of 1824, 1876, 1888 and 2000, the candidate who had the greatest popular vote did not win the greatest Electoral College vote and so lost the presidency.

On the first Monday after the second Wednesday in December, the electors cast their ballots. At least 270 electoral votes are required to elect a President. If this majority is not reached, the House of Representatives chooses the President.

7. THE PRESIDENT IS INAUGURATED.

On January 20, the President enters office in a ceremony that is known as the Inauguration and takes the presidential oath: "I do solemnly swear (or affirm) that I will faithfully execute the office of President of the United States, and will to the best of my ability, preserve, protect and defend the Constitution of the United States."

Electoral votes by state in the 2004 election

Voted for Bush
286 electoral votes

Voted for Kerry*
251 electoral votes

*one elector form Minnesota voted for John Edwards

go Play election games and learn about the 2004 presidential election at timeforkids.com/election04

Government

Once voters decide on a candidate, how do they actually make their choice official? Americans vote in five different ways. Here's a look at the voting systems used around the country, listed in order of how common they are.

OPTICAL-SCAN SYSTEMS
This method is similar to the one used for standardized tests. Voters fill in a small bubble by a candidate's name. The paper is later scanned by a machine that adds up the votes.

ELECTRONIC MACHINES
Like ATMs, these gadgets let voters touch a screen to select the name of their chosen candidate.

PUNCH CARDS
To select a candidate this way, voters use a special hole puncher to mark a spot by the name of the person they want to elect.

LEVER MACHINES
Voters pull a lever next to the name of the nominee they support. Their vote is recorded on a wheel behind the machine.

In many locations, people touch computer screens to cast their votes.

PAPER BALLOTS
Voters place a piece of paper marked with their preferred candidate's name in a sealed box. The ballots are later counted by hand.

TFK Mystery Person

CLUE 1: I was born in Boston, Massachusetts, in 1882.

CLUE 2: In 1933, President Franklin D. Roosevelt named me Secretary of Labor. I was the first woman to serve in a U.S. Cabinet position.

CLUE 3: Throughout my career, I defended the interests of working people and helped develop fair labor rules.

WHO AM I?

(See Answer Key that begins on page 342.)

Pay Day

Considering that many business leaders make millions each year, the salaries of government officials seem quite low in comparison.

POSITION	2005 SALARY
President	$400,000
Vice President	$202,900
Senator	$158,000
U.S. Representative	$158,000
Majority and Minority Leaders	$175,600
Speaker of the House	$202,900
Chief Justice, U.S. Supreme Court	$202,900
Associate Justice, U.S. Supreme Court	$194,200

Source: U.S. Office of Personnel Management

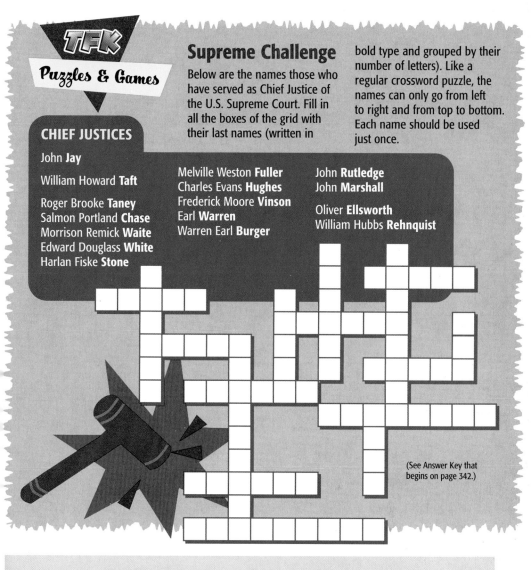

Supreme Challenge

Below are the names those who have served as Chief Justice of the U.S. Supreme Court. Fill in all the boxes of the grid with their last names (written in bold type and grouped by their number of letters). Like a regular crossword puzzle, the names can only go from left to right and from top to bottom. Each name should be used just once.

CHIEF JUSTICES

John **Jay**

William Howard **Taft**

Roger Brooke **Taney**
Salmon Portland **Chase**
Morrison Remick **Waite**
Edward Douglass **White**
Harlan Fiske **Stone**

Melville Weston **Fuller**
Charles Evans **Hughes**
Frederick Moore **Vinson**
Earl **Warren**
Warren Earl **Burger**

John **Rutledge**
John **Marshall**

Oliver **Ellsworth**
William Hubbs **Rehnquist**

(See Answer Key that begins on page 342.)

The Presidential Succession

Who would take over if the President died, resigned or was removed from office? The list of who is next in line is known as presidential succession.

★ Vice President
★ Speaker of the House
★ President Pro Tempore of the Senate
★ Secretary of State
★ Secretary of the Treasury
★ Secretary of Defense
★ Attorney General
★ Secretary of the Interior
★ Secretary of Agriculture
★ Secretary of Commerce
★ Secretary of Labor

★ Secretary of Health and Human Services
★ Secretary of Housing and
   Urban Development
★ Secretary of Transportation
★ Secretary of Energy
★ Secretary of Education
★ Secretary of Veterans Affairs
★ Secretary of Homeland Security*

* In July 2005, the Senate passed a law moving the Homeland Security Secretary to number 8 on the list. This law requires House approval.

Who on the current Cabinet was not born in the U.S. and therefore cannot become President?

(See Answer Key that begins on page 342.)

Government

95

HEALTH & BODY

Sleepy Heads

Researchers debate why sleep is so essential to our health

All through the animal kingdom, for the survival of the species, sleep ranks right up there with eating and mating. Everybody does it, from fruit flies to humans. Yet scientists still don't know exactly what sleep is for.

Is it to refresh the body? Not really. Researchers have yet to find any important function of the body that sleep helps. As far as anyone can tell, muscles don't need sleep, just time to relax. The rest of the body chugs along without being aware of whether the brain is asleep or awake.

Is it to refresh the mind? Maybe. The brain benefits from a good night's sleep. But sleep researchers don't agree about how it benefits.

One theory is that sleep allows the brain to review and bring together all the information it gathered while awake. Another theory suggests that we sleep in order to allow the brain to stock up on fuel and flush out wastes. A third is that sleep operates in some mysterious way to help you master various skills, such as how to play the piano and ride a bike.

How much sleep should you get? Most researchers tell us to use common sense.

A good night's sleep is good for us.

"If you feel sleepy the following day," says Dr. Pierre-Hervé Luppi at the University of Lyons in France, "if you have episodes of sleepiness or a feeling of major fatigue throughout the day, it means you're not sleeping enough."

You don't have to know what sleep is for to know that it's good for you!

—By Christine Gorman

HOW TO GET A GOOD NIGHT'S SLEEP

Set your body clock by keeping the same sleep schedule, seven days a week. Don't try to catch up by sleeping late on weekends.

Create an environment that will help you sleep—cool, dark and uncluttered. White noise, eyeshades or ear plugs can help.

No caffeine (including cola and chocolate) in the p.m. Avoid spicy foods. Finish eating at least three hours before bedtime.

Warm milk is a fine sleep aid.

No computers, TV or arguments half an hour before bed. Soothing music and mysteries are O.K., but avoid the scarier tales and music with a fast tempo.

If you're still awake after 20 minutes in bed, get up, go to another room and do a quiet activity. Repeat as needed.

Health & Body

A facelift for the food Pyramid

Grains	Vegetables	Fruits	Milk	Meat & Beans
Make half your grains whole	Vary your veggies	Focus on fruits	Get your calcium-rich foods	Go lean with protein

◊ **Oils** Oils are not a food group, but you need some for good health. Get your oils from fish, nuts, and liquid oils such as corn oil, soybean oil, and canola oil.

In 2005, the Department of Agriculture introduced a new food pyramid. Pyramids, to be precise. Instead of a one-size-fits-all pyramid, there are now 12 different versions. Each one is slightly different, depending on a person's age, gender and level of physical activity. The pyramids are designed to help people with different lifestyles and nutritional needs live healthier lives. The new nutritional guideline system is called MyPyramid.

The new version is color-coded: orange for grains, green for vegetables, red for fruits, yellow for fats and oils, blue for milk and purple for meats and beans. It also features a person climbing a staircase to symbolize the importance of exercising for at least 30 minutes every day.

For an 11-year-old girl who exercises for 30 to 60 minutes each day, the pyramid recommends that she eat:

• about six ounces of grains, including three ounces of whole grains rather than products made out of white flour

• three servings (one cup equals one serving) of fruit and five servings of vegetables

• three cups of milk

• 5 ounces of lean meat or beans

• a small amount of fats and oils and added sugars

Check out *www.mypyramid.gov* to see what it recommends for you.

Counting Calories

A calorie is a type of measurement that indicates how much energy we get from food. Nutrition labels tell you how many calories a food contains. In general, kids ages 7 to 12 should take in about 2,200 calories each day. Teenage girls need about 2,200 calories, while teenage boys require about 2,800.

Exercise: It's Good for You

Not only is exercise fun, but it also helps your mind, body and overall well-being. Kids who exercise regularly often do better in school, sleep better, are less likely to be overweight or obese, and are stronger than less-active kids. Exercise can also relieve stress and improve your mood.

Federal health officials recently reported that most kids spend a shocking 4½ hours each day watching TV, using a computer or playing video games! They recommend that kids exercise for at least 30 minutes almost every day. So get up and get moving!

There are two types of exercise, **aerobic** and **anaerobic**. When you do aerobic exercises, such as running, swimming, biking and playing soccer, you increase your heart rate and the flow of oxygen-rich blood to your muscles. Aerobic exercise also builds endurance and burns fat and calories. Anaerobic exercise, such as weight-lifting, involves short bursts of effort. It also helps to build strength and muscle mass.

Playing on a team is a great way to exercise and meet new friends, but it's not for everyone. If you prefer to work out alone, try dancing, jumping rope, jogging, yoga, swimming or roller skating.

Don't let bad weather stop you from working up a sweat. Run up and down the stairs in your house or set up an indoor obstacle course. Head to your local YMCA for a swim or a game of hoops.

Kids on the Move

Age	% of kids who participate in an organized physical activity	% of kids who participate in a free-time physical activity
9	36.1%	75.8%
10	37.5	77.0
11	43.1	78.9
12	37.7	77.5
13	38.1	78.0

Source: U.S. Centers for Disease Control and Prevention

Calorie Consumption

Here's a look at how many calories you can burn per hour when doing certain activities.

ACTIVITY	CALORIES BURNED
SLEEPING	90
DANCING	210
WALKING (4 M.P.H.)	240
DOWNHILL SKIING	288
HIKING	288
ROLLER SKATING (9 M.P.H.)	336
PLAYING SOCCER	360
PLAYING BASKETBALL	380
JOGGING (6 M.P.H.)	790

Did You Know?

About 15% of kids ages 6 to 19 are obese and 20% are overweight. Obesity can lead to serious health problems, such as heart disease, stroke, diabetes and high blood pressure.

The Doctor Is In

Fact Monster asked pediatrician Brian Orr to answer some questions kids often ask about their bodies.

WHY DO SOME PEOPLE HAVE FRECKLES?

Freckles are small birthmarks. They are made of collections of melanocytes, or skin cells, that produce pigment. Most people inherit a tendency to have freckles from their parents. Like many other birthmarks, freckles are not usually present at birth but instead develop over time.

WHAT CAUSES A BURP?

When we eat, we swallow air along with our food. Our stomach already has air in it from bacteria that produce gas and from chemical reactions caused by digestive enzymes. When there is too much air to fit in our stomach, we force some out in what we call a burp. It's funny that something considered impolite occurs so naturally.

WHY DO WE GET BODY ODOR?

Most people think we get body odor from sweat. That's only partially true. Much of our body odor comes from bacteria that live on us and grow in our warm sweat. A bunch of bacteria clinging together in close quarters creates an unpleasant odor. When we bathe, we wash away the bacteria—and the smell.

WHY ARE PEOPLE ALLERGIC TO THINGS?

Allergens are things, such as pollen from trees or hair from animals, that trick our bodies into thinking we are fighting a cold or virus. These allergens make people who are prone to allergies have symptoms like runny noses, watery eyes and coughs. Not everyone, however, is prone to allergies. But if you are, allergies can be a pain in the neck.

WHY ARE OUR MOUTHS DRY IN THE MORNING?

When we sleep, we relax all of our muscles, including our jaw muscles. When these muscles relax, our mouths usually fall open, and the air we breathe dries out our mouths. So have that glass of water ready in the morning because no matter what you do, your mouth will be dry when you wake up.

Ouch!

Millions of kids are rushed to the emergency room every year when they get hurt playing a sport. Here are the sports that send the most kids to the hospital.

1. **Basketball**
2. **Cycling**
3. **Football**
4. **Baseball or softball**
5. **Ice skating, inline skating or skateboarding**

Source: National Center for Health Statistics

Homework Tip!

Review your homework to see if it's complete. Ask someone to check it for you.

For tips on staying healthy:
www.factmonster.com/healthtips

The Five Senses

Each person has five sense organs that take in information from the environment and send it to the brain. The brain then processes the information and tells your body how to respond. The sense organs are your eyes, ears, nose, tongue and skin.

SENSE	ORGAN	JOB
Sight	Eyes	Detect color and light
Hearing	Ears	Detect sound
Smell	Nose	Detects scents
Taste	Tongue	Detects tastes: sweet, salty, sour and bitter
Touch	Skin	Detects pain, pressure, heat and cold

Did You Know?

Each year, about half a million Americans die from smoking-related illnesses. Cigarettes contain nicotine, a highly addictive drug. Nicotine is also a poison! Arsenic, formaldehyde, hydrogen cyanide, tar and carbon monoxide are some of the other poisons found in cigarettes. No wonder smoking is linked to heart disease and cancer.

What Scares You?

Are you afraid of spiders or heights? Don't worry—you're not alone. Many people have a fear of something. When the fear is constant and without good reason, it's called a phobia. Here are some common—and not-so-common—phobias.

PHOBIA	WHAT'S FEARED
Acrophobia	heights
Agoraphobia	crowds, public places or open areas
Ailurophobia	cats
Anglophobia	England or anything English
Arachnophobia	spiders
Aviophobia	airplanes
Brontophobia	thunderstorms
Claustrophobia	closed or small spaces
Thalassophobia	the sea
Triskadekaphobia	the number 13
Xylophobia	wooden objects or forests

TFK Top 5 Ways Kids Handle Stress

In a recent poll of kids, most said they had more than one activity that helped them calm down. Here are the most common ways that kids deal with stress.*

1. Play or do something active—455 kids
2. Listen to music—385
3. Watch TV or play a video game—368
4. Talk to a friend—263
5. Try not to think about it—254

*Figures show the number of kids who chose the activity as something they do "a lot" when they are stressed.

Source: KidsHealth KidsPoll "How Kids Handle Stress," 2005

For trivia about your body: www.factmonster.com/bodycount

Health & Body

Your Body

If you could peek inside your own body, what would you see? Hundreds of bones, miles of blood vessels and trillions of cells, all of which are constantly working together.

LIGAMENTS

MAIN JOB: To hold joints together. These bands of tough tissue are strong and flexible.

SKIN

MAIN JOB: To protect your internal organs from drying up and to prevent harmful bacteria from getting inside your body

HOW MUCH: The average person has about six pounds of skin.

MAIN LAYERS:
- Epidermis: Outer layer of skin cells, hair, nails and sweat glands
- Dermis: Inner layer of living tissue, containing nerves and blood vessels

TENDONS

MAIN JOB: To hold your muscles to your bones

DID YOU KNOW? Tendons look like rubber bands.

JOINTS

MAIN JOB: To allow bones to move in different directions

DID YOU KNOW? Bones don't bend. Joints allow two bones next to each other to move.

CELLS

MAIN JOB: To perform the many jobs necessary to stay alive, such as moving oxygen around your body, taking care of your energy supply and waste removal

DID YOU KNOW? There are 26 billion cells in a newborn baby and 50 trillion cells in an adult.

SOME DIFFERENT CELLS:
- Bone cells produce the fibers and minerals from which bone is made.
- Fat cells contain fat, which is burned to create energy.
- Muscle cells are organized into muscles, which move body parts.
- Nerve cells pass nerve messages around your body.
- Red blood cells carry oxygen around your body.

MUSCLES

MAIN JOB: To make body movement possible

HOW MUCH: Your body has more than 650 muscles.

KINDS OF MUSCLES:
- Skeletal muscles help the body move. You have about 400 skeletal muscles.
- Smooth muscles are located inside organs, like the stomach.
- The cardiac muscle is found only in the heart.

go ▸ Show what you know about staying healthy at timeforkids.com/triviafever

GLANDS

MAIN JOB: To manufacture substances that help your body to function

KINDS OF GLANDS:
- Endocrine glands make hormones, which tell the different parts of your body when to work.
- Oil glands keep your skin from drying out.
- Salivary glands make saliva, which helps you to digest and swallow food.
- Sweat glands make perspiration, which regulates your body temperature.

BONES

MAIN JOB: To give shape and support to your body

HOW MANY: At birth you had more than 300 bones in your body. As an adult you'll have 206, because some bones fuse together.

DID YOU KNOW? The largest bone in the body is the femur, or thighbone. In a 6-foot-tall person, it is 20 inches long. The smallest bone is the stirrup bone in the ear. It is one-tenth of an inch long.

KINDS OF BONES:
- Long bones are thin; they are found in your legs, arms and fingers.
- Short bones are wide and chunky; they are found in your feet and wrists.
- Flat bones are flat and smooth, like your shoulder blades.
- Irregular bones, like the bones in your inner ear and the vertebrae in your spine, come in many different shapes.

Pearly Whites

We use our teeth to bite and chew food—the first stage in digestion. Babies start to get their first teeth, called milk or deciduous teeth, at about six months. By around age 2, children have 20 teeth: four central incisors, four lateral incisors, four canines and eight premolars. These teeth begin to fall out at around age 6, and adult, or permanent teeth, replace them.

Adults usually have 32 teeth: eight incisors, four canines, eight bicuspids, eight molars and four wisdom teeth. Wisdom teeth sometimes don't appear until age 25, and in some cases, they never break through the gums.

VISCERA

This term refers to the organs that fill your body's chest and abdominal cavity.

MAIN JOB: To provide your body with food and oxygen and to remove waste

PARTS: The viscera include the trachea (windpipe), lungs, liver, kidneys, gallbladder, spleen, stomach, large intestine, small intestine and bladder.

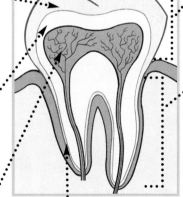

ENAMEL: The strong, white covering of the tooth. Enamel is the hardest thing in the human body.

DENTIN: A yellow bonelike material under the enamel and cementum. It contains nerve fibers.

PULP: The soft center of the tooth. It contains blood vessels and nerves. It nourishes the tooth and sends signals to the brain.

CROWN: The part of the tooth that's visible.

ROOT: The part of the tooth that extends into the jawbone. It makes up about two-thirds of the tooth.

CEMENTUM: A layer of hard, tough tissue that covers most of the root. It helps attach the tooth to the jawbone. It contains the **PERIODONTAL LIGAMENT,** the soft layer between the cementum and the jawbone.

Body Systems

CIRCULATORY SYSTEM

The circulatory system transports blood throughout the body. The heart pumps the blood, and the arteries and veins transport it. Blood is carried away from the heart by arteries. The biggest artery, called the aorta, branches from the left side of the heart into smaller arteries, which then branch into even smaller vessels that travel all over the body. When blood enters the smallest of these vessels, which are called capillaries, it gives nutrients and oxygen to cells and takes in carbon dioxide, water and waste. The blood then returns to the heart through veins. Veins carry waste products away from cells and bring blood back to the heart, which pumps it to the lungs to pick up oxygen and eliminate waste carbon dioxide.

DIGESTIVE SYSTEM

The digestive system breaks down food into protein, vitamins, minerals, carbohydrates and fats, which the body needs for energy, growth and repair. After food is chewed and swallowed, it goes down a tube called the esophagus and enters the stomach, where it is broken down by powerful acids. From the stomach the food travels into the small intestine, where it is broken down into nutrients. The food that the body doesn't need or can't digest is turned into waste and eliminated from the body through the large intestine.

ENDOCRINE SYSTEM

The endocrine system is made up of glands that produce hormones, sometimes called the body's long-distance messengers. Hormones are chemicals that control body functions, such as metabolism and growth. The glands, which include the pituitary gland, thyroid gland, adrenal glands, pancreas, ovaries and testes, release hormones into the bloodstream, which then transports the hormones to organs and tissues throughout the body.

IMMUNE SYSTEM

The immune system is our body's defense system against infections and diseases. It works to respond to dangerous organisms, such as viruses or bacteria, and substances that may enter the body. There are three types of response systems in the immune system:

- The anatomic response physically prevents dangerous substances from entering your body. The anatomic system includes the skin and the mucous membranes.
- The inflammatory system eliminates the invaders from your body. Sneezing and fever are examples of the inflammatory system at work.
- The immune response is made up of white blood cells, which fight infection by gobbling up toxins, bacteria and other threats.

MUSCULAR SYSTEM

The muscular system is made up of fibrous tissues that work with the skeletal system to control movement of the body. Some muscles—like the ones in your arms, legs, mouth and tongue—are voluntary, meaning that you decide when to move them. Other muscles, like the ones in your stomach, heart, blood vessels and intestines, are involuntary. This means that they're controlled by the nervous system and hormones, and you often don't even realize they're at work.

Muscles control your facial expression.

NERVOUS SYSTEM

The nervous system is made up of the brain, the spinal cord and nerves. The nervous system sends and receives nerve impulses that tell your muscles and organs what to do. There are three parts to your nervous system that work together.

- The central nervous system consists of the brain and spinal cord. It sends out nerve impulses and receives sensory information, which tells your brain about things you see, hear, smell, taste and feel.

- The peripheral nervous system includes the nerves that branch off from the brain and the spinal cord. It carries the nerve impulses from the central nervous system to the muscles and glands.

- The autonomic nervous system regulates involuntary action, such as heartbeat and digestion.

SKELETAL SYSTEM

The skeletal system is made up of bones, ligaments and tendons. It shapes the body and protects organs. The skeletal system works with the muscular system to help the body move.

The skeleton acts as the body's frame.

RESPIRATORY SYSTEM

The respiratory system brings air into the body and removes carbon dioxide. It includes the nose, trachea (windpipe) and lungs. When you inhale, air enters your nose and goes down the trachea. The trachea branches into two bronchial tubes, which go to the lungs. These tubes branch off into even smaller bronchial tubes, which end in air sacs. Oxygen follows this path and passes through the air sacs and blood vessels and enters the bloodstream. At the same time, carbon dioxide passes into the lungs and is exhaled.

TFK Mystery Person

CLUE 1: I am a health-care reformer who was born in Maine in 1802.

CLUE 2: During the Civil War, I was in charge of all women nurses who worked in Union hospitals. Thanks to my leadership, nurses were treated better and wounded soldiers got better care.

CLUE 3: In the 19th century, mentally ill people were cruelly mistreated. I spent my life working to improve their living conditions and helped start up many mental institutions.

WHO AM I?

(See Answer Key that begins on page 342.)

Health & Body

105

HISTORY

Milestones of the Civil Rights Movement

1954 The U.S. Supreme Court rules in *Brown v. Board of Education* that segregation in public schools is unconstitutional.

1955 Rosa Parks is arrested for refusing to give up her seat on a bus to a white passenger. She becomes known as "the mother of the civil rights movement."

Civil-rights pioneer Rosa Parks died in 2005.

1960 Four black students begin a sit-in at a segregated Woolworth's lunch counter. Six months later, the original four protesters are served lunch at the same Woolworth's.

1961 "Freedom Riders" test new laws that prohibit segregation on buses and other modes of transportation.

1963 About 200,000 people join the March on Washington, D.C., where Martin Luther King Jr. delivers his famous "I Have a Dream" speech.

 Play the Fight for Rights history challenge at timeforkids.com/rights

Teens Make History

In 1957, the Little Rock Nine, as they later came to be called, were the first black teenagers to attend all-white Central High School in Little Rock, Arkansas.

Brown v. Board of Education outlawed segregation in schools, but many school systems defied the law. Little Rock's Central High School was a notorious example. The Little Rock Nine were determined to attend the school and receive the same education offered to white students.

Things grew frightening right away. On the first day of school, the Governor of Arkansas ordered the state's National Guard to block the black students from entering the school. Imagine what it must have been like to be a student confronted by armed soldiers!

President Eisenhower sent federal troops to protect the students. That was only the beginning of their ordeal. Every morning on their way to school, angry crowds of whites taunted and insulted the Little Rock Nine—they even received death threats.

As scared as they were, the students wouldn't give up, and several went on to graduate from Central High School. Nine black teenagers challenged a racist system and defeated it.

LITTLE ROCK CENTRAL HIGH

RAY   ROBERTS   PATTILLO   THOMAS   WALLS

MOTHERSHED   BROWN   ECKFORD   GREEN

The Little Rock Nine (above) were blocked from entering Central High.

1964 President Lyndon Johnson signs the Civil Rights Act of 1964. The law prohibits discrimination of all kinds based on race, color, religion or national origin.

1965 Congress passes the Voting Rights Act of 1965, making it easier for Southern blacks to register to vote.

1968 Martin Luther King Jr. is shot and killed by James Earl Ray.

2003 The U.S. Supreme Court rules that race can be one of many factors considered by colleges when selecting their students.

TFK

Puzzles & Games

Who Said That?

We celebrate Martin Luther King Jr.'s birthday in January. The civil rights leader and other famous African Americans said many memorable things. Read each quotation. Then unscramble and write the name of the person who said it.

1. "I have a dream that my four little children will one day live in a nation where they will not be judged by the color of their skin. . . ." TRAIMN EHTULR GKNI

2. "Talent wins games, but teamwork and intelligence win championships." EALICHM ARDJON

3. "The only thing better than singing is more singing." EALL LAIZFTREGD

4. "The night is beautiful,/So the faces of my people." GNOSTALN EGSUHH

5. "You don't make progress by standing on the sidelines, whimpering and complaining." LYERSHI MSIHLOCH

(See Answer Key that begins on page 342.)

History

107

3000–2000 B.C.

10,000–4000 B.C.	In Mesopotamia, settlements develop into cities, and people learn to use the wheel.
4500–4000 B.C.	Earliest known civilization arises in Sumer.
3000–2000 B.C.	The rule of the **pharaohs** begins in Egypt. King Khufu completes construction of the Great Pyramid at Giza (ca.* 2680 B.C.), and King Khafre builds the Great Sphinx of Giza (ca. 2540 B.C.).
3000–1500 B.C.	The Indus Valley civilization flourishes in what is today Pakistan. In Britain, Stonehenge is erected.
1500–1000 B.C.	Moses leads the Israelites out of Egypt and delivers the Ten Commandments. Chinese civilization develops under the Shang Dynasty.
1000–900 B.C.	Hebrew elders begin to write the books of the Hebrew Bible.
900–800 B.C.	Phoenicians establish Carthage (ca. 810 B.C.). The *Iliad* and the *Odyssey* are composed, probably by the Greek poet Homer.
800–700 B.C.	The first recorded Olympic games (776 B.C.) take place.
700–600 B.C.	Lao-tse, Chinese philosopher and founder of Taoism, is born (604 B.C.).
600–500 B.C.	Confucius (551–479 B.C.) develops his philosophy in China. Buddha (ca. 563–483 B.C.) founds Buddhism in India.
500–400 B.C.	Greek culture flourishes during the age of **Pericles** (450–400 B.C.). The Parthenon is built in Athens as a temple of the goddess Athena (447–432 B.C.).
400–300 B.C.	Alexander the Great (356–323 B.C.) destroys Thebes (335 B.C.), conquers Tyre and Jerusalem (332 B.C.), occupies Babylon (330 B.C.) and invades India.
300–250 B.C.	The **Temple of the Sun** is built at Teotihuacán, Mexico (ca. 300 B.C.).
250–200 B.C.	The Great Wall of China is built (ca. 215 B.C.).
100–31 B.C.	Julius Caesar (100–44 B.C.) invades Britain (55 B.C.) and conquers Gaul (France) (ca. 50 B.C.). Cleopatra rules Egypt (51–31 B.C.).
44 B.C.	Julius Caesar is murdered.

500–400 B.C.

300–250 B.C.

* ca. stands for *circa*, which means *around*.

A.D. 300-349

CONSTANTIN LE GRAND

A.D. 500-549

A.D. 800-849

ca. A.D. 1-30 ▶ Life of Jesus Christ. Emperor Kuang Wu Ti founds Han dynasty in China. Buddhism introduced to China.

50-99 ▶ Jews revolt against the Romans; Jerusalem destroyed (A.D. 70).

100-149 ▶ The great Emperor Hadrian rules Rome (A.D. 117-138).

150-199 ▶ The earliest Mayan temples are built in Central America.

200-249 ▶ Goths invade Asia Minor (ca. A.D. 220).

250-299 ▶ Mayan civilization (A.D. 250-900) has advances in art, architecture and science.

300-349 ▶ **Constantine the Great** (rules A.D. 312-337) unites eastern and western Roman empires, with new capital at Constantinople (A.D. 330).

350-399 ▶ Huns (Mongols) invade Europe (ca. A.D. 360).

400-449 ▶ St. Patrick returns to Ireland (A.D. 432) and brings Christianity to the island.

450-499 ▶ Vandals destroy Rome (A.D. 455).

500-549 ▶ **Arthur,** king of the Britons, is killed (ca. A.D. 537).

550-599 ▶ After killing about half the European population, plague subsides (A.D. 594).

600-649 ▶ Muhammad, founder of Islam, flees from Mecca to Medina (the Hegira, A.D. 622). Arabs conquer Jerusalem (A.D. 637) and destroy the Alexandrian library (A.D. 641).

650-699 ▶ Arabs attack North Africa (A.D. 670) and destroy Carthage (A.D. 697).

700-749 ▶ Arab empire extends from Lisbon to China (by A.D. 716).

750-799 ▶ City of Machu Picchu flourishes in Peru.

800-849 ▶ **Charlemagne** is crowned first Holy Roman Emperor in Rome (A.D. 800).

850-899 ▶ Russian nation is founded by Vikings under Prince Rurik (A.D. 855-879).

900-949 ▶ Vikings discover Greenland (ca. A.D. 900). Arab Spain under Abd al-Rahman III becomes center of learning (A.D. 912-961).

950-999 ▶ Erik the Red establishes the first Viking colony in Greenland (A.D. 982).

History

ca. 1000

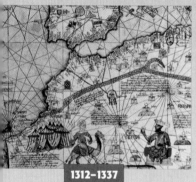

1312–1337

1428

ca. 1000–1300	▶	The Pueblo period of Anasazi culture flourishes; cliff dwellings are built.
ca. 1000	▶	Viking raider **Leif Eriksson** reaches North America.
ca. 1008	▶	Murasaki Shikibu finishes *The Tale of Genji*, the world's first novel.
1066	▶	William of Normandy invades England; is crowned William I "the Conqueror."
1096	▶	Pope Urban II launches the First Crusade, one of at least eight European military campaigns between 1095 and 1291 to take the Holy Land from the Muslims.
ca. 1150	▶	The temple complex of Angkor Wat is completed in Cambodia.
1211	▶	Genghis Khan invades China, captures Peking (1214), conquers Persia (1218) and invades Russia (1223).
1215	▶	Britain's King John is forced by barons to sign the Magna Carta, limiting royal power.
1231	▶	The Inquisition begins as the Roman Catholic Church fights heresy; torture is used.
1251	▶	Kublai Khan governs China.
1271	▶	Marco Polo of Venice travels to China; visits court of Kublai Khan (1275–1292).
1312–1337	▶	The **Mali Empire** reaches its height in Africa under King Mansa Musa.
ca. 1325	▶	Aztecs establish Tenochtitlán on the site of modern Mexico City.
1337–1453	▶	In the Hundred Years' War, English and French kings fight for control of France.
1347–1351	▶	At least 25 million people die in Europe's Black Death (bubonic plague).
1368	▶	The Ming Dynasty begins in China.
ca. 1387	▶	Geoffrey Chaucer writes *The Canterbury Tales*.
1428	▶	**Joan of Arc** leads the French against the English.
1438	▶	The Incas rule in Peru.
1450	▶	Florence, Italy, becomes the center of Renaissance art and learning.
1453	▶	The Turks conquer Constantinople, beginning the Ottoman Empire.
1455	▶	Johannes Gutenberg invents the movable type printing press.
1462	▶	Ivan the Great rules Russia until 1505 as first Czar.
1492	▶	Christopher Columbus reaches the New World.

1519

1588

1846

1501	▶	The first African slaves are brought to America, to the Spanish colony of Santo Domingo.
ca. 1503	▶	Leonardo da Vinci paints the *Mona Lisa*.
1509	▶	Henry VIII takes the English throne. Michelangelo begins painting the ceiling of the Sistine Chapel.
1517	▶	Martin Luther objects to wrongdoing in the Catholic Church; start of Protestantism.
1519	▶	**Hernando Cortés** conquers Mexico for Spain.
1520	▶	Suleiman I "the Magnificent" becomes Sultan of Turkey.
1522	▶	Portuguese explorer Ferdinand Magellan's expedition circumnavigates the globe.
1543	▶	Copernicus publishes his theory that Earth revolves around the Sun.
1547	▶	Ivan IV "the Terrible" is crowned Czar of Russia.
1588	▶	The **Spanish Armada** is defeated by the English.
1609	▶	Galileo makes the first astronomical observations using a telescope.
1618	▶	Thirty Years' War begins. European Protestants revolt against Catholic oppression.
1620	▶	Pilgrims, after a three-month voyage aboard the *Mayflower*, land at Plymouth Rock.
1775	▶	The American Revolution begins with the Battle of Lexington and Concord.
1776	▶	The U.S. Declaration of Independence is signed.
1783	▶	The American Revolution ends with the Treaty of Paris.
1789	▶	The French Revolution begins with the storming of the Bastille.
1819	▶	Simón Bolívar leads wars for independence throughout South America.
1824	▶	Mexico becomes a republic, three years after declaring independence from Spain.
1846	▶	Failure of potato crop causes **famine in Ireland.**
1861	▶	The U.S. Civil War begins as attempts to reach a compromise on slavery fail.
1865	▶	The U.S. Civil War ends.
1884	▶	The Berlin West Africa Conference is held; Europe colonizes the African continent.
1893	▶	New Zealand becomes the first country in the world to give women the right to vote.
1898	▶	The Spanish-American War begins.

History

1903

1914

1949

1903	▶	The **Wright brothers** fly the first powered airplane at Kitty Hawk, North Carolina.
1904	▶	The Russo-Japanese War begins, as competition for Korea and Manchuria heats up.
1909	▶	U.S. explorers Robert E. Peary and Matthew Henson reach the North Pole. The National Association for the Advancement of Colored People (NAACP) is founded in New York City.
1912	▶	The *Titanic* sinks on its maiden voyage; more than 1,500 drown.
1914	▶	**World War I begins.**
1917	▶	U.S. enters World War I. Russian Revolution begins.
1918	▶	World War I fighting ends. A worldwide flu epidemic strikes; by 1920, about 20 million are dead.
1919	▶	Mahatma Gandhi begins his nonviolent resistance against British rule in India.
1924	▶	Joseph Stalin begins his rule as Soviet dictator, which lasts until his death in 1953.
1929	▶	In the U.S., stock market prices collapse and the Depression begins.
1933	▶	Adolf Hitler is appointed German Chancellor; Nazi oppression begins. Franklin Delano Roosevelt is inaugurated U.S. President; he launches the New Deal.
1937	▶	The Nazis open their first concentration camp (Buchenwald); through 1945, the Nazis murder some 6 million Jews in what is now called the Holocaust.
1939	▶	World War II begins.
1941	▶	A Japanese attack on the U.S. fleet at Pearl Harbor in Hawaii (December 7) brings U.S. into World War II. Manhattan Project (atom bomb research) begins.
1945	▶	War ends in Europe on V-E Day (May 8). The U.S. drops the atom bomb on Hiroshima, Japan (August 6), and Nagasaki, Japan (August 9). The war ends in the Pacific on V-J day (September 2).
1947	▶	The U.S. Marshall Plan is proposed to help Europe recover from the war. India and Pakistan gain independence from Britain.
1948	▶	The existence of the nation of Israel is proclaimed.
1949	▶	The North Atlantic Treaty Organization (NATO) is founded. Communist People's Republic of China is proclaimed by Chairman Mao Zedong. **South Africa sets up apartheid** (a policy of discrimination against nonwhites).
1950	▶	Korean War begins when North Korean Communist forces invade South Korea. It lasts three years.
1957	▶	Russians launch *Sputnik I*, the first Earth-orbiting satellite; the space race begins.

WORLD HISTORY 1960-PRESENT

1963

1963 ▶ Martin Luther King Jr. delivers his "I have a dream" speech in Washington, D.C. **President John F. Kennedy is killed** by a sniper in Dallas.

1965 ▶ U.S. planes begin combat missions in Vietnam War.

1967 ▶ Israeli and Arab forces battle; Six-Day War ends with Israel occupying Sinai Peninsula, Golan Heights, Gaza Strip and part of the Suez Canal.

1969 ▶ *Apollo 11* astronauts take man's first walk on the Moon.

1973 ▶ Vietnam War ends with the signing of peace pacts. The Yom Kippur War begins as Egyptian and Syrian forces attack Israel.

1979 ▶ Muslim leader Ayatollah Khomeini takes over Iran, where U.S. citizens are seized and held hostage.

1981 ▶ Scientists identify the AIDS virus.

1989 ▶ Thousands rallying for democracy are killed in Tiananmen Square, China. After 28 years, the Berlin Wall that divided Germany is torn down.

1990 ▶ South Africa frees Nelson Mandela, who was imprisoned 27 years. Iraqi troops invade Kuwait, setting off nine-month Persian Gulf War.

1991 ▶ The Soviet Union breaks up after President Mikhail Gorbachev resigns. In Yugoslavia, Slovenia and Croatia secede; a four-year war with Serbia begins.

1994 ▶ South Africa holds first interracial national election; **Nelson Mandela** is elected President.

2000 ▶ Elections in Yugoslavia formally end the brutal rule of Slobodan Milosevic.

2001 ▶ **On Sept. 11, hijackers crash two jetliners into New York City's World Trade Center,** another into the Pentagon and a fourth in rural Pennsylvania. In response, U.S. and British forces attack the Taliban government and bomb al-Qaeda terrorist camps in Afghanistan.

2003 ▶ The **U.S. and Britain lead an invasion of Iraq.** Their forces topple Saddam Hussein's government within weeks. U.S. troops capture the former dictator.

2004 ▶ The U.S. transfers power of Iraq to an interim Iraqi government. Hamid Karzai is elected President of Afghanistan. An underwater earthquake in the Indian Ocean causes a raging tsunami that devastates several Asian countries and parts of East Africa; more than 225,000 people die in the disaster.

2005 ▶ Iraqi voters elect a 275-seat National Assembly, approve a constitution and elect a Parliament.

1994

2001

2003

go 🖱 **Learn about the terrible tsunami at timeforkids.com/tsunami**

History

1770

1789

1804

1607 ▶	Jamestown, the first permanent English settlement in America, is established in Virginia.
1620 ▶	After a three-month voyage aboard the *Mayflower*, the Pilgrims land at Plymouth in Massachusetts.
1770 ▶	In the **Boston Massacre,** British troops fire into a mob, killing five men.
1773 ▶	A group of colonists dump tea into Boston Harbor to protest the British tea tax. The event becomes known as the Boston Tea Party.
1775 ▶	The American Revolution begins with the Battle of Lexington and Concord.
1776 ▶	The Continental Congress adopts the Declaration of Independence; the United States is born.
1783 ▶	The American Revolution officially ends with the signing of the Treaty of Paris.
1787 ▶	Delegates from 12 of the original 13 colonies meet in Philadelphia to draft the U.S. Constitution.
1789 ▶	**George Washington** is unanimously elected President of the U.S. The U.S. Constitution goes into effect.
1791 ▶	The first 10 Amendments to the Constitution, known as the Bill of Rights, are ratified.
1803 ▶	The U.S. purchases the Louisiana Territory from France, nearly doubling the size of the U.S.
1804 ▶	**Meriwether Lewis and William Clark** set out from St. Louis, Missouri, to explore the West and to find a route to the Pacific Ocean.
1805 ▶	Lewis and Clark reach the Pacific Ocean.
1812 ▶	The U.S. declares war on Britain for interfering with American shipping and westward expansion. It becomes known as the War of 1812.
1814 ▶	Francis Scott Key writes the "Star-Spangled Banner." The Treaty of Ghent ends the War of 1812.
1819 ▶	The U.S acquires Florida from Spain.
1823 ▶	President Monroe declares in the Monroe Doctrine that the Americas are to be off-limits for further colonization by European powers.

1836

1849

1861

1836	Texas declares its independence from Mexico. All the Texan defenders of the **Alamo** are killed in a siege by the Mexican Army.
1838	More than 15,000 Cherokee Indians are forced to march from Georgia to Indian Territory in present-day Oklahoma. About 4,000 die from starvation and disease along the "Trail of Tears."
1845	Texas becomes a state.
1846	The U.S. declares war on Mexico to gain territory in the Southwest.
1848	The Mexican War ends; the U.S. gains territory comprising present-day California, Nevada, Utah, most of New Mexico and Arizona and parts of Colorado and Wyoming.
1849	**Gold** is discovered at Sutter's Mill in California.
1854	Congress establishes the territories of Kansas and Nebraska. Tensions rise between those who want them to be free states and those who want them to be slave states.
1857	Abolitionist John Brown and 21 followers try to spark a slave revolt by capturing a government arms depot in Harpers Ferry, West Virginia.
1860	Following the election of Abraham Lincoln as President, South Carolina secedes from the U.S.
1861	More Southern states secede from the U.S. and form the Confederate States of America, with Jefferson Davis as President. The **Civil War,** a conflict between the North (the Union) and the South (the Confederacy) over the expansion of slavery, begins when the Confederates attack Fort Sumter in Charleston, South Carolina.
1863	Lincoln issues the Emancipation Proclamation, freeing slaves in the Confederate states.
1865	The Civil War ends with the surrender of Confederate general Robert E. Lee to Union general Ulysses S. Grant. Lincoln is assassinated by John Wilkes Booth. The 13th Amendment to the Constitution is ratified, prohibiting slavery.
1867	The U.S. purchases Alaska from Russia.
1869	The Central Pacific and Union Pacific railroads are joined at Promontory, Utah, creating the first transcontinental (cross-country) railroad.

History

1890	▶	The last major battle of the Indian Wars occurs at Wounded Knee in South Dakota.
1898	▶	The U.S.S. *Maine* is blown up in Havana harbor, which leads the U.S. to declare war on Spain. As a result of winning the Spanish-American War, the U.S. acquires Puerto Rico, Guam and the Philippines.
1917	▶	The U.S. enters World War I by declaring war on Germany and Austria-Hungary.
1920	▶	The 19th Amendment to the Constitution is ratified, giving women the right to vote.
1929	▶	The U.S. stock market crashes, and the **Great Depression** begins.
1933	▶	President Franklin Roosevelt's economic recovery measures, known as the New Deal, are enacted by Congress.
1941	▶	Japan attacks the U.S. naval base at **Pearl Harbor,** Hawaii, leading to the U.S.'s entry into World War II.
1945	▶	Germany surrenders, marking the end of World War II in Europe. The U.S. drops two atom bombs on Japan. Japan surrenders, and World War II ends in the Pacific.
1950	▶	The Korean War begins as the U.S. sends troops to defend South Korea against communist North Korea.
1953	▶	The Korean War ends.
1954	▶	The Supreme Court decision *Brown v. Board of Education of Topeka, Kansas*, declares that racial segregation of schools is unconstitutional.
1955	▶	Rosa Parks refuses to give up her bus seat to a white passenger. Martin Luther King Jr. leads a black boycott of the Montgomery, Alabama, bus system.
1963	▶	President John F. Kennedy is assassinated in Dallas, Texas.
1965	▶	**The first U.S. combat troops arrive in South Vietnam.**
1968	▶	Martin Luther King Jr. is assassinated in Memphis, Tennessee.
1969	▶	Astronauts Neil Armstrong and Edwin Aldrin Jr. become the first men to land on the moon.
1973	▶	The U.S., North Vietnam, South Vietnam and the National Liberation Front (Viet Cong) sign peace pacts in Paris. The U.S. withdraws from Vietnam.

1929

1941

1965

1986

1991

1998

2005

1974 ▶ President Nixon resigns as a result of the Watergate scandal.

1979 ▶ Iranian students storm the U.S. embassy in Tehran and hold 66 people hostage.

1981 ▶ The U.S. hostages held in Iran are released after 444 days in captivity.

1986 ▶ The space shuttle *Challenger* explodes 73 seconds after liftoff.

1991 ▶ The U.S. and its allies fight in the first **Persian Gulf War,** driving the Iraqis out of Kuwait.

1992 ▶ President George H.W. Bush and Russian President Boris Yeltsin formally declare an end to the cold war.

1998 ▶ The House of Representatives votes to impeach **President Bill Clinton.**

1999 ▶ The Senate acquits Clinton of impeachment charges.

2000 ▶ The presidential contest between Al Gore and George W. Bush is one of the closest elections in U.S. history. The U.S. Supreme Court determines the outcome, and Bush is declared the winner.

2001 ▶ Hijackers crash two jetliners into New York City's World Trade Center and another into the Pentagon. A fourth hijacked plane crashes in rural Pennsylvania. President Bush declares war on terrorism, and U.S. and British forces topple the Taliban government and attack Osama bin Laden's al-Qaeda terrorist camps in Afghanistan.

2002 ▶ A wave of corporate accounting scandals rocks the U.S. economy as Enron and several other companies are investigated by federal authorities.

2003 ▶ Seven astronauts die when the space shuttle *Columbia* explodes upon re-entry into the Earth's atmosphere. The U.S. and Britain lead a war in Iraq and topple dictator Saddam Hussein. Troops capture Hussein in December.

2004 ▶ The U.S. transfers control of Iraq to an interim Iraqi government.

2005 ▶ Hurricane Katrina hits the Gulf Coast, leveling entire cities in Mississippi. Parts of New Orleans are destroyed when two levees break and water submerges 80% of the city. It's the worst natural disaster in the nation's history.

For more events in U.S. history:
www.factmonster.com/ustimeline

History

How to Write a Narrative Essay

The first important thing to remember about a narrative essay is that it tells a story. You may write about:

- ✔ an experience or event from your past.
- ✔ a recent or an ongoing experience or event.
- ✔ something that happened to somebody else, such as a parent or a grandparent.

> **Learning something new can be a scary experience. One of the hardest things I've ever had to do was to learn how to swim. I was always afraid of the water, but I decided that swimming was an important skill that I should learn.**

The second important thing is that in a narrative essay the story should have a point. In the final paragraph, you should come to a conclusion about the story you told.

> **Learning to swim was not easy for me, but in the end my efforts paid off. Now when I am faced with a new situation I am not so nervous. I may feel uncomfortable at first, but I know that as my skills improve, I will feel more and more comfortable.**

The conclusion is where the author reflects on the larger meaning of the experience described. In this case, the author concludes that learning to swim has helped her to feel more confident about herself in new situations. The idea that self-confidence comes from conquering your fears is something that anyone can relate to. It is the point of this essay.

Get Personal!

The writing in an essay should be lively and engaging. Try to keep the reader's interest by adding details or observations. Sharing your thoughts invites the reader into your world and makes the story more personal and more interesting.

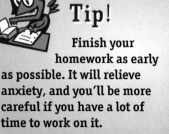

Homework Tip!

Finish your homework as early as possible. It will relieve anxiety, and you'll be more careful if you have a lot of time to work on it.

go See sample papers and writing checklists at timeforkids.com/homeworkhelper

For more tips on writing: www.factmonster.com/writingtips

Homework Helper

How to Write a Persuasive Essay

The purpose of a persuasive essay is to convince the reader to agree with your viewpoint or to accept your recommendation for a course of action. For instance, you might argue that the salaries of professional athletes are too high. Or you might suggest that vending machines be banned from your school cafeteria. A successful persuasive essay will use evidence to support your viewpoint, consider opposing views and present a strong conclusion.

Some people worry that adopting a school-uniform policy would be too expensive for families. However, there are ways to lessen the cost. For example, in Seattle, Washington, local businesses pay for uniforms at South Shore Middle School. In Long Beach, California, graduating students donate or sell their old uniforms to other students.

Use evidence to support your viewpoint. Statistics, facts, quotations from experts and examples will help you build a strong case for your argument. Appeal to the reader's sense of logic by presenting specific and relevant evidence in a well-organized manner.

Consider opposing views. Try to anticipate the concerns and questions that a reader might have about your subject. Responding to these points will give you the chance to explain to the reader why your viewpoint or recommendation is the best one.

Present a strong conclusion. All your evidence and explanations should build toward a strong ending in which you summarize your view in a clear and memorable way. The conclusion in a persuasive essay might include a call to action.

Remember:

Use a pleasant, reasonable tone in your essay. Sarcasm and arrogance weaken an argument. Logic and fairness will help to keep it strong.

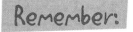

EXHIBIT
A

Tackle a Descriptive Essay

The purpose of a descriptive essay is to write about a person, place or thing in such vivid detail that the reader can easily form a mental picture. You may accomplish this by using words that create a mood, making interesting comparisons and describing images that appeal to the senses.

> I have always been fascinated by carnival rides. My first experience with a carnival ride was a Ferris wheel at a local fair. It was huge, smoky and noisy. Ever since that first impression years ago, these rides have reminded me of mythical beasts carrying off their screaming passengers. Even the droning sound of their engines brings to mind the great roar of a fire-breathing dragon.

Mood Words The author uses words that create excitement, like "fascinated," "great roar" and "fire-breathing dragon."

Interesting Comparisons One way the author makes his subject interesting is by comparing the Ferris wheel to a mythical beast.

Sensory Details The author uses his senses for details about how the Ferris wheel looks, sounds and feels. The ride is "huge, smoky and noisy," and its engines "drone."

Like any essay, a descriptive essay should be well organized. This essay began with a general statement—that the author has always been fascinated by carnival rides. The body of the essay is made of paragraphs that describe the subject. The conclusion restates the main idea—in this case, that the author continues to find carnival rides fascinating.

> A trip on the Ferris wheel never fails to thrill me. The fascination I have for Ferris wheels comes back with each and every ride.

TFK Writing Tip

"As both a writer and an editor, I like details. When I'm editing someone else's writing, I try to point out specific details that I think are working and not working. I always begin with the positive. If I like the way words are used, I let the writer know and try to explain why. If there's a section that isn't clear, I tell the writer why I am confused and give suggestions for how it might be changed."

—Nicole Iorio is a senior editor at TIME For Kids magazine.

For research and study tips:
www.factmonster.com/hwtips

Homework Helper

Compare-and-Contrast Essay

A compare-and-contrast essay shows the differences and similarities between two people, places or things.

To write a compare-and-contrast essay, follow the steps below:

✔ Find two things to compare and contrast. For example, you can compare and contrast two animals, two jobs, two characters or two stories.

✔ Take notes on your topics. Ask yourself: What is the same about both things? What is different?

✔ Write a title. Be sure your title lets the reader know the two things that you will be comparing and contrasting.

✔ Write an introduction. Briefly tell your reader about the two things you will be comparing and contrasting.

✔ Write a paragraph in which you discuss how your topics are different. Use specific examples. Use words and phrases that show contrast, such as *however*, *but*, *on the other hand* or *on the contrary*.

✔ Write a paragraph in which you discuss how your topics are similar. Use specific examples to show the similarities.

✔ Write a conclusion. Be careful not to repeat ideas that you have already discussed in your essay. Ask yourself: What do I want my reader to remember? What can my reader learn from the ideas discussed in the essay?

✔ Once you have finished your paper, be sure to review your writing.

TFK Writing Tip

"The conclusion reinforces what the reader read and why they were reading it. For example, in a research paper, a conclusion summarizes the key information and facts so the reader can remember them. In a persuasive essay, it reminds the reader what the author is trying to get at so it's imprinted in the reader's mind. In a narrative paper, it restates the highlights of the story. In a compare-and-contrast paper, it shows the connection between the items being compared, in case the reader couldn't pick them out."

—Zack Dale is a TFK Kid Reporter from Ohio.

Did You Know?

More than 790,000 kids in the United States are homeschooled.

 Get writing, research and organizing tips at timeforkids.com/homeworkhelper

How-to Article

A how-to article explains the way something is done. It often presents the information in steps.

To write a how-to article, follow the steps below:

✔ Choose a favorite activity, sport or hobby that you could teach someone about (for example, how to use a telescope, play a board game or follow a recipe).

✔ Write a title for your article.

✔ Write an introduction that tells your reader what you will be explaining and why it is useful to know.

✔ Think about what your reader might already know about this subject. Assume your reader has never done this activity before!

✔ List all the materials needed to do this activity.

✔ Picture the activity in your mind, or do the activity yourself. Make a list of the steps you take in order to complete the activity.

✔ Begin writing. To help your reader follow directions, use time-order words such as *first, second, third, fourth, now, next, then* and *finally*.

✔ Include any hints, drawings or photos you think would be useful to your reader.

✔ Use specific words to help your reader understand each step.

✔ Write a conclusion to end your paper.

Once you have finished writing, be sure to review your work.

TFK Writing Tip

"It's easy to get distracted by a new or interesting idea as you write. Create an outline, which is one way to organize facts and details that you want to include in your story. An outline will force you to think about the main points you're going to be making. Then you can check your writing against your outline to make sure each sentence or paragraph you write relates to or supports your main idea."

—Jeremy Caplan is a reporter at TIME.

Did You Know?

In 1900, there were about 15.5 million kids in public schools. About 15 million of them were in grades pre-K through grade 8. In 2004, there were about 48 million kids in school, with about 33 million of them in grades pre-K through grade 8.

Don't Copy This

Plagiarism means you used someone else's work without giving them credit. In your writing, you must give credit whenever you use information that you found in a source, unless it is common knowledge (see below).

ALWAYS GIVE YOUR SOURCE FOR:

- quotations (exact words).

- paraphrased information. Simply changing a few words of someone else's writing is unacceptable.

- summarized information.

- facts that are not common knowledge.

- ideas, including opinions and thoughts about what particular facts mean.

- maps, charts, graphs, data and other visual or statistical information.

Common knowledge is information that is widely available. If you saw the same fact repeated in most of your sources, and if your reader is likely to already know this fact, it is probably common knowledge. For example, the fact that Vladimir Putin was elected President of Russia in 2000 is common knowledge.

ACCIDENTAL PLAGIARISM

Sometimes, plagiarism is obvious. Copying a lab report from another student and buying a research paper over the Internet are clear examples of plagiarism. But plagiarism can also be accidental. Close paraphrasing and not giving proper credits are the most common causes of accidental plagiarism. These tips will help you avoid accidental plagiarism.

- In your research, when you copy words from a source, put quotation marks around them so that you do not forget that they were not your own words.

- When your notes include an idea, write in parentheses whether it is the source's idea or your own idea.

- Check your final text against your notes. Make sure that you did not accidentally use wording or other content without giving credit for it.

Homework Tip!

Use one folder for carrying homework to and from school.

How to Give an Oral Report

In many ways, planning an oral report is similar to planning a written report.

✔ **Choose a subject that is interesting to you.** What do you care about? What would you like to learn more about? Follow your interests, and you'll find your topic.

✔ **Be clear about your purpose.** Do you want to persuade your audience? Inform them about a topic? Or just tell an entertaining story?

To present an effective oral report, follow these four steps:

An oral report also has the same three basic parts as a written report.

✔ The **introduction** should "hook" your audience. Catch their interest with a question, a dramatic tale or a personal experience that relates to your topic.

✔ The **body** is the main part of your report and will take up most of your time. Make an outline of the body so that you can share information in an organized way.

✔ The **conclusion** is the time to summarize and get across your most important point. What do you want the audience to remember?

1. Research!

It's important to really know your subject and be well organized. If you know your material, you will be confident and able to answer questions. If your report is well organized, the audience will find it informative and easy to follow.

Too much information can seem overwhelming, and too little can be confusing. Organize your outline around your key points, and focus on getting them across.

Remember—enthusiasm is contagious! If you're interested in your subject, the audience will be interested too.

2. Rehearse!

Practicing your report is a key to success. At first, some people find it helpful to go through the report alone. You might practice in front of a mirror or in front of your stuffed animals. Then try out your report in front of a practice audience—friends or family. Ask your practice audience:

- Could you follow my presentation?
- Did I seem knowledgeable about my subject?
- Was I speaking clearly? Could you hear me? Did I speak too fast or too slowly?

If you are using visual aids, such as posters or overhead transparencies, practice using them while you rehearse. Also, you might want to time yourself to see how long your report actually takes. The time will probably go by faster than you expect.

3. Report!

Stand up straight. Hold your upper body straight, but not stiff, and keep your chin up. Try not to distract your audience by shifting around or fidgeting.

Make eye contact. You will seem more sure of yourself, and the audience will listen more closely, if you make eye contact during your report.

Use gestures. Your body language can help you make your points and keep the audience interested. Lean forward at key moments, and use your hands and arms for emphasis.

Use your voice effectively. Vary your tone, and speak clearly. If you're nervous, you might speak too fast. If you find yourself hurrying, take a breath and try to slow down.

4. Nerves!

Almost everyone is nervous when speaking before a group. Being well prepared is the best way to prevent nerves from getting the better of you. Also, try breathing deeply before you begin your report.

Book Report

A book report tells a reader about a particular book. It often gives the writer's opinion about the book.

To write a book report, follow the steps below:

✔ **Choose a book to write about.** You could write about a book in any genre or category: adventure, mystery, fantasy, biography, fiction or nonfiction.

✔ **Take notes about the book.**

✔ **Write an introductory paragraph.** You may want to start with a question to get your reader interested. Be sure to include the title and author of the book and let the reader know what type of story it is: funny, exciting, scary or sad.

✔ **Write a title.** The title could include the name of the book.

✔ **Write a paragraph summarizing the plot.** Be sure to give the names of the main characters and tell a little about them. You could explain the problem they face in the book and what they are doing to overcome it. Be careful not to give away the ending!

✔ **Write a paragraph that gives the reader your opinion of the book.** Here you might want to write about your favorite part or what you learned.

✔ **Write a conclusion that lets the reader know if you recommend this book.** Tell the reader why he or she should or should not read this book.

Once you have finished your paper, be sure to review your writing.

TFK Writing Tip

"A good introduction makes the reader want to read more! It should grab the reader's attention. When working on an introduction, I ask myself what makes the story interesting. Is there a surprising anecdote or an unusual fact that stands out? If so, introducing the information in the lead sentence will make the reader curious. Try to introduce the story in such a way that the reader feels he or she is in the thick of things—and can't wait to see what happens next."

Kathryn Satterfield is a senior editor at TIME For Kids magazine.

Homework Tip!

Try to do your homework in the same place and at the same time every day.

The title should include the name of the book being reviewed.

THE BAD BEGINNING: A TERRIBLE TALE

Includes the title and author of the book in the introduction

Engages the reader with a question

Do you enjoy happy endings? If so, *The Bad Beginning* by Lemony Snicket is a book you'll want to avoid. This is a story with a bad beginning, a bad middle and a bad ending. Why would anyone want to read such a thoroughly bad book? It's all in good fun!

Provides a brief summary of the plot

The Bad Beginning is a story about the suffering of three orphaned siblings at the hands of their uncle, Count Olaf. Although Violet, Klaus and Sunny are the inheritors of an enormous fortune, they cannot claim the money until they are older. For now, they must live with Olaf and cook and clean for him and his terrible theater friends. Why would such a cruel character take in three orphans? He wants to steal their fortune, of course.

Includes details about a problem the characters face

States an opinion about the book

I can't tell you how the story ends, but I can tell you what I enjoyed most about the book. Snicket makes his readers laugh and want to continue reading, even in the most terrible situations. For example, he constantly warns his reader to put down the book because nothing good could possibly come of the orphans' unfortunate situation. He writes: "It is my sad duty to write down these unpleasant tales, but there is nothing stopping you from putting this book down at once..." Of course, Snicket's warnings only made me even more curious to find out what would become of the siblings in the end.

Provides examples from the book to support the opinion

Gives reasons for recommending (or not recommending) the book

Will Olaf's evil plot win out? Or will these three crafty kids outwit him? If you're not afraid of a little misery and a whole lot of mischief, then I recommend you read *The Bad Beginning* and find out for yourself.

How to Write a Research Paper

Writing a research paper involves all of the steps for writing an essay plus some additional ones. To write a research paper you must first do some research; that is, investigate your topic by reading about it in different sources, including books, magazines, newspapers and on the Internet. The information you gather is used to support the points you make in your paper.

Eight Steps to a Great Research Paper

1. Find your topic. Try to pick a topic that's fun and interesting. If your topic genuinely interests you, chances are that you'll enjoy working on it.

2. Look for sources. Take a trip to the library. Use the electronic catalog or browse the shelves to look for books on your topic. If you find a book that is useful, check the bibliography (list of sources) in the back of that book for other books or articles on that topic. If you need help finding sources, ask a librarian.

Keep a list of all the sources that you use. Include the title of the source, the author, publisher and place and date of publication.

3. Read your sources and take notes. After you've gathered your sources, begin reading and taking notes. Use 3 x 5 index cards, writing one fact or idea per card. This way related ideas from different sources can be easily grouped together. Be sure to note the source and the page number on each card.

4. Make an outline. Organize your index cards by topic, then develop an outline to organize your ideas. An outline shows your main ideas and the order in which you are going to write about them.

5. Write a first draft. Every essay or paper is made up of three parts: the introduction, the body and the conclusion.

- **The introduction is the first paragraph. It often begins with a general statement about the topic and ends with a more specific statement of your main idea.**

- **The body of the paper follows the introduction. It has a number of paragraphs in which you develop your ideas in detail. Limit yourself to one main idea per paragraph, and use examples and quotations to support your ideas.**

- **The conclusion is the last paragraph of the paper. Its purpose is to sum up your points—leaving out specific examples—and to restate your main idea.**

6. **Use footnotes or endnotes.** These identify the sources of your information. If you are using footnotes, the note will appear on the same page as the information you are documenting, at the bottom (or foot) of the page. If you are using endnotes, the note will appear together with all other notes on a separate page at the end of your report, just before the bibliography. Since there are different formats, be sure to use the one your teacher prefers.

   The National Beagle Club held its first show in 1891.[1]

   [1] Samantha Lopez, *For the Love of Beagles* (New York: Ribbon Books, 1993), p. 24.

7. **Revise your draft.** After you've completed your first draft, you'll want to make some changes.

8. **Proofread your final draft.** When you are happy with your revision, print it and check spelling, punctuation and grammar. It is good to do this more than once, checking for different kinds of mistakes each time.

How to Write a Biography

A biography is the story of a life. Biographers (people who write biographies) use primary and secondary sources.

✓ Primary sources convey firsthand experience. They include letters, diaries, interview tapes and other accounts of personal experience.

✓ Secondary sources convey secondhand experience. They include articles, textbooks, reference books and other sources of information.

To write a biography, you should:

1. Select a person you find interesting.

2. Find out the basic facts of the person's life. You might want to start by looking in an encyclopedia.

3. Think about what else you would like to know about the person.

   ✓ What makes this person special or interesting?

   ✓ What kind of effect did he or she have on the world?

   ✓ What are the adjectives you would use to describe the person?

   ✓ What examples from the person's life show those qualities?

   ✓ What events shaped or changed this person's life?

Taking Notes

Hearing something once is not enough to really learn it, and that's why note taking is so important. Clearly written, accurate notes help to capture information for later study and review. Taking notes also helps you to focus and learn during class time.

TAKING NOTES IN CLASS

- Keep your notes neat and organized. Use a separate spiral-bound notebook for each subject, or use dividers in your loose-leaf notebook to make individual sections for each subject.

- Begin each note-taking session at the top of a fresh page. Start by writing the date.

- Don't try to write down everything the teacher says, but try to record as many facts and ideas as you can. Mark important facts or main ideas with a star or underline them.

- Use short sentences and phrases and easily remembered abbreviations and symbols. Some commonly used abbreviations and symbols are:

cf	(compare)
i.e.	(that is)
e.g.	(for example)
w/	(with)
w/o	(without)
&, +	(and)
=	(equals, is)

- Write clearly, and leave lots of blank space in the left margin or between ideas in case you need to add information later.

- Read over your notes as soon as you can after class. If there is anything you don't understand, ask the teacher at the next class.

TAKING NOTES FROM TEXTBOOKS

- Organize your paper the same way you would for class notes.

- Write down the name of the book and the chapter or section from which you will be taking notes.

- Keep textbook notes separate from class notes.

- Get a general idea of what the reading is about.

- Read the introduction, headings and subheadings and any paragraphs that summarize the content.

- Look at any illustrations or graphs and charts and read the captions.

- Go back and read the chapter or section carefully. Look for the main ideas.

- Try not to copy information directly from the textbook into your notes. Instead, summarize the information in your own words. This will help you to concentrate and learn.

- If you do copy directly from the textbook, use quotation marks to indicate that it is a direct quotation. Take care to copy the quotation exactly.

- Summarize the main ideas at the end of your notes, and circle them.

Homework Tip!

Bring all the supplies you will need to the library, including your assignment, books, pens, paper and change for the photocopier. Remember to ask the librarian if you need help finding resources.

Giving Credit Where It Is Due: Putting Together a Bibliography

A bibliography is a list of the sources you used to get information for your report. It is included at the end of your report. You will find it easy to prepare your bibliography if you keep track of each source you use as you are reading and taking notes.

When putting together a final bibliography, list your sources (texts, articles, interviews and so on) in alphabetical order by authors' last names. Sources that don't have authors should be alphabetized by title. There are different formats for bibliographies, so be sure to use the one your teacher prefers.

Book

Author (last name first). *Title of the book*. City: Publisher, Date of publication.
Dahl, Roald. *The BFG*. New York: Farrar, Straus and Giroux, 1982.

Encyclopedia

Encyclopedia title, edition, date. Volume number, "Article title," page numbers.
Encyclopædia Britannica, 1997. Volume 7, "Gorillas," pp. 50–51.

Magazine

Author (last name first), "Article title." *Name of magazine*. Volume number, (Date): page numbers.
Jordan, Jennifer, "Filming at the Top of the World." *Museum of Science Magazine*. Volume 47, No. 1 (Winter 1998): p. 11.

Newspaper

Author (last name first), "Article title." *Name of newspaper,* city, state of publication. (Date): edition if available, section, page number(s).
McGrath, Charles, "A Rigorous Intellectual Dressed in Glamour." The New York *Times*, New York, N.Y. (12/29/04): New England Edition, The Arts, p. B1.

Person

Full name (last name first). Occupation. Date of interview.
Nerow, Jayce. Police officer. January 5, 2006.

CD-ROM

Disc title: version, date. "Article title," pages if given. Publisher.
Compton's Multimedia Encyclopedia: Macintosh version, 1995.
"Civil rights movement," p. 3. Compton's Newsmedia.

Internet

Author (last name first) (date). "Article title." Date work retrieved, name and URL of website.
Brunner, Borgna (2001). "Earthquakes!" Retrieved January 27, 2003, from www.infoplease.com/spot/earthquake1.html.

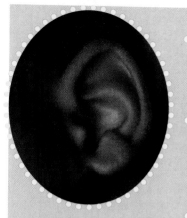

Listening Skills

Being a good listener is a key to success in the classroom. Follow these tips and you won't miss a beat.

- Give your full attention to the person who is speaking. **Don't look out the window or at what else is going on in the room.**

- Make sure your mind is focused. **If you feel your mind wandering, change the position of your body and try to concentrate on the speaker's words.**

- Let yourself finish listening before you begin to speak! **You can't really listen if you are busy thinking about what you want to say next.**

- Listen for main ideas. **The main ideas are the most important points the speaker wants to get across. They may be mentioned at the start or end of a talk, and repeated a number of times. Pay special attention to statements that begin with phrases such as "My point is..." or "The thing to remember is..."**

- Ask questions. **If you are not sure you understand what the speaker has said, just ask. It is a good idea to repeat in your own words what the speaker said so that you can be sure your understanding is correct.**

- Give feedback. **Sit up straight and look directly at the speaker. Now and then, nod to show that you understand. At appropriate points you may also smile, frown or laugh. Remember, you listen with your face as well as with your ears!**

Beating the Block

Do you ever find yourself staring at a blank computer screen or blank piece of paper? Writer's block—a condition that leaves you unable to put your thoughts on paper—can be very frustrating. Here's how a *TIME For Kids* editor tackles the problem.

"I've tried many things for writer's block, from reading other writers' great works to exercising! The best way to snap out of it is to just write something! For example, if you can't think of a good opening, write another section of your story. Beginning to write anything tends to jump-start the writing part of your brain so you can keep going. Eventually, you'll think of exactly what you need to say."

— Martha Pickerill is the managing editor of TIME For Kids magazine.

 **go** Get more tips on beating writer's block at timeforkids.com/writing

Business Letter

Write a business letter when you want to:

- request information.
- order a product.
- make a complaint about a product or service.
- share your opinion with your school, a public official or a local newspaper.

When you write a business letter, be sure to thank the person or organization for reading your letter. Remember to write a closing such as *Sincerely* or *Best regards* and add a comma after it. And don't forget to write your signature above your typewritten name! Below is a sample business letter.

1520 Sixth Avenue
New York, NY 10980 ← **Heading**

May 1, 2006 ← **Date**

Principal Valerie Sanchez
Redwood Elementary School ← **Name and address of the person who is receiving the letter**
New York, NY 10980

Dear Ms. Sanchez: ← **Greeting**

I am a fifth-grade student. I think that students in our school should be allowed to wear uniforms. We need to spend less time and money worrying about our school clothes and spend more time and energy on our studies. ← **Explanation of who the writer is and why he is writing this letter**

If students were allowed to wear uniforms, parents would spend less money on clothes. Parents could then spend money on more important things that kids need like food, books and medical care. ← **Gives the writer's opinion on the topic**

If students wore uniforms, it would make it easier for them to get to school on time. I spend a lot of time in the morning deciding what clothes to wear. But if I wore a uniform, then I wouldn't waste my time thinking about clothes. I could focus more on getting to school. ← **Describes the writer's experience in support of his opinion**

Students wouldn't worry so much about fitting in if they wore uniforms. Kids are under a lot of pressure to wear the right clothes, brands and styles. Uniforms would show kids that it's more important to be judged on who they are rather than on what they wear.

I really think this is an important issue. Students in our school should be allowed to decide if they want to wear uniforms or not. ← **Tells Ms. Sanchez what action the writer would like her to take**

Thank you, Ms. Sanchez, for reading my letter. I hope you will consider my suggestion. ← **Closing**

Sincerely,

Thomas James ← **Signature**

Thomas James

Homework Helper

133

How to Study for Tests

Tests are a way for you and your teacher to measure how well you have learned the material covered in class. Think of them as a challenge!

Before the Test

1. If possible, find out what material the test will cover and what type of test it will be (multiple choice, true or false, short answer or essay).

2. Study at a time when you are alert and not hungry or sleepy.

3. Don't wait until the last minute! Short, daily study sessions are better than cramming the night before the test.

4. Set a goal for each study period. If you are being tested on three chapters, set up four study sessions—one for each chapter and one for a review of all three.

5. Repeat, repeat, repeat! Read and reread your notes and the key parts of the textbook.

6. While reviewing your notes, cover them up and summarize them aloud.

Group Study

Working in a group can be a great way to study. Here's one plan for getting the most out of it.

1. First, compare your notes and review old homework.

2. Next, drill each other on facts you need to memorize. For example: What are the four stages of a butterfly's life cycle?

3. Finally, take the time to discuss "why" questions. For example: Why do monarch butterflies migrate?

REMEMBER—BE PREPARED!

A study group is a place to share your understanding of a subject. The other people in the group aren't there to teach you facts that you should already know.

10 Tips for Taking Tests

1. Read the instructions carefully. Never assume you will know what they will say! Ask the teacher if you are unsure about anything.

2. Read the entire test through before you start to answer it. Notice the point value of each section. This will help you to pace yourself.

3. Answer the easiest questions first, then the ones with the highest point value. You don't want to spend 20 minutes trying to figure out a two-point problem!

4. Keep busy! If you get stuck on a question, go back to it later. The answer might come to you while you are working on another part of the test.

5. If you aren't sure how to answer a question fully, try to answer at least part of it. You might get partial credit.

6. Need to guess on a multiple-choice test? First, eliminate the answers that you know are wrong. Then take a guess. Because your first guess is most likely to be correct, you shouldn't go back and change an answer later unless you are certain you were wrong.

7. On an essay test, take a moment to plan your writing. First, jot down the important points you want to make. Then number these points in the order you will cover them.

8. Keep it neat! If your teacher can't read your writing, you might lose points.

9. Don't waste time doing things for which you will not receive credit, such as rewriting test questions.

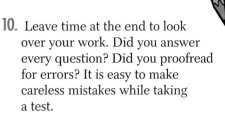

10. Leave time at the end to look over your work. Did you answer every question? Did you proofread for errors? It is easy to make careless mistakes while taking a test.

After the Test

✔ Read the teacher's comments carefully and try to learn from your mistakes.

✔ Save tests to review for end-of-term tests.

Homework Tip!
Study with a friend by giving each other little quizzes, or review work with flash cards.

Spelling Tips

This may be the best-known spelling rule:

i before *e*, except after *c* (or when sounded like *ay* as in *neighbor* and *weigh*)

Examples: ie words: *believe, field*
cei words: *ceiling, deceit*
ei words: *freight, reign*

Silent *e* helps a vowel say its name.

This means that when a word ends with a vowel followed by a consonant and then silent *e*, the vowel has a long sound. For example, the *a* in *rate* has a long *a*. The *a* is short in *rat*. The *i* in *hide* is long. The *i* is short in *hid*.

When two vowels go walking, the first one usually does the talking.

This means that when there are two vowels in a row, the first has a long sound and the second is silent. For example, the *o* in *coat* is long, and the *a* is silent.

Make sure that you are pronouncing words correctly.

This can help you to avoid some common spelling errors, such as *canidate* instead of *candidate, jewelery* instead of *jewelry*, and *libary* instead of *library*.

Make up funny memory aids.

For example, do you have trouble remembering which has two s's—*desert* (arid land) or *dessert* (a sweet treat)? Remember that with *dessert*, you'd like two of them. Similarly, do you have trouble remembering how to spell *separate*? Remember that there's *a rat* in the middle.

Break a word into syllables.

Look for prefixes, suffixes and roots. Practice each short part and then the whole word.

dis-ap-pear-ing
tra-di-tion-al

After you break apart a work, ask yourself: How is this word like other words I know? Spelling the word *traditional* may make you think of spelling *functional* and *national*. Finding patterns among words is one of the best ways to learn spelling.

Plural Spelling
Here are some general rules for spelling plural nouns.

NOUNS	PLURAL	EXAMPLES
Most nouns	add *s*	book, books; cup, cups
Most nouns that end in *ch, sh, s, x* or *z*	add *es*	box, boxes; bush, bushes; fez, fezes
Most nouns that end in a vowel and *y*	add *s*	boy, boys; day, days; key, keys
Most nouns that end in a consonant and *y*	*y* becomes *ies*	baby, babies; country, countries; spy, spies
Most nouns that end in *f* or *fe*	*f* or *fe* becomes *ves*	elf, elves; loaf, loaves; thief, thieves
Most nouns that end in *o*	add *s*	kangaroo, kangaroos; piano, pianos
Certain nouns that end in a consonant and *o*	add *es*	hero, heroes; potato, potatoes; volcano, volcanoes

Transitions

Good writers arrange their ideas and information in sentences that are woven together to tell a story. Sometimes the relationship between ideas is obvious, so the writer does not need to point out how they connect. Other times, authors use transitional words or phrases to show how ideas are related. *However, although, but* and *first* are common transition words.

Below is a TFK story accompanied by comments from the story's author, Martha Pickerill. Martha explains how she tries to connect her ideas.

I used the transition word "But" here because I wanted to set up a contrast between this paragraph and the preceding paragraph: how widely recognized Levi's once was compared to today.

"From now on" and "Last week" are transitional phrases that help the reader understand the time frame in the story. Both of these phrases let the reader know I am moving on to talk about current events at Levi's.

In the previous paragraph, I mention that plants will be closing. Alvarado's quote provides personal details to support the information in the preceding paragraph. Therefore, I didn't need any transitional words or phrases.

Here, I felt the connection between paragraphs was clear enough. But if I had had a little more space, I would have used a question to make a transition, such as, "How did Levi's get in such bad shape? Brands like..."

LEVI'S MAKERS HAVE THE BLUES

As a symbol of America, Levi's jeans have always been instantly recognized around the world, just like Coca-Cola and McDonald's.

But the jeans that were once the uniform of American kids aren't such hot pants anymore. From now on, most Levi's won't even be made in the U.S. Last week Levi Strauss announced that it will close 10 U.S. plants in the next eight months. Some 5,900 Levi's workers in the U.S. will lose their jobs. More Levi's will be made overseas, where it's cheaper to run a factory. Levi's needs to cut costs. Its sales have been dropping.

"I've been working here for about 20 years," said Thomas Alvarado, 55, a Levi's worker at an El Paso, Texas, plant who will lose his job. "You know, it's like a family."

Brands like Gap, Old Navy and Tommy Hilfiger are taking over. Critics say Levi's missed some major trends, including cargo pants. But the company says it has big plans to get "cool" again.

INVENTIONS & TECHNOLOGY

The Coolest Inventions of 2005

Each year, writers and reporters at TIME magazine research hundreds of new gadgets, then select the very best. Here are some of 2005's brightest inventions. How have we survived until now without them?

CHESHIRE GRIN

iCat has an expressive face that takes robotic pets to a new level. Tell her to go away, and iCat will look sad. Praise her, and she'll smile. Thirteen electric motors move her eyes, eyebrows, eyelids, mouth and head. iCat can communicate in eight languages so far. She can also connect to the Internet and read online text aloud. For now, iCat is a lab pet, for research only.

THE LAST STRAW

LifeStraw uses seven types of filters to purify dirty water. Costing only $3, the super-straw can prevent illnesses, such as diarrhea, that kill at least 2 million people every year in places

iCat

138

LifeStraw

with unsafe drinking water. It can also provide clean drinking water for survivors of hurricanes, earthquakes or other disasters. And it's handy for hikers who want to drink water straight from the source.

OPEN SESAME

Fukuda's Automatic Door opens just enough to match the shape of the person or object passing through. The door's sensitive motion detector tells it how far to open. This helps save energy by keeping too much hot or cold air from coming in. It can also keep out dirt—but not your little brother or sister.

Automatic Door

TRAINING WHEELS

Learning to ride a bike can be tricky, but the new Shift tricycle makes this challenge easier. Shift's rear wheels move toward each other as the rider picks up speed. The wheels separate for easier balance at slower speeds or when the rider comes to a stop. The 25-pound aluminum trike will go on sale for $100 in late 2006.

Shift tricycle

TUNNEL VISION

AntWorks is a new kind of ant farm that replaces the sand found in older models with a clear, seaweed-based gel. The goo is packed with all the tasty sugar, water and nutrients that ants need to live. Just pop in some ants, close the lid and watch the insects tunnel through the blue-tinted goo. It contains a magnifying glass to let you zoom in on the tireless workers.

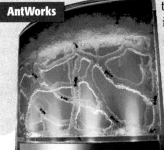

AntWorks

Waterproof paper

WRITE ON!

Chemist Sally Ramsey made an accidental discovery while experimenting with a new protective coating for plastic. She invented waterproof paper! The paper resists mildew and is easy to write on even when wet. For those who like to write in the shower, it will be on the market in 2007.

LandRoller

WHEELY AMAZING

These new LandRoller skates are made for beginners. They are designed to make sure a skater doesn't topple over on cracked pavement or uneven surfaces. LandRoller's two wheels, bigger than those of other inline skates, are angled inward to help beginners keep their balance. The cost: $249.

Great Ideas from

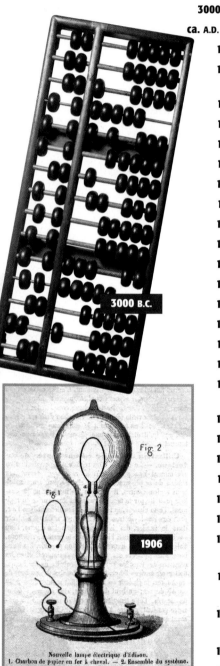

3000 B.C.

ca. 3800–3600 B.C.	▶	Wheel
3000 B.C.	▶	Abacus
ca. A.D. 100	▶	Paper
1608	▶	Telescope
1623	▶	Mechanical calculator
1709	▶	Piano
1752	▶	Lightning rod
1753	▶	Hot-air balloon
1783	▶	Steamship
1829	▶	Braille
1831	▶	Lawn mower
1832	▶	Matches
1839	▶	Rubber
1850	▶	Refrigerator
1866	▶	Dynamite
1868	▶	Typewriter
1869	▶	Vacuum cleaner
1870	▶	Chewing gum
1876	▶	Telephone
1877	▶	Phonograph (record player)
1885	▶	Bicycle
1888	▶	Ballpoint pen
1889	▶	Handheld camera
1891	▶	Zipper
1893	▶	Motion pictures (movies)
1895	▶	X ray
1899	▶	Aspirin
		Tape recorder
1901	▶	First transatlantic radio signals
		Electric washing machine
1903	▶	First motorized plane (Wright brothers)
		Windshield wipers
1904	▶	Ice-cream cone
1906	▶	Lightbulbs

1891

1906

Fig. 2

Fig I

Nouvelle lampe électrique d'Edison.
1. Charbon de papier en fer à cheval. — 2. Ensemble du système.

For the inductees into the Inventors Hall of Fame: www.factmonster.com/inventors

Great Minds

Inventions & Technology

These Robots Are Wild!

Weird-looking robots may one day work for you

Most people think that cockroaches are nasty pests. But not Roy Ritzmann. "They're fast and they're agile," Ritzmann says.

Ritzmann, a biologist at Case Western Reserve University, in Cleveland, Ohio, is helping other scientists at the school use bugs as models for robots. The scientists hope that new, insectlike robots will be able to operate in places that other robots can't.

"Many engineers now realize that much can be learned from biology," Roger Quinn, the director of Case Western Reserve's Biorobotics Laboratory, told TFK. More and more robotics designers believe that the behaviors and physical structures that help animals thrive could also make machines more useful.

Arthropods are especially

good robot models. Rugged arthropods include insects; crustaceans, such as lobsters; and arachnids, such as scorpions. Biologists and robotics scientists say arthropods can travel quickly over rocky or uneven ground.

Arthropods also have sensors on the outside of their bodies, including antennas and sensitive hairs that help the creatures respond quickly to changes in their environment.

Using animal-like sensors, the new robots will be able to react naturally in an unpredictable environment.

Quinn (above) and Ritzmann look at an early version of the roachlike Robot V.

Joseph Ayers (left) holds one of the real lobsters that inspired RoboLobster, shown in tank in mid-design.

They may find a path through a collapsed building to survivors of an earthquake, for example. They have the ability to climb, crawl or swim into dangerous situations or places.

NASA scientists are thinking of sending multilegged robots, modeled on scorpions and cockroaches, to explore Mars. They will travel over big boulders and into tight spots where today's wheeled rovers cannot. By behaving like bugs, the new generation of robots may help humans unlock the mysteries of the universe.

—By Kathryn R. Satterfield

Rise of the Robots

1961
Unimate, the first industrial robot, joins the assembly line at a General Motors plant. The robotic arm performs such basic tasks as stacking metal.

1966
The Stanford Research Institute, in California, creates Shakey, the first mobile robot controlled by artificial intelligence. It took Shakey hours to perform basic tasks.

1974
A researcher at the Massachusetts Institute of Technology (MIT) creates the Silver Arm. Its delicate sensors allow it to work like human fingers to assemble small items.

1994
Dante II, built by scientists from Carnegie Mellon University, collects samples in Mount Spurr volcano in Alaska.

1997
Researchers at MIT begin developing Kismet, a robotic head that can interact with humans through facial expressions.

1999
Sony introduces its electronic toy dog AIBO.

2000
Honda introduces ASIMO. It is the first humanoid robot that can walk forward and backward and turn while walking.

2002
Roomba, a vacuuming robot, gets down to work.

Did You Know?

Kids can be just as creative as adults when it comes to dreaming up cool inventions. Jeanie Low was 11 years old when she received a patent in 1992, for inventing the Kiddie Stool—a foldup stool that fits under the sink. Kids can unfold it, stand on it and reach the sink on their own!

Mobile Magic

More than 182 million people in the U.S. subscribe to cellphones. Here's what these multimedia machines can do.

Ringtones With every call comes brief bits of music or a celebrity voice. You can choose a different song for different callers.

Games Bowling and card games are cellphone hits, but versions of console games are also popular. Some companies offer multiplayer gaming via phone.

Television Phones can show such small TV bites as music videos, highlights from sports events or previews of new episodes of shows. Fox is producing "mobisodes" of the TV show 24, with original scripts and different actors.

Bloggers New technology allows phones to send text and upload photos to a blog that other people can view via phone.

Pictures "Picturemail" lets you send camera-phone snapshots like e-mail. Another service turns photos from high-quality camera phones into prints.

TFK Mystery Person

CLUE 1: Born to former slaves in 1877 in Kentucky, I became a pioneering African American inventor.

CLUE 2: In 1912, I invented a gas mask. A version of it is still used by soldiers and firefighters.

CLUE 3: I was the first person to receive a patent for an automatic traffic signal, in 1923. It made driving cars a lot safer.

WHO AM I?

(See Answer Key that begins on page 342.)

Sports Sports fans can get game highlights, scores, stats and text messaging from other fans.

Wallpaper This is a way to personalize the phone with an image of a favorite actor, singer or work of art. You can even choose a picture to pop up for a specific caller.

Inventions & Technology

 go Check out kids' favorite technology websites at timeforkids.com/tech

KIDS OF THE WORLD

MEXICO

LOCATION Central America

SCHOOL Large schools hold two shifts—one group of children attends in the morning, and one attends in the afternoon. Uniforms are usually required.

The school year typically runs from the beginning of September through the end of June.

PLAY Lotería, a game similar to bingo, is played with picture cards and song. Jump rope and other outdoor games are very popular.

Soccer is the top sport in Mexico. Other favorites include baseball and jai alai, a game similar to handball that originated in Spain.

FAMILY Many homes in Mexico include not just parents and children but also grandparents, aunts, uncles, cousins or other family members.

Children have two last names. Their father's last name is the first part, and their mother's last name is the second part.

FAVORITE FOODS Mole is a sauce that is made with as many as 24 ingredients. It typically includes peppers and spices, such as cinnamon and chocolate.

Another favorite is tamal (plural: tamales). Corn dough is stuffed with meat, cheese or a sweet filling, then wrapped in a corn husk and steamed.

Did You Know? Spanish is Mexico's official language, but more than 60 native languages are spoken. The top native languages are Náhuatl (about 2.5 million speakers) and Maya (about 1.5 million speakers).

RUSSIA

LOCATION Eastern Europe and Central Asia

SCHOOL Russian children have nine years of elementary education. The school day usually runs from 8:30 A.M. to 2:30 P.M.; lunch is eaten at school.

School uniforms were abolished in the 1990s. Nowadays, kids dress for warmth—they sometimes even wear fur coats!

PLAY Chess is a national obsession. Other pastimes include the card game *Durak* (Russian Fool) and the computer game Tetris, which was invented in Russia.

Soccer is the top sport in Russia. Ice hockey and ice skating are also popular in this chilly country.

FAMILY About three-quarters of Russian families live in small city apartments. Some families also have a country cottage, which is called a dacha.

In Russia, grandmothers—babushkas—are famous for the strong role they play in families, public life and fairy tales.

FAVORITE FOODS Borscht is a beet soup served hot or cold, topped with sour cream and sprinkled with dill or chopped green scallions.

Pelmen are small, moist dumplings filled with chopped meat. They are served with butter, sour cream and vinegar.

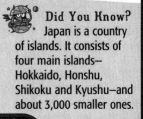 **Did You Know?** Russia is the world's largest country. It covers 6.6 million square miles (17 million sq km) and 11 time zones and is part of two continents—Europe and Asia.

JAPAN

LOCATION East Asia

SCHOOL Schools in Japan are very competitive, and the pressure to score well begins early. Even preschoolers may attend "cram schools" to prepare for exams.

The Japanese school year typically begins in April and lasts until March. There is a summer break of about six weeks, but kids have homework during that time.

PLAY Comic books have been popular in Japan since the 1700s. Comics now account for about 40% of all published material in Japan.

Kite flying is enjoyed by people of every age. Each year Japan hosts many kite festivals that feature giant, colorful handmade kites.

FAMILY Homes in Japan are small—on average, less than 1,000 square feet (compared with 2,400 square feet in the U.S.). The typical family of four lives in five small rooms.

Most fathers in Japan work long hours. As a result, some kids only see their fathers on weekends or holidays.

FAVORITE FOODS Fish! Fish may be eaten at breakfast, lunch or dinner. On average, each person in Japan eats about 150 pounds of fish a year.

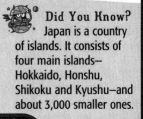 **Did You Know?** Japan is a country of islands. It consists of four main islands—Hokkaido, Honshu, Shikoku and Kyushu—and about 3,000 smaller ones.

Kids of the World

go Learn about cultures around the world at timeforkids.com/goplaces

ETHIOPIA

LOCATION East Africa

SCHOOL Because much of Ethiopia is rural, kids who attend school may have to walk several miles each way.

Unlike most other African nations, school in Ethiopia is free. However, many kids work to help support their families. Fewer than half are still enrolled by grade 5.

PLAY *Gebeta*, a game of strategy, has been popular for hundreds of years. It is played using seeds or pebbles and a board with rows of cups.

Many kids learn the lively *eskista* dance, which is performed almost entirely with the shoulders. Soccer is the most popular sport.

FAMILY Most families live in rural areas. It is common for an extended family to live in a cluster of houses and farm together.

Traditionally, parents and children do not share a last name. Most kids take their father's first name as their last name.

FAVORITE FOODS *Injera* is a pancake-like bread used to scoop up spicy dishes such as *doro wat* (chicken stew) and *mesir wat* (lentil stew).

Did You Know? Ethiopia is the only African country that was never colonized. Formerly called Abyssinia, it was the site of powerful ancient kingdoms.

IRAN

LOCATION Middle East

SCHOOL Girls and boys are educated separately until the university level. Girls usually have only female teachers, and boys typically have only male teachers.

Since Iran has an official religion—Islam—religious study is part of public-school education at all grades.

PLAY Backgammon—*takhteh nard*, "battle on wood"—is an old favorite. Archeologists recently found a 5,000-year-old backgammon board in southeastern Iran.

Soccer is the No. 1 sport in Iran. Both girls and boys enjoy playing the game at school, though usually only men may attend professional games.

FAMILY It is traditional for families to eat meals together on the floor, gathered around dishes of food spread on a kind of tablecloth called a *sofreh*.

Many children grow up in a home with at least one grandparent. If not, they are likely to have grandparents living close by.

FAVORITE FOODS *Khoresh* is a fragrant stew of meat, fruit or vegetables, nuts and spices. It is usually served with fluffy white rice.

Did You Know? Iran was known as Persia until 1935. It is the site of some of the world's oldest villages. They were built near the Caspian Sea at least 6,000 years ago.

Home of Hope

FROM TFK MAGAZINE

A unique school in India gives children a path out of poverty

What do you want to be when you grow up? Like many kids, the students at the Shanti Bhavan school in Baliganapalli, a small village in southern India, have no difficulty answering this question. "An astronaut!" screams 9-year-old Naceraj. Shashi, 10, wants to be a professional athlete. Nikhil, a fourth-grader, wants to be an engineer.

A few years ago, no one would have bothered to ask these kids about their hopes and dreams. They are members of India's poorest class, called untouchables.

Most Indians are Hindus. The Hindu faith teaches that people are born into distinct social classes, called castes (*kasts*). The lowest class is the untouchable caste. Traditionally, jobs are determined by caste. Untouchables have the worst jobs. Modern laws ban discrimination against untouchables, but in many parts of India, families from this caste still suffer.

Ten years ago, Abraham George, a New Jersey businessman, bought a barren plot of land in Baliganapalli. George wanted to help the poorest people in India, the country where he was born. He invested $15 million and turned the dry land into a world-class boarding school called Shanti Bhavan, which means "home of peace."

George built modern classrooms and playgrounds and hired teachers. The children at the school live in cheerful rooms and have clean clothes, nutritious meals and quality health care. Best of all, Shanti Bhavan is free.

By the time they are in fourth grade, students at the school are fluent in three languages. "I've never seen kids who love learning so much," says Lindsay Oishi, a teacher from Hawaii. "Their enthusiasm is contagious."

Karthika, 12, has been at Shanti Bhavan for six years. She visits her mother twice a year. Karthika's home is a small shack. She says. "Once I'm old enough, I'll be able to help my whole family so they don't have to live like this."

—By Ritu Upadhyay

On a visit home, Karthika (left) spends time with her mom.

TFK Mystery Person

CLUE 1: I was born in Romania in 1988 but have lived in France since age 2. By the time I was 14, I had published a best-selling novel.

CLUE 2: I go to school and lead a normal life, despite the fact that my book has sold more than 50,000 copies in Europe and was published in the U.S.

CLUE 3: My fantasy novel, *The Prophesy of the Stones*, is a story about a girl who dreams up a magical world.

WHO AM I?

(See Answer Key that begins on page 342.)

Kids of the World

Say It in Another Language!

If you want to impress your friends, try greeting them in a foreign language.

Language	Hello	Good-bye	Please	Thank you	Yes	No
German	hallo (hal-lo)	auf Wiedersehen (owf vee-der-zay-en)	bitte (BIT-the)	danke (DAHN-keh)	ja (yah)	nein (nine)
Dutch	hallo (hal-lo)	tot ziens (TOTE-ZEANS)	alstublieft (ALS-TU-BLEAFT)	dank u wel (dahnk ye well)	ja (yah)	nee (nay)
Swedish	hej (hey)	hejdå (hey da)	tack (tahk)	tack (tahk)	ja (yah)	nej (nay)
French	bonjour (bong-zhoor)	au revoir (oh rer-vwahr)	s'il vous plaît (seel voo play)	merci (mair-see)	oui (wee)	non (nong)
Spanish	hola (oh-lah)	adiós (ah-dyos)	por favor (pohr fah-vohr)	gracias (GRAH-syahs)	sí (see)	no (noh)
Italian	ciao (chow)	arrivederci (ah-ree-veh-DAIR-chee)	per favore (PAIR fah-VO-reh)	grazie (GRAH-zy-eh)	si (see)	no (noh)

The Latest Lingo

FROM TFK MAGAZINE

How new words make it into the dictionary

Do you Google in the snain? Don't bother to look for these words in *Merriam-Webster's Collegiate Dictionary*. Snain, meaning "a mix of snow and rain," never caught on. Google, meaning "to search the Internet," may be added in an upcoming edition.

Some 1,000 new words or usages enter the English language each year. Some go into the dictionary. Others fade from use. "Our language is a living thing," Jim Lowe, an editor at Merriam-Webster, told TFK. "It keeps growing."

Merriam-Webster first published the *Collegiate Dictionary* in 1898. Since then, at least 100,000 words have been added. As the world changes, we need new words to describe it.

The dictionary's editors look in everything from catalogs to comic books for the latest lingo. New words go on index cards that note when and where they first appeared.

Lowe reviews these words for the editor's annual updates. Every 10 years, the dictionary gets a total makeover. Lowe and the other editors review the 1 million or so new terms they have found. About 10,000 make it in. For a word to be added, it must show up regularly in a lot of places.

Lowe is no longer surprised by the words he finds. "When I first saw *spam*, I thought it was unusual," he says. "It's hard to associate meats with e-mail." But there it is on page 1,195, in black and white.

—By Kathryn Satterfield

These are some of the 30 new entries added recently. Don't know what they mean? Now you can look them up!

- brain freeze
- chick flick
- cybrarian
- Wi-Fi

Word Watch: Merriam-Webster editors review words and records of their origins.

Did You Know?

There are more than 2,700 languages in the world. In addition, there are more than 7,000 dialects. A dialect is a regional variety of a language that has its own pronunciation, vocabulary or meaning.

Language

149

A GUIDE TO EASILY CONFUSED WORDS

Not sure when to use "effect" and "affect"?
You're not alone. Here's a guide to some easily confused words.

AFFECT / EFFECT

Affect is usually a verb that means to have an influence on: "His loud humming was affecting my ability to concentrate."

Effect is usually a noun that means a result or the ability to produce a result: "The sound of the falling rain had a calming effect, nearly putting me to sleep."

CAPITAL / CAPITOL

The city or town that is a state or country's seat of government is called the **capital.** Capital can also refer to money or to an uppercase letter.

The building in which the legislative assembly meets is the **capitol.**

COMPLEMENT / COMPLIMENT

Complement is a noun or verb that means something that completes or makes up a whole: "The red sweater is a perfect complement to the outfit."

Compliment is a noun or verb that means an expression of praise or admiration: "I received many compliments about my new outfit."

FARTHER / FURTHER

Farther is an adjective and adverb that means at a more distant point: "Tomorrow, we will travel 100 miles farther than we did today."

Further is an adjective and adverb that means to or at a greater extent: "We won't be able to find a solution until we analyze the problem further."

FEW / LESS

Few is an adjective that means small in number. It is used with countable objects: "This store has few kids' movies."

Less is an adjective that means small in amount or degree: "Which jar holds less water?"

IT'S / ITS

It's is a contraction for *it is*: "It's a shame that we cannot talk about its size."

Its is the possessive form of *it*: "The school needed money for its new gym."

PRINCIPAL / PRINCIPLE

Principal is a noun that means a person who holds a high position or plays an important role: "The school principal has 20 years of teaching experience." Remember that your principal is your pal. Principal is also an adjective that means chief or leading: "The principal reason my dad turned down the job offer was because I didn't want to change schools."

Principle is a noun that means a rule or standard: "They refused to compromise their principles."

PRINCIPLE'S OFFICE

For a list of Latin and Greek word elements:
www.factmonster.com/wordroots

Bee Season

Every year millions of students participate in spelling competitions around the country. Some dread these events and are relieved to drop out in the early rounds. Others, however, study for hours a day, hoping to take part in

Anurag Kashyap (left) won the 2005 Spelling Bee.

the glory of "Bee Week"—the National Spelling Bee finals.

Bee Week isn't all spelling. Competitors also enjoy sightseeing, ice-cream socials, barbecues and a talent show. In 2005, Anurag Kashyap of Poway, California, took home $28,000 in cash and other prizes for correctly spelling "appoggiatura," a term in music.

The National Spelling Bee dates back to 1925. Over the years, the Bee has grown from a mere nine contestants to a high of 273 in 2005. Here are some tongue-twisting words that made students into National Spelling Bee champs.

1990	fibranne	1998	chiaroscurist
1991	antipyretic	1999	logorrhea
1992	lyceum	2000	demarche
1993	kamikaze	2001	succedaneum
1994	antediluvian	2002	prospicience
1995	xanthosis	2003	pococurante
1996	vivisepulture	2004	autochthonous
1997	euonym	2005	appoggiatura

 **Homework Tip!** If there are questions in a reading assignment, read the questions before reading the text. It will make answering them easier.

Palindromes

A **palindrome** is a word, phrase or sentence that reads the same forward and backward. Here are some examples of palindromes.

A daffodil slid off Ada.

Boston did not sob.

Dee saw a seed.

Kayak

Ma is as selfless as I am.

Never odd or even.

Step on no pets.

A nut for a jar of tuna.

Flee to me, remote elf.

Madam, I'm Adam.

Name no one man.

Not New York, Roy went on.

Can you think of other palindromes?

TFK

Puzzles & Games

Making Change

Can you transform the word HARD into the word SOFT? Start with HARD and change one letter to create a different four-letter word. Do that five more times until you've come up with SOFT. For example, here's how to change HEAD into TAIL in five moves: HEAD > HEAL > TEAL > TELL > TALL > TAIL. Hint: Each image below represents one of the five words you have to come up with to change HARD into SOFT.

(See Answer Key that begins on page 342.)

LARD

American Sign Language (ASL) and the American Manual Alphabet

American Sign Language (ASL) was developed at the American School for the Deaf, which was founded in 1817 in Hartford, Connecticut. Teachers at the school created ASL by combining French Sign Language with several American visual languages. ASL includes signs, gestures, facial expressions and the **American Manual Alphabet** shown below. Today, it is the fourth most used language in the U.S.

A B C D E F G
H I J K L M N
O P Q R S T U
V W X Y Z

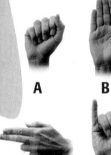

THE WORLD'S 10 MOST SPOKEN LANGUAGES

1. Chinese (Mandarin)
2. English
3. Hindustani
4. Spanish
5. Russian
6. Arabic
7. Bengali
8. Portuguese
9. Malay-Indonesian
10. French

Source: Ethnologue

Did You Know?

The three most popular foreign languages studied in the U.S. are Spanish, French and German.

go ➡ Hear foreign languages spoken at timeforkids.com/goplaces

"ONYMS"

ACRONYMS ·····► are words or names formed by combining the first letters of words in a phrase. For example, **SCUBA** comes from **s**elf-**c**ontained **u**nderwater **b**reathing **a**pparatus.

ANTONYMS ·····► are words with opposite meanings. **Hot** and **cold** are antonyms.

EPONYMS ·····► are words based on or derived from a person's name. For example, the word **diesel** was named after Rudolf **Diesel,** who invented the **diesel** engine.

HETERONYMS ·····► are words with identical spellings but different meanings and pronunciations. For example, **bow** and arrow, and to **bow** on stage.

HOMONYMS ·····► are words that sound alike (and are sometimes spelled alike) but name different things. **Die** (to stop living) and **dye** (color) are homonyms.

PSEUDONYMS ·····► are false names or pen names used by an author. The word comes from the Greek **pseud** (false) and **onym** (name). Mark Twain is a pseudonym for Samuel Langhorne Clemens.

SYNONYMS ·····► are words with the same or similar meanings. **Cranky** and **grumpy** are synonyms.

Most Common Words

Here are the 50 words used most often in English.

the	his	when
of	they	we
and	at	there
a	be	can
to	this	an
in	from	your
is	I	which
you	have	their
that	or	said
it	by	if
he	one	do
for	had	will
was	not	each
on	but	about
are	what	how
as	all	up
with	were	

Source: *American Heritage Word Frequency Book*

TFK Mystery Person

CLUE 1: I was born in South Africa in 1892 and grew up in Birmingham, England.

CLUE 2: I helped write the *Oxford English Dictionary*, and in my spare time I invented an imaginary language spoken by elves.

CLUE 3: I created a fictional world inhabited by small people who live in a place called Middle-earth. The first book about them is titled *The Hobbit*. My most famous work is *The Lord of the Rings*.

WHO AM I?

(See Answer Key that begins on page 342.)

Language

153

MATH

$$c_v(c) = \frac{\exp\left[-\frac{hs}{KT}\right.}{c_v(c)} + \ldots$$

$$(E)_Q = \varepsilon \sum_{n=0}^{\infty} n e - nx$$

$$z^0$$

$$A(t) = A_0\left(\ldots + \frac{r}{n}\right)^{\ldots}$$

Famous Math Minds

Imagine solving difficult math problems before computers were invented! Many of the world's greatest mathematicians came up with complicated theories and inventions well before high-tech tools were developed.

ARCHIMEDES This brilliant Greek is regarded as one of the most influential mathematicians of all time—amazing, considering he was born around 287 B.C.! He discovered buoyancy (he's said to have yelled "Eureka"—which means "I found it!"—in delight when he figured out why some things float). He also devised many weapons of war, several formulas for measuring capacity and pi.

ALBERT EINSTEIN Probably the most famous genius of all time, Einstein changed history when he scribbled $E=mc^2$ in 1905. His theory of relativity says that the speed of light inside a vacuum is the fastest speed in the universe. Einstein's discoveries became the foundation for much of modern science. Einstein was born in Germany in 1879 and became a U.S. citizen in 1940.

ADA BYRON LOVELACE Born in England in 1815, Lovelace, the daughter of British poet Lord Byron, is considered the world's first computer programmer. After studying plans for mechanical calculating machines imagined by Charles Babbage, Lovelace saw that the machines could be improved and used to compose music and perform complicated problems. In 1979, the U.S. Department of Defense named a software program "Ada" in her honor.

SIR ISAAC NEWTON Considered one of the greatest mathematicians and physicists in history, Newton was born in England in 1643. He discovered the mathematical laws of gravity and solved difficult problems in geometry. Newton also invented a type of math called calculus.

PYTHAGORAS This mysterious Greek figure, who lived around 580 B.C.–510 B.C, led a secret society. His followers, called Pythagoreans, believed he had magical powers and treated him like a god. He made important discoveries in the relationship between numbers and music. The Pythagorean theorem—the sum of the angles of a triangle is equal to two right angles—is an important concept in geometry. Pythagoreans were also the first to teach that the Earth is a round planet that spins on its axis.

Integers

Integers are whole numbers. They include positive numbers, negative numbers and zero, but not fractions, decimals or percents. Here are some rules to remember when you add, subtract, multiply and divide integers.

✔ Adding a negative number is the same as subtracting a positive number.

$$3 + (-4) = 3 - 4$$

✔ Subtracting a negative number is the same as adding a positive number. The two negatives cancel out each other.

$$3 - (-4) = 3 + 4$$

✔ If you multiply or divide two positive numbers, the result will be positive.

$$6 \times 2 = 12$$

✔ If you multiply or divide a positive number with a negative number, the result will be negative.

$$6 \times (-2) = -12$$

✔ If you multiply or divide two negative numbers, the result will be positive—the two negatives cancel out each other.

$$(-6) \times (-2) = 12$$

Math

Metric Weights

Most of the world uses the metric system. The only countries not on this system are the U.S., Myanmar (formerly called Burma) and Liberia.

The metric system is based on **10s.** For example, 10 decimeters make a meter.

Length

UNIT	VALUE
millimeter (mm)	0.001 meter
centimeter (cm)	0.01 meter
decimeter (dm)	0.1 meter
meter (m)	1 meter
dekameter (dam)	10 meters
hectometer (hm)	100 meters
kilometer (km)	1,000 meters

Metric Conversions

MULTIPLY	BY	TO FIND
centimeters	.3937	inches
feet	.3048	meters
gallons	3.7853	liters
grams	.0353	ounces
inches	2.54	centimeters
kilograms	2.2046	pounds
kilometers	.6214	miles
liters	1.0567	quarts
liters	.2642	gallons
meters	3.2808	feet
meters	1.0936	yards
miles	1.6093	kilometers
ounces	28.3495	grams
pounds	.4536	kilograms
quarts	.946	liters
square kilometers	.3861	square miles
square meters	1.196	square yards
square miles	2.59	square kilometers
square yards	.8361	square meters
yards	.9144	meters

Mass & Weight

UNIT	VALUE
milligram (mg)	0.001 gram
centigram (cg)	0.01 gram
decigram (dg)	0.1 gram
gram (g)	1 gram
dekagram (dag)	10 grams
hectogram (hg)	100 grams
kilogram (kg)	1,000 grams
metric ton (t)	1,000,000 grams

Capacity

UNIT	VALUE
milliliter (ml)	0.001 liter
centiliter (cl)	0.01 liter
deciliter (dl)	0.1 liter
liter (l)	1 liter
dekaliter (dal)	10 liters
hectoliter (hl)	100 liters
kiloliter (kl)	1,000 liters

CENTIMETERS

U.S. Weights and Measures

Measuring Length

12 inches	= 1 foot
3 feet	= 1 yard
5 1/2 yards	= 1 rod
40 rods	= 1 furlong
8 furlongs	= 1 mile

Measuring Area

144 square inches	= 1 square foot
9 square feet	= 1 square yard
30 1/4 square yards	= 1 square rod
160 square rods	= 1 acre
640 acres	= 1 square mile

Measuring Weight

16 ounces	= 1 pound
2,000 pounds	= 1 ton

Measuring Liquid

2 cups	= 1 pint
2 pints	= 1 quart
4 quarts	= 1 gallon
8 ounces	= 1 cup
16 ounces	= 1 pint

Cooking Measures

3 teaspoons	= 1 tablespoon
4 tablespoons	= 1/4 cup
5 tablespoons + 1 teaspoon	= 1/3 cup
16 tablespoons	= 1 cup

Did You Know?

Troy weight is used to measure precious metals. The grain is the smallest unit in troy weight. Long ago, gold was weighed against grains or the seeds of a plant.

In the United States, we use the U.S. customary system to measure things. Here are some of the units of measurement in the system.

LENGTH	WEIGHT	CAPACITY
mile (mi.)	ton (t. or tn.)	gallon (gal.)
yard (yd.)	pound (lb.)	quart (qt.)
foot (ft.)	ounce (oz.)	pint (pt.)
inch (in.)	dram (dr.)	cup (c.)

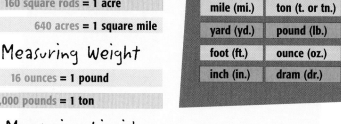

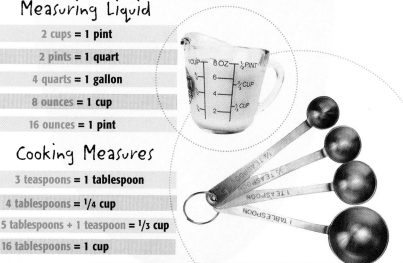

For more measurement tables:
www.factmonster.com/measurement

Rounding Numbers

A **rounded number** has about the same value as the number you start with, but it is less exact. For example, 341 rounded to the nearest hundred is 300. That is because 341 is closer in value to 300 than to 400.

Rules for Rounding

Here are the general rules for rounding:

- If the number you are rounding ends with 5, 6, 7, 8 or 9, round the number up.

  Example: 38 rounded to the nearest 10 is 40.

- If the number you are rounding ends with 0, 1, 2, 3 or 4, round the number down.

  Example: 33 rounded to the nearest 10 is 30.

What Are You Rounding To?

When rounding a number, ask: What are you rounding it to? Numbers can be rounded to the nearest 10, the nearest 100, the nearest 1,000 and so on. Consider the number 4,827:

- 4,827 rounded to the nearest 10 is 4,830.

- 4,827 rounded to the nearest 100 is 4,800.

- 4,827 rounded to the nearest 1,000 is 5,000.

Rounding Decimals

Rounding decimals works exactly the same way as rounding whole numbers. The only difference is that you round to tenths, hundredths, thousandths and so on.

- 7.8899 rounded to the nearest tenth is 7.9.

- 1.0621 rounded to the nearest hundredth is 1.06.

- 3.8792 rounded to the nearest thousandth is 3.879.

Did You Know?

When rounding long decimals, look only at the number in the place you are rounding to and the number that follows it. For example, to round 5.3874791 to the nearest hundredth, just look at the number in the hundredths place—8—and the number that follows it—7. Then you can easily round it up to 5.39.

How to Reduce a Fraction

Divide the numerator (the top part) and the denominator (the bottom part) by their **greatest common factor (GCF),** which is the largest whole number that can be divided evenly into each of the numbers.

Example: $6/15$
The greatest common factor is 3, so
$(6 \div 3) / (15 \div 3) = 2/5$

Or
Divide the numerator and the denominator by a common **factor.** A factor is any number that divides a number evenly without a remainder. Keep dividing until you can no longer divide either the numerator or the denominator evenly by the common factor.

Example: $8/20$, using 2 as the factor:
$(8 \div 2) / (20 \div 2) = 4/10 =$
$(4 \div 2) / (10 \div 2) = 2/5$

To change

A fraction to a decimal:

Divide the numerator by the denominator.
$1/4 = 1.00 \div 4 = 0.25$

A fraction to a percent:

Multiply the fraction by 100 and reduce it. Then, attach a percent sign.
$1/4 = 1/4 \times 100/1 = 100/4 = 25/1 = 25\%$

A decimal to a fraction:

Starting from the decimal point, count the decimal places. If there is one decimal place, put the number over 10 and reduce. If there are two places, put the number over 100 and reduce. If there are three places, put it over 1,000 and reduce, and so on.
$0.25 = 25/100 = 1/4$

A decimal to a percent:

Move the decimal point two places to the right. Then, attach a percent sign.
$0.25 = 25\%$

A percent to a decimal:

Move the decimal point two places to the left. Then, drop the percent sign.
$25\% = 0.25$

A percent to a fraction:

Drop the percent sign.
Put the number over 100 and reduce.
$25\% = 25/100 = 1/4$

Did You Know?

To add or subtract decimals, line up the decimal points and use zeros to fill in the blanks:

$9 - 2.67 =$

$$\begin{array}{r} 9.00 \\ - 2.67 \\ \hline 6.33 \end{array}$$

Math

159

Prime Numbers

A **prime number** is a number that can be divided, without a remainder, only by itself and by 1. For example, 17 is a prime number. It can be divided only by 17 and by 1.

Some facts:

- **The only even prime number is 2. All other even numbers can be divided by 2.**

- **No prime number greater than 5 ends in a 5. Any number greater than 5 that ends in a 5 can be divided by 5.**

- **Zero and 1 are not considered prime numbers.**

- **Except for 0 and 1, a number is either a prime number or a composite number. A composite number is any number greater than 1 that is not prime.**

To prove whether a number is a prime number, first try dividing it by 2 and see if you get a whole number. If you do, it can't be a prime number. If you don't get a whole number, next try dividing it by 3, then by 5, then by 7 and so on, always dividing by a prime number.

Here's a list of prime numbers between 1 and 100: 2, 3, 5, 7, 11, 13, 17, 19, 23, 29, 31, 41, 43, 47, 53, 59, 61, 67, 71, 73, 79, 83, 89 and 97.

3 29 73
11 59 97

Multiplication Table

To find the answer to a multiplication problem, pick one number from the top of the box and one number from the left side. Follow each row into the center. The place where they meet is the answer.

X	0	1	2	3	4	5	6	7	8	9	10	11	12
0	0	0	0	0	0	0	0	0	0	0	0	0	0
1	0	1	2	3	4	5	6	7	8	9	10	11	12
2	0	2	4	6	8	10	12	14	16	18	20	22	24
3	0	3	6	9	12	15	18	21	24	27	30	33	36
4	0	4	8	12	16	20	24	28	32	36	40	44	48
5	0	5	10	15	20	25	30	35	40	45	50	55	60
6	0	6	12	18	24	30	36	42	48	54	60	66	72
7	0	7	14	21	28	35	42	49	56	63	70	77	84
8	0	8	16	24	32	40	48	56	64	72	80	88	96
9	0	9	18	27	36	45	54	63	72	81	90	99	108
10	0	10	20	30	40	50	60	70	80	90	100	110	120
11	0	11	22	33	44	55	66	77	88	99	110	121	132
12	0	12	24	36	48	60	72	84	96	108	120	132	144

Squares and Square Roots

A square of a number is that number times itself.

For example:

$4^2 = 16$: 4 x 4 = 16

$6^2 = 36$: 6 x 6 = 36

Finding a square root is the **inverse operation** of squaring. Inverse operations are two operations that do the opposite, such as multiplication and division. The square root of 4 is 2, or:

$\sqrt{4}$ is 2: 2 x 2 = 4

$\sqrt{9}$ is 3: 3 x 3 = 9

Here's a table of squares and square roots for numbers from 1 to 20.

Number	Square	Square Root
1	1	1.00
2	4	1.414
3	9	1.732
4	16	2.000
5	25	2.236
6	36	2.449
7	49	2.646
8	64	2.828
9	81	3.000
10	100	3.162
11	121	3.317
12	144	3.464
13	169	3.606
14	196	3.742
15	225	3.873
16	256	4.000
17	289	4.123
18	324	4.243
19	361	4.359
20	400	4.472

Did You Know?

A cardinal number shows quantity—it tells how many.

- 8 puppies
- 10 friends

To learn how to find square roots:
www.factmonster.com/findingsqroots

Powers & Exponents

A power is the product of multiplying a number by itself.

Usually, a power is represented with a **base number** and an **exponent.** The base number tells what number is being multiplied. The exponent, a small number written above and to the right of the base number, tells how many times the base number is being multiplied.

For example, "6 to the 5th power" may be written as 6^5. Here, the base number is 6 and the exponent is 5. This means that 6 is being multiplied by itself 4 times:

6 x 6 x 6 x 6 x 6

6 x 6 x 6 x 6 x 6 = 7,776 or $6^5 = 7{,}776$

BASE NUMBER	2ND POWER	3RD POWER	4TH POWER	5TH POWER
1	1	1	1	1
2	4	8	16	32
3	9	27	81	243
4	16	64	256	1,024
5	25	125	625	3,125
6	36	216	1,296	7,776
7	49	343	2,401	16,807
8	64	512	4,096	32,768
9	81	729	6,561	59,049
10	100	1,000	10,000	100,000

ROMAN NUMERALS

The ancient Romans gave us this numbering system. The year 2007 in Roman numerals is MMVII.

King Louis the ___?
(See Answer Key that begins on page 342.)

One	I
Two	II
Three	III
Four	IV
Five	V
Six	VI
Seven	VII
Eight	VIII
Nine	IX
Ten	X
Eleven	XI
Twelve	XII
Thirteen	XIII
Fourteen	XIV
Fifteen	XV
Sixteen	XVI
Seventeen	XVII
Eighteen	XVIII
Nineteen	XIX
Twenty	XX
Thirty	XXX
Forty	XL
Fifty	L
Sixty	LX
Seventy	LXX
Eighty	LXXX
Ninety	XC
One hundred	C
Five hundred	D
One thousand	M

Can you figure out the year on this building?
(See Answer Key that begins on page 342.)

THE • YEAR • MDCCCLXXI

Geometric Terms

ANGLE: two rays joined by the same endpoint

ACUTE ANGLE: an angle that measures less than 90°

CONGRUENT FIGURES: two figures with the same size and shape

ENDPOINT: the end of a line segment

EQUILATERAL TRIANGLE: a triangle with all sides of the same length

HYPOTENUSE: the side of a right triangle opposite the right angle

ISOSCELES TRIANGLE: a triangle with at least two equal sides

LINE SEGMENT: a part of a line that has two endpoints

OBTUSE ANGLE: an angle that measures more than 90°

PARALLEL LINES: two lines that are the same distance apart and will never intersect

PARALLELOGRAM: a quadrilateral with both pairs of sides parallel and the same length

PERPENDICULAR LINES: two lines that meet to form a right angle

QUADRILATERAL: a figure with four sides

RAY: a straight line with only one endpoint

RHOMBUS: a parallelogram with all four sides of equal length

RIGHT ANGLE: an angle that measures 90°

RIGHT TRIANGLE: a triangle having a right angle

SCALENE TRIANGLE: a triangle with each side being a different length

TRAPEZOID: a quadrilateral with one set of parallel sides

VERTEX: the point on an angle where two rays meet

For rules on working with Roman numerals:
www.factmonster.com/romannumerals

Polygons:
How Many Sides?

A geometrical figure with three or more sides is called a polygon or a polyhedron. Here are the names of some polygons.

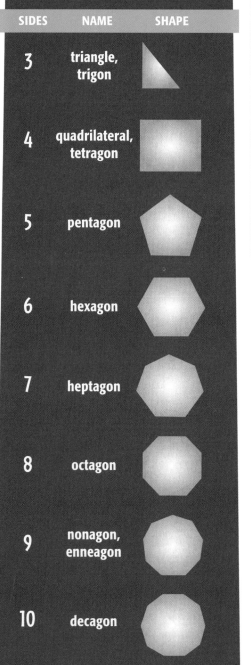

SIDES	NAME	SHAPE
3	triangle, trigon	
4	quadrilateral, tetragon	
5	pentagon	
6	hexagon	
7	heptagon	
8	octagon	
9	nonagon, enneagon	
10	decagon	

Common Formulas

Finding Area

Area is the amount of surface within fixed lines.

SQUARE
Multiply the length of one side by itself. (For example, if the side is 6 inches long, multiply 6 x 6.)

RECTANGLE
Multiply the base by the height.

CIRCLE
Multiply the radius by itself, then multiply the result by 3.1416.

TRAPEZOID
Add the two parallel sides, multiply by the height and divide by 2.

TRIANGLE
If you know the base and the height, multiply them and then divide by 2.

Finding Circumference and Perimeter

The **circumference** of a circle is the complete distance around it. To find the circumference of a circle, multiply its diameter by 3.1416.

The **perimeter** of a geometrical figure is the complete distance around that figure. To find the perimeter, simply add up the lengths of the figure's sides.

A prefix is an element at the beginning of a word. A numerical prefix lets you know how many there are of a particular thing. You can use these prefixes to figure out how many sides a figure has. For example, a hexagon has six sides, and a heptagon has seven.

Prefix	Meaning	Example
uni-	1	**unicorn:** mythical creature with one horn
mono-	1	**monorail:** train that runs on one track
bi-	2	**bicycle:** two-wheeled vehicle
tri-	3	**triceratops:** three-horned dinosaur
quadr-	4	**quadruped:** four-footed animal
quint-	5	**quintuplets:** five babies born at a single birth
penta-	5	**pentagon:** figure with five sides
hex-	6	**hexapod:** having six legs—an insect, for example
sex-	6	**sextet:** group of six musicians
hept-	7	**heptathlon:** athletic contest with seven events
sept-	7	**septuagenarian:** a person between ages 70 and 79
octo-	8	**octopus:** sea creature with eight arms
nove-	9	**novena:** prayers said over nine days
deka- or deca-	10	**decade:** a period of 10 years
cent-	100	**century:** a period of 100 years
hecto-	100	**hectogram:** 100 grams
milli-	1,000	**millennium:** a period of 1,000 years
kilo-	1,000	**kilogram:** 1,000 grams
mega-	1,000,000	**megaton:** 1 million tons
giga-	1,000,000,000	**gigabyte:** 1 billion bytes

More Than a Million

Numbers don't stop at the millions, billions or trillions. In fact, they go on and on and on. Here's what some really big numbers look like:

10 million	10,000,000
100 million	100,000,000
billion	1,000,000,000
trillion	1,000,000,000,000
quadrillion	1,000,000,000,000,000
quintillion	1,000,000,000,000,000,000
sextillion	1,000,000,000,000,000,000,000
septillion	1,000,000,000,000,000,000,000,000
octillion	1,000,000,000,000,000,000,000,000,000
nonillion	1,000,000,000,000,000,000,000,000,000,000
googol	1 followed by 100 zeroes
centillion	1 followed by 303 zeroes
googolplex	1 followed by a googol of zeroes

Mean and Median

The **mean** is also called the average. To find the mean of a series of numbers, add up all the numbers. Then divide the sum by the amount of numbers in the group. For example, in the series 1, 3, 5, 18, 19, 20, 25, the mean, or average, is 13: $91 \div 7$.

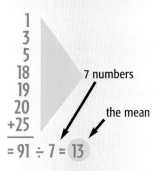

1
3
5
18   7 numbers
19
20   the mean
+25
_____
= 91 ÷ 7 = 13

The **median** of a series is the number that falls in the middle when the numbers are placed in order from least to greatest. In the above series, the median is 18. When there are two numbers in the middle, the median is the mean of the two numbers. For example, in the series 1, 3, 6, 18, 19, 20, the middle numbers are 6 and 18. The median is 12: $6 + 18 = 24$. $24 \div 2 = 12$.

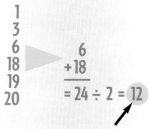

1
3
6   6
18   +18
19   _____
20   = 24 ÷ 2 = 12

the median

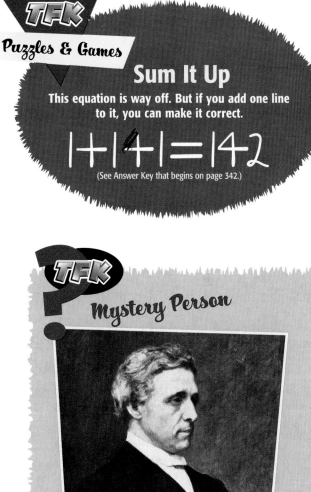

TFK Puzzles & Games

Sum It Up

This equation is way off. But if you add one line to it, you can make it correct.

$$1 + 141 = 142$$

(See Answer Key that begins on page 342.)

TFK

Mystery Person

CLUE 1: I was a 19th century English mathematician who earned fame as a novelist.

CLUE 2: I lectured in mathematics at Oxford University and wrote books on math and logic using my real name, Charles Lutwidge Dodgson.

CLUE 3: Under a pen name, I wrote two famous children's books that turned logic and language on their head. The heroine of both books was based on Alice Liddel, the young daughter of a friend.

WHO AM I?

(See Answer Key that begins on page 342.)

Math

165

MILITARY & WAR

AMERICA'S WARS

From the American Revolution to the war in Iraq, the U.S. has fought in 12 major conflicts. Do you know their names, where they were fought and why, and who won? Here's a quick look.

The American Revolution
1775-1783

CAUSE: Great Britain forced its 13 American colonies to pay taxes but did not give them any representation in the British Parliament. "Taxation without representation" and other injustices led the colonies to seek independence.

OUTCOME: The U.S. declared its independence on July 4, 1776. It achieved formal recognition when the Treaty of Paris was signed with Britain in 1783.

 During the battle at Yorktown, which marked the end of the Revolution and victory

for the Americans, French soldiers outnumbered Americans nearly three to one: 29,000 French fighters to 11,000 American troops.

The War of 1812
1812-1815

CAUSE: The British obstructed American trade overseas and forced American sailors to serve on British ships. Some members of Congress, called "war hawks," encouraged the war because they hoped to gain some of Britain's territory in North America.

OUTCOME: Trade issues between the two countries remained unresolved, but Britain gave up claims to some of its land on the North American continent.

The British burned the White House during the War of 1812. The building was restored, and the smoke-stained walls were painted white.

The Mexican War
1846-1848

CAUSE: Mexico was angered by the U.S.'s annexation of Texas, which had belonged to Mexico. The U.S. wanted to gain more of Mexico's land, especially California.

OUTCOME: Mexico received $15 million from the U.S. in damages but was forced to give up two-fifths of its territory. This land eventually became the states of California, Nevada, Arizona, New Mexico and Utah.

 The war was fought in the name of "manifest destiny," the belief that the U.S. should possess the entire continent from the Atlantic Ocean to the Pacific Ocean.

The Civil War
1861-1865

CAUSE: The Northern states (the Union) and the Southern states (the Confederacy) fought over slavery and states' rights. Eleven states (South Carolina, Mississippi, Florida, Alabama, Georgia, Louisiana, Texas, Arkansas, North Carolina, Virginia and Tennessee) seceded from the Union to form a separate nation called the Confederate States of America.

OUTCOME: The Union victory led to the reunification of the country and ended slavery.

More than 180,000 black soldiers fought in the Union Army. By the end of the war, they made up 10% of the Union troops. Both free African Americans and runaway slaves volunteered as soldiers.

Homework Tip!

Tell friends and family when you are doing your homework, and ask them to leave you alone until you're finished.

The Spanish-American War
1898

CAUSE: The U.S. supported Cuba's desire for independence from Spanish rule. It saw the war as an opportunity to expand its own power in other parts of the world.

OUTCOME: Cuba was freed from Spanish rule, and the U.S. gained several former Spanish territories: Puerto Rico, Guam and the Philippines.

 Before the war began, an explosion in Havana Harbor sank the U.S. battleship *Maine*, killing 260 crew members. "Remember the Maine!" became the war's most famous slogan.

World War I
1914-1918

CAUSE: Rivalries over power, territory and wealth led to the Great War. The U.S. joined the Allies (Britain, France, Russia, Italy and Japan), who were at war with the Central Powers (Germany, Austria-Hungary, Bulgaria and Turkey), after German submarines began sinking unarmed ships— notably the *Lusitania.*

OUTCOME: About 10 million soldiers died and 20 million were wounded. Germany was forced to admit guilt for the war, pay the other countries for the damage it caused and return territory it claimed during the war.

 World War I was characterized by trench warfare. Each army dug protective trenches—long, deep rows of ditches in the ground. The troops slept, ate and fought against the enemy in these trenches.

World War II
1939-1945

CAUSE: The Axis powers— Hitler's Germany, along with the dictatorships of Italy and Japan—attempted to dominate the world. The Allies (the U.S., Britain, France, the U.S.S.R. and others) fought to stop them.

OUTCOME: Germany surrendered on May 7, 1945, and Japan surrendered on September 2, 1945, after the U.S. dropped atom bombs on the cities of Hiroshima and Nagasaki.

 Combat aircraft, both bombers and fighter planes, changed the nature of war during World War II. Air superiority was critical to victory. The British Spitfire, American Mustang and the German Messerschmitt were among the most famous fighter planes of the war.

The Korean War
1950-1953

CAUSE: Communist North Korea, supported by China, invaded non-communist South Korea. U.N. forces, mostly made up of U.S. troops, fought to protect South Korea.

OUTCOME: South Korea maintained its independence from North Korea.

 The Korean War was the first armed conflict in the global struggle between democracy and communism—the cold war.

The Vietnam War
1955-1975

CAUSE: Communist North Vietnam invaded noncommunist South Vietnam in an attempt to unify the country and impose communist rule. The United States fought on the side of South Vietnam to keep it independent.

OUTCOME: The United States withdrew its combat troops in 1973. In 1975, North Vietnam succeeded in taking control of South Vietnam.

 Vietnam was the longest conflict the U.S. ever fought and the first war it lost.

Persian Gulf War
1991

CAUSE: Iraq invaded the country of Kuwait. The U.S., Britain and other countries came to Kuwait's aid.

OUTCOME: Iraq withdrew from Kuwait.

 The Desert Bar was made by Hershey for the soldiers in Desert Storm, another name for the Persian Gulf War. The chocolate bar was designed to withstand heat up to 140°F.

Afghanistan War
2002

CAUSE: Afghanistan's Taliban government harbored Osama bin Laden and members of the al-Qaeda terrorist group, who were responsible for the September 11, 2001, attacks on the U.S. After it refused to turn over bin Laden, U.S. and U.N. coalition forces attacked.

OUTCOME: The Taliban government was ousted, and many terrorist camps in Afghanistan were destroyed.

 **The Taliban surrendered within two months, much earlier than expected.**

Iraq War
2003

CAUSE: Dictator Saddam Hussein's supposed possession of illegal weapons of mass destruction and Iraq's suspected ties to terrorism prompted the U.S. and Britain to invade and topple his government. The Bush Administration acknowledged in 2005 that no WMDs were found in Iraq.

OUTCOME: Saddam Hussein was removed from power. American troops remain in Iraq, fighting and rebuilding.

 In December 2003, U.S. troops captured Saddam Hussein. They found him hiding in an 8-foot hole on a farm near his hometown of Tikrit. He had been on the run for nearly nine months.

Did You Know?

Weapons of mass destruction (WMD) include biological, chemical and nuclear weapons that are designed to kill many people over a large area.

The Meaning Behind Memorial Day

Though spring doesn't end until late June, many people consider Memorial Day—the last Monday of May—to be the real start of summer. That's when people heat up the grill, catch the biggest movies and hit the road. But Memorial Day has the word *memorial* in it for a reason!

Originally called Decoration Day, the holiday got started on May 30, 1868, when U.S. General John A. Logan declared the day an occasion to decorate the graves of Civil War soldiers. Twenty years later, the name was changed to Memorial Day. President Richard Nixon declared it a federal holiday in 1971. Over time it has become an occasion to honor the men and women who died in all wars.

Some people confuse Memorial Day with Veterans Day, which is celebrated on November 11.

A soldier places flags on graves at Arlington National Cemetery in Virginia.

Originally, Veterans Day was called Armistice Day, because it celebrated the end of World War I. Later, it was decided that Armistice Day should honor all servicemen—living and dead—who fought in America's wars, and the name was changed.

One Memorial Day tradition is for the President or Vice President to give a speech and lay a wreath on soldiers' graves in Arlington National Cemetery in Virginia.

—*By Carolyn Buchanan*

This memorial at Pearl Harbor honors the 1,102 Americans who died there on December 7, 1941, during a Japanese attack.

Animals in Uniform

For centuries, animals have been used to help fight wars. Before tanks were invented, soldiers rode their horses into battle. Pack animals, such as camels and horses, carried ammunition and supplies. Many other animals have been called for duty. Here's a look at a few of them.

- In the 16th century, Emperor Akbar of India used elephants in battle. The elephants wore bells to sound frightening, and poisoned daggers were attached to the end of their trunks as weapons.

- The Greek king Pyrrhus and his men rode elephants into battle against the Romans. Although the Greeks won, many men and elephants died. Today "Pyrrhic victory" means a victory won at great cost.
- In the 15th century, the Spanish used dog warriors. The dogs wore quilted overcoats into battle.
- Dogs helped Christopher Columbus fight Native Americans.
- Carrier pigeons delivered messages between ships at sea during World War I.
- During World War I, cats lived with soldiers in trenches, where they killed mice.

THE BRANCHES OF THE MILITARY

There are five branches of the U.S. military: the Air Force, Army, Coast Guard, Marine Corps and Navy. Each branch, except the Coast Guard, is part of the Department of Defense. The Coast Guard falls under the authority of the Department of Homeland Security.

AIR FORCE The U.S. Air Force, the newest branch, was created in 1947. Its main function is to protect the country from the air and from space. It uses fighter, bomber and transport aircraft as well as helicopters. The Air Force also controls the country's nuclear missiles.

MARINE CORPS The U.S. Marine Corps was organized in 1775 to help the Navy. It became its own branch in 1798. The Marine Corps is amphibious— that is, it has responsibilities both on land and in the sea. During wartime, the Marine Corps carries out operations that clear the way for attacks by other branches, usually the Navy. Recently, Marines have expanded their role in ground operations. The Marine Corps has its own tanks and other armor, artillery and aircraft.

U.S. MILITARY

ARMY The U.S. Army, the oldest and largest branch, was created in 1775 by the Continental Congress. It is a ground force, meaning it operates only on land. Its main role is to protect and defend the country, using troops, tanks and artillery (large guns and other heavy weapons).

NAVY The U.S. Navy was also created in 1775 by the Continental Congress. Its main role is to make sure the United States has access to the sea when and where necessary. The Navy also has a fleet of aircraft that it sends from its largest ships, called aircraft carriers, in areas where there are no available runways. Navy ships and submarines are used to attack the enemy.

COAST GUARD The U.S. Coast Guard was originally established in 1790 as the Revenue Cutter Service. In 1915, it was reorganized as the Coast Guard. During peacetime, the Coast Guard enforces the laws of the sea and rescues people and vessels in trouble. During war, the President of the United States can transfer Coast Guard resources to the Navy.

Countries with the Largest Military Budgets

These countries spend the most money each year on their military. The figures are given in U.S. dollars.

COUNTRY	BUDGET
1. UNITED STATES	$417,400,000,000
2. JAPAN	46,900,000,000
3. UNITED KINGDOM	37,100,000,000
4. FRANCE	35,000,000,000
5. CHINA	32,800,000,000

Source: Stockholm International Peace Research Institute

MONEY

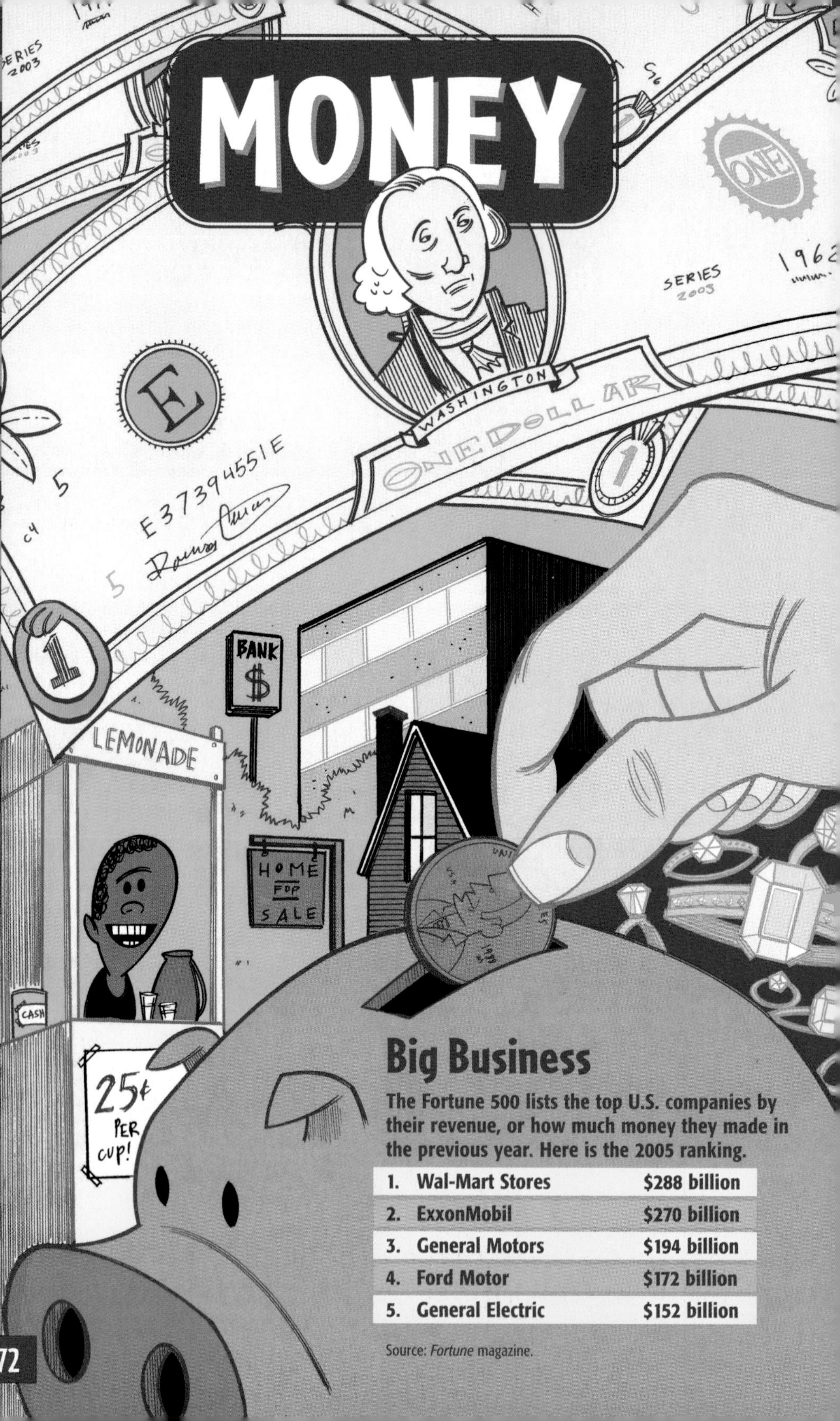
SERIES 2003
ONE
WASHINGTON
ONE DOLLAR
E37394551E
BANK $
LEMONADE
HOME FOR SALE
CASH
25¢ PER CUP!

Big Business

The Fortune 500 lists the top U.S. companies by their revenue, or how much money they made in the previous year. Here is the 2005 ranking.

1.	Wal-Mart Stores	$288 billion
2.	ExxonMobil	$270 billion
3.	General Motors	$194 billion
4.	Ford Motor	$172 billion
5.	General Electric	$152 billion

Source: *Fortune* magazine.

FROM TFK MAGAZINE

Kid$ Selling to Kids

Young people are signing up to help pitch new products to their peers

After lunch in her school in Tallahassee, Florida, 16-year-old Jenny Lieb hands out sticks of Big Red gum to her friends. Nothing unusual here, except that Jenny is taking notes on her friends' reactions to the gum.

Jenny is an agent for a marketing firm called BzzAgent. This company and others recruit young people to help spread excitement about products: music, movies, soft drinks, cellphones and more. The phenomenon is called peer-to-peer marketing.

Agents receive free products to share with their friends.

In return, they fill out surveys and record their friends' reactions. While BzzAgent's nearly 100,000 agents range in age from 16 to 89, other companies, including Alloy, Tremor and the Girls Intelligence Agency, recruit much younger agents.

Why are marketers eager to sign up kids like Jenny? Money! Kids ages 12 through 19 spent $169 billion in 2004, says Michael Wood, the vice president of Teenage Research Unlimited.

"Most of my friends and I have never felt that commercials drew us in," Jenny says. "But with [peer-to-peer], you're actually seeing the product and trying it out on the spot."

The trend has critics. "You won't know whether your friends hang out with you because they like you or because it's their job," says Marilyn Cohen, the director of Teen Futures Media Network.

—By Brenda Iasevoli

WILL IT SELL? Jenny Lieb (left) shares new kinds of snacks with her friend, Susan Jacobs.

Jobs That Parents Hope Their Kids Will Have

The U.S. celebrates Labor Day every September. The holiday honors all workers. In a recent poll, 504 parents of kids ages 5 to 17 named the job they would choose for their kids.

1. Start a business 25%
2. Doctor 18%
3. Teacher 11%
4. Chief of a big company 9% (tie)
4. Professional athlete 9% (tie)
5. Lawyer 4%

Source: Office Depot Back-to-School Survey conducted by Harris Interactive

Money

U.S. CURRENCY

The U.S. Mint, created by Congress in 1792, makes all of the country's coins. The Bureau of Engraving and Printing (BEP), established in 1861, designs and prints U.S. bills. It also prints U.S. postage stamps. Both the Mint and the BEP are parts of the U.S. Treasury Department.

U.S. PAPER MONEY

BILL*	PORTRAIT	DESIGN ON BACK
$1	Washington	ONE between images of the front and back of the Great Seal of the U.S.
$2 (1998)	Jefferson	The signing of the Declaration of Independence
$5 (2000)	Lincoln	Lincoln Memorial
$10 (2000)	Hamilton	U.S. Treasury Building
$20 (2003)	Jackson	White House
$50 (2004)	Grant	U.S. Capitol
$100 (1996)	Franklin	Independence Hall in Philadelphia, Pennsylvania

*Date in parentheses indicates when new versions of the bills were introduced.

- In 1929, the size of paper money was reduced by one-third. Portraits and back designs of currency were established at this time.
- The Bureau of Engraving and Printing produces 37 million notes a day, worth about $696 million.
- If you had 10 billion $1 notes and spent one every second of the day, it would take 317 years to spend them all.
- The $100 bill is the largest that is now in circulation.
- About half the bills printed every year are $1 bills. These bills wear out in about 18 months, faster than any other.
- The Treasury first printed paper money in 1862 during a coin shortage. The bills were issued in denominations of 1¢, 5¢, 25¢ and 50¢.

U.S. COINS

COIN	PORTRAIT	DESIGN ON BACK
Cent	Lincoln	Lincoln Memorial
Nickel	Jefferson	Commemoration of the Louisiana Purchase
Dime	F.D. Roosevelt	Torch, olive branch, oak branch
Quarter	Washington	Eagle*
Half-dollar	J.F. Kennedy	Presidential coat of arms
Dollar	Sacajawea and her infant son	Eagle in flight

*The 50 State Quarters Program features new quarters with unique designs on the back. Five coins have debuted each year since 1999, and five new quarters will be released every year through 2008.

- The U.S. Mint produces about 13 billion coins each year for general circulation.
- During World War II, steel pennies were issued to conserve copper.
- "In God we trust" first appeared on U.S. coins in 1864, on the 2¢ coin.
- Lincoln is the only President on a coin who faces right.
- The dime is the only coin that does not say how much it's worth.

Kid Work

Don't fear if you're too young to get a job at a restaurant or store. There are plenty of ways to earn money to buy that hot new CD, video game or pair of jeans. Try selling these products and services to your parents, friends or neighbors. Be sure to check with your parents before you start your business. Tip: If you put $5 a week into a bank account that pays interest, you'll save about $266 a year.

- Organize photographs, bookshelves or recipes
- Entertain kids at birthday parties with a beauty parlor or sports games
- Make personalized stationery on your computer
- Clean and organize attics and basements
- Teach computer skills
- Type papers
- Water plants when neighbors are away
- Wash windows
- Shovel snow
- Rake leaves
- Walk or take care of dogs
- Tutor
- Wrap gifts
- Baby-sit
- Wash cars
- Deliver newspapers

TFK
Puzzles & Games

Showing Their Age

These five corporate symbols have advertised their products for many years. Can you name each one? As a bonus, put them in the order they first appeared, from earliest to latest.

(See Answer Key that begins on page 342.)

Did You Know?

In 2007 the U.S. Mint will start producing new dollar coins that feature portraits of the presidents. Four coins will be issued each year in the order the presidents served.

Richest Americans

Each year, *Forbes* magazine makes a list of the wealthiest people in the United States. Four of the people in the top five made their fortunes in the computer industry.

NAME, OCCUPATION	NET WORTH
1. **Bill Gates**, cofounder of Microsoft	$51 billion
2. **Warren Buffett**, chairman of Berkshire Hathaway, a company that owns and runs dozens of other companies	$40 billion
3. **Paul Allen**, cofounder of Microsoft	$22.5 billion
4. **Michael Dell**, founder of Dell computer	$18 billion
5. **Lawrence Ellison**, founder of Oracle software company	$17 billion

go See how you're handling your money at timeforkids.com/budget

A World of Money

Here are the currencies of some countries around the world.

COUNTRY	CURRENCY
Australia	Dollar
Brazil	Real
China	Yuan
Denmark	Krone
Guatemala	Quetzal
India	Rupee
Israel	Shekel
Japan	Yen
Mexico	Peso
Russia	Ruble
South Africa	Rand
Sweden	Krona
Thailand	Baht
Vietnam	Dong

Money

175

Can Disney Get the Magic Back?

The studio that invented hand-drawn films finally joins the computer-animation age

THE SKY IS FALLING! Disney made a big change with the film *Chicken Little*.

Walt Disney's *Snow White and the Seven Dwarfs* cast a spell in 1937. The world's first animated film had charming hand-drawn characters, original songs and a fairy-tale ending. It's a formula that Disney followed for decades as the company built an animated-film kingdom.

But for the past 10 years, computer-generated (CG) animation has ruled. Artists at Pixar pioneered the use of computers to create three-dimensional animated films. *Toy Story*, Pixar's first movie, was released in 1995. Since then, CG films have taken over at the box office.

Although CG threatened their kingdom, many old-school Disney animators would not change their ways. "Walt was well known for being an innovative guy," says Oscar-winning animator Eric Armstrong. "A lot of people thought it was funny that Disney didn't want to try the same experimentation." Since 1994's *The Lion King*, Disney's own hand-drawn films have struggled.

In 2005, Disney animators finally changed their 'toons. The studio's bright, sassy first CG film, *Chicken Little*, arrived.

To get *Chicken Little* and the next three CG films made, animation chief David Stainton had to convince his artists that CG could free their creativity. Among those he persuaded was Glen Keane, the animator of *Aladdin* and *Pocahontas*. "Everybody wanted me to really fight for hand drawn," Keane told TIME. "Many of the traditional artists thought that I had betrayed them." Keane, who is directing *Rapunzel Unbraided*, added that the computer "forced me to be a better artist."

In 2006, Disney found another way to reanimate the Magic Kingdom: They bought Pixar. The digital animation talents and storytelling skills of Pixar are sure to give inspiration to Disney's own animators.

—*By Richard Corliss*

1937 *SNOW WHITE* It all started with hand-drawn dwarfs, birds and royalty.

2008 *RAPUNZEL UNBRAIDED* Animator Glen Keane gives his heroine CG freckles.

2006 *MEET THE ROBINSONS* A boy genius is taken in by a futuristic family.

2007 *AMERICAN DOG* The canine star is stranded in the desert, but he thinks he's on TV.

Movies & TV

177

Sulley

Top Money-Making Animated Films of All Time*

MOVIE	MONEY EARNED IN THE U.S.
1. Shrek 2	$436,471,036
2. Finding Nemo	339,714,978
3. The Lion King	328,539,505
4. Shrek	267,665,011
5. The Incredibles	261,437,578
6. Monsters, Inc.	255,870,172
7. Toy Story 2	245,852,179
8. Aladdin	217,350,219
9. Madagascar	193,202,933
10. Toy Story	191,780,865

*Through January 23, 2006
Source: Exhibitor Relations Co., Inc.

For the history of film:
www.factmonster.com/movietimeline

Reel Facts

- Sulley, the gentle giant in *Monsters, Inc.*, has 2,320,413 hairs in his fur coat.

- In the film *Because of Winn-Dixie*, the pooch of the title was played by two different Picardy shepherds, a rare breed from France.

- In the *Star Wars* films, the "TIE" in TIE Fighter is an acronym for Twin Ion Engines.

- In 2002, *Shrek* won the first Oscar for Best Animated Feature Film.

- Alfonso Cuarón, the director of *Harry Potter and the Prisoner of Azkaban*, had never read the Harry Potter books or seen the first two movies when he was offered the job of director.

- The word *vader* means *father* in Dutch.

Source: Internet Movie Database

Big Bucks

We hear a lot about how much movies earn at the box office. That's because they cost millions to make, and studios hate to lose money when a movie tanks. Here are the most expensive movies ever made.

MOVIE	YEAR OF RELEASE	COST TO MAKE*
Superman Begins	2006	$250 million
Spider-Man 2	2004	200 million
Titanic	1997	200 million
Terminator 3	2003	175 million
Waterworld	1995	175 million
Wild Wild West	1999	170 million
Van Helsing	2004	160 million
The Polar Express	2004	150 million
War of the Worlds	2005	132 million
Harry Potter and the Goblet of Fire	2005	130 million

*Estimated   Source: Internet Movie Database

SPIDER-MAN

Lines to Remember

Here are some of filmdom's most memorable lines. Can you match the quote to the film in which it was spoken? May the Force be with you! (*Star Wars*, of course).

1. "To infinity and beyond."
2. "Snakes. Why did it have to be snakes?"
3. "No capes!"
4. "Oh, they're gonna squeeze her."
5. "Yo, Adrian!"
6. "If you build it, he will come."
7. "Hello, my name is Inigo Montoya."
8. "Toto, I've got a feeling we're not in Kansas anymore."
9. "Houston, we have a problem."
10. "You're gonna need a bigger boat."

A. *Field of Dreams*
B. *Princess Bride*
C. *Jaws*
D. *The Wizard of Oz*
E. *Toy Story*
F. *Raiders of the Lost Ark*
G. *Apollo 13*
H. *Rocky*
I. *Charlie and the Chocolate Factory*
J. *The Incredibles*

(See Answer Key that begins on page 342.)

Top Kids Movies of All Time*

MOVIE	MONEY EARNED IN THE U.S.
1. *Star Wars*	$460,998,007
2. *Shrek 2*	436,471,036
3. *E.T.–The Extra-Terrestrial*	434,949,459
4. *Star Wars: Episode I–The Phantom Menace*	431,088,295
5. *Finding Nemo*	339,714,978
6. *The Lion King*	328,539,505
7. *Harry Potter and the Sorcerer's Stone*	317,575,550
8. *Star Wars: Episode I–The Attack of the Clones*	310,676,740
9. *Return of the Jedi*	309,205,079
10. *The Empire Strikes Back*	290,271,960

Source: Exhibitor Relations Co., Inc.   *Through January 23, 2006

Top Kids Movies of 2005*

MOVIE	MONEY EARNED IN THE U.S.
1. *The Chronicles of Narnia: The Lion, the Witch and the Wardrobe*	$271,852,138
2. *Charlie and the Chocolate Factory*	206,459,076
3. *Madagascar*	193,202,933
4. *Chicken Little*	133,394,202
5. *Robots*	128,200,012
6. *The Pacifier*	113,006,880
7. *Are We There Yet?*	82,674,398
8. *Cheaper By the Dozen 2*	78,070,178
9. *March of the Penguins*	77,413,017
10. *Herbie: Fully Loaded*	66,002,004

Source: Exhibitor Relations Co., Inc.   *Through January 23, 2006

Top Honors

The Academy Awards honor the best in moviemaking. Winning an Oscar is considered the highest honor for filmmakers, actors and actresses.

Although most nominees and winners are adults, kids have also made their mark in Oscar history. Check out these young Oscar contenders. (People whose names are in white won an Oscar.)

ACTOR	AGE	FILM	YEAR
Justin Henry	8	*Kramer vs. Kramer*	1979
Jackie Cooper	9	*Skippy*	1931
Mary Badham	10	*To Kill a Mockingbird*	1962
Quinn Cummings	10	*The Goodbye Girl*	1977
Patty McCormack	10	*The Bad Seed*	1956
Tatum O'Neal	10	*Paper Moon*	1973
Brandon De Wilde	11	*Shane*	1953
Haley Joel Osment	11	*The Sixth Sense*	1999
Anna Paquin	11	*The Piano*	1993
Keisha Castle-Hughes	13	*Whale Rider*	1999
Patty Duke	16	*The Miracle Worker*	1962
Jack Wild	16	*Oliver!*	1968

Movies & TV

179

TV Facts and Figures

Did you ever keep track of how much time
you spend in front of the television?
Try it—you might be surprised or even shocked!

92% of all U.S. households own a VCR or DVD player.

On average, kids ages 6 to 11 watch 19 hours, 49 minutes of TV each week.

On average, girls ages 12 to 17 watch 19 hours, 49 minutes of TV each week. Boys watch 20 hours, 14 minutes.

The average American youth spends 1,023 hours each year watching TV and 900 hours in school.

The average household has 2.4 TV sets. 98% of all U.S. households own at least one set. 79% have more than one TV set.

56% of children ages 8 to 16 have a TV in their bedroom; 36% of kids ages 6 and under do.

40% of Americans always or often watch television while eating dinner.

Homework Tip!

Turn off the television while you're studying. If you like to listen to music while doing schoolwork, try playing classical music.

Top-Selling DVDs of 2005

1. *Star Wars* Trilogy
2. *Napoleon Dynamite*
3. *Band of Brothers*
4. *Family Guy:* Seasons 1 and 2
5. *Harry Potter and the Prisoner of Azkaban*
6. *24:* Season 1
7. *Star Wars: Episode I— The Phantom Menace*
8. *The Incredibles*
9. *Star Wars: Episode II— The Attack of the Clones*
10. *Shrek 2*

Source: *Video Business*

Most-Rented Videos of 2005

1. *National Treasure*
2. *Meet the Fockers*
3. *Hitch*
4. *Ladder 49*
5. *The Notebook*
6. *Without a Paddle*
7. *The Longest Yard*
8. *Guess Who*
9. *The Pacifier*
10. *Monster-in-Law*

Source: *Video Business*

Top-Rated Kid Shows*

KIDS 2 TO 11

NETWORK SHOWS
1. *American Idol*–Tuesday (Fox)
2. *American Idol*–Wednesday (Fox)
3. *Survivor: Palau* (CBS)
4. *Survivor: Vanuatu* (CBS)
5. *Extreme Makeover: Home Edition* (ABC)

CABLE SHOWS
1. *Jimmy Neutron Boy Genius* (Nickelodeon)
2. *SpongeBob SquarePants* (Nickelodeon)
3. *Fairly OddParents* (Nickelodeon)
4. *Drake & Josh* (Nickelodeon)
5. *Ned Declassified* (Disney)

KIDS 12 TO 17

NETWORK SHOWS
1. *American Idol*–Wednesday (Fox)
2. *American Idol*–Tuesday (Fox)
3. *The Simpsons* (Fox)
4. *The O.C.* (Fox)
5. *Simple Life 3* (Fox)

CABLE SHOWS
1. *Real World XIV* (MTV)
2. *WWE Entertainment* (Spike)
3. *The Cheetah Girls* (Disney)
4. *Wildfire* (ABC Family)
5. *Zoey 101* (Nickelodeon)

*September 2004–September 2005
Source: Nielsen Media Research

TV Land

The United States may be called the entertainment capital of the world, but China can claim the honor of being television capital of the world.

COUNTRY	NUMBER OF TELEVISION SETS
1. China	400,000,000
2. United States	219,000,000
3. Japan	86,500,000
4. India	63,000,000
5. Russia	60,500,000
6. Germany	51,400,000
7. Brazil	36,500,000
8. France	34,800,000
9. United Kingdom	30,500,000
10. Italy	30,300,000

Source: CIA World Factbook

TFK Mystery Person

CLUE 1: A big Hollywood star, I was born in Miami in 1927 and grew up in the Bahamas.

CLUE 2: I starred in *Guess Who's Coming to Dinner* and *In the Heat of the Night.*

CLUE 3: In 1963, I became the first African American actor to win an Academy Award, for *Lilies of the Field.* I also won an Oscar for Lifetime Achievement in 2002. My career has opened doors for other black performers.

WHO AM I?

(See Answer Key that begins on page 342.)

Did You Know?

There are more than 1,700 television stations in the United States.

Movies & TV

MUSIC

Songs Most Downloaded in 2005

SONG, ARTIST	NUMBER OF DOWNLOADS
1. "Hollaback Girl," Gwen Stefani	1,171,672
2. "Gold Digger," Kayne West	1,089,665
3. "Beverly Hills," Weezer	961,988
4. "Since U Been Gone," Kelly Clarkson	960,341
5. "My Humps," Black Eyed Peas	917,807
6. "Mr. Brightside," Killers	889,323
7. "Sugar, We're Goin' Down," Fall Out Boy	830,835
8. "Don't Phunk with My Heart," Black Eyed Peas	815,753
9. "You and Me," Lifehouse	808,991
10. "Boulevard of Broken Dreams," Green Day	803,790

Source: Nielsen SoundScan

Songs Most Played on the Radio in 2005

SONG	ARTIST
1. "We Belong Together"	Mariah Carey
2. "Boulevard of Broken Dreams"	Green Day
3. "Let Me Love You"	Mario
4. "Since U Been Gone"	Kelly Clarkson
5. "1, 2 Step"	Ciara, featuring Missy Elliott
6. "Let Me Go"	3 Doors Down
7. "You and Me"	Lifehouse
8. "Behind These Hazel Eyes"	Kelly Clarkson
9. "Hollaback Girl"	Gwen Stefani
10. "Disco Inferno"	50 Cent

Source: Nielsen SoundScan

GENRES OF MUSIC

BLUES A style of music that evolved from southern African-American work songs and secular (nonreligious) songs. Blues influenced the development of rock, rhythm-and-blues and country music. Some blues musicians include **Bessie Smith, Muddy Waters** and **Robert Johnson.**

CLASSICAL Music that is usually more sophisticated and complex than other styles of music. Many classical compositions are instrumentals, which means there are no words in the songs. Classical music has its roots in Europe. It includes symphonies, chamber music, sonatas and ballets. Some important classical-music composers are **Wolfgang Amadeus Mozart, Ludwig van Beethoven** and **Johann Sebastian Bach.**

COUNTRY-AND-WESTERN

A form of American music that originated in the Southwest and the Southeast in the 1920s. Early country songs often told stories of poor people facing difficult lives. Recent country songs are often hard to tell apart from pop-music songs. **Johnny Cash, Willie Nelson, Faith Hill** and **Keith Urban** are popular country-music singers.

Keith Urban

ELECTRONICA

Music created using electronic equipment, such as synthesizers, samplers, computers, keyboards and drum machines. Electronica is popular dance music. This style of sound became popular in the early 1990s. **Moby, Fatboy Slim** and the **Chemical Brothers** are popular electronica artists.

FOLK A style of music that has been passed down orally within cultures or regions. It is known for its simple melodies and the use of acoustic instruments. Modern folk music is based on traditional folk music and often contains political lyrics. **Bob Dylan, Pete Seeger, Woody Guthrie** and **Joan Baez** are folk performers.

JAZZ American music born in the early part of the 20th century from African rhythms and slave chants. It has spread from its African-American roots to become a worldwide style. Jazz forms include improvisation (unrehearsed playing), swing, bebop and cool jazz. **Benny Goodman, Miles Davis, Cassandra Wilson** and **Keith Jarrett** are famous jazz musicians.

POP Popular music is a genre that covers a wide range of music, is often softer than rock and is driven by melody. Pop usually appeals to a broad assortment of listeners. Some famous pop musicians include **Frank Sinatra, John Mayer, Hilary Duff** and **Beyoncé.**

RAP Urban, typically African-American music that features lyrics—usually spoken over sampled sounds or drum loops—often about social or political issues. Hip-hop, a style of music similar to rap, blends rock, jazz and soul with sampled sounds. **Jay-Z, Run-D.M.C., Missy Elliott** and **Eminem** are rappers.

Missy Elliott

ROCK One of the most popular forms of 20th century music, rock combines African-American rhythms, urban blues, folk and country music. It developed in the early 1950s and has inspired—and been inspired by—many other styles, such as grunge, ska and heavy metal. Some important rock bands are **Buddy Holly and the Crickets, The Beatles,** the **Rolling Stones, Nirvana** and **U2.**

GOOD VIBRATIONS

Musical instruments are grouped into families based on how they make sounds. In an orchestra, musicians sit together in these family groupings. But not every instrument fits neatly into a group. For example, the piano has strings that vibrate and hammers that strike. Is it a stringed instrument or a percussion instrument? Some say it is both!

BRASS

Brass instruments are made of brass or some other metal and make sounds when air is blown inside. The musician's lips must buzz, as though making a "raspberry" noise against the mouthpiece. Air then vibrates inside the instrument, which produces a musical sound. **Brass instruments include the trumpet, trombone, tuba, French horn, cornet and bugle.**

PERCUSSION

Most percussion instruments, such as drums and tambourines, make sounds when they are hit. Others, like maracas, are shaken, and still others may be scratched, rubbed or whatever else makes the instrument vibrate and produce a sound. **Percussion instruments include drums, cymbals, triangles, chimes, bells and xylophones.**

STRINGS

Yes, the sounds of stringed instruments come from their strings. The strings may be plucked (guitar and harp); bowed (cello and violin); or struck (piano). This creates a vibration that causes a unique sound.

Stringed instruments include the violin, viola, cello, bass, double bass, harp, lute, banjo, guitar and dulcimer.

WOODWINDS

Woodwind instruments produce sound when air (wind) is blown inside. Air might be blown across an edge (flute); between a reed and a surface (clarinet); or between two reeds (bassoon). The sound happens when the air vibrates inside. **Woodwind instruments include the flute, piccolo, clarinet, recorder, bassoon and oboe.**

Big Hits

These musicians and bands have sold the most albums in the United States.

ARTIST	NUMBER OF ALBUMS SOLD (IN MILLIONS)
The Beatles	168.5
Elvis Presley	116.5
Led Zeppelin	107.5
Garth Brooks	105.0
Eagles	89.0
Billy Joel	78.5
Pink Floyd	73.5
Barbra Streisand	70.5
Elton John	69.0
AC/DC	66.0

Source: Recording Industry Association of America

Top-Selling Albums of 2005

	ALBUM	ARTIST	UNITS SOLD
1.	*Emancipation of Mimi*	Mariah Carey	4,968,606
2.	*Massacre*	50 Cent	4,852,744
3.	*Breakaway*	Kelly Clarkson	3,496,192
4.	*American Idiot*	Green Day	3,360,394
5.	*Monkey Business*	Black Eyed Peas	3,037,251
6.	*X&Y*	Coldplay	2,615,280
7.	*Feels Like Today*	Rascal Flatts	2,511,209
8.	*Love.Angel.Music.Baby*	Gwen Stefani	2,505,390
9.	*Late Registration*	Kayne West	2,413,580
10.	*Documentary*	Game	2,275,646

Source: Nielsen SoundScan

For inductees into the Rock and Roll Hall of Fame: www.factmonster.com/rockhall

American Idols

Several top performers on the hit TV show *American Idol* have gone on to become, well, American idols. Here's a look at the most successful AI alumni.

DOUBLE-PLATINUM ALBUMS
(sold 2 million copies)

Thankful, Kelly Clarkson (winner, season 1)

Breakaway, Kelly Clarkson

Measure of a Man, Clay Aiken (runner-up, season 2)

PLATINUM ALBUMS
(sold 1 million copies)

Soulful, Ruben Studdard (winner, season 2)

Merry Christmas With Love, Clay Aiken

Free Yourself, Fantasia (winner, season 3)

Some Hearts, Carrie Underwood (winner, season 4)

GOLD ALBUMS
(sold 500,000 copies)

Josh Gracin, Josh Gracin (4th place, season 2)

Kelly Clarkson

MOVERS AND SHAKERS

Here's a look at some of the world's most famous and most talented dancers.

FRED ASTAIRE (1899–1987) He danced in many famous Hollywood musicals, often with Ginger Rogers as his partner. His elegance and grace as a dancer made him one of the most popular movie stars of all time.

MIKHAIL BARYSHNIKOV (b. 1948) Latvian-born dancer and choreographer who is considered one of the best male classical dancers of the 20th century. He is also involved in modern dance and leads his own modern-dance company, the White Oak Dance Project.

GEORGE BALANCHINE (1904–1983) Russian-born American dancer and choreographer who is considered the greatest choreographer of modern dance. He co-founded the New York City Ballet and the School of American Ballet.

SAVION GLOVER (b. 1973) American tap dancer who made his Broadway debut at age 12, playing the title role in *The Tap Dance Kid*. He won a Tony Award for his 1996 Broadway show, *Bring In Da Noise, Bring In Da Funk*.

MARTHA GRAHAM (1894–1991) American modern dancer and choreographer whose unique dances required that her performers be very flexible and disciplined. Her dance troupe is the oldest in the United States.

MARIA TALLCHIEF (b. 1925) American-Indian ballet dancer who is one of the greatest ballerinas of all time. She was the first U.S.-born dancer to be named top ballerina at the New York City Ballet.

TWYLA THARP (b. 1941) American dancer and choreographer whose dances combine ballet, jazz and modern dance. She often includes pop culture in her high-energy dances.

TFK Mystery Person

CLUE 1: I was born in a poor area of New Orleans in 1901. The city is known as the birthplace of jazz.

CLUE 2: I was an amazing trumpet player and one of the most influential jazz artists in history. My hits include "What a Wonderful World."

CLUE 3: My recording of the song "Hello, Dolly" in 1963 knocked The Beatles off the top of the music charts.

WHO AM I?

(See Answer Key that begins on page 342.)

Music

MYTHOLOGY

THE OLYMPIAN GODS AND GODDESSES

In Greek mythology, 12 gods and goddesses ruled the universe from atop Greece's Mount Olympus. All the Olympians are related to one another. The Romans adopted most of these gods and goddesses, but with new names (given below in parentheses).

Zeus

The most powerful of all was Zeus (Jupiter), god of the sky and the king of Olympus. His temper affected the weather; he threw thunderbolts when he was unhappy. He was married to Hera.

Hera (Juno) was goddess of marriage and the queen of Olympus. She was Zeus's wife and sister. Many myths tell of how she got back at Zeus for his many insults.

186

Poseidon (Neptune) was god of the sea. He was the most powerful god after his brother, Zeus. He lived in a beautiful palace under the sea and caused earthquakes when he was in a rage.

Hades (Pluto) was king of the dead. He lived in the underworld, the heavily guarded land that he ruled. He was the husband of Persephone (daughter of the goddess Demeter), whom he kidnapped.

Aphrodite (Venus) was the goddess of love and beauty. Some people believe she was a daughter of Zeus. Others believe she rose from the sea.

Apollo (same Roman name) was the god of music and healing. He was also an archer and hunted with a silver bow.

Ares (Mars) was the god of war. He was both cruel and a coward. Ares was the son of Zeus and Hera, but neither of his parents liked him.

Hephaestus (Vulcan) was the god of fire and the forge (a furnace in which metal is heated). Although he made armor and weapons for the gods, he loved peace.

Artemis (Diana) was the goddess of the hunt and the protector of women in childbirth. She loved all wild animals.

Athena (Minerva) was the goddess of wisdom. She was also skilled in the art of war. Athena sprang full-grown from the forehead of Zeus and became his favorite child.

Hestia (Vesta) was the goddess of the hearth (a fireplace at the center of the home). She was the oldest Olympian.

Hermes (Mercury) was the messenger god, a trickster and a friend to thieves. He was the son of Zeus. The speediest of all gods, he wore winged sandals and a winged hat.

THESE OLYMPIANS ARE SOMETIMES INCLUDED IN THE LIST OF RULERS:

Demeter (Ceres) was the goddess of the harvest. The word *cereal* comes from her Roman name.

Dionysus (Bacchus) was the god of wine. In ancient Greece, he was honored with springtime festivals that centered on theater.

Apollo

Ares

Artemis

Dionysus

Mythology

For more gods and goddesses,
www.factmonster.com/deities

Odin

Aztec

COATLICUE was the goddess of the Earth and the mother of all the gods. She also gave birth to the Moon and stars. The Aztecs carved a gigantic stone statue of her wearing a necklace made of human hearts and hands.

HUITZILOPOCHTLI was the god of the Sun and of war. He was the patron god of the Aztec capital of Tenochtitlán, where Mexico City now stands. The Aztecs built a great temple there in his honor and sacrificed many humans to him.

CHICOMECOATL was the goddess of corn and fertility. So important was corn to the Aztecs that she was also known as "the goddess of nourishment."

Aztec priests

Egyptian

RA was the supreme god and the god of the Sun. The early pharaohs claimed to be descended from him. He sometimes took the form of a hawk or a lion.

NUT represented the heavens and helped to put the world in order. She had the ability to swallow stars and the pharaohs and cause them to be born again. She existed before all else had been created.

OSIRIS was the god of the underworld and the judge of the dead. He was associated with the cycle of life and was often shown wearing mummy wrappings.

ISIS invented agriculture. She was the goddess of law, healing, motherhood and fertility. She came to be seen as a Mother Earth figure.

HORUS was a sky god who loved goodness and light. The son of Osiris and Isis, he was often shown as a young child.

THOTH was the god of wisdom and magic. He was believed to have invented writing, astronomy and other arts, and served as a scribe, or writer, to the gods.

NEPHTHYS was the goddess of the dead. She was a kind friend to the newly dead as well as to those left behind.

Norse

ODIN was the supreme god and, along with his brothers Vili and Ve, the creator of the world. He was also the ruler of war and wisdom.

FRIGG was the goddess of the sky, marriage and motherhood. It was believed that she knew the fate of each person, but she kept it a close secret.

LOKI was the god of mischief and death. He liked to invent horrible ways to harm the other gods. His nastiness and trickery earned him many enemies.

FREYJA was the goddess of love and fertility. She was very beautiful and enjoyed music and song. Fairies were among her most beloved companions.

BALDER was the god of light, peace and joy. A kind and gentle god, he was slain in a plot hatched by Loki. He was greatly mourned, especially by his parents, Odin and Frigg.

GREEK HEROES

Odysseus

ACHILLES

Achilles was the strongest and most fearless warrior in the war between the Greeks and the Trojans. As an infant, his mother held him by his heel and dipped him into the River Styx. This made him nearly invincible—only his heel remained vulnerable. Achilles died when Paris wounded him in the heel. Today, the tendon that connects the calf muscles to the heel bone is called the Achilles tendon. A small but dangerous weakness is known as an "Achilles heel."

ODYSSEUS

King of Ithaca and a celebrated warrior, Odysseus helped the Greeks win the Trojan War. His journey home to Ithaca and to his wife, Penelope, took nearly 10 years. Along the way Odysseus's courage and cleverness saved him and his men from such monsters as the Cyclops Polyphemus, the Sirens, and Scylla and Charybdis. His adventures are told in Homer's epic poem, the *Odyssey*.

HERCULES

Brave and powerful Hercules is perhaps the most loved of all Greek heroes. The son of Zeus and Alcmene, Hercules grew up to become a famous warrior. Hera, Zeus's wife, was angry that Zeus had a child with another woman. She made Hercules temporarily insane, and he killed his wife and children. As punishment Hercules performed 12 seemingly impossible labors.

Hercules

PERSEUS

The son of Zeus and Danaë, Perseus completed dangerous feats with his quick thinking and talents as a warrior. Because looking directly at the monstrous Medusa would turn a man to stone, Perseus beheaded her while watching her reflection in a mirror. He kept her head in his satchel. Later, to save the princess Andromeda from being eaten by a sea monster, Perseus pulled out Medusa's head and turned the creature to stone.

THESEUS

Theseus was known for his triumph over numerous monsters, especially the Minotaur, which lived in a labyrinth (a maze) on the island of Crete. Every year the people of Athens had been forced to send 14 young people to Crete for the Minotaur to eat alive. But Theseus, using a ball of magic thread from the princess Ariadne, found his way in and out of the labyrinth and killed the beast.

Theseus

JASON

Jason was the leader of the Argonauts, the 50 heroes who sailed in search of the Golden Fleece. Jason's uncle Pelias had stolen the kingdom that should have been Jason's. He promised to return it only if Jason would bring home the Golden Fleece—the wool from the magical winged ram. On their journey Jason and the Argonauts faced down such dangers as Harpies—half human, half bird. They ultimately captured the fleece with the help of the sorceress Medea, who became Jason's wife.

Mythology

PRESIDENTS

1 GEORGE WASHINGTON (SERVED 1789–1797)
Born: Feb. 22, 1732, in Virginia; died: Dec. 14, 1799
Political Party: None (first term), Federalist
Vice President: John Adams
DID YOU KNOW? Washington was the only President unanimously elected. He received all 69 electoral votes.
FIRST LADY: Martha Dandridge Custis

2 JOHN ADAMS (SERVED 1797–1801)
Born: Oct. 30, 1735, in Massachusetts; died: July 4, 1826
Political Party: Federalist
Vice President: Thomas Jefferson
DID YOU KNOW? Adams was the first President to live in the White House.
FIRST LADY: Abigail Smith

3 THOMAS JEFFERSON (SERVED 1801–1809)
Born: April 13, 1743, in Virginia; died: July 4, 1826
Political Party: Democratic-Republican
Vice Presidents: Aaron Burr, George Clinton
DID YOU KNOW? **In signing the 1803 Louisiana Purchase, Jefferson nearly doubled the size of the U.S.**
FIRST LADY: Martha Wayles Skelton

4 JAMES MADISON (SERVED 1809–1817)
Born: March 16, 1751, in Virginia; died: June 28, 1836
Political Party: Democratic-Republican
Vice Presidents: George Clinton, Elbridge Gerry
DID YOU KNOW? **Madison was the only President to have two Vice Presidents die in office. Clinton died in 1812 and Gerry died in 1814.**
FIRST LADY: Dorothy "Dolley" Payne Todd

5 JAMES MONROE (SERVED 1817–1825)
Born: April 28, 1758, in Virginia; died: July 4, 1831
Political Party: Democratic-Republican
Vice President: Daniel D. Tompkins
DID YOU KNOW? **The Monroe Doctrine forbade foreign countries like Spain and Russia from expanding into North and South America.**
FIRST LADY: Elizabeth "Eliza" Kortright

6 JOHN QUINCY ADAMS (SERVED 1825–1829)
Born: July 11, 1767, in Massachusetts; died: Feb. 23, 1848
Political Party: Democratic-Republican
Vice President: John C. Calhoun
DID YOU KNOW? **In 1843, Adams became the first President to have his photograph taken.**
FIRST LADY: Louisa Catherine Johnson

7 ANDREW JACKSON (SERVED 1829–1837)
Born: March 15, 1767, in South Carolina; died: June 8, 1845
Political Party: Democratic
Vice Presidents: John C. Calhoun, Martin Van Buren
DID YOU KNOW? **Jackson took several bullets while fighting in duels—an activity for which he was famous.**
FIRST LADY: Rachel Donelson Robards

8 MARTIN VAN BUREN (SERVED 1837–1841)
Born: Dec. 5, 1782, in New York; died: July 24, 1862
Political Party: Democratic
Vice President: Richard M. Johnson
DID YOU KNOW? **Van Buren was the first President born a U.S. citizen rather than a British subject.**
FIRST LADY: Hannah Hoes

9 WILLIAM HENRY HARRISON (SERVED 1841)
Born: Feb. 9, 1773, in Virginia; died: April 4, 1841
Political Party: Whig
Vice President: John Tyler
DID YOU KNOW? **Harrison had the shortest presidency: he died after only a month in office.**
FIRST LADY: Anna Tuthill Symmes

10 JOHN TYLER (SERVED 1841–1845)
Born: March 29, 1790, in Virginia; died: Jan. 18, 1862
Political Party: Whig
Vice President: None
DID YOU KNOW? **Tyler was the first President to marry in office. He was also the President with the most children (15).**
FIRST LADY: Letitia Christian (d. 1842); Julia Gardiner

11 JAMES KNOX POLK (SERVED 1845–1849)
Born: Nov. 2, 1795, in North Carolina; died: June 15, 1849
Political Party: Democratic
Vice President: George M. Dallas
DID YOU KNOW? **Polk's inauguration was the first one to be reported by telegraph.**
FIRST LADY: Sarah Childress

12 ZACHARY TAYLOR (SERVED 1849–1850)
Born: Nov. 24, 1784, in Virginia; died: July 9, 1850
Political Party: Whig
Vice President: Millard Fillmore
DID YOU KNOW? **Taylor never voted until he was 62 years old.**
FIRST LADY: Margaret Mackall Smith

13 MILLARD FILLMORE (SERVED 1850–1853)
Born: Jan. 7, 1800, in New York; died: March 8, 1874
Political Party: Whig
Vice President: None
DID YOU KNOW? **Fillmore and his first wife, Abigail, started the White House Library.**
FIRST LADY: Abigail Powers (d. 1853); Caroline Carmichael McIntosh

14 FRANKLIN PIERCE (SERVED 1853–1857)
Born: Nov. 23, 1804, in New Hampshire; died: Oct. 8, 1869
Political Party: Democratic
Vice President: William R. King
DID YOU KNOW? **Pierce was the only elected President not re-nominated by his party for a second term.**
FIRST LADY: Jane Means Appleton

15 JAMES BUCHANAN (SERVED 1857–1861)

Born: April 23, 1791, in Pennsylvania; died: June 1, 1868
Political Party: Democratic
Vice President: John C. Breckinridge
DID YOU KNOW? **Buchanan was the only President to never marry. His niece Harriet Lane was his First Lady.**
FIRST LADY: None

16 ABRAHAM LINCOLN (SERVED 1861–1865)

Born: Feb. 12, 1809, in Kentucky; died: April 15, 1865
Political Party: Republican
Vice Presidents: Hannibal Hamlin, Andrew Johnson
DID YOU KNOW? **Lincoln's Gettysburg Address and Second Inaugural Address are among the greatest presidential speeches.**
FIRST LADY: Mary Todd

17 ANDREW JOHNSON (SERVED 1865–1869)

Born: Dec. 29, 1808, in North Carolina; died: July 31, 1875
Political Parties: Union, Democratic
Vice President: None
DID YOU KNOW? **Johnson was the first President to be impeached. The Senate found him not guilty, however, and he remained President.**
FIRST LADY: Eliza McCardle

18 ULYSSES S. GRANT (SERVED 1869–1877)

Born: April 27, 1822, in Ohio; died: July 23, 1885
Political Party: Republican
Vice Presidents: Schuyler Colfax, Henry Wilson
DID YOU KNOW? **Grant's much-praised *Memoirs* has been in print since 1885.**
FIRST LADY: Julia Boggs Dent

19 RUTHERFORD B. HAYES (SERVED 1877–1881)

Born: Oct. 4, 1822, in Ohio; died: Jan. 17, 1893
Political Party: Republican
Vice President: William A. Wheeler
DID YOU KNOW? **The first telephone was installed in the White House while Hayes was President.**
FIRST LADY: Lucy Ware Webb Hayes

20 JAMES A. GARFIELD (SERVED 1881)

Born: Nov. 19, 1831, in Ohio; died: Sept. 19, 1881
Political Party: Republican
Vice President: Chester A. Arthur
DID YOU KNOW? **Garfield was the first President who campaigned in two languages—English and German.**
FIRST LADY: Lucretia Rudolph

Presidents

21 CHESTER A. ARTHUR (SERVED 1881–1885)

Born: Oct. 5, 1829, in Vermont; died: Nov. 18, 1886
Political Party: Republican
Vice President: None
DID YOU KNOW? A stylish dresser, Arthur was nicknamed
"Gentleman Boss" and "Elegant Arthur."
FIRST LADY: Ellen Lewis Herndon

22 GROVER CLEVELAND (SERVED 1885–1889)

Born: March 18, 1837, in New Jersey; died: June 24, 1908
Political Party: Democratic
Vice President: Thomas A. Hendricks
DID YOU KNOW? Cleveland was the only President to be defeated and
then re-elected, serving two non-consecutive terms.
FIRST LADY: Frances Folsom

23 BENJAMIN HARRISON (SERVED 1889–1893)

Born: Aug. 20, 1833, in Ohio; died: March 13, 1901
Political Party: Republican
Vice President: Levi P. Morton
DID YOU KNOW? Benjamin Harrison was the only President who was
a grandson of a President (William Henry Harrison).
FIRST LADY: Caroline Lavina Scott (d. 1892); Mary Scott Lord Dimmick

24 GROVER CLEVELAND (SERVED 1893–1897)

Born: March 18, 1837, in New Jersey; died: June 24, 1908
Political Party: Democratic
Vice President: Adlai E. Stevenson
DID YOU KNOW? Cleveland was the only President to be married in
the White House.
FIRST LADY: Frances Folsom

25 WILLIAM McKINLEY (SERVED 1897–1901)

Born: Jan. 29, 1843, in Ohio; died: Sept. 14, 1901
Political Party: Republican
Vice Presidents: Garret A. Hobart, Theodore Roosevelt
DID YOU KNOW? During his presidency, Hawaii was annexed and the
Philippines, Guam and Puerto Rico became U.S. territories.
FIRST LADY: Ida Saxton

26 THEODORE ROOSEVELT (SERVED 1901–1909)

Born: Oct. 27, 1858, in New York; died: Jan. 6, 1919
Political Party: Republican
Vice President: Charles W. Fairbanks
DID YOU KNOW? Theodore Roosevelt was the first President to ride
in an automobile, an airplane and a submarine.
FIRST LADY: Edith Kermit Carow

go Learn fun facts about Theodore Roosevelt
at timeforkids.com/bio/troosevelt

27 WILLIAM H. TAFT (SERVED 1909–1913)
Born: Sept. 15, 1857, in Ohio; died: March 8, 1930
Political Party: Republican
Vice President: James S. Sherman
DID YOU KNOW? **Taft was the only President who went on to serve on the Supreme Court as Chief Justice.**
FIRST LADY: Helen Herron

28 WOODROW WILSON (SERVED 1913–1921)
Born: Dec. 28, 1856, in Virginia; died: Feb. 3, 1924
Political Party: Democratic
Vice President: Thomas R. Marshall
DID YOU KNOW? **Wilson was the first President to hold a news conference. About 125 members of the press attended the event on March 15, 1913.**
FIRST LADY: Ellen Louise Axson (d. 1914); Edith Bolling Galt

29 WARREN G. HARDING (SERVED 1921–1923)
Born: Nov. 2, 1865, in Ohio; died: Aug. 2, 1923
Political Party: Republican
Vice President: Calvin Coolidge
DID YOU KNOW? **Harding was a newspaper publisher before he was President.**
FIRST LADY: Florence King

30 CALVIN COOLIDGE (SERVED 1923–1929)
Born: July 4, 1872, in Vermont; died: Jan. 5, 1933
Political Party: Republican
Vice President: Charles G. Dawes
DID YOU KNOW? **Coolidge was the first President to be sworn in by his father, a justice of the peace.**
FIRST LADY: Grace Anna Goodhue

31 HERBERT C. HOOVER (SERVED 1929–1933)
Born: Aug. 10, 1874, in Iowa; died: Oct. 20, 1964
Political Party: Republican
Vice President: Charles Curtis
DID YOU KNOW? **An asteroid, Hooveria, was named for Hoover.**
FIRST LADY: Lou Henry

32 FRANKLIN D. ROOSEVELT (SERVED 1933–1945)
Born: Jan. 30, 1882, in New York; died: April 12, 1945
Political Party: Democratic
Vice Presidents: John Garner, Henry Wallace, Harry S. Truman
DID YOU KNOW? **Franklin D. Roosevelt was the only President elected to four terms.**
FIRST LADY: Anna Eleanor Roosevelt

 Read an expert on Franklin D. Roosevelt at timeforkids.com/bio/fdr

33 HARRY S. TRUMAN (SERVED 1945–1953)

Born: May 8, 1884, in Missouri; died: Dec. 26, 1972
Political Party: Democratic
Vice President: Alben W. Barkley
DID YOU KNOW? **Truman was a farmer, a hatmaker and a judge before entering politics.**
FIRST LADY: Elizabeth "Bess" Virginia Wallace

34 DWIGHT D. EISENHOWER (SERVED 1953–1961)

Born: Oct. 14, 1890, in Texas; died: March 28, 1969
Political Party: Republican
Vice President: Richard M. Nixon
DID YOU KNOW? **Eisenhower was a five-star general in World War II before becoming President.**
FIRST LADY: Marie "Mamie" Geneva Doud

35 JOHN F. KENNEDY (SERVED 1961–1963)

Born: May 29, 1917, in Massachusetts; died: Nov. 22, 1963
Political Party: Democratic
Vice President: Lyndon B. Johnson
DID YOU KNOW? **Kennedy was the first Roman Catholic President.**
FIRST LADY: Jacqueline Lee Bouvier

36 LYNDON B. JOHNSON (SERVED 1963–1969)

Born: Aug. 27, 1908, in Texas; died: Jan. 22, 1973
Political Party: Democratic
Vice President: Hubert H. Humphrey
DID YOU KNOW? **Lyndon Johnson was the first person to take the oath of office on an airplane. It was the presidential jet.**
FIRST LADY: Claudia Alta "Lady Bird" Taylor

37 RICHARD M. NIXON (SERVED 1969–1974)

Born: Jan. 9, 1913, in California; died April 22, 1994
Political Party: Republican
Vice Presidents: Spiro T. Agnew, Gerald R. Ford
DID YOU KNOW? **Nixon was the only President to resign.**
FIRST LADY: Thelma Catherine "Pat" Ryan

38 GERALD R. FORD (SERVED 1974–1977)

Born: July 14, 1913, in Nebraska
Political Party: Republican
Vice President: Nelson A. Rockefeller
DID YOU KNOW? **After college, Ford was a football coach, a park ranger and a male model.**
FIRST LADY: Elizabeth "Betty" Anne Bloomer Warren

39 JIMMY CARTER (SERVED 1977–1981)
Born: Oct. 1, 1924, in Georgia
Political Party: Democratic
Vice President: Walter F. Mondale
DID YOU KNOW? **Carter won the Nobel Peace Prize in October 2002.**
FIRST LADY: Rosalynn Smith

40 RONALD W. REAGAN (SERVED 1981–1989)
Born: Feb. 6, 1911, in Illinois; died: June 5, 2004
Political Party: Republican
Vice President: George H.W. Bush
DID YOU KNOW? **Reagan worked for nearly 30 years as a Hollywood actor.**
FIRST LADY: Nancy Davis

41 GEORGE H.W. BUSH (SERVED 1989–1993)
Born: June 12, 1924, in Massachusetts
Political Party: Republican
Vice President: J. Danforth Quayle
DID YOU KNOW? **Bush was the first President to spend a holiday with troops overseas: Thanksgiving in Saudi Arabia.**
FIRST LADY: Barbara Pierce

42 WILLIAM J. CLINTON (SERVED 1993–2001)
Born: Aug. 19, 1946, in Arkansas
Political Party: Democratic
Vice President: Albert Gore Jr.
DID YOU KNOW? **Clinton was the second of two Presidents to be impeached. The Senate acquitted him.**
FIRST LADY: Hillary Rodham

43 GEORGE W. BUSH (SERVED 2001–)
Born: July 6, 1946, in Connecticut
Political Party: Republican
Vice President: Richard B. Cheney
DID YOU KNOW? **George W. Bush was an owner of the Texas Rangers baseball team from the late 1980s until 1998.**
FIRST LADY: Laura Welch

go **Take a quiz on Ronald Reagan at timeforkids.com/bio/reagan**

For biographies of the Presidents:
www.factmonster.com/presidents

Presidents

Early Jobs of Presidents

Of course, every U.S. President had another job before being elected. John Adams was a teacher. Andrew Johnson was a tailor. Most were lawyers or members of the military—and 14 Presidents were both! Here are the jobs held by the most U.S. Presidents.

General Washington, ready for battle

1. Military – 28 Presidents
2. Lawyers – 23
3. Educators – 12
4. Businessmen – 6
5. Journalists – 4
Farmers – 4

Grading the Presidents

Over the years, many polls have tried to determine the best and the worst American Presidents. In 1948 historian Arthur Schlesinger Sr. asked 55 of his colleagues to rate each President. Not surprisingly, Abraham Lincoln, George Washington and Franklin D. Roosevelt scored as great Presidents, while Ulysses Grant and Warren Harding fell into the failure category. More recently, C-SPAN asked 58 historians to grade the Presidents. Here's how they ranked.

Did You Know?

Eight U.S. Presidents were born in Virginia, more than any other state. Ohio comes in at a close second, with seven.

THE BEST

1. Abraham Lincoln
2. Franklin D. Roosevelt
3. George Washington
4. Theodore Roosevelt
5. Harry Truman

THE WORST

1. James Buchanan
2. Andrew Johnson
3. Franklin Pierce
4. Warren G. Harding
5. William Henry Harrison

Source: C-SPAN

Unfortunate Endings and Close Calls

Since the earliest days of government, leaders have had loyal fans as well as harsh critics. Most people have chosen to voice their opinions at the ballot box. A few others, however, have taken drastic measures. Four U.S. Presidents were shot and killed by assassins' bullets, and four others survived assassination attempts.

Abraham Lincoln was shot on April 14, 1865, at Ford's Theatre in Washington, D.C., by actor John Wilkes Booth. Lincoln died the next day.

James Garfield was shot on July 2, 1881, at the Baltimore and Potomac Railway Depot in Washington, D.C., by Charles Guiteau, a mentally ill man who was denied a position in Garfield's administration. Garfield died 80 days later, on September 19, in New Jersey.

William McKinley was shot on September 6, 1901, at the Pan American Expo in Buffalo, New York, by Leon Czolgosz, a factory worker who believed there should be no government. McKinley died on September 14.

John F. Kennedy was shot on November 22, 1963, in Dallas, Texas, while riding in a motorcade. Most people agree that Lee Harvey Oswald shot Kennedy from a nearby building. Kennedy died later that day. Oswald was shot and killed two days later by Jack Ruby.

The following presidents escaped assassination attempts while in office:

Andrew Jackson (1835)   **Harry Truman** (1950)

Gerald Ford (two attempts in 1975)   **Ronald Reagan** (1981)

Mystery Person

CLUE 1: I served as the 33rd President of the U.S. from 1945 to 1953.

CLUE 2: When communist North Korea launched an attack against South Korea in 1950, I sent U.S. troops to help U.N. forces defend South Korea.

CLUE 3: My actions helped limit the spread of the Korean War, which ended with a peace agreement in 1953.

WHO AM I?

(See Answer Key that begins on page 342.)

For a list of presidential pets:
www.factmonster.com/presidentpets

Presidents

199

RELIGION

U.S. Religious Groups by Membership

About 140 million Americans belong to religious groups. Here's a breakdown.

RELIGIOUS GROUP	MEMBERS
1. Protestant	66 million
2. Catholic	62 million
3. Jewish	6 million
4. Mormon	4 million
5. Muslim	1.6 million

Source: Religious Congregation and Membership

Major Organized Religions of the World

	RELIGION	MEMBERS	% OF WORLD POPULATION
1.	Christianity	2.1 billion	33.0 %
2.	Islam	1.3 billion	20.1
3.	Hinduism	851 million	13.3
4.	Buddhism	375 million	5.9
5.	Sikhism	25 million	0.4

Source: *Encyclopedia Britannica*

Religious Holidays 2007

CHRISTIAN HOLIDAYS

Ash Wednesday
February 21
The first day of Lent

Easter April 8
The resurrection of Jesus

Pentecost May 27
The feast of the Holy Spirit

First Sunday in Advent
December 2
The start of the Christmas season

Christmas December 25
The birth of Jesus

JEWISH HOLIDAYS

All Jewish holidays begin at sundown the day before the dates listed here.

Purim March 4
The feast of the lots

Passover April 3
The feast of unleavened bread

Shavuot May 23
The feast of first fruits

Rosh Hashanah September 13
The Jewish New Year

Yom Kippur September 22
The day of atonement

Sukkot September 27
The feast of the tabernacles

Simchat Torah October 4
The rejoicing of the law

Hanukkah December 5
The beginning of the festival of lights

MUSLIM HOLIDAYS

All Muslim holidays begin at sundown the day before the dates listed here.

Muharram January 20
The Muslim New Year

Mawlid al-Nabi
March 31
The prophet Muhammad's birthday

Ramadan
September 13
The month of fasting

Eid al-Fitr October 13
Ramadan ends

Eid al-Adha December 20
The festival of sacrifice

A Monumental Ruling

FROM TFK MAGAZINE

In 2005, the Supreme Court ruled on two controversial cases. The rulings will guide future decisions on placing religious displays on government property. The nation's highest court decided that the Ten Commandments can be displayed on government land, but not inside courthouses.

Many Christians, Jews and Muslims consider the Ten Commandments to be the rules of behavior that God expects of all people. Some say the monuments violate the Constitution by promoting religion in a government building.

The U.S. Constitution calls for the separation of church and state. That means the government is not to support or promote religion. The Supreme Court said that each display of the Ten Commandments should be looked at separately.

One case involved the placement of a 6-foot-tall granite monument with the Ten Commandments written on it on the grounds of the Texas capitol. It was decided that it is a legitimate marker of the nation's legal and religious history.

The other case involved the hanging of framed copies of the Ten Commandments in two Kentucky courthouses. The Supreme Court said those documents promote religion and must be removed. The justices said the placement of the Ten Commandments inside a courthouse violates the Constitution because it promotes religion in a public government building.

—By Jill Egan

Noel Scott holds a sign as he protests in front of the Supreme Court in Washington, D.C.

Texas Attorney General Greg Abbott is happy about the Supreme Court's decision.

Religion

201

THE FIVE MAJOR FAITHS

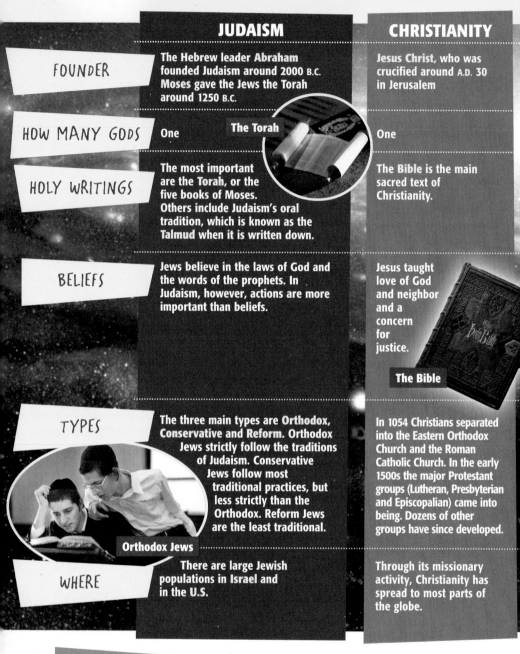

	JUDAISM	CHRISTIANITY
FOUNDER	The Hebrew leader Abraham founded Judaism around 2000 B.C. Moses gave the Jews the Torah around 1250 B.C.	Jesus Christ, who was crucified around A.D. 30 in Jerusalem
HOW MANY GODS	One	One
HOLY WRITINGS	The most important are the Torah, or the five books of Moses. Others include Judaism's oral tradition, which is known as the Talmud when it is written down.	The Bible is the main sacred text of Christianity.
BELIEFS	Jews believe in the laws of God and the words of the prophets. In Judaism, however, actions are more important than beliefs.	Jesus taught love of God and neighbor and a concern for justice.
TYPES	The three main types are Orthodox, Conservative and Reform. Orthodox Jews strictly follow the traditions of Judaism. Conservative Jews follow most traditional practices, but less strictly than the Orthodox. Reform Jews are the least traditional.	In 1054 Christians separated into the Eastern Orthodox Church and the Roman Catholic Church. In the early 1500s the major Protestant groups (Lutheran, Presbyterian and Episcopalian) came into being. Dozens of other groups have since developed.
WHERE	There are large Jewish populations in Israel and in the U.S.	Through its missionary activity, Christianity has spread to most parts of the globe.

The Torah

The Bible

Orthodox Jews

Holy Places

Throughout the world there are places of special significance to different religious groups. Here's a sampling of some of the world's most sacred spots.

• The Holy Land, a collective name for Israel, Jordan and Egypt, is a place of pilgrimage for Muslims, Jews and Christians.

• The Ganges River in India is sacred to Hindus. They drink its water, bathe in it and scatter the ashes of their dead in it.

202

ISLAM	HINDUISM	BUDDHISM
Muhammad, who was born in A.D. 570 at Mecca, in Saudi Arabia	Hinduism has no founder. The oldest religion, it may date to prehistoric times.	Siddhartha Gautama, called the Buddha, in the 4th or 5th century B.C. in India
One	Many	None, but there are enlightened beings (Buddhas)
The Koran is the sacred book of Islam.	The most ancient are the four Vedas.	The most important are the Tripitaka, the Mahayana Sutras, Tantra and Zen texts.
The Five Pillars, or main duties, are: 1. Profession of faith 2. Prayer 3. Charitable giving 4. Fasting during the month of Ramadan 5. Pilgrimage to Mecca (called Hajj) at least once	Reincarnation is the belief that all living things are in a cycle of death and rebirth. Life is ruled by the laws of karma, in which rebirth depends on moral behavior.	The Four Noble Truths: 1. All beings suffer. 2. Desire for possessions, power and so on causes suffering. 3. Desire can be overcome. 4. The path that leads away from desire is the Eightfold Path (the Middle Way).
Almost 90% of Muslims are Sunnis. Shiites are the second-largest group. The Shiites split from the Sunnis in 632, when Muhammad died.	No single belief system unites Hindus. A Hindu can believe in only one god, in many or in none.	Theravada (Way of the Elders) and Mahayana (Greater Vehicle) are the two main types.
Islam is the main religion of the Middle East, Asia and North Africa.	Hinduism is practiced by more than 80% of India's population.	Buddhism is the main religion in many Asian countries.

The god Ganesha

Hajj

Buddha

- The Black Hills of South Dakota are a holy place for some Native American people, who travel there in "vision quests"—searches for peace and oneness with the universe.

- Mount Fai Shan is China's sacred mountain. It is thought to be a center of living energy—a holy place for Buddhists.

- The Sacred Mosque in Mecca, Saudi Arabia, is sacred to Muslims. Muslims around the world face in the direction of Mecca five times a day to pray.

Religion

203

SCIENCE

Woof, Woof! Who's Next?

FROM **TFK** MAGAZINE

Meet Snuppy, the first cloned puppy

Since Dolly the sheep was cloned in 1996, scientists have cloned many types of animals, but nobody had ever created a genetic double of man's best friend. That is, not until South Korean researcher Woo Suk Hwang and his team at Seoul National University brought Snuppy the puppy into the world in 2005. The animal was cloned from a single cell from the ear of a 3-year-old Afghan hound.

The Korean achievement proves that cloning a dog is possible but difficult. John Sperling, who co-founded Genetic Savings & Clone (GS&C), of Sausalito, California, spent seven years and more than $19 million trying without success to clone a dog. Texas A&M researcher Mark Westhusin cloned a cat on his second try in 2001. But he and his team gave up the dog-cloning project because of the time and effort it took.

Cloning Snuppy (the name comes from "Seoul National University puppy") took nearly three years and cost millions of dollars. GS&C still wants to capture the Fido-cloning market, though, and company scientists are trying to make it easier to do so. Even if they manage to clone a dog, says Ben Carlson, a company spokesman, it won't be cheap. "We're charging $32,000 for a cat," he says, "and it will be more for dogs."

Snuppy, a copy of his dad, was borne by a surrogate mom.

What comes next? GS&C has stored the DNA of several rare or endangered animals, including two types of antelope, in its cryogenic freezers. Hwang, who has since admitted to faking research on cloned human cells, won't say what he's planning, but some people think the next step would be to clone a chimp or other primate. Human cloning is still off limits, but the world seems to be inching closer.

—*By Michael D. Lemonick*

Cloning Milestones

Dolly

1996 Scientists in Scotland clone the world's first sheep from adult cells. The lamb born in July 1996 is named Dolly.

1997 Scientists at Oregon Regional Primate Research Center clone two rhesus monkeys. They call them Neti and Ditto.

2000 Scientists in Virginia clone five baby piglets from an adult pig.

Japanese scientists clone a baby bull from a bull that was a clone itself. It was the first time a large mammal was re-cloned.

cc

2002 Scientists introduce the world's first cloned cat, called cc.

2005 South Korean researchers clone a dog and call it Snuppy.

2000 mL

Science

205

EARTH'S TIMELINE

Life on Earth began about 2 billion years ago, but there are no good fossils from before the Cambrian Period, which began 550 million years ago. The largely unknown past before then is called the Precambrian. It is divided into the Lower (older) and Upper (younger) Precambrian—also called the Archeozoic and Proterozoic Eras.

The history of Earth since the Cambrian Period began is divided into three giant chunks of time, or eras, each of which includes a number of shorter periods.

PALEOZOIC ERA

This era began 550 million years ago and lasted for 305 million years. It is sometimes called Early Life.

PERIOD	MILLIONS OF YEARS AGO	CREATURES THAT APPEARED
CAMBRIAN	550–510	INVERTEBRATE SEA LIFE
ORDOVICIAN	510–439	FIRST FISH
SILURIAN	439–409	GIGANTIC SEA SCORPIONS
DEVONIAN	409–363	MORE FISH AND SEA LIFE
CARBONIFEROUS	363–290	EARLY INSECTS AND AMPHIBIANS
PERMIAN	290–245	EARLIEST TURTLES

MESOZOIC ERA

This era began 245 million years ago and lasted for 180 million years. It is sometimes called Middle Life or the Age of Reptiles.

PERIOD	MILLIONS OF YEARS AGO	CREATURES THAT APPEARED
TRIASSIC	245–208	EARLY REPTILES AND MAMMALS
JURASSIC	208–146	EARLY DINOSAURS; FIRST BIRDS
CRETACEOUS	146–65	MORE DINOSAURS, BIRDS; FIRST MARSUPIALS

CENOZOIC ERA

This era began 65 million years ago and includes the geological present. It is sometimes called Recent Life or the Age of Mammals.

PERIOD	MILLIONS OF YEARS AGO	CREATURES THAT APPEARED
TERTIARY	65–2	LARGER MAMMALS; MANY INSECTS; BATS
QUATERNARY	2–PRESENT	EARLY HUMANS TO MODERN HUMANS

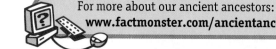

For more about our ancient ancestors:
www.factmonster.com/ancientancestors

Why do stars twinkle?

We see the stars through the atmosphere. Their light passes through miles of constantly moving pockets and streams of air, which distort the image of the stars. The distortions make it seem as if the shining lights are moving or blinking. In outer space, where there is no atmosphere, the stars do not twinkle.

Why don't the oceans freeze?

Actually, in the Arctic and Antarctic, the oceans do freeze. The icecap at the North Pole is entirely over ocean; the ice is about 30 feet thick. Oceans don't freeze completely because they contain an enormous amount of water, which is constantly circulating around the globe. In addition, water flowing from warmer oceans (and from areas near underwater volcanoes) takes off some of the chill. Another important factor is that oceans contain salt-water, which has a lower freezing temperature than freshwater.

Why do boats float?

A steel bar dropped into water sinks, but a huge boat made of steel floats. Why? Most of the space in the boat is taken up by air. The air makes the boat less dense than water. Objects of lesser density float on top of liquids of greater density. (Try the experiment on page 209 to see how this works.) This is also why holes in the bottom of a boat cause it to sink: as air floods out of the boat and water rushes in, the overall density of the boat increases to become more dense than the surrounding water.

Why do I have brown eyes?

The genes we inherit from our parents determine things like our height, looks, hair color and eye color. This passing of characteristics from parent to child is called heredity. If your mother has brown eyes, and your father has blue eyes, there's a good chance you'll have brown eyes. That's because the brown-eye gene is dominant and the blue-eye gene is recessive. The dominant gene usually prevails over the recessive one. It's possible, however, for you to have blue eyes if both your parents have brown eyes. They probably inherited recessive blue-eye genes from their parents and passed them on to you.

Science

SUPER SCIENCE DISCOVERIES

In 1543, while on his deathbed, Polish astronomer **Nicolaus Copernicus** published his theory that the Sun is a motionless body at the center of the solar system, with the planets revolving around it. Before the Copernican system was introduced, astronomers believed Earth was at the center of the universe.

When **Charles Darwin**, the British naturalist, came up with the theory of evolution in 1859, he changed our idea of how life on Earth developed. Darwin argued that organisms often evolve, or change, very slowly over time. These changes are adaptations that sometimes help a species to survive in its environment. These adaptations happen by chance. If a species doesn't adapt, it may become extinct. Darwin called this process natural selection, but it is often called survival of the fittest.

Wilhelm Roentgen, a German physicist, discovered X rays in 1895. X rays go right through some substances, like flesh and wood, but are stopped by others, such as bones and lead. This allows X rays to be used to see broken bones or explosives inside suitcases, which makes them useful for doctors and security officers. For this discovery, Roentgen was awarded the first-ever Nobel Prize in Physics, in 1901.

In 1983 and 1984, **Luc Montagnier** of France and **Robert Gallo** of the U.S. discovered the HIV virus and determined that it was the cause of AIDS. Scientists have since developed tests to determine if a person has HIV. Drugs are now available to keep HIV and AIDS under control. The hope is that further research will lead to the development of a cure.

An atom bomb destroyed Hiroshima.

The atom bomb ended World War II, but it also started the nuclear-arms race. Some of the greatest scientists of the time, including J. Robert Oppenheimer and Hans Bethe, gathered in the early 1940s to figure out how to refine uranium and build an atom bomb. Their work was called the **Manhattan Project**. In 1945, the U.S. dropped atom bombs on the Japanese cities of Hiroshima and Nagasaki. Tens of thousands of people were instantly killed, and Japan surrendered.

Wilhelm Roentgen discovered X rays.

Cladistics Rules

Cladistics is a way of classifying groups of animals by the physical traits they share. The traits can be anything from feathers to bone structure. Because animals that share traits probably descended from the same ancestor, cladistics also shows us the evolutionary history of animals. For example, vertebrates are animals that have a backbone. Because fish, amphibians, mammals and reptiles share this feature, they must have a common ancestor, which also had a backbone. When these vertebrates evolved, they added new features.

Amphibians, mammals and reptiles added the feature of four limbs. Like the backbone, this trait was inherited from a common ancestor. Fish do not share that trait and so did not evolve from that ancestor. From yet another common ancestor, mammals and reptiles inherited the ability to produce waterproof eggs that could be laid on land.

Amphibians don't share that trait—nor that particular ancestor.

A cladogram is a diagram that shows this evolutionary history. It is a series of branching lines that extend from points called nubs. The nub represents an ancestor that developed a special feature, such as four limbs. A line leads from the ancestor to its descendants.

FISHES   AMPHIBIANS   REPTILES   MAMMALS

WATERPROOF EGGS

FOUR LIMBS

BACKBONE

Source: American Museum of Natural History

FACTMONSTER

YOUR TURN: Loopy Liquids

CREATE COLORFUL LAYERS OF LIQUID IN A JAR
Materials
- 1/2 cup light corn syrup
- 1/2 cup glycerin (you can find this oily substance in drug stores)
- 1/2 cup water
- 1/2 cup vegetable oil
- 4 small cups
- 1 tall, clear glass or jar that can hold more than 2 cups of liquid
- two different colors of food coloring
- a funnel
- a spoon

What to do
1. Pour the light corn syrup, glycerin, water and vegetable oil into four separate cups.
2. Add a few drops of one color of the food coloring to the water and mix.
3. Add a few drops of the other color to the corn syrup and mix.
3. Pour the colored corn syrup into the jar. Pour it into the middle of the jar to keep it from running down the sides.
4. Using the funnel, carefully and slowly pour the glycerin into the jar. Try not to upset the layer of corn syrup.

5. Wash the funnel.
6. Repeat step 4, but pour the colored water into the jar.
7. Wash the funnel.
8. Repeat step 4, this time pouring the vegetable oil.

What happens
The liquids remain in separate layers. (If they got mixed, try again, being careful not to shake the jar or disturb the layers while pouring liquid into the jar.) They stayed layered because you poured the liquids into the jar from the highest density to the lowest density. The oil is least dense, so it floats on top.

For science project tips:
www.factmonster.com/scienceprojects

THE ELEMENTS

Elements are the building blocks of nature. Water, for example, is created from two basic ingredients: the element hydrogen and the element oxygen. Each element is a substance made up of only one type of **atom.** For example, all the atoms in a bar of pure gold are the same. Elements cannot be split up into any simpler substances. (When elements combine, they form substances called **compounds.** Water is a compound.)

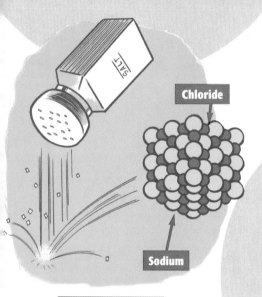

Chloride

Sodium

Table salt is made up of sodium and chloride atoms.

A water molecule is made up of one oxygen and two hydrogen atoms.

Oxygen

Hydrogen

An atom, however, is made up of even smaller particles. These are known as subatomic particles. The most important are:

- **protons,** which have positive electrical charges.
- **electrons,** which have negative electrical charges.
- **neutrons,** which are electrically neutral.

The **atomic number** of an element is the number of protons in one atom of the element. Each element has a different atomic number. For example, the atomic number of hydrogen is 1, and the atomic number of oxygen is 8.

Did You Know?

The Periodic Table *(see page 211)* is based on the 1869 Periodic Law proposed by Russian chemist Dmitry Mendeleyev. He had noticed that when arranged by atomic weight, the chemical elements lined up to form groups with similar properties. He was able to use this to predict the existence of undiscovered elements and note errors in atomic weights. In 1913 Henry Moseley of England rearranged the elements of the table by their atomic number.

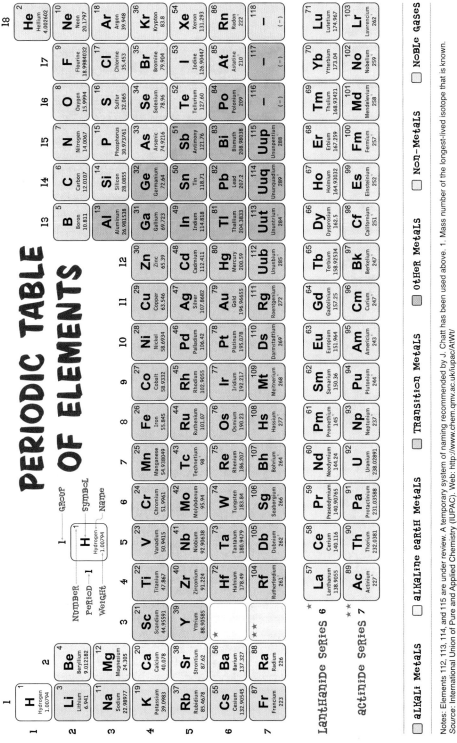

PERIODIC TABLE OF ELEMENTS

Number — 1
Period — H
Symbol — Hydrogen
Name — 1.00794
Weight

Group 1

H 1	Hydrogen 1.00794
Li 3	Lithium 6.941
Na 11	Sodium 22.98977
K 19	Potassium 39.0983
Rb 37	Rubidium 85.4678
Cs 55	Cesium 132.90545
Fr 87	Francium 223

Group 2

Be 4	Beryllium 9.012182
Mg 12	Magnesium 24.305
Ca 20	Calcium 40.078
Sr 38	Strontium 87.62
Ba 56	Barium 137.327
Ra 88	Radium 226

Lanthanide Series 6 ★

La 57	Lanthanum 138.9055	
Ce 58	Cerium 140.116	
Pr 59	Praseodymium 140.90765	
Nd 60	Neodymium 144.24	
Pm 61	Promethium 145	
Sm 62	Samarium 150.36	
Eu 63	Europium 151.964	
Gd 64	Gadolinium 157.25	
Tb 65	Terbium 158.92534	
Dy 66	Dysprosium 162.5	
Ho 67	Holmium 164.93032	
Er 68	Erbium 167.259	
Tm 69	Thulium 168.93421	
Yb 70	Ytterbium 173.04	
Lu 71	Lutetium 174.967	

Actinide Series 7 ★★

Ac 89	Actinium 227	
Th 90	Thorium 232.0381	
Pa 91	Protactinium 231.03588	
U 92	Uranium 238.02891	
Np 93	Neptunium 237	
Pu 94	Plutonium 244	
Am 95	Americium 243	
Cm 96	Curium 247	
Bk 97	Berkelium 247	
Cf 98	Californium 251	
Es 99	Einsteinium 252	
Fm 100	Fermium 257	
Md 101	Mendelevium 258	
No 102	Nobelium 259	
Lr 103	Lawrencium 262	

Groups 3–18 (transition metals and main group):

- Sc 21 Scandium 44.95591
- Ti 22 Titanium 47.867
- V 23 Vanadium 50.9415
- Cr 24 Chromium 51.9961
- Mn 25 Manganese 54.938049
- Fe 26 Iron 55.845
- Co 27 Cobalt 58.9332
- Ni 28 Nickel 58.6934
- Cu 29 Copper 63.546
- Zn 30 Zinc 65.39
- Y 39 Yttrium 88.90585
- Zr 40 Zirconium 91.224
- Nb 41 Niobium 92.90638
- Mo 42 Molybdenum 95.94
- Tc 43 Technetium 98
- Ru 44 Ruthenium 101.07
- Rh 45 Rhodium 102.9055
- Pd 46 Palladium 106.42
- Ag 47 Silver 107.8682
- Cd 48 Cadmium 112.411
- Hf 72 Hafnium 178.49
- Ta 73 Tantalum 180.9479
- W 74 Tungsten 183.84
- Re 75 Rhenium 186.207
- Os 76 Osmium 190.23
- Ir 77 Iridium 192.217
- Pt 78 Platinum 195.078
- Au 79 Gold 196.96655
- Hg 80 Mercury 200.59
- Rf 104 Rutherfordium 261
- Db 105 Dubnium 262
- Sg 106 Seaborgium 266
- Bh 107 Bohrium 264
- Hs 108 Hassium 277
- Mt 109 Meitnerium 268
- Ds 110 Darmstadtium 269
- Rg 111 Roentgenium 272
- Uub 112 Ununbium 285
- B 5 Boron 10.811
- Al 13 Aluminum 26.981538
- Ga 31 Gallium 69.723
- In 49 Indium 114.818
- Tl 81 Thallium 204.3833
- Uut 113 Ununtrium 284
- C 6 Carbon 12.0107
- Si 14 Silicon 28.0855
- Ge 32 Germanium 72.64
- Sn 50 Tin 118.71
- Pb 82 Lead 207.2
- Uuq 114 Ununquadium 289
- N 7 Nitrogen 14.0067
- P 15 Phosphorus 30.973761
- As 33 Arsenic 74.9216
- Sb 51 Antimony 121.76
- Bi 83 Bismuth 208.98038
- Uup 115 Ununpentium 288
- O 8 Oxygen 15.9994
- S 16 Sulfur 32.065
- Se 34 Selenium 78.96
- Te 52 Tellurium 127.60
- Po 84 Polonium 209
- Uuh 116 (–)
- F 9 Fluorine 18.9984032
- Cl 17 Chlorine 35.453
- Br 35 Bromine 79.904
- I 53 Iodine 126.90447
- At 85 Astatine 210
- Uus 117 (–)
- He 2 Helium 4.002602
- Ne 10 Neon 20.1797
- Ar 18 Argon 39.948
- Kr 36 Krypton 83.8
- Xe 54 Xenon 131.293
- Rn 86 Radon 222
- Uuo 118 (–)

Legend:
- Alkali Metals
- Alkaline Earth Metals
- Transition Metals
- Other Metals
- Non-Metals
- Noble Gases

Notes: Elements 112, 113, 114, and 115 are under review. A temporary system of naming recommended by J. Chatt has been used above. 1. Mass number of the longest-lived isotope that is known.
Source: International Union of Pure and Applied Chemistry (IUPAC). Web: http://www.chem.qmv.ac.uk/iupac/AtWt/

PLANTS

Without plants, nearly all life on Earth would end. Plants provide not only oxygen for humans and animals to breathe, but also food for many animals to eat. There are about 260,000 plant species in the world today. They are found on land, in oceans and in freshwater. They were among the first living things on Earth.

Plants and animals are organisms, or living things. Three features distinguish plants from animals: plants have chlorophyll, a green pigment necessary for photosynthesis; they are fixed in one place (they don't move); and their cell walls are made sturdy by a material called cellulose.

Plants are broadly divided into two groups: flower- and fruit-producing plants, and those that do not produce flowers or fruits. Flowering and fruiting plants include all garden flowers, agricultural crops, grasses, shrubs and most leaf trees. Nonflowering plants include pines, ferns, mosses and conifers (evergreen trees and shrubs that produce cones).

Plant Hall of Fame

Biggest Flower: *Rafflesia arnoldii.* Each bloom can be up to 3 feet wide and weigh as much as 24 pounds. Found in Southeast Asia, the reddish-brown flower gives off an incredibly stinky odor.

Most Massive Living Thing: The giant sequoia. One tree found in California's Sierra Nevada is almost 275 feet tall with a circumference of 103 feet at the base. It is estimated to weigh nearly 1,400 tons and contains enough timber to build 120 average-size houses. It is believed to be around 2,100 years old.

Biggest Leaves: Raffia Palm. Native to tropical Africa, its huge leaves can grow as long as 80 feet.

Oldest Trees: Bristlecone pines. These trees are found in California, Nevada and Utah. The oldest-known living bristlecone pine is more than 4,700 years old.

Biggest Fungus: *Armillaria ostoyae,* or the honey mushroom. Not only is this the largest fungus, it's also probably the biggest living organism in the world. Located in Malheur National Forest in eastern Oregon, the fungus lives three feet underground and spans 3.5 miles.

Deadliest: The castor-bean plant. The source of castor oil, it also contains ricin, which is lethal to humans (but the oil is not). A single castor-bean seed can kill.

Photosynthesis

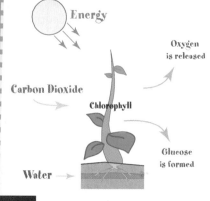

Energy

Oxygen is released

Carbon Dioxide

Chlorophyll

Glucose is formed

Water

Photosynthesis is a process by which green plants (and some bacteria) use **energy** from the Sun, **carbon dioxide** from the air and **water** from the ground to make **oxygen** and **glucose.** Glucose is a sugar that plants use for energy and growth.

Chlorophyll is what makes the process of photosynthesis work.

Chlorophyll, a green pigment, traps the energy from the Sun and helps to change it into glucose.

Photosynthesis is one example of how people and plants depend on each other. It provides us with most of the oxygen we need in order to breathe. We, in turn, exhale the carbon dioxide needed by plants.

Rocks

Rocks are everywhere. Beach sand, mountains and soil are all made of rock. Rocks are classified into three categories, based on how they are formed.

IGNEOUS ROCKS are formed when molten rock (magma) from within the Earth cools and solidifies. There are two kinds: intrusive igneous rocks solidify beneath Earth's surface; extrusive igneous rocks solidify at the surface. Examples: granite, basalt, obsidian

Obsidian

Schist

METAMORPHIC ROCKS are sedimentary or igneous rocks that have been transformed by heat, pressure or both. Metamorphic rocks are usually formed deep within Earth, during a process like mountain building. Examples: schist, marble, slate

SEDIMENTARY ROCKS are formed when sediment (bits of rock plus material such as shells and sand) gets packed together. These rocks can take millions of years to form. Most rocks that you see on the ground are sedimentary. Examples: limestone, sandstone, coal

Coal

Minerals and Gems

MINERALS are solid, inorganic (not living) substances that are found in and on Earth. Most are chemical compounds, which means they are made up of two or more elements. For example, the mineral sapphire is made up of aluminum and oxygen. A few minerals, such as gold, silver and copper, are made from a single element. Minerals are considered the building blocks of rocks.

Copper

Many minerals, such as gold and platinum, are very valuable because they are beautiful and rare. Quartz is the most common mineral.

GEMS are minerals or other organic substances that have been cut and polished. Valuable gems include diamonds, rubies and emeralds.

Magma that cools at the surface is extrusive igneous rock.

Weathering breaks the rock into sediment. Erosion causes the sediment to collect underwater and to move to other locations.

Rock Cycle

The rock cycle explains how the different types of rock form.

Magma that cools and hardens underground forms intrusive igneous rock.

The three types of rock at Earth's mantle melt into magma.

Pressure squeezes the sediment together, forming sedimentary rock.

Heat and pressure deep underground change igneous and sedimentary rock into metamorphic rock.

SPACE

Our Solar System

The Sun

The solar system is made up of the Sun (*solar* means related to the Sun) at its center, nine planets and the various moons, asteroids, comets and meteors controlled primarily by the Sun's gravitational pull.

The Sun, our closest star, is thought to be about 4.6 billion years old. This fiery ball measures 870,000 miles (1,392,000 km) across, and its temperature is estimated to be more than 27,000,000°F (15,000,000°C) at its core. More than a million Earth-size planets could fit inside it. The Sun's great mass exerts a powerful gravitational pull on everything in our solar system, including Earth.

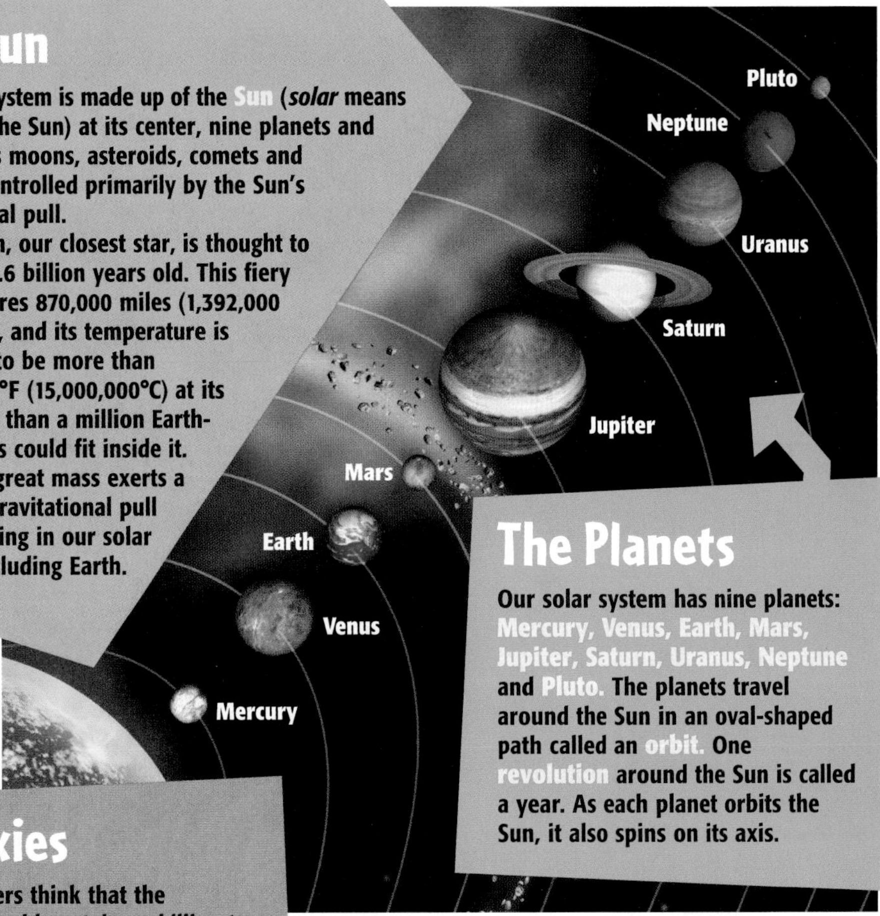

Pluto
Neptune
Uranus
Saturn
Jupiter
Mars
Earth
Venus
Mercury

The Planets

Our solar system has nine planets: Mercury, Venus, Earth, Mars, Jupiter, Saturn, Uranus, Neptune and Pluto. The planets travel around the Sun in an oval-shaped path called an orbit. One revolution around the Sun is called a year. As each planet orbits the Sun, it also spins on its axis.

Galaxies

Astronomers think that the universe could contain 40 billion to 50 billion galaxies—huge systems with billions of stars. Our own galaxy is the Milky Way. It contains about 200 billion stars.

The Moon

The Moon travels around Earth in an oval orbit at 22,900 miles (36,800 km) per hour. Temperatures range from -299°F (-184°C) during its night to 417°F (214°C) during its day, except at the poles, where the temperature is a constant -141°F (-96°C). The Moon's gravity affects our planet's ocean tides. The closer the Moon is to Earth, the greater the effect. The time between high tides is about 12 hours 25 minutes.

Space

215

The Planets

MERCURY

Named for a Roman god (a winged messenger), this planet zooms around the Sun at 30 miles per second!

SIZE
Two-fifths the size of Earth

DIAMETER
3,032.4 miles (4,880 km)

SURFACE
The surface's plains, cliffs and craters are covered by a dusty layer of minerals.

ATMOSPHERE
A thin mixture of helium (95%) and hydrogen

TEMPERATURE
The sunlit side reaches 950°F (510°C). The dark side drops to -346°F (-210°C).

MEAN DISTANCE FROM THE SUN
36 million miles (57.9 million km)

REVOLUTION TIME (IN EARTH DAYS OR YEARS)
88 Earth days

MOONS: 0
RINGS: 0

VENUS

Named after the Roman goddess of love and beauty, Venus is also known as the morning star and evening star since it is visible at these times.

SIZE
Slightly smaller than Earth

DIAMETER
7,519 miles (12,100 km)

SURFACE
A rocky, dusty expanse of mountains, canyons and plains, with a 200-mile river of hardened lava

ATMOSPHERE
Carbon dioxide (95%), nitrogen, sulfuric acid and traces of other elements

TEMPERATURE
Ranges from 55°F (13°C) to 396°F (202°C) at the surface

MEAN DISTANCE FROM THE SUN
67.24 million miles (108.2 million km)

REVOLUTION TIME (IN EARTH DAYS OR YEARS)
243.1 Earth days

MOONS: 0
RINGS: 0

EARTH

Our planet is not perfectly round. It bulges at the equator and is flatter at the poles.

SIZE
Four planets in our solar system are larger and four are smaller than Earth.

DIAMETER
7,926.2 miles (12,756 km)

SURFACE
Earth is made up of water (70%) and solid ground.

ATMOSPHERE
Nitrogen (78%), oxygen (20%), other gases

TEMPERATURE
Averages 59°F (15°C) at sea level

MEAN DISTANCE FROM THE SUN
92.9 million miles (149.6 million km)

REVOLUTION TIME (IN EARTH DAYS OR YEARS)
365 days, 5 hours, 46 seconds

MOONS: 1
RINGS: 0

MARS

Because of its blood-red color (which comes from iron-rich dust), this planet was named for the Roman god of war.

SIZE
About one-half the size of Earth

DIAMETER
4,194 miles (6,794 km)

SURFACE
Canyons, dunes, volcanoes and polar caps of water ice and carbon dioxide ice

ATMOSPHERE
Carbon dioxide (95%)

TEMPERATURE
Between 80°F and -199°F (27°C and -128°C)

MEAN DISTANCE FROM THE SUN
141.71 million miles (227.9 million km)

REVOLUTION TIME (IN EARTH DAYS OR YEARS)
687 Earth days

MOONS: 2 RINGS: 0

JUPITER

The largest planet in our solar system was named for the most important Roman god.

SIZE
11 times the diameter of Earth

DIAMETER
88,736 miles (142,800 km)

SURFACE
A ball of gas and liquid

ATMOSPHERE
Whirling clouds of colored dust, hydrogen, helium, methane, water and ammonia

TEMPERATURE
-234°F (-148°C) average

MEAN DISTANCE FROM THE SUN
483.88 million miles (778.3 million km)

REVOLUTION TIME (IN EARTH DAYS OR YEARS)
11.9 Earth years

MOONS: 63 RINGS: 3

SATURN

Named for the Roman god of farming, the second largest planet has many majestic rings surrounding it.

SIZE
About 10 times larger than Earth

DIAMETER
74,978 miles (120,660 km)

SURFACE
Liquid and gas

ATMOSPHERE
Hydrogen and helium

TEMPERATURE
-288°F (-178°C) average

MEAN DISTANCE FROM THE SUN
887.14 million miles (1,427 million km)

REVOLUTION TIME (IN EARTH DAYS OR YEARS)
29.5 Earth years

MOONS: 47 RINGS: ABOUT 1,000

TURN THE PAGE FOR MORE PLANETS

The Planets

URANUS

This greenish-blue planet is named for an ancient Greek sky god.

SIZE
About four times larger than Earth

DIAMETER
32,193 miles (51,810 km)

SURFACE
Little is known.

ATMOSPHERE
Hydrogen, helium and methane

TEMPERATURE
Uniform temperature of -353°F (-214°C)

MEAN DISTANCE FROM THE SUN
1,783,980,000 miles (2,870,000,000 km)

REVOLUTION TIME (IN EARTH DAYS OR YEARS)
84 Earth years

MOONS: 27
RINGS: 11

NEPTUNE

This stormy blue planet is named for an ancient Roman sea god.

SIZE
About four times the size of Earth

DIAMETER
30,775 miles (49,528 km)

SURFACE
A liquid layer covered with thick clouds and raging storms

ATMOSPHERE
Hydrogen, helium, methane and ammonia

TEMPERATURE
-353°F (-214°C)

MEAN DISTANCE FROM THE SUN
2,796,460,000 miles (4,497,000,000 km)

REVOLUTION TIME (IN EARTH DAYS OR YEARS)
164.8 Earth years

MOONS: 13
RINGS: 4

PLUTO

Named for the Roman god of the underworld, Pluto is the coldest and smallest planet. Some astronomers think it is actually a large comet orbiting the Sun.

SIZE
Less than one-fifth the size of Earth

DIAMETER
1,423 miles (2,290 km)

SURFACE
A giant snowball of methane and water mixed with rock

ATMOSPHERE
Methane

TEMPERATURE
Between -369°F and -387°F (-223°C and -233°C)

MEAN DISTANCE FROM THE SUN
3,666,000,000 miles (5,900,000,000 km)

REVOLUTION TIME (IN EARTH DAYS OR YEARS)
248.5 Earth years

MOONS: 3
RINGS: UNKNOWN

go Click through an interactive space suit at timeforkids.com/spacesuit

Moons Over Pluto

FROM TFK MAGAZINE

These are the first images of the two new moons of Pluto.

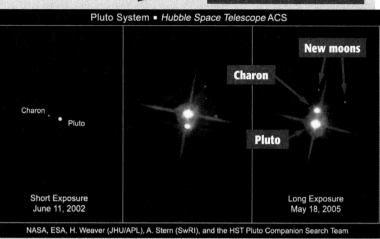

Pluto System ▪ *Hubble Space Telescope* ACS

New moons
Charon
Pluto

Charon
Pluto

Short Exposure
June 11, 2002

Long Exposure
May 18, 2005

NASA, ESA, H. Weaver (JHU/APL), A. Stern (SwRI), and the HST Pluto Companion Search Team

It turns out that Pluto, the smallest and most distant planet in the solar system, isn't as lonely as we thought. In 2005, astronomers announced that they had spotted two more small moons circling the pint-size planet. Before the discovery, Pluto had only one known moon, Charon (kare-uhn).

The scientific spotlight on Pluto doesn't end there. Astronomers are also trying to figure out what makes a planet a planet. Recently several Pluto-size objects have been found orbiting the Sun at even greater distances than Pluto. Should these chunks of rock and ice join in the roll call of planets?

The size of a space object isn't the only thing that makes it a planet. Many moons that orbit known planets are bigger than the small objects that scientists are discovering. If astronomers decide that the distant, orbiting objects are truly little planets, we may add more than 20 newcomers to our solar neighborhood.

Astronomers will debate it, and that may not be a bad thing, says Neil deGrasse Tyson, the head of the Hayden Planetarium, in New York City. "The point," Tyson told TIME "is that the solar system is a lot more interesting than just a list of nine planets."

—By David Bjerklie

An artist's view of how Pluto and its moons might look

Space

The Constellations

For more than 5,000 years, people have looked into the night sky and seen the same stars we see today. They noticed groups of stars that stayed in the same shape and connected them with imaginary lines.

These groups are known as **constellations**. They help astronomers quickly locate other objects in the sky. There are 88 recognized constellations. The constellations on these pages appear in the sky over North America during the summer.

LIBRA
(THE SCALES)

BOÖTES
(THE HERDSMAN)

OPHIUCHUS
(THE SERPENT BEARER)

AQUILA
(THE EAGLE)

CEPHEUS
(THE KING)

DRACO
(THE DRAGON)

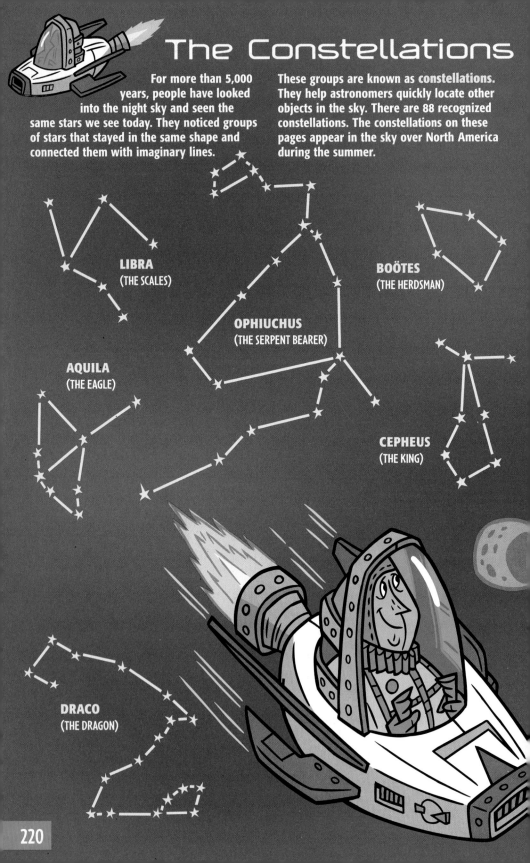

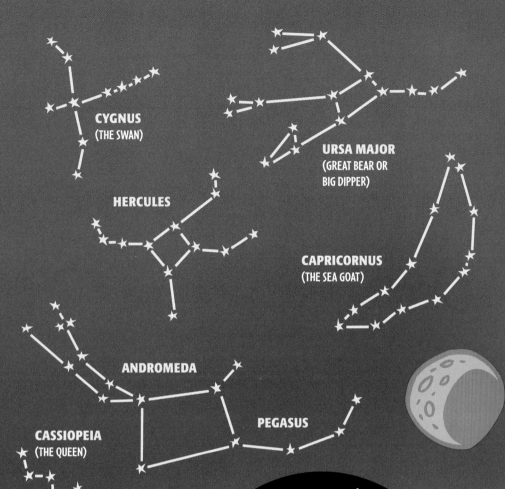

CYGNUS
(THE SWAN)

URSA MAJOR
(GREAT BEAR OR
BIG DIPPER)

HERCULES

CAPRICORNUS
(THE SEA GOAT)

ANDROMEDA

CASSIOPEIA
(THE QUEEN)

PEGASUS

URSA MINOR
(LITTLE BEAR OR
LITTLE DIPPER)

The Zodiac

**As Earth revolves around the Sun,
a different part of the sky becomes
visible. The dates below show when
the constellations can be seen on the
horizon in North America.**

CONSTELLATION	ENGLISH NAME	DATES
Aquarius	Water bearer	Jan. 20–Feb. 19
Pisces	Fish	Feb. 20–March 20
Aries	Ram	March 21–April 19
Taurus	Bull	April 20–May 20
Gemini	Twins	May 21–June 20
Cancer	Crab	June 21–July 22
Leo	Lion	July 23–Aug. 22
Virgo	Virgin	Aug. 23–Sept. 22
Libra	Scales	Sept. 23–Oct. 22
Scorpio	Scorpion	Oct. 23–Nov. 21
Sagittarius	Archer	Nov. 22–Dec. 21
Capricorn	Sea goat	Dec. 22–Jan. 19

1961

1957	▶	The Soviet Union launches *Sputnik*, the first satellite.
1961	▶	Soviet Yuri Gagarin is the first space traveler. Less than a month later, **Alan Shepard Jr.** becomes the first American in space.
1962	▶	John Glenn is the first American to orbit Earth.
1963	▶	Soviet Valentina Tereshkova becomes the first woman in space.
1965	▶	Soviet cosmonaut Alexei Leonov makes the first space walk.
1969	▶	*Apollo 11* astronaut Neil Armstrong becomes the first human to walk on the Moon.
1971	▶	The Soviet Union launches the world's first space station, *Salyut 1*.
1973	▶	The United States sends its first space station, *Skylab*, into orbit.
1976	▶	The U.S.'s *Viking I* is the first spacecraft to land on Mars.
1981	▶	U.S. space shuttle *Columbia*, the world's first reusable spacecraft, is launched.
1986	▶	The U.S. space shuttle *Challenger* explodes 73 seconds after liftoff. Six astronauts and civilian Christa McAuliffe die.
1990	▶	The U.S.'s Hubble Space Telescope is put into orbit.
1995	▶	American Eileen Collins becomes the first woman to pilot a space shuttle.
1998	▶	The Russian *Proton* rocket makes the first flight to the International Space Station. The U.S. space shuttle *Endeavor* follows.
2000	▶	The first crew reaches the International Space Station.
2003	▶	The space shuttle *Columbia* breaks up over Texas during re-entry; seven astronauts die.
		An image taken by a powerful satellite confirms that the universe is 13.7 billion years old and supports the theory that the universe formed in a giant burst of energy called the Big Bang.
2004	▶	The U.S. rovers *Spirit* and *Opportunity* send detailed color images of the surface of Mars back to Earth.
2005	▶	The space shuttle program is temporarily grounded after problems with the *Discovery* shuttle flight.

1971

Skylab

1973

UNITED STATES OF AMERICA

FACT MONSTER

U.S. Space Shuttle Tragedies

On February 1, 2003, the *Columbia* space shuttle broke up as it was preparing to land at the Kennedy Space Center in Florida. All seven astronauts aboard the shuttle died, including six Americans and Israel's first astronaut. As the shuttle was re-entering Earth's atmosphere, hot gases filled the wing, leading to the spacecraft's destruction.

Seventeen years earlier, on January 28, 1986, the *Challenger* exploded 73 seconds after liftoff. All seven people aboard the shuttle died, including six NASA astronauts and Christa McAuliffe, a schoolteacher who was to be the first civilian in space. A booster fuel leak had ignited, causing the tragedy.

The *Columbia* breaks apart.

2004

Astronomical Terms

Between the orbits of Mars and Jupiter are an estimated 30,000 pieces of rocky debris, known collectively as the **asteroids**, or planetoids (small planets). **Ceres** was the first asteroid discovered, on New Year's night in 1801.

Scientists believe that the universe began about 13.7 billion years ago with a massive explosion called the **Big Bang**. In 1927 Georges Lemaître proposed the Big Bang theory of the universe. The theory says that all the matter in the universe was originally compressed into a tiny dot. In a fraction of a second, the dot expanded, and all the matter instantaneously filled what is now our universe. The event marked the beginning of time.

A **black hole** is a mysterious dense object with a gravity so strong that even light cannot escape from it. That's why black holes are almost impossible to see.

A **comet** is a large "snowball" of frozen gases (mostly carbon dioxide, methane and water vapor). Comets originate in the outer solar system. As comets move toward the Sun, heat from the Sun turns some of the snow into gas, which begins to glow and is seen as the comet's tail.

A **galaxy** is a collection of gas and millions of stars held together by gravity. Almost everything you see in the sky belongs to our galaxy, the Milky Way.

Gravity is the force that draws objects to each other. On Earth, gravity pulls things down, toward the center of the planet. That's why things fall.

A **light year** is the distance light travels in one year. It equals 5.88 trillion miles.

A **meteoroid** is a small piece of cosmic matter. When a meteoroid enters our atmosphere, it is called a meteor. It is also known as a shooting star, because it burns while passing through the air. Larger meteors that survive the journey through the atmosphere and land on Earth are called meteorites.

Ceres

A meteor

Space

223

SPORTS

Ouch!

Many young athletes are pushing too hard and getting injured

Acute injuries are common in football.

Ashley Deutsch and her athletic trainer work on her ankle.

Ashley Deutsch, 12, plays basketball at her school in West Lafayette, Indiana. But two hours of practice every day caused her ankles to swell. So Ashley started to visit her school's athletic trainer for physical therapy. For three weeks, she iced and wrapped her injured ankles.

Ashley is just one of 30 million U.S. kids who play competitive sports. As the number of young athletes grows, so does the number of injuries. Annually, about 3.5 million American kids younger than 15 are treated for sports-related injuries.

More and more of these young athletes are being treated for overuse injuries, which require lengthy rehabilitation and care. Overuse injuries include cracked kneecaps, sore shoulders, torn tendons, back pain and damaged growth plates, the fast-growing areas in kids' bones.

Experts call these ailments overuse injuries because they occur when frequent and repetitive motion places stress on a part of the body. Changes in the way kids participate in sports have helped contribute to the surge in such injuries.

In today's win-at-all-costs sports culture, many young athletes never rest. They specialize in one sport, competing year-round. Single-sport athletes often practice the same skills over and over. The nonstop effort leaves no recovery time for the body and puts athletes who are still growing at greater risk of injury. "A single area of the body gets used exclusively, and other areas are not strengthened," said Angela Smith, an orthopedic surgeon.

"Young athletes would be better off playing on only one team," says orthopedic expert James Beaty, "and spending the rest of the time being a kid." What a good game plan!

—*Joe McGowan*

Where Does It Hurt?

Here's a look at some hot spots for overuse injuries and the activities that can cause them.

SHOULDERS Swimming, pitching and tennis can injure the rotator cuff, a group of muscles that helps move the shoulder in an arc.

ELBOW Repetitive throwing can put too much pressure on the muscles, tendons and cartilage near the elbow. A painful condition known as Little League elbow afflicts kids in many sports, not just baseball.

BACK Excessive flexing and stretching in such sports as ice-skating and gymnastics can affect the spine, causing back pain.

LEGS AND FEET Running and dancing can cause a stress fracture, a hairline break in a bone. Most stress fractures occur in the foot or the bones of the lower leg.

KNEES AND HEELS Too much jumping and running in such sports as track, basketball and soccer can cause torn tendons in the legs. Tendons connect muscles to bones.

Sports

225

BASEBALL

Many people believe that baseball was invented in 1839 by Abner Doubleday at Cooperstown, New York, the site of the Hall of Fame and National Museum of Baseball. But research has proved that a game called "base ball" was played in the U.S. and in England before 1839. In fact, Jane Austen mentioned the game in her 1817 novel *Northanger Abbey*.

The first baseball game as we know it was played at Elysian Fields, Hoboken, New Jersey, on June 19, 1846, between the Knickerbockers and the New York Nine.

LITTLE LEAGUE
WORLD SERIES
CHAMPIONS

The Little League World Series

The Little League World Series—the sport's annual world-championship tournament—has been played in Williamsport, Pennsylvania, every year since 1947. In 2005, the Ewa Beach team from West Oahu, Hawaii, defeated 2004's champions from Willemsted, Curaçao, 7-6. The Hawaii team was down three runs in the sixth inning but rallied to tie the game. For only the third time in Little League World Series history, the game went into a seventh inning. Michael Memea slugged a walk-off solo homer to win it for Hawaii—the second time in series history that a home run won the championship.

This was the first time a team from Hawaii won the series. U.S. teams have won 28 times. The 1952 series introduced the first non-U.S. team—Montreal, Canada—which sent their boys (girls weren't allowed until 1974). Monterrey, Mexico, was the first non-American team to take the championship, in 1957. Taiwan, with 16 championships, holds more wins than any other foreign country.

2005 World Series

The past few seasons have been lucky ones for baseball teams with a "curse." In 2004, the Boston Red Sox finally won the World Series. Then in 2005, the American League's Chicago White Sox erased an 88-year drought and swept the Houston Astros 4 games to 0 to take home the World Series trophy. The last time the Windy City Sox won was in 1917. Two years later the baseball world was rocked by the "Black Sox" scandal. Eight members of the 1919 team were caught throwing the World Series. Could the White Sox's neighbor, the Chicago Cubs, be the next team to break a long dry spell? Its last Series win was in 1908!

Like Father, Like Son

Through the years, many fathers and sons have played Major League baseball. But it wasn't until 1989 that Ken Griffey Sr. and Ken Griffey Jr. became the first father and son to play in the major leagues at the same time. One year and one trade later, Ken Jr. and Ken Sr. became the only father and son to play on the same team. And to top it all off, on September 14, 1990, they became the only father-son pair to hit back-to-back home runs in a game. Junior has compiled better statistics and won more awards than his father, but Ken Sr. won World Series titles with Cincinnati in 1975 and 1976. Ken Jr. has never played in a World Series.

TOP PLAYERS OF 2005

MOST VALUABLE PLAYER
A.L.—Alex Rodriguez, New York Yankees
N.L.—Albert Pujols, St. Louis Cardinals

CY YOUNG AWARD (BEST PITCHER)
A.L.—Bartolo Colon, Los Angeles Angels
N.L.—Chris Carpenter, St. Louis

ROOKIE OF THE YEAR
A.L.—Huston Street, Oakland Athletics
N.L.—Ryan Howard, Philadelphia Phillies

HOME-RUN CHAMPIONS
A.L.—Alex Rodriguez, New York Yankees, 48 home runs
N.L.—Andruw Jones, Atlanta Braves, 51 home runs

BATTING CHAMPIONS
A.L.—Michael Young, Texas Rangers, .331 batting average
N.L.—Derrek Lee, Chicago Cubs, .335 batting average

BASKETBALL

In 1891, Dr. James Naismith invented basketball in Springfield, Massachusetts. The game was originally played with a soccer ball and two peach bushel baskets, which is how the game got its name. Twelve of the 13 rules Naismith created are still part of the game. One thing has changed: originally there were nine players on each team; now there are only five. The Basketball Hall of Fame is named in Naismith's honor.

Wilt Chamberlain

2005 Basketball Championships

NBA San Antonio Spurs beat the Detroit Pistons, 4 games to 3

WNBA Sacramento Monarchs beat the Connecticut Sun, 3 games to 1

Tim Duncan

The Monarchs win!

WNBA Hot Shots— 2005 Scoring Leaders

	GAMES	POINTS	AVERAGE
Sheryl Swoopes, Houston	33	614	18.6
Lauren Jackson, Seattle	34	597	17.6
Chamique Holdsclaw, Los Angeles	33	561	17.0

2005 NBA Scoring Leaders

	GAMES	POINTS	AVERAGE
Allen Iverson, Philadelphia	75	2,302	30.7
Kobe Bryant, Los Angeles Lakers	66	1,819	27.6
LeBron James, Cleveland	80	2,175	27.2

Did You Know?

The Basketball Hall of Fame began inducting members in 1959, but it wasn't until 1992 that the first women were inducted. They were Nera White, a 10-time Most Valuable Player in Amateur Athletic Union tournaments, and Lucia Harris-Stewart, who played on the first U.S. Olympic women's basketball team, in 1976.

Facts of the Court

- Two leagues called the National Basketball League (NBL) and the Basketball Association of America (BAA) merged after the 1948–49 season to become today's National Basketball Association (NBA).

- The Boston Celtics have won the most NBA championships (16), including seven straight from 1960 to 1966.

- Kareem Abdul-Jabbar, who played 20 seasons in the NBA, holds the record for the most points scored in a career—38,387.

- On March 2, 1962, Philadelphia Warriors center Wilt Chamberlain scored 100 points in one game against the New York Knicks. That is the most a pro player has ever scored in one game.

- The NBA introduced the three-pointer for the 1979–80 season, an idea it borrowed from the American Basketball Association.

- Basketball became an official Olympic event at the Summer Games in Berlin, Germany, in 1936.

Sports

PRO FOOTBALL

Originally a game played by colleges, professional football became popular in America in the 1920s. The National Football League (NFL) was established in 1922 and merged with the American Football League in 1970 to form a 26-team league. With the addition of the Houston Texans in 2002, the NFL now consists of 32 teams.

Packers and Chiefs at the first Super Bowl

The Trivia Bowl

- The NFL Pro Bowl, pro football's version of an All-Star game, has been played at Aloha Stadium in Honolulu, Hawaii, since 1980.

- Jay Berwanger, the first winner of the Heisman trophy, was the NFL's first No. 1 pick in the college draft, when it was established in 1936.

- The Green Bay Packers defeated the Kansas City Chiefs in the first Super Bowl, which was held in Los Angeles in January 1967.

- Don Shula, who coached with the Baltimore Colts and the Miami Dolphins, won 347 games in his career. That's more than any other coach in NFL history.

- Jim Brown led the NFL in rushing more times than any other running back in history. He led the league eight times from 1957 to 1965.

Super-Size Super Bowl

Super Bowl XL (40) proved to be "extra large" for the Pittsburgh Steelers, who beat the Seattle Seahawks 21-10. This gave Pittsburgh its fifth trophy, tying Dallas and San Francisco for the most Super Bowls wins. The last time the Steelers won the title was back in 1980. This was Seattle's first trip to the big game. Pittsburgh wide receiver Hines Ward was named the Most Valuable Player.

Upcoming Super Bowl Sites

2007	Super Bowl XLI (41)	Miami, Florida
2008	Super Bowl XLII (42)	Glendale, Arizona
2009	Super Bowl XLIII (43)	Tampa, Florida

Jim Brown of the Cleveland Browns

Football Phenomena

MOST POINTS SCORED IN A GAME: 113
- The Washington Redskins beat the New York Giants, 72–41, on November 27, 1966.

LONGEST FIELD GOAL: 63 YARDS (TIE)
- Tom Dempsey, New Orleans Saints vs. Detroit Lions, November 8, 1970
- Jason Elam, Denver Broncos vs. Jacksonville Jaguars, October 25, 1998

LONGEST TOUCHDOWN RUN: 99 YARDS
- Tony Dorsett, Dallas Cowboys vs. Minnesota Vikings, January 3, 1983

COLLEGE BASKETBALL

March Madness

Fans describe the end of college-basketball season as March Madness. That's because the men's and women's championship tournaments are held in March and feature more than 100 of the best teams in the country.

Tennessee holds the most women's titles (six), but the 2004 women's champ, the University of Connecticut, is catching up, with five titles. UCLA has won the most men's championships (11).

In 2006 the University of Florida Gators won its first NCAA men's championship, defeating the UCLA Bruins 73–57. In the women's tournament, the University of Maryland Terrapins beat the Duke Blue Devils in an overtime thriller, 78–75.

Florida's Joakim Noah was named the Most Outsanding Player in the Final Four.

COLLEGE FOOTBALL

Vince Young

Horns Hook 'Em!

The University of Texas Longhorns upset 2005's national champs, the University of Southern California Trojans, with a game-winning touchdown late in the fourth quarter that put Texas up 41–38. With the win, Texas claimed the national crown. Before 1998, polls of writers and coaches named the unofficial champ. Now the BCS (Bowl Championship Series) combines polls and computer averages to rank the teams and decide which ones advance to the bowl games. A new twist to the BCS for the 2007 bowl season has the four major bowls (Rose, Orange, Fiesta and Sugar) taking place January 1-3, with a fifth bowl game on January 8 for the championship.

OTHER 2006 BOWL GAMES

ORANGE BOWL *(Miami, Florida)* Penn State 26, Florida State 23

FIESTA BOWL *(Tempe, Arizona)* Ohio State 34, Notre Dame 20

SUGAR BOWL *(usually in New Orleans, played in Atlanta, Georgia, in 2006)* West Virginia 38, Georgia 35

COTTON BOWL *(Dallas, Texas)* Alabama 13, Texas Tech 10

GATOR BOWL *(Jacksonville, Florida)* Virginia Tech 35, Louisville 24

OUTBACK BOWL *(Tampa, Florida)* Florida 31, Iowa 24

Top Dog

The Heisman Trophy is an annual award given since 1935 to the outstanding college-football player in the country. Several Heisman winners have gone on to success in the NFL and been elected to the Pro Football Hall of Fame after retiring. Current NFL players Charles Woodson (1997) and Carson Palmer (2002) are recent winners. In 2005 tailback Reggie Bush of the University of Southern California won the award with the second most votes in Heisman history. Only O.J. Simpson in 1968 got more votes than Reggie did.

Reggie Bush

For sports superstitions:
www.factmonster.com/spot/superstitions

Sports

SOCCER

Soccer is the world's most popular sport. Known as football throughout the rest of the world, soccer is played by boys, girls, men and women of nearly all ages. Hundreds of millions of people play the game.

The World Cup

The world's biggest soccer tournament is called the World Cup. It's played every four years by teams made up of each country's best players.

Germany won the women's World Cup in 2003, while Brazil was the winner of the men's World Cup in 2002.

Germany hosted the men's World Cup in 2006. China will host the women's World Cup in 2007.

Brazil in 2002

Get Your Kicks

Sneakers go back a long way. In the late 18th century, people wore rubber-soled shoes called plimsols, but they were pretty crude—for one thing, there was no right foot or left foot. Around 1892, the U.S. Rubber Company came up with more comfortable rubber sneakers with canvas tops, called Keds. (The shoes were called sneakers because they were so quiet, a person wearing them could sneak up on someone.)

In 1917, Marquis Converse produced the first shoe made just for basketball, called Converse All-Stars. In 1923, an Indiana hoops star named Chuck Taylor endorsed the shoes, and they became known as Chuck Taylor All-Stars. These are the best-selling basketball shoes of all time.

Sneakers went international in 1924. That's when a German man named Adi Dassler created a sneaker that he named after himself: Adidas. This brand soon became the most popular athletic shoe in the world.

During the first half of the 20th century, sports shoes were worn mostly to play sports. But in the 1950s, kids began wearing them as fashion statements. Even more teens followed the fad after seeing James Dean in sneakers in the popular movie *Rebel Without a Cause*.

Sneaker sales really took off in 1984, when Nike signed Michael Jordan to endorse Air Jordans—the most famous sneaker ever made. During the 1980s, sneakers became fashionable footwear for kids and adults. Companies like Nike, Reebok and Adidas produced sneakers in wild styles, and new technologies supposedly improved their performance. For example, Reebok's Pump lets wearers pump air into the shoes to make them fit snugly. Of course, innovations like these come with a price: athletic shoes often cost well over $100 a pair!

WORLD-CUP CHAMPIONS

WOMEN	MEN
1991 U.S.A.	1930 Uruguay
1995 Norway	1934 Italy
1999 U.S.A.	1938 Italy
2003 Germany	1942, 1946 not held
	1950 Uruguay
	1954 West Germany
	1958 Brazil
	1962 Brazil
	1966 England
	1970 Brazil
	1974 West Germany
	1978 Argentina
	1982 Italy
	1986 Argentina
	1990 West Germany
	1994 Brazil
	1998 France
	2002 Brazil

HOCKEY

Ice hockey, by birth and upbringing a Canadian game, is an offshoot of field hockey. Some historians say that the first ice-hockey game was played in Montreal in December 1879 between two teams composed almost exclusively of McGill University students. But others believe that earlier hockey games took place in Kingston, Ontario, or Halifax, Nova Scotia.

In the Montreal game of 1879, there were 15 players on a side. The players used an assortment of sticks to keep the puck in motion. Early rules allowed nine men on a side, but the number was reduced to seven in 1886 and later to six.

In the winter of 1894–1895, a group of college students from the United States visited Canada and saw hockey played. Enthusiastic about the game, they introduced it as a winter sport when they returned home.

On the Ice Again

When National Hockey League players returned to the ice in 2005 after a season-long lockout, they returned to a changed game. New rules were adopted to speed up the game, increase goal scoring and attract new fans. The shootout, the biggest change to the game, eliminates ties. If neither team scores during a five-minute overtime, each team takes three shots at the goal. Whichever team makes the most shots gets the extra point—if still tied, the shootout becomes sudden death. Other changes include more penalties for fighting, changed lines on the rink and smaller goaltender gear.

In addition, many players will be earning less money. Their salaries are being rolled back 24%, and there's a salary cap. But there was good news for the lowest-paid players—the minimum salary was increased from $180,000 to $450,000.

NHL All-Time Career Point Scorers

PLAYER	GOALS	ASSISTS	POINTS
1. WAYNE GRETZKY	894	1,963	2,857
2. MARK MESSIER	694	1,193	1,887
3. GORDIE HOWE	801	1,049	1,850
4. RON FRANCIS	549	1,249	1,798
5. MARCEL DIONNE	731	1,040	1,771

Did You Know?

Gordie Howe, known as "Mr. Hockey," played professional hockey until he was 52—the oldest player in NHL history. He led the Detroit Red Wings to four Stanley Cup titles in the 1940s and 1950s. He retired in the early 1970s but returned to play on the same team as his two sons, Mark and Marty. He left the game for good in 1982.

Top Goalies

These goaltenders have won the most games.

	PLAYER	GAMES	WINS	LOSSES	TIES
1.	PATRICK ROY	1,029	551	315	131
2.	TERRY SAWCHUK	971	447	330	172
3.	JACQUES PLANTE	837	435	247	146
4.	ED BELFOUR	856	435	281	111
5.	TONY ESPOSITO	886	423	306	152

The Stanley Cup

Each player on the team that wins the NHL championship gets his name engraved on the **Stanley Cup,** along with all the previous winners. The original cup was only seven inches high; now it stands more than three feet tall. The Montreal Canadiens have won the most titles with 23. The Tampa Bay Lightning won the 2004 Stanley Cup. Because of the lockout, there was no Stanley Cup in 2005.

Sports

GOLF

Tee Time

It may be that golf originated in Holland—historians believe it did—but certainly Scotland developed the game and is famous for it. Formal competition began in 1860 with the British Open championship.

The four major events in men's professional golf (the Grand Slam) are:

The Masters
British Open
U.S. Open
PGA Championship

The four major events in women's professional golf (the Women's Grand Slam) are:

LPGA Championship
U.S. Women's Open
Nabisco Championship
Women's British Open

The **Ryder Cup** is the most prestigious team golf event in the world. It is played every two years between a team of American golfers and a team of European golfers.

WINNERS OF MAJORS IN 2005
MEN:
The Masters: Tiger Woods
British Open: Tiger Woods
U.S. Open: Michael Campbell
PGA Championship:
  Phil Mickelson
U.S. Amateur Champion:
  Edoardo Molinari

WOMEN:
LPGA Championship:
  Annika Sorenstam
U.S. Open:
  Birdie Kim
Nabisco Championship:
  Annika Sorenstam
British Open: Jeong Jang
U.S. Amateur Champion:
  Morgan Pressel

Tiger Woods

Did You Know?

Tiger Woods won the 1997 Masters Tournament when he was just 21 years old, with a record score of 270. He was the first person of color to win the tournament since it began in 1934.

CYCLING

In 2005, Lance Armstrong won his seventh consecutive Tour de France and became the first person to ever win seven times. His closest competitor followed 4 minutes and 40 seconds behind him. Armstrong retired from professional racing after his 2005 Tour de France win. In 1996 Armstrong was diagnosed with cancer. He not only beat the disease, he also became the greatest cyclist in history.

Lance Armstrong

OLYMPICS

The first Olympic Games were held in Olympia, Greece, around 777 B.C. Only men were allowed to compete. Events included boxing, wrestling and chariot racing. No medals were awarded. Instead, winners received a crown of olive leaves. The Games went on for more than 1,000 years, but were cancelled in 393 A.D.

In 1894, French educator Pierre de Coubertin proposed a revival of the ancient Games. He believed that a modern Olympics with competitors from around the world would promote peace and understanding among nations. That year, Coubertin formed the International Olympic Committee to help bring back the games.

The modern Olympics premiered in Athens, Greece, in 1896. Only summer events were included. Figure skating was part of the Summer Olympics in 1908. The sport later became part of the Winter Games, which started in Chamonix, France, in 1924.

The spirit of the ancient Olympics is still alive today. The Games are a source of national pride and peaceful competition for countries all over the world.

Opening ceremonies at the Athens 2002 Summer Olymmpics

UPCOMING OLYMPIC GAMES

2008	(SUMMER)	Beijing, China
2010	(WINTER)	Vancouver, British Columbia
2012	(SUMMER)	London, England

Sprinter Justin Gatlin

Michael Phelps swims for gold.

TFK Top 5 All-Time Winter Olympic Medal Winners

COUNTRY	MEDALS
1. Germany*	328
2. Russia/USSR**	293
3. Norway	280
4. United States	216
5. Austria	185

*East Germany and West Germany competed separately from 1968 until 1988.
**The USSR broke up into 15 countries, including Russia, in 1991.
Source: The International Olympic Committee

All-Time Summer Olympic Medal Winners

COUNTRY	GOLD	SILVER	BRONZE	TOTAL
UNITED STATES	896	690	604	2,190
RUSSIA/USSR*	553	463	447	1,463
GERMANY**	401	424	453	1,278
GREAT BRITAIN	198	251	249	698
FRANCE	210	211	243	664

*Includes competing as the United Team immediately after the breakup of the Soviet Union.
**Includes Germany before, during and after its breakup into East and West Germany.

Source: Wikipedia

Sports

233

Alpine Skiing

The Norwegians, Swedes and Lapps (people from Finland) used skis for many centuries before skiing became a sport. Emigrants from these countries introduced skis to the United States. The first skier of record in the U.S. was a Norwegian mailman named "Snowshoe" Thompson, who moved to the U.S. around 1850 and used skis when carrying mail.

Ski clubs sprang up in the U.S. more than 100 years ago in Wisconsin and Minnesota, and ski contests were held there in 1886. In 1936, Franz Pfnur and Christi Cranz, both of Germany, won the first alpine-skiing Olympic gold medals.

These are the events held in most present-day alpine competitions:

Downhill features the longest course and is the fastest of the alpine events. Skiers can reach speeds of more than 90 miles per hour as they race down the slope. Downhill racing includes turns, jumps and gliding stages.

In the **slalom**, the shortest race, single poles, called gates, are placed closely together on the course. It's the most technically challenging event, as skiers must make quick, sharp turns through the gates.

On a **giant slalom** course, gates span the length of the run. They are spaced more widely apart than the slalom gates. This makes for a faster run with wider turns than the slalom. Each gate is made of two poles connected by a piece of fabric.

Super giant slalom, the newest alpine event, was introduced into competitions in 1987. It has a much longer course than either the slalom or giant slalom and the gates are the most widely spaced of the slaloms. Super-GS skiers "tuck" into a low, scrunched position to get the most speed from their run.

Bode Miller

Snowboarding

Sherman Poppen is generally considered to be the inventor of the snowboard. In 1965, he fastened two skis together so his daughter could "surf" down a snow-covered slope near their Michigan home. He called the sport *snurfing,* a combination of *snow* and *surfing*.

Early snowboarders, mostly male teens, were often viewed as rebels. Now, males and females of all ages are seen cruising down the slopes on snowboards.

Snowboarding debuted as an Olympic sport in 1988. Men and women compete in halfpipe, giant slalom and snowboard cross events. The halfpipe is a U-shaped course carved into a mountain. Competitors are scored for their technique. In the parallel giant slalom, snowboarders race against each other on separate slalom courses. Snowboard cross features a long course with turns and jumps.

Shaun White

EXTREME SPORTS

The X Games were dreamed up by the sports television network ESPN. They debuted during the summer of 1994 in Newport and Providence, Rhode Island. The games were supposed to take place every two years. But the first games were so popular, organizers made it an annual competition.

The summer games include bicycle stunts, Moto X, skateboarding, surfing, inline skating and wakeboarding.

Probably the most famous "extreme" athlete is skateboarder Tony Hawk. He was the first skateboarder to land a 900 trick in the halfpipe competition. A 900 is 2½ complete midair rotations on the skateboard. It's called a 900 because one complete spin is 360° around (like a circle) and 2½ x 360 = 900.

The winter games include snowboarding, skiing, snowmobiling and Moto X. At the 2005 Winter Games in Aspen, Colorado, Canadian Charles Gagnier ended American Tanner Hall's quest for a fourth gold in ski slopestyle.

Elissa Steamer

2005 SUMMER X GAMES WINNERS
LOS ANGELES, CALIFORNIA
AUGUST 4–7, 2005

Skateboard: Danny Way (men's big air), Pierre-Luc Gagnon (men's vert), Elissa Steamer (women's street), Cara-Beth Burnside (women's vert), Bob Burnquist (men's vert best trick)

BMX: Jamie Bestwick (vert), Dave Mirra (park), Corey Bohan (dirt), Jamie Bestwick (best trick)

Moto X: Jeremy Stenberg (best trick), Doug Henry (super moto), Tommy Clowers (step up), Travis Pastrana (freestyle)

Wakeboard: Dallas Friday (women), Danny Harf (men)

Surfing: Team East

GYMNASTICS

Gymnastics is one of the most physically demanding sports, not to mention one of the most popular at the Summer Olympics.

The Fédération Internationale de Gymnastique (FIG) is the organization that oversees gymnastics throughout the world. The FIG recognizes seven gymnastic areas: men's artistic gymnastics, women's artistic gymnastics, rhythmic gymnastics, trampoline, sports aerobics, sports acrobatics and noncompetitive general gymnastics.

Nastia Liukin

Gymnastic Stars

Olga Korbut, a Soviet gymnast, inspired many girls to take up gymnastics after she won three gold medals at the 1972 Olympics in Munich. Romanian gymnast Nadia Comaneci became the first woman to score a perfect 10, at the 1976 summer games in Montreal, Canada.

Kerri Strug provided one of the most exciting events of the 1996 Olympics— and gymnastics history—when she nailed her vault on an injured ankle to ensure a gold medal for the U.S. team.

At the 2004 Olympics in Athens, Paul Hamm and Carly Patterson of the United States earned gold in the all-around competition. The U.S. team won a total of nine gymnastic medals in Athens.

Sports

235

AUTO RACING

Automobile racing originated in France in 1894 and appeared in the U.S. the next year.

Jimmie Johnson

Racing, Anyone?

The National Association for Stock Car Auto Racing's **Nextel Cup Series** is the most popular auto-racing series in the U.S. The NASCAR season runs from February to November. The biggest Nextel Cup race of the year is the **Daytona 500**. Jimmie Johnson won the 2006 Daytona 500. Tony Stewart was the 2005 NASCAR Nextel points champion.

Formula One World Champions

Germany's Michael Schumacher won his seventh Formula One driver's world championship in 2004, giving him two more titles than his nearest competitor on the all-time list, Argentina's Juan-Manuel Fangio.

TOP TITLE WINNERS

7–	**MICHAEL SCHUMACHER (Germany)**
5–	**JUAN-MANUEL FANGIO (Argentina)**
4–	**ALAIN PROST (France)**

Our Need for Speed

The biggest and oldest race held in the U.S. is the **Indianapolis 500.** It's held every year at the oval-shaped Indianapolis Motor Speedway in Indiana. Dan Wheldon was the 2005 Indy 500 winner.

Dan Wheldon

Rising Star

Danica Patrick's performance at the Indianapolis 500 increased fan interest in open-wheel racing. But NASCAR, the more popular circuit, is grooming a female phenom of its own. Erin Crocker, 24, started racing when she was 7 and in 2004 became the first woman to win a grueling World of Outlaws sprint-car race. She then signed with legendary NASCAR crew chief Ray Evernham, who guided Jeff Gordon to three Winston Cup titles.

Though Crocker has risen quickly through the stock-car ranks, Evernham won't rush his prized talent. He had scheduled Crocker to drive full time in the Busch Series, NASCAR's top minor-league circuit, but after crashes in her first two Busch starts, she will get more experience at a lower level. Expect to see her in the Nextel Cup Series before long. Although Crocker couldn't find a sponsor to drive an Indy car, as did Patrick, she's happy where she is. "If you want to reach the big leagues," says Crocker, who graduated from Rensselaer Polytechnic Institute, "NASCAR is the place to be."

Erin Crocker

TENNIS

The four biggest tournaments in tennis make up the Grand Slam. Here are the recent winners.

Venus Williams

Tennis Champions

AUSTRALIAN OPEN (2006)
Men: **Roger Federer**
Women: **Amelie Mauresmo**
FRENCH OPEN (2005)
Men: **Rafael Nadal**
Women: **Justine Henin-Hardenne**
WIMBLEDON (2005)
Men: **Roger Federer**
Women: **Venus Williams**
U.S. OPEN (2005)
Men: **Roger Federer**
Women: **Kim Clijsters**

Did You Know?

Maureen Connolly (in 1953), Margaret Smith Court (in 1970) and Steffi Graf (in 1988) are the only three women tennis players to win all four Grand Slam tournaments in one year.

SWIMMING

Style Points

The five swimming areas used in competition are:
- Breaststroke
- Backstroke
- Butterfly
- Freestyle
- Medley (all four strokes)

Michael Phelps

Making a Splash

Michael Phelps entered the 2004 Summer Olympics poised to tie or break Mark Spitz's record of seven gold medals. While he didn't accomplish the Olympian feat, he did bring home eight medals (six were gold). That tied him with Russian gymnast Aleksandr Dityatin as the winningest athlete at a single Olympic Games.

Homework Tip!

If you have sports practice or a game after school, take a break and have a meal or snack before you start your homework. You need the time to fuel up and rest before starting in on homework.

TFK Mystery Person

CLUE 1: I was born in Mobile, Alabama, in 1906. Because the major leagues were segregated, I had to spend most of my career pitching in the Negro Leagues.

CLUE 2: At age 42, I finally got to play in the major leagues and became the American League's oldest rookie. Four years later, I was picked for the All-Star team.

CLUE 3: I am known for my funny sayings, one of which is "Don't look back. Something may be gaining on you."

WHO AM I?
(See Answer Key that begins on page 342.)

Sports

237

TRANSPORTATION

Top-Selling Cars and Trucks of 2005

RANK	MAKE AND MODEL
1.	Ford F-Series pickup
2.	Chevy Silverado-C/K pickup
3.	Toyota Camry
4.	Dodge Ram pickup
5.	Honda Accord
6.	Toyota Corolla
7.	Honda Civic
8.	Nissan Altima
9.	Ford Explorer
10.	Chevrolet TrailBlazer

Source: Reuters

Most Expensive Cars

RANK	MAKE AND MODEL	PRICE
1.	Saleen S7	$562,700
2.	Mercedes-Benz SLR McLaren	452,750
3.	Porsche Carrera GT	443,000
4.	Maybach 62	377,750
5.	Maybach 57	327,750
6.	Rolls-Royce Phantom	320,000
7.	Lamborghini Murciélago	281,000
8.	Aston Martin V12 Vanquish	256,350
9.	Ferrari 612 Scaglietti	254,150
10.	Ferrari 575M Maranello	225,090

NOTE: Prices are for 2005 models.
Includes only vehicles currently sold in the U.S.
Source: Forbes.com

Car Names

Dodge Viper, Jeep Cherokee, Subaru Brat. Some car names are really cool. The automobile industry has gone into overdrive to come up with names that attract consumers. Below are some of the more inventive car names and the images they try to convey.

THE WILD, WILD WEST Ford Bronco, Jeep Wrangler, Dodge Dakota, GMC Yukon

RUGGED ADVENTURE Nissan Frontier, GMC Safari, Toyota Tundra, Ford Expedition

HIGH TECH Infiniti FX45, Cadillac SRX, Audi S4, Jaguar X-Type

COSMIC Pontiac Solstice, Chevrolet Equinox, Dodge Aries, Saturn Sky

ROYALTY Buick Regal, Lincoln Continental, Dodge St. Regis, Buick Park Avenue

FRENCH Lincoln Versailles, Pontiac Parisienne, Buick LeSabre, Chrysler LeBaron

ANIMAL MAGNETISM Ford Mustang, Mercury Cougar, Corvette Stingray, Plymouth Barracuda

HIP Pontiac Vibe, Ford Freestyle, Dodge Neon, Toyota Matrix

CUTE AS A BUTTON Renault Le Car, Mini Cooper, VW Bug, Nissan Cube

DON'T MESS WITH ME Lamborghini Diablo, Chrysler Crossfire, Aston Martin Vanquish, Plymouth Fury

MYSTERIOUS Dodge Stealth, Mitsubishi Mirage, Dodge Shadow

ThrustSSC

SPEED THRILLS

Here are speed records set by some of the world's fastest-moving vehicles. Many of these vehicles were specially built and operated under test conditions—so don't try this at home!

Land car Andy Green, behind the wheel of ThrustSSC (Super-Sonic Car), zoomed at a speed of 763.05 m.p.h. in Black Rock Desert, Nevada, on October 15, 1997. It took him only a few seconds to travel one mile.

Railed vehicle The fastest conventional train (one built to carry passengers) is France's TGV (*tres grande vitesse*, which means *very great speed*). On a test run in 1990, it barreled along the tracks at a top speed of 456 m.p.h. while carrying just a few cars. The record for a train on a scheduled route goes to a TGV that travels between Lyon and Aix-en-Provence, in France. It reaches a top speed of 198.83 m.p.h. and cruises at an average speed of 163.60 m.p.h.

Non-conventional vehicle In 2003, an unmanned sled train propelled by a rocket motor traveled 6,453 m.p.h.—more than eight times the speed of sound—at Holloman Air Force Base in New Mexico.

Water-born vehicle In 1998, the *Spirit of Australia,* steered by Aussie Ken Warby, raced over the waters of Blowering Dam, Australia, at an average speed of 317.18 m.p.h. Warby not only piloted his jet-powered hydroplane, but he also built it from scratch in his backyard.

Motorcycle American Dave Campos rode Easyriders, his 23-foot-long streamliner-style motorcycle, at an average speed of 322.87 m.p.h. He sped his supercycle over the Bonneville Salt Flats in Utah in 1990.

Bicycle In 1995, Fred Rompelberg of the Netherlands pedaled his way to history. The professional cyclist reached a speed of 167.04 m.p.h., also on Utah's Bonneville Salt Flats.

Favorite Car Colors

1. Silver	2. White	3. Red	4. Blue	5. Light brown
18%	16%	14%	11%	11%

Transportation

239

FAMOUS AVIATORS

WRIGHT BROTHERS

Aviation was born on the sand dunes at Kitty Hawk, North Carolina, on December 17, 1903. On that day Orville Wright crawled between the wings of the plane he and his brother, Wilbur, had built and took to the air. He covered 120 feet in 12 seconds. In a fourth attempt that day, Wilbur stayed up 59 seconds and covered 852 feet. These were the first controlled, sustained flights in a power-driven airplane.

CHARLES LINDBERGH

Lindbergh made the world's first nonstop solo flight across the Atlantic Ocean. On May 20, 1927, he took off in his plane, *The Spirit of St. Louis*, traveling 3,610 miles from Long Island, New York, to Paris, France. He landed 33 hours later, greeted by a mob of 100,000 cheering Parisians. "Lucky Lindy" instantly became an international hero for his daring flight.

AMELIA EARHART

Amelia Earhart is the most celebrated female pilot in history. As America's "Lady of the Air," she set many aviation records. Earhart became the first woman (and second person after Lindbergh) to fly solo across the Atlantic, in 1932, and the first person to fly alone across the Pacific, from Honolulu, Hawaii, to Oakland, California, in 1935. In 1937, during an attempt to circumnavigate the globe, she disappeared somewhere in the South Pacific. Her fate remains a mystery.

CHUCK YEAGER

On October 14, 1947, Chuck Yeager, a famous World War II pilot, accomplished what was then a mind-boggling feat—he became the first person to fly faster than the speed of sound. His successful attempt to break the sound barrier required enormous courage. No one knew whether the rocket-powered X-1 fighter plane—or its pilot—would survive. In 1953 he went on to set yet another world speed record of 1,650 m.p.h. A best-selling book, *The Right Stuff*, and the film of the same title told of Yeager's extraordinary achievements.

Hartsfield

World's Busiest Airports

These are the airports that served the most passengers in 2004.

1. Atlanta (Hartsfield)
2. Chicago (O'Hare)
3. London (Heathrow)
4. Tokyo (Haneda)
5. Los Angeles
6. Dallas/Fort Worth
7. Frankfurt-Main
8. Paris (Charles de Gaulle)
9. Amsterdam
10. Denver

Source: Airports Council International World Headquarters, Geneva, Switzerland

Milestones in Flight

1783	Hot-air balloon
	Parachute
1852	Dirigible
1900	Zeppelin
1903	First airplane flight
1911	Hydroplane
1926	Liquid-fueled rocket
1939	First successful helicopter flight
1955	Hovercraft
1968	Supersonic transport (SST)
1970	Jumbo jet
1981	Solar-powered airplane Launch of the first space shuttle, *Columbia*
2004	First private staffed ship, *SpaceShipOne*, leaves the atmosphere

VEHICLE HALL OF FAME

FAMOUS TRAINS

Trans-Siberian Express Traveling between Moscow and Vladivostok, Russia, the Trans-Siberian Express makes the longest regular train trip, stopping at 91 stations in nine days.

Japanese Bullet Train

Super Chief Beginning in 1936, the Super Chief ran from Chicago to Los Angeles. It was famous for its gourmet food and movie-star passengers.

Orient Express In 1883 the Orient Express began service from Paris to Istanbul, crossing six countries.

Bullet Train The Japanese Shinkansen, or Bullet Train, runs at speeds of more than 100 m.p.h. over special tracks with very few curves. In 1997 a newer version of the Bullet Train became at that time the fastest scheduled train in the world, regularly reaching speeds of up to 186 m.p.h.

FAMOUS SHIPS

The _Titanic_ This doomed ship set out on its first—and last—voyage from Southampton, England, to New York City in 1912. In the early hours of April 15, the ship hit a massive iceberg. Only 705 of its 2,227 passengers and crew survived.

The _Titanic_

The _Bounty_ On April 28, 1789, on a voyage from England to Tahiti and then to the West Indies, first mate Fletcher Christian mutinied against the ship's hated Captain Bligh. Bligh and 18 loyal sailors were set adrift in a lifeboat and survived a seven-week, 3,600-mile voyage to safety and were later rescued. The mutineers settled on remote Pitcairn Island in the South Pacific. Their descendants still live on the tiny island.

The _Lusitania_ Germany and Britain were already at war on May 7, 1915, when the British luxury liner _Lusitania_ was sunk off the Irish coast by a German submarine. Among the 1,195 who died were 128 U.S. citizens. Americans were outraged by the incident, and two years later, the U.S. entered World War I.

The _Endurance_ On December 5, 1914, Irish explorer Ernest Shackleton and 27 men set sail on the _Endurance_ for Antarctica. The crew planned to make a trans-Antarctic land crossing. Sixty miles from their landing point, the _Endurance_ became trapped in the ice, unable to break free. Shackleton navigated a lifeboat to a whaling station 800 miles away. Thanks to his daring mission, he was able to save his entire crew.

TFK Mystery Person

CLUE 1: I am an award-winning German engineer who was born in 1832.

CLUE 2: In 1876, I invented an amazing new kind of engine. It was a gas-powered, four-stroke engine that was quieter, more efficient and more reliable than other gas-powered or steam engines. It was the first of its kind.

CLUE 3: My engine led to the development of those used in cars, trucks and airplanes today.

WHO AM I?

(See Answer Key that begins on page 342.)

TFK Top 5 Longest Subway Systems

The Green Line, in Boston, Massachusetts, is the oldest subway line in the U.S. It started in 1897. The New York City subway, which opened in 1904, is the longest system in the U.S. Riders can travel 230 miles. That's longer than the distance between New York City and Boston! Here are the world's longest subways.

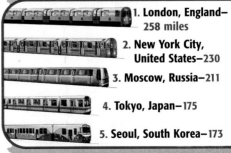

1. **London, England— 258 miles**

2. **New York City, United States—230**

3. **Moscow, Russia—211**

4. **Tokyo, Japan—175**

5. **Seoul, South Korea—173**

Source: Jane's Urban Transport Systems

Transportation

UNITED STATES

They Paint the Sky Red

Fireworks on the fourth of July are as American as apple pie. And one of America's greatest creators of these sky shows is a company called Fireworks by Grucci. A major Grucci show usually costs $40,000 and lasts 16 minutes. Six pyrotechnicians, or fireworks experts, are needed to wire and fire thousands of shells. Here's an inside look at what happens before the rockets' red glare.

1. THE BIG GUNS

Mortars (right) brought from the Grucci warehouse on Long Island, New York, are placed on a 90-foot-long barge. Each tube holds a single shell.

Sometimes one accidentally goes off inside its solid-steel casing. But the evenly spaced grid keeps other shells from igniting on the ground.

2. THE AMMO

Chief pyrotechnician Jeff Engel (top of middle column) carefully lowers a six-inch, five-pound shell into one of the mortars. It rests on top of several ounces of black powder, called a lift charge. When the powder is ignited, the firework is blasted skyward. It takes about three seconds for the firework to reach its peak, 300 to 600 feet up. That's when the shell explodes and you see a flash. Each burst's colors come from metallic compounds packed inside the shell: strontium nitrate erupts into red, barium nitrate shows as green and copper becomes blue.

3. IN THE BUNKER

Engineer Joe Russo (below) checks wiring in "the Hut." This command center, protected by thick steel walls, sits on a separate barge. Twelve hours before showtime, technicians start linking the fireworks through 5,000 feet of wiring to a firing panel in the Hut. During the show, the Hut crew taps by hand a launch sequence on a laptop computer, creating the display. Some operations still launch fireworks the old-fashioned way: people light fuses with a flare and get out the way…fast.

4. READY, AIM...

With all the tubes loaded and circuits tested, a tugboat nudges the barges into their offshore positions. The mortars (below) have been aimed in various directions—some straight up,

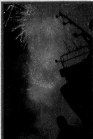

some angled—to paint an exciting picture on the largest possible canvas. Since what goes up must come down, every show has a "fallout zone." This is the distance that ensures that the spectators will be safe from ash and debris if a shell bursts too early or late.

5. ...FIRE!

All great fireworks shows build through "scenes"—a blue scene, a gold scene—toward a climax. The last salvo is the "finale rack," a rapid-fire sequence of dozens of smaller shells that create one huge, noisy, multicolored fantasia. On a typical July fourth, there are 10,000 public fireworks displays nationwide. Hard work and passion go into making each one look effortless and magnificent.

—*Johnny Dwyer*

THE U.S. FLAG

In 1777 the Continental Congress decided that the flag would have 13 alternating red and white stripes, for the 13 colonies, and 13 white stars on a blue background. A new star has been added for every new state. Today the flag has 50 stars. Shown here is an early version of the flag.

THE GREAT SEAL
OF THE UNITED STATES

Benjamin Franklin, John Adams and Thomas Jefferson began designing the Great Seal in 1776. The Great Seal is printed on the back of the $1 bill and is used on certain government documents, such as foreign treaties.

The bald eagle, our national bird, is at the center of the seal. It holds a banner in its beak. The motto says *E pluribus unum*, which is Latin for "out of many, one." This refers to the colonies that united to make a nation. In one claw, the eagle holds an olive branch for peace; in the other claw, it carries arrows for war.

THE PLEDGE OF ALLEGIANCE TO THE FLAG

The original pledge was published in the September 8, 1892, issue of *The Youth's Companion* in Boston. For years, there was a dispute over who should get credit for writing the pledge, James B. Upham or Francis Bellamy, both members of the magazine's staff. In 1939, the United States Flag Association decided that Bellamy deserved the credit.

Here's the original version of the pledge:

> **I pledge allegiance to my Flag and the Republic for which it stands— one nation indivisible—with liberty and justice for all.**

OTHER SYMBOLS
OF THE UNITED STATES

The **bald eagle** has been our national bird since 1782. The Founding Fathers had been unable to agree on which native bird should have the honor—Benjamin Franklin strongly preferred the turkey! Besides appearing on the Great Seal, the bald eagle is also pictured on coins, the $1 bill, all official U.S. seals and the President's flag.

The image of **Uncle Sam,** with his white hair and top hat, first became famous on World War I recruiting posters. The artist, James Montgomery Flagg, used himself as a model. But the term dates back to the War of 1812, when a meat-packer nicknamed Uncle Sam supplied beef to the troops. The initials for his nickname were quite appropriate!

THE LIBERTY BELL

The Liberty Bell was cast in England in 1752 for the Pennsylvania Statehouse (now named Independence Hall) in Philadelphia. It arrived in Philadelphia with a crack, and it was recast in 1753. The bell, which weighs about 2,000 pounds, is inscribed with a passage from Leviticus (a book of the Bible): "Proclaim liberty throughout all the land unto all the inhabitants thereof." The bell was rung on July 8, 1776, for the first public reading of the Declaration of Independence. The bell cracked again on July 8, 1835, while tolling the death of Chief Justice John Marshall. It has not been rung since.

A LOOK AT THE U.S. POPULATION*

U.S. POPULATION:
281,421,906

MALES: 138,053,563 (49.1% of population)
FEMALES: 143,368,343 (50.9% of population)
NUMBER OF KIDS AGES 5 TO 9: 20,549,505
NUMBER OF KIDS AGES 10 TO 14: 20,528,072
AVERAGE FAMILY SIZE: 3.14 people
MEDIAN AGE OF THE POPULATION: 35.3

RACE

75.1% of Americans are white.

12.5% are of Hispanic origin (they may be of any race).

12.3% are black.

3.6% are Asian, Native Hawaiian or Pacific Islander.

0.9% are Native American or Alaskan Native.

KIDS AT HOME

ABOUT 71% of kids live with two parents.

ABOUT 25% live with one parent.

NEARLY 4% live with neither parent.

ABOUT 5.5% live in a home maintained by a grandparent.

*Figures are based on Census 2000.

A LOOK BACK AT THE U.S. POPULATION

The figures do not include overseas armed forces.

1790	3,929,214	1900	75,994,575
1800	5,308,483	1920	105,710,620
1820	9,638,453	1950	150,697,361
1850	23,191,876	1980	226,545,805
1880	50,155,783	1990	248,709,873

Ancestry of the U.S. Population

The United States is indeed a big melting pot, made up of people of different ethnicities and cultures. Here are the top ancestries of U.S. citizens, according to the U.S. Census Bureau.

1. German
2. Irish
3. African American
4. English
5. American
6. Mexican
7. Italian
8. Polish
9. French
10. American Indian

Foreign-Born Americans

The term *foreign born* refers to Americans who were not born in this country. Below is a list of the top 10 places where these Americans were born.

1. Mexico
2. China
3. Philippines
4. India
5. Cuba
6. Vietnam
7. El Salvador
8. Korea
9. Dominican Republic
10. Canada

Source: Immigration and Naturalization Service

Did You Know?

When the nation was founded, the average American could expect to live to age 35. By 1900, the life expectancy had increased to 47.3; in 2003, the life expectancy for men was 74.8 years and 80.1 for women.

United States

245

Most Common First Names in the United States

Is your name Jacob or Michael, Sarah or Olivia? If it is, you have one of the most popular names in the country! Here's a list of the most popular first names.

GIRLS
1. Emily
2. Madison
3. Hannah
4. Emma
5. Alexis
6. Ashley
7. Abigail
8. Sarah
9. Samantha
10. Olivia

BOYS
1. Jacob
2. Michael
3. Joshua
4. Matthew
5. Ethan
6. Joseph
7. Andrew
8. Christopher
9. Daniel
10. Nicholas

TWINS
1. Jacob, Joshua
2. Taylor, Tyler
3. Matthew, Michael
4. Daniel, David
5. Faith, Hope
6. Madison, Morgan
7. Ethan, Evan
8. Mackenzie, Madison
9. Alexander, Andrew
10. Nathan, Nicholas

Did You Know?
Every year since 1940, there has been an average of 91,685 more boys born in the United States than girls.

International Adoptions

Each year, thousands of American families adopt infants and young children from all over the world. Here's a look at where children were born who were adopted from foreign countries in 2004.

RANK	COUNTRY OF BIRTH	NUMBER
1.	CHINA	7,044
2.	RUSSIA	5,865
3.	GUATEMALA	3,264
4.	SOUTH KOREA	1,716
5.	KAZAKHSTAN	826
6.	UKRAINE	723
7.	INDIA	406
8.	HAITI	356
9.	ETHIOPIA	289
10.	COLOMBIA	287

Source: U.S. State Department

Road Trip

Can you get the Bumpkin Family to Bellystone National Park? Begin the trip on the box near *Start*. Move two spaces down. Whenever you land on a new space, read the number next to the arrow and move that many spaces in the arrow's direction. If there are two directions, pick one. Remember: driving down the wrong path will drive you crazy!

(See Answer Key that begins on page 342.)

AMERICAN INDIANS

There are more than 550 federally recognized American Indian tribes in the United States, including 223 village groups in Alaska. *Federally recognized* means these tribes and groups have a special legal relationship with the U.S. government.

A Cherokee in traditional garb

AMERICAN INDIAN POPULATION BY STATE

Here are the states with the highest American Indian populations.

STATE	POPULATION
1. Oklahoma	252,420
2. California	242,164
3. Arizona	203,527
4. New Mexico	134,355
5. Washington	81,483
6. North Carolina	80,155
7. Texas	65,877
8. New York	62,651
9. Michigan	55,638
10. South Dakota	50,575

Source: U.S. Census Bureau

LARGEST AMERICAN INDIAN TRIBES

TRIBE NAME	POPULATION
1. Cherokee	729,533
2. Navajo	298,197
3. Latin American Indian	180,940
4. Choctaw	158,774
5. Sioux	153,360
6. Chippewa	149,669
7. Apache	96,833
8. Blackfeet	85,750
9. Iroquois	80,822
10. Pueblo	74,085

Source: U.S. Census Bureau

Largest Cities in the U.S.

CITY	POPULATION*
1. New York, New York	8,008,278
2. Los Angeles, California	3,694,820
3. Chicago, Illinois	2,896,016
4. Houston, Texas	1,953,631
5. Philadelphia, Pennsylvania	1,517,550
6. Phoenix, Arizona	1,321,045
7. San Diego, California	1,223,400
8. Dallas, Texas	1,188,580
9. San Antonio, Texas	1,144,646
10. Detroit, Michigan	951,270

*Figures are based on Census 2000.

Manhattan is a borough of New York City.

EXTREME Points of the U.S.

EXTREME POINTS	LATITUDE	LONGITUDE	DISTANCE (from the geographic center of the U.S. in Castle Rock, South Dakota)
Northernmost: Point Barrow, Alaska	71°23' N	156°29' W	2,507 miles (4,034 km)
Easternmost: West Quoddy Head, Maine	44°49' N	66°57' W	1,788 miles (2,997 km)
Southernmost: Ka Lae (South Cape), Hawaii	18°55' N	155°41' W	3,463 miles (5,573 km)
Westernmost: Cape Wrangell, Alaska (Attu Island)	52°55' N	172°27' E	3,625 miles (5,833 km)

Minutes Degrees Direction

PARK IT HERE!

There are 388 parks, monuments and recreation areas in the National Park System. Here are a few sites that are less well known but fascinating.

Much of Jewel Cave remains unexplored.

Biscayne National Park
Biscayne, Florida
This park in eastern Florida covers 270 square miles, and 95% of it is underwater. Divers and snorkelers hit the ocean to explore shipwrecks and a bright coral reef.

Women's Rights National Historical Park
Seneca Falls, New York
The Wesleyan Chapel, site of the first Women's Rights Convention in 1848, is part of this historical park. So is the home of women's rights leader Elizabeth Cady Stanton.

Biscayne National Park contains ancient coral reefs—and shipwrecks.

Cape Cod National Seashore
Wellfleet, Massachusetts
With its 40-mile stretch of beach and historic lighthouses, including Nauset Light and Highland Light, this park is a great place to swim in the Atlantic, explore nature trails and learn about our nation's seafaring past and present.

Hawaii Volcanoes National Park
Near Hilo, Hawaii
Visitors will find the Earth's most massive volcano, 13,677-foot Mauna Loa, and watch bubbling lava flow from the world's most active volcano, Kilauea.

Alcatraz Island
San Francisco, California
Sitting in the middle of San Francisco Bay, "the Rock" was the home of America's most famous federal prison.

Brown vs. Board of Education National Historic Site
Topeka, Kansas
The Supreme Court case that ended segregation in public schools originated in Topeka, Kansas. This site honors the decision. On view is a segregated elementary school once reserved for African-American kids.

Alaska's Mount Saint Elias is 18,008 feet high.

Jewel Cave
Black Hills, South Dakota
At 133 miles long, this is the third-longest cave in the world. It got its name because of its glittering calcite crystals, called popcorn, that look like green jewels. The cave was discovered relatively recently (1900), so it is one of the most unspoiled in the U.S. Visitors can see spectacular stalactites, stalagmites and other formations shaped like drapes, frost and balloons.

Wrangell-St. Elias
Copper Center, Alaska
At more than 9.6 million acres (the size of six Yellowstones), this is the largest unit in the National Park System. Four mountain ranges meet here and include nine of the 16 highest peaks in U.S. You could spend months exploring its lakes and rivers and viewing animals such as caribou, moose and bear. The park is the site of Malaspina Glacier, which is bigger than Rhode Island. This is more than a park—it's a spectacular world.

For more National Parks:
www.factmonster.com/nationalparks

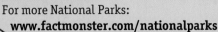

Lewis & Clark Slept Here

Two centuries after the famed explorers reached the Pacific Ocean, their feat has been marked by America's newest national park. The Lewis and Clark National Historical Park is made up of a dozen sites that sit along the Washington-Oregon border. The new park rings a huge outlet of the Columbia River and extends along 40 miles of beach and Pacific coast.

The park's 53.8 miles of trails wind through coastal rain forests. Hikers and bicyclists can retrace Lewis's final push to the sea on the eight-mile discovery trail. In other areas, visitors can see all kinds of Pacific animals, including beavers, bald eagles and Roosevelt elk. One of the most scenic sites is Ecola State Park, in Oregon, where surfers ride chilly waves. The Lower Columbia River Water Trail is a 146-mile water route that runs to the ocean.

Another part of the park is Oregon's Indian Beach. This stretch of coast is where Clark, Sacajawea and 12 other expedition members hiked to view the remains of a beached whale. You can also visit Washington's Cape Disappointment, where Clark led a team of 11 men to get their first close-up look at the Pacific. The view hasn't changed since then, but there's more to do now—the oceanfront is great for camping, whale watching, picnicking and fishing.

Source: LIFE magazine

American Firsts

- **Bank established:** Bank of North America, Philadelphia, 1781
- **Birth in America to English parents:** Virginia Dare, born on Roanoke Island, N.C., 1587
- **African American elected to U.S. Senate:** Hiram Revels, 1870, Mississippi
- **African American elected to U.S. House of Representatives:** Jefferson Long, Georgia, 1870
- **African American associate Justice of U.S. Supreme Court:** Thurgood Marshall; appointed October 2, 1967
- **College:** Harvard, founded 1636
- **Five and Dime store:** Founded by Frank Woolworth, Utica, N.Y., 1879

- **Newspaper published daily:** *Pennsylvania Packet and General Advertiser,* Philadelphia, September 1784
- **Postage stamps issued:** 1847
- **Public school:** Boston Latin School, Boston, 1635
- **Skyscraper:** Home Insurance Co., Chicago, 1885

Hiram Revels

- **Woman member of U.S. House of Representatives:** Jeannette Rankin of Montana; elected November 1916
- **Woman member of U.S. Senate:** Rebecca Latimer Felton of Georgia; appointed October 3, 1922
- **Woman member of U.S. Supreme Court:** Sandra Day O'Connor; appointed July 1981
- **Woman cabinet member:** Frances Perkins, Secretary of Labor; appointed 1933

Harvard

Fort DeSoto Park–North Beach is a sandy paradise.

Beach Hall of Fame

Each year since 1991, Dr. Stephen P. Leatherman, also known as " Dr. Beach," has put together a list of the top 10 beaches in the United States. These are the ones that have earned the No. 1 slot.

YEAR	NAME	LOCATION
2005	Fort DeSoto Park–North Beach	Florida
2004	Hanauma Bay	Hawaii
2003	Kaanapali	Hawaii
2002	Saint Joseph Peninsula State Park	Florida
2001	Poipu Beach Park	Hawaii

ROUSING RIDES

About 328 million people visit U.S. amusement parks each year, where roller coasters are the top attraction. Here are some of the wildest thrill rides around.

Hydra

KINGDA KA

Six Flags Great Adventure Jackson, New Jersey

The world's tallest and fastest. It rockets from a dead stop to 128 m.p.h. in 3.5 seconds, then shoots to a 456-foot crest. One roller-coaster expert calls it "one of the most exhilarating thrills around."

SHEIKRA

Busch Gardens Tampa Bay, Tampa

This "Dive" coaster plunges riders 200 vertical feet, twists them through an inverted loop, then drops them another 138 feet—into an underground tunnel. For a finale, riders shoot through a wall of water.

HYDRA: THE REVENGE

Dorney Park Allentown, Pennsylvania

You don't ride Hydra, you dangle from it—through narrow canyons, around zero-gravity corkscrews, into a winding "cobra roll." One thrill ride expert calls it "the best of floorless coasters."

POWDERKEG

Silver Dollar City Branson, Missouri

The ride is called family friendly, but families will be pushing almost 4 g's, tilting through banked turns and rattling over three massive hills on this ride through the Ozarks.

HADES

Mt. Olympus Water and Theme Park Wisconsin Dells, Wisconsin

This wooden-racked newcomer features a 140-foot drop and coasterdom's longest below-surface tunnel. A thrill-ride veteran says, "Some of the most extreme banking I've ever seen on a woodie."

Source: LIFE magazine

ROADSIDE ATTRACTIONS

Going on a road trip? If you prefer offbeat destinations, check out these roadside attractions and odd museums.

World's Largest Ball of Paint

Alexandria, Indiana

In 1977, Michael Carmichael started painting over a baseball, adding layers of paint, day after day, year after year. After more than 20,000 coats of paint, the ball weighs more than 1,300 pounds. Visitors can paint the ball themselves and become part of ball-of-paint history.

Scale Model of the Solar System

Peoria, Illinois

The Lakeview Museum Community Solar System is home to the biggest little solar system in the world. The planets and their orbits are in scale (42 feet equals 1 million miles). The museum's planetarium, a big yellow dome 36 feet in diameter, stands in for the Sun. Forty miles away, astronaut-tourists can find Pluto, with a diameter of one inch. Distant comets are located as far away as the South Pole!

Barney Smith's Toilet Seat Art Museum

San Antonio, Texas

Nearly 700 toilet seats—all painted or engraved by Barney Smith—are on display at this unusual museum. Many have objects glued on them, such as model trains, dog licenses and Boy Scout badges. Smith sees himself as an artist who just happens to use a different type of canvas.

Topiary Painting

Columbus, Ohio

A Sunday on the Island of La Grande Jatte is a famous painting by Georges Seurat. It shows people relaxing by a river. Artist James T. Mason has reproduced this work, using electric clippers instead of a brush. Mason's art is topiary—the cutting and trimming of trees and bushes into shapes. His green version of the painting consists of 54 topiary people, as well as eight boats, three dogs, a monkey and a cat. The tallest figure is 12 feet tall. They all appear in a park by a small lake, where strollers can become part of the "picture."

PEZ Museum

Easton, Pennsylvania

It's a PEZ lover's dream. Nearly 1,500 PEZ dispensers fill the museum, including a Disney PEZ dispenser that sits in a 10-foot-high castle; Halloween-themed PEZ dispensers are in a haunted house; and a psychedelic PEZ dispenser is next to a real Volkswagen Beetle car that seems to be crashing through a wall. The hand-held candy dispensers were first produced more than 50 years ago, and today collectors covet them. The museum displays such PEZ prizes as NFL, *Star Wars,* Charlie Brown, Elton John and Santa Claus dispensers. Best of all, you can buy PEZ at the museum and start your own collection.

Paper House

Rockport, Massachusetts

In 1922, Swedish immigrant Ellis Stenman began building a two-room cottage made almost entirely out of newspaper. The house is framed with wood, but the walls are made of 215 layers of newspaper. Stenman made his own glue, out of flour, water and apple peels. The inside walls are decorated with intricately folded and quilted newspapers. Even the furniture and curtains are made of newspaper. Stenman wrapped paper around wire to build chairs, desks and lamps. In all, he used about 100,000 newspapers. Talk about recycling!

PACIFIC
OCEAN

Seattle
Tacoma
Olympia
Spokane

Washington

Portland
Great Falls
Montana
Missouri River
Bisma

Salem
Helena
Billings

Eugene

Oregon
Boise
Idaho
—Yellowstone
National
Park
Rapid City
P

Wyoming

California

Reno
Nevada
*Great
Salt
Lake*
Salt Lake City
Cheyenne

Santa Rosa
Sacramento
Carson City

San Francisco
Modesto
Utah
Denver

San Jose
*Yosemite
National
Park*
Colorado Springs

Fresno
Colorado
Pueblo

*Death
Valley*
Las Vegas

Los Angeles
*Grand
Canyon*
Flagstaff
Santa Fe

Escondido
Phoenix
Albuquerque
Amarillo

San Diego
Lubbock

Arizona
New Mexico
At

Tucson

El Paso
Texa

Kauai

Oahu
Hawaii
Honolulu
Maui

PACIFIC
OCEAN
Hawaii

ARCTIC OCEAN

RUSSIA

MEXICO

Alaska
CANADA

**BERING
SEA**
Anchorage
Juneau

Aleutian Islands

0 mi.   300 mi.   600 mi.

0 km   400 km   800 km

PACIFIC OCEAN

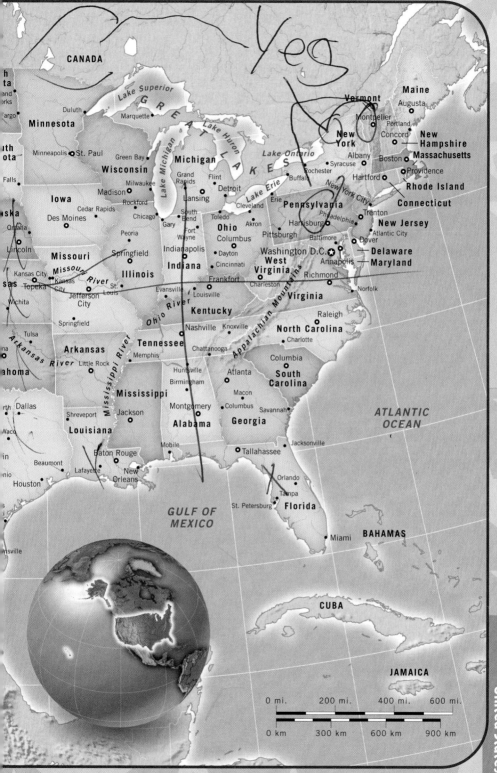

ALABAMA

★ CAPITAL: **MONTGOMERY** ★ ABBREVIATION: **ALA.**
★ LARGEST CITY: **BIRMINGHAM** ★ POSTAL CODE: **AL**

Origin of name: **May come from a Choctaw word meaning "thicket-clearers"**

Entered union (rank): **December 14, 1819 (22)**

Motto: *Audemus jura nostra defendere* **(We dare defend our rights)**

Tree: **southern longleaf pine**

Flower: **camellia**

Bird: **yellowhammer (yellow-shafted flicker)**

Other: **dance: square dance; nut: pecan**

Song: **"Alabama"**

Nickname: **Yellowhammer State**

Residents: **Alabamian, Alabaman**

Land area: **50,750 square miles (131,443 sq km)**

Population (2005): **4,530,182**

Home of: **George Washington Carver, who discovered more than 300 uses for peanuts**

Did You Know?
The Confederacy was founded in Montgomery in 1861.

ALASKA

★ CAPITAL: **JUNEAU** ★ ABBREVIATION: **ALASKA**
★ LARGEST CITY: **ANCHORAGE** ★ POSTAL CODE: **AK**

Origin of name: **From an Aleut word meaning "great land" or "that which the sea breaks against"**

Entered union (rank): **January 3, 1959 (49)**

Motto: **North to the future**

Tree: **Sitka spruce**

Flower: **forget-me-not**

Bird: **willow ptarmigan**

Other: **sport: dog mushing**

Song: **"Alaska's Flag"**

Nicknames: **The Last Frontier and Land of the Midnight Sun**

Residents: **Alaskan**

Land area: **570,374 square miles (1,477,267 sq km)**

Population (2005): **655,435**

Home of: **The longest coastline in the U.S., 6,640 miles, which is greater than that of all other states combined**

Did You Know?
When it was purchased for about 2¢ an acre in 1867, Alaska was called "Seward's Folly."

ARIZONA

Origin of name: **From the Native American Arizonac, meaning "little spring"**

Entered union (rank): **February 14, 1912 (48)**

Motto: *Ditat deus* (God enriches)

Tree: palo verde

Flower: flower of saguaro cactus

Bird: cactus wren

Other: gemstone: turquoise; neckwear: bolo tie

Song: "Arizona"

Nickname: Grand Canyon State

Residents: Arizonan, Arizonian

Land area: 113,642 square miles (296,400 sq km)

Population (2005): 5,743,834

Home of: The most telescopes in the world, in Tucson

Phoenix

Did You Know?
London Bridge was shipped to Lake Havasu City and rebuilt there stone-by-stone.

ARKANSAS

Origin of name: **From the Quapaw Indians**

Entered union (rank): **June 15, 1836 (25)**

Motto: *Regnat populus* (The people rule)

Tree: pine

Flower: apple blossom

Bird: mockingbird

Other: fruit and vegetable: pink tomato; insect: honeybee

Song: "Arkansas"

Nickname: Natural State

Residents: Arkansan

Land area: 52,075 square miles (134,874 sq km)

Population (2005): 2,752,629

Home of: The only active diamond mine in the U.S.

Little Rock

Did You Know?
Arkansas's Hattie Caraway was the first woman elected to the U.S. Senate.

CALIFORNIA

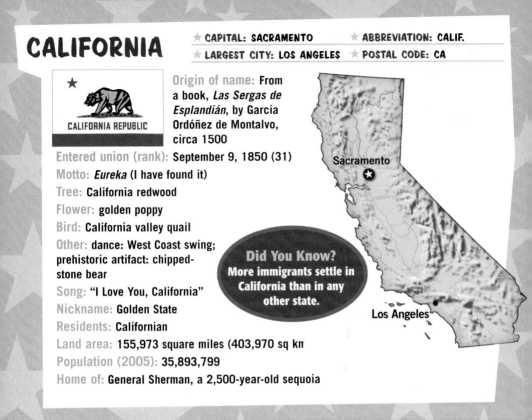

CALIFORNIA REPUBLIC

Origin of name: From a book, *Las Sergas de Esplandián*, by Garcia Ordóñez de Montalvo, circa 1500

Entered union (rank): September 9, 1850 (31)

Motto: *Eureka* (I have found it)

Tree: California redwood

Flower: golden poppy

Bird: California valley quail

Other: dance: West Coast swing; prehistoric artifact: chipped-stone bear

Song: "I Love You, California"

Nickname: Golden State

Residents: Californian

Land area: 155,973 square miles (403,970 sq km

Population (2005): 35,893,799

Home of: General Sherman, a 2,500-year-old sequoia

Sacramento

Los Angeles

Did You Know?
More immigrants settle in California than in any other state.

COLORADO

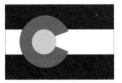

Origin of name: From the Spanish, "ruddy" or "red"

Entered union (rank): August 1, 1876 (38)

Motto: *Nil sine numine* (Nothing without providence)

Tree: Colorado blue spruce

Flower: Rocky Mountain columbine

Bird: lark bunting

Other: fossil: *Stegosaurus;* gemstone: aquamarine

Song: "Where the Columbines Grow"

Nickname: Centennial State

Residents: Coloradan, Coloradoan

Land area: 103,730 square miles (268,660 sq km)

Population (2005): 4,601,403

Home of: The world's largest silver nugget (1,840 pounds), found in 1894 near Aspen

Denver

Did You Know?
There are 54 peaks in the Rocky Mountains that rise above 14,000 feet.

CONNECTICUT

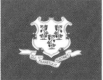

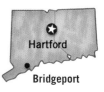

★ CAPITAL: HARTFORD ★ ABBREVIATION: CONN.
★ LARGEST CITY: BRIDGEPORT ★ POSTAL CODE: CT

Origin of name: From the Mohegan Indian word Quinnehtukqut, meaning "beside the long tidal river"

Entered union (rank): January 9, 1788 (5)

Motto: *Qui transtulit sustinet* (He who transplanted still sustains)

Tree: white oak

Flower: mountain laurel

Bird: American robin

Other: hero: Nathan Hale; heroine: Prudence Crandall

Song: "Yankee Doodle"

Nickname: Nutmeg State

Residents: Nutmegger

Land area: 4,845 square miles (12,550 sq km)

Population (2005): 3,503,604

Home of: The first American cookbook—*American Cookery* by Amelia Simmons—published in Hartford in 1796

Did You Know?
The U.S. Constitution was modeled after Connecticut's colonial laws.

DELAWARE

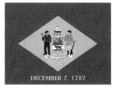

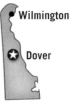

★ CAPITAL: DOVER ★ ABBREVIATION: DEL.
★ LARGEST CITY: WILMINGTON ★ POSTAL CODE: DE

Origin of name: From Delaware River and Bay, named for Sir Thomas West, Baron De La Warr

Entered union (rank): December 7, 1787 (1)

Motto: Liberty and independence

Tree: American holly

Flower: peach blossom

Bird: blue hen chicken

Other: colors: colonial blue and buff; insect: ladybug

Song: "Our Delaware"

Nicknames: Diamond State, First State and Small Wonder

Residents: Delawarean

Land area: 1,955 square miles (5,153 sq km)

Population (2005): 830,364

Home of: The first log cabins in North America, built in 1683 by Swedish immigrants

Did You Know?
Delaware was the first of the original 13 colonies to ratify the U.S. Constitution.

FLORIDA

★ CAPITAL: **TALLAHASSEE**

★ LARGEST CITY: **JACKSONVILLE**

★ ABBREVIATION: **FLA.**

★ POSTAL CODE: **FL**

Tallahassee

Jacksonville

Origin of name: **From the Spanish, meaning "feast of flowers"**

Entered union (rank): **March 3, 1845 (27)**

Motto: **In God we trust**

Tree: **Sabal palm**

Flower: **orange blossom**

Bird: **mockingbird**

Other: **shell: horse conch; soil: Myakka fine sand**

Song: **"The Sewanee River"**

Nickname: **Sunshine State**

Residents: **Floridian, Floridan**

Land area: **54,153 square miles (140,256 sq km)**

Population (2005): **17,397,161**

Home of: **U.S. spacecraft launchings from Cape Canaveral, formerly Cape Kennedy**

Did You Know?
There are two rivers in Florida with the name Withlacoochee.

GEORGIA

★ CAPITAL: **ATLANTA**

★ LARGEST CITY: **ATLANTA**

★ ABBREVIATION: **GA.**

★ POSTAL CODE: **GA**

Origin of name: **In honor of George II of England**

Entered union (rank): **January 2, 1788 (4)**

Atlanta

Motto: **Wisdom, justice and moderation**

Tree: **live oak**

Flower: **Cherokee rose**

Bird: **brown thrasher**

Other: **crop: peanut; fossil: shark tooth**

Song: **"Georgia on My Mind"**

Nicknames: **Peach State and Empire State of the South**

Residents: **Georgian**

Land area: **57,919 square miles (150,010 sq km)**

Population (2005): **8,829,383**

Home of: **One of the world's largest college campuses, Berry College, in Rome**

Did You Know?
During the Civil War, Atlanta was burned and nearly destroyed by Union troops.

HAWAII

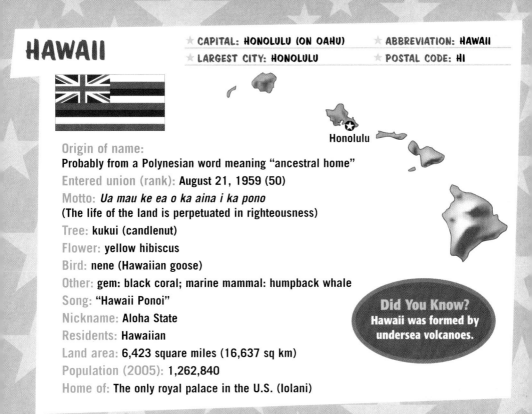

Honolulu

Origin of name:
Probably from a Polynesian word meaning "ancestral home"

Entered union (rank): August 21, 1959 (50)

Motto: *Ua mau ke ea o ka aina i ka pono*
(The life of the land is perpetuated in righteousness)

Tree: kukui (candlenut)

Flower: yellow hibiscus

Bird: nene (Hawaiian goose)

Other: gem: black coral; marine mammal: humpback whale

Song: "Hawaii Ponoi"

Nickname: Aloha State

Residents: Hawaiian

Land area: 6,423 square miles (16,637 sq km)

Population (2005): 1,262,840

Home of: The only royal palace in the U.S. (Iolani)

Did You Know?
Hawaii was formed by undersea volcanoes.

IDAHO

Origin of name: Although popularly believed to be a Native American word, it is an invented name whose meaning is unknown.

Did You Know?
Idaho produces about 25% of the country's potato crop.

Boise

Entered union (rank): July 3, 1890 (43)

Motto: *Esto perpetua* (It is forever)

Tree: white pine

Flower: lilac

Bird: mountain bluebird

Other: fish: cutthroat trout; horse: Appaloosa

Song: "Here We Have Idaho"

Nickname: Gem State

Residents: Idahoan

Land area: 82,751 square miles (214,325 sq km)

Population (2005): 1,393,262

Home of: The longest Main Street in America, 33 miles, in Island Park

United States

ILLINOIS

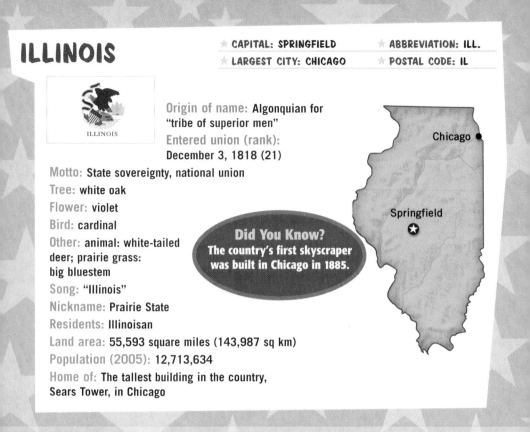

Origin of name: Algonquian for "tribe of superior men"

Entered union (rank): December 3, 1818 (21)

Motto: State sovereignty, national union

Tree: white oak

Flower: violet

Bird: cardinal

Other: animal: white-tailed deer; prairie grass: big bluestem

Song: "Illinois"

Nickname: Prairie State

Residents: Illinoisan

Land area: 55,593 square miles (143,987 sq km)

Population (2005): 12,713,634

Home of: The tallest building in the country, Sears Tower, in Chicago

Did You Know?
The country's first skyscraper was built in Chicago in 1885.

Chicago ●

Springfield ✪

INDIANA

★ CAPITAL: INDIANAPOLIS ★ ABBREVIATION: IND.
★ LARGEST CITY: INDIANAPOLIS ★ POSTAL CODE: IN

Origin of name: Means "land of Indians"

Entered union (rank): December 11, 1816 (19)

Motto: The crossroads of America

Tree: tulip tree

Flower: peony

Bird: cardinal

Other: river: Wabash; stone: limestone

Song: "On the Banks of the Wabash, Far Away"

Nickname: Hoosier State

Residents: Indianan, Indianian

Land area: 35,870 sq miles (92,904 sq km)

Population (2005): 6,237,569

Home of: The famous car race, the Indianapolis 500

Indianapolis ✪

Did You Know?
Wabash, Indiana, was the first U.S. city to be lighted by electricity.

IOWA

Origin of name: Probably from an Indian word meaning "this is the place"

Entered union (rank): December 28, 1846 (29)

Motto: Our liberties we prize and our rights we will maintain

Tree: oak

Flower: wild rose

Bird: eastern goldfinch

Other: fossil: crinoid; rock: geode

Song: "Song of Iowa"

Nickname: Hawkeye State

Residents: Iowan

Land area: 55,875 square miles (144,716 sq km)

Population (2005): 2,954,451

Home of: The shortest and steepest railroad in the U.S., in Dubuque: 296 feet, 60° incline

Des Moines

Did You Know?
The Eskimo Pie, the first chocolate-covered ice-cream bar, was invented in Onawa in 1921.

KANSAS

Origin of name: From a Sioux word meaning "people of the south wind"

Entered union (rank): January 29, 1861 (34)

Motto: *Ad astra per aspera* (To the stars through difficulties)

Tree: cottonwood

Flower: sunflower

Bird: western meadowlark

Other: animal: buffalo; reptile: ornate box turtle

Song: "Home on the Range"

Nicknames: Sunflower State and Jayhawk State

Residents: Kansan

Land area: 81,823 square miles (211,922 sq km)

Population (2005): 2,735,502

Home of: Helium, discovered by scientists in 1905 at the University of Kansas

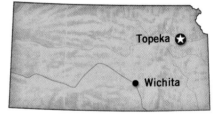

Topeka

Wichita

Did You Know?
The world's largest ball of twine is in Cawker City.

United States

261

KENTUCKY

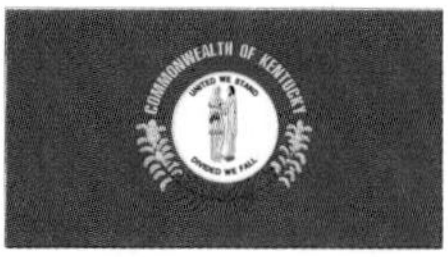

Origin of name: From an Iroquoian word (Kentahten) meaning "land of tomorrow"

Entered union (rank): June 1, 1792 (15)

Motto: United we stand, divided we fall

Tree: tulip poplar

Flower: goldenrod

Bird: Kentucky cardinal

Other: bluegrass song: "Blue Moon of Kentucky"; horse: Thoroughbred

Song: "My Old Kentucky Home"

Nickname: Bluegrass State

Residents: Kentuckian

Land area: 39,732 square miles (102,907 sq km)

Population (2005): 4,145,922

Home of: The largest underground cave in the world, the Mammoth-Flint Cave system, over 300 miles long

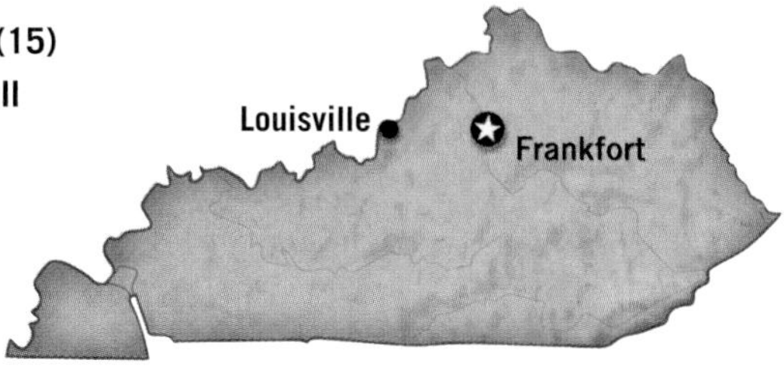

Louisville · Frankfort

Did You Know?
"Happy Birthday to You" was written by two Louisville teachers.

LOUISIANA

Origin of name: In honor of Louis XIV of France

Entered union (rank): April 30, 1812 (18)

Motto: Union, justice and confidence

Tree: bald cypress

Flower: magnolia

Bird: eastern brown pelican

Other: crustacean: crawfish; dog: Catahoula leopard hound

Songs: "Give Me Louisiana" and "You Are My Sunshine"

Nickname: Pelican State

Residents: Louisianan, Louisianian

Land area: 43,566 square miles (112,836 sq km)

Population (2005): 4,515,770

Home of: About 98% of the world's crawfish

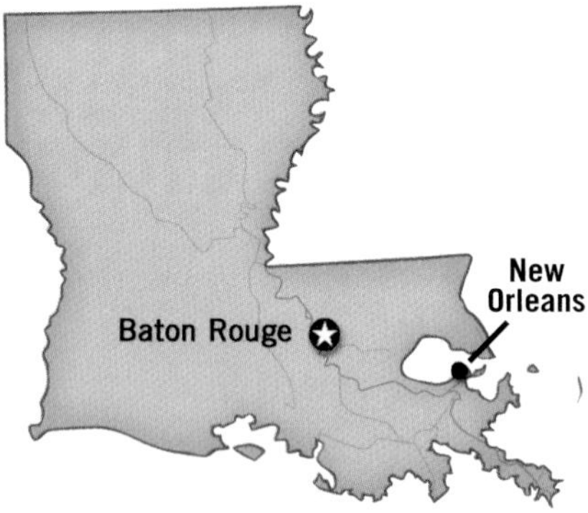

New Orleans

Baton Rouge

Did You Know?
Tourists have been flocking to New Orleans for Mardi Gras since 1838.

MAINE

Origin of name: **First used to distinguish the mainland from the coastal islands**

Entered union (rank): **March 15, 1820 (23)**

Motto: *Dirigo* **(I lead)**

Tree: **white pine**

Flower: **white pine cone and tassel**

Bird: **chickadee**

Other: **animal: moose; cat: Maine coon cat**

Song: **"State of Maine Song"**

Nickname: **Pine Tree State**

Residents: **Mainer**

Land area: **30,865 square miles (79,939 sq km)**

Population (2005): **1,317,253**

Home of: **The most easterly point in the U.S., West Quoddy Head**

Did You Know?
Maine is the world's largest producer of blueberries.

MARYLAND

Origin of name: **In honor of Henrietta Maria (Queen of Charles I of England)**

Entered union (rank): **April 28, 1788 (7)**

Motto: *Fatti maschii, parole femine* **(Manly deeds, womanly words)**

Tree: **white oak**

Flower: **black-eyed Susan**

Bird: **Baltimore oriole**

Other: **crustacean: Maryland blue crab; sport: jousting**

Song: **"Maryland! My Maryland!"**

Nicknames: **Free State and Old Line State**

Residents: **Marylander**

Land area: **9,775 square miles (25,316 sq km)**

Population (2005): **5,558,058**

Home of: **The first umbrella factory in the U.S., opened in 1828, in Baltimore**

Did You Know?
During the Civil War, Maryland was a slave state but part of the Union.

United States

263

MASSACHUSETTS

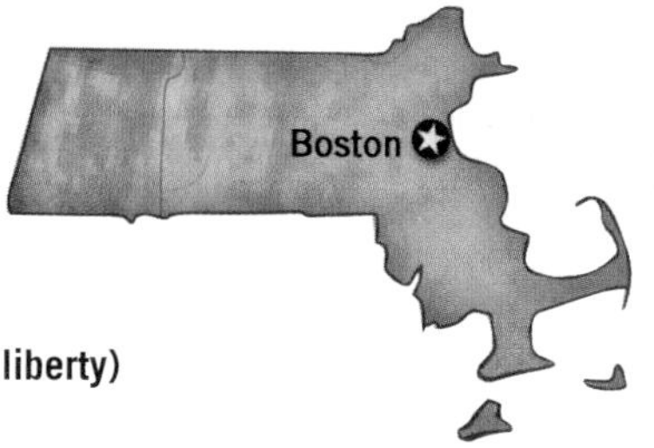

Origin of name: From the Massachusett Indian tribe, meaning "at or about the great hill"

Boston ✪

Entered union (rank): February 6, 1788 (6)

Motto: *Ense petit placidam sub libertate quietem*
(By the sword we seek peace, but peace only under liberty)

Tree: American elm

Flower: mayflower

Bird: chickadee

Other: beverage: cranberry juice; dessert: Boston cream pie

Song: "All Hail to Massachusetts"

Nicknames: Bay State and Old Colony State

Residents: Bay Stater

Land area: 7,838 square miles (20,300 sq km)

Population (2005): 6,416,505

Home of: The first World Series, played between the Boston Pilgrims and the Pittsburgh Pirates in 1903

Did You Know?
The first basketball game was played in Springfield, Massachusetts, in 1891.

MICHIGAN

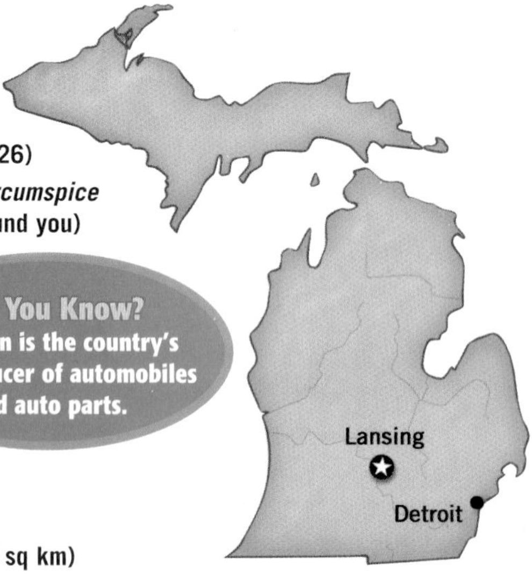

Origin of name: From an Indian word (Michigana) meaning "great or large lake"

Entered union (rank): January 26, 1837 (26)

Motto: *Si quaeris peninsulam amoenam circumspice*
(If you seek a pleasant peninsula, look around you)

Tree: white pine

Flower: apple blossom

Bird: robin

Other: reptile: painted turtle; wildflower: Dwarf Lake iris

Song: "Michigan, My Michigan"

Nickname: Wolverine State

Residents: Michigander, Michiganian

Land area: 56,809 square miles (147,135 sq km)

Population (2005): 10,112,620

Home of: Battle Creek, "Cereal City," producer of most of the breakfast cereal in the U.S.

Did You Know?
Michigan is the country's top producer of automobiles and auto parts.

Lansing ✪

Detroit

MINNESOTA

* CAPITAL: **ST. PAUL**
* LARGEST CITY: **MINNEAPOLIS**
* ABBREVIATION: **MINN.**
* POSTAL CODE: **MN**

Origin of name: From a Dakota Indian word meaning "sky-tinted water"

Entered union (rank): May 11, 1858 (32)

Motto: *L'Étoile du nord* (The north star)

Tree: red (or Norway) pine

Flower: lady slipper

Bird: common loon

Other: drink: milk; mushroom: morel

Song: "Hail Minnesota"

Nicknames: North Star State, Gopher State and Land of 10,000 Lakes

Residents: Minnesotan

Land area: 79,617 square miles (206,207 sq km)

Population (2005): 5,100,958

Home of: One of the world's oldest rocks, 3.8 billion years old

Did You Know? Although it's called "Land of 10,000 Lakes," Minnesota has more than 15,000 lakes.

MISSISSIPPI

* CAPITAL: **JACKSON**
* LARGEST CITY: **JACKSON**
* ABBREVIATION: **MISS.**
* POSTAL CODE: **MS**

Origin of name: From an Indian word meaning "Father of Waters"

Entered union (rank): December 10, 1817 (20)

Motto: *Virtute et armis* (By valor and arms)

Tree: magnolia

Flower: magnolia

Bird: mockingbird

Other: stone: petrified wood; water mammal: bottlenose dolphin

Song: "Go, Mississippi"

Nickname: Magnolia State

Residents: Mississippian

Land area: 46,914 square miles (121,506 sq km)

Population (2005): 2,902,966

Home of: Coca-Cola, first bottled in 1894 in Vicksburg

Did You Know? Hernando de Soto explored the Mississippi River in 1540.

MISSOURI

Origin of name: Named after the Missouri Indian tribe; means "town of the large canoes"

Entered union (rank): August 10, 1821 (24)

Motto: *Salus populi suprema lex esto* (The welfare of the people shall be the supreme law)

Tree: flowering dogwood

Flower: hawthorn

Bird: bluebird

Other: musical instrument: fiddle; tree nut: eastern black walnut

Song: "Missouri Waltz"

Nickname: Show-Me State

Residents: Missourian

Land area: 68,898 square miles (178,446 sq km)

Population (2005): 5,754,618

Home of: Mark Twain and some of his characters, such as Tom Sawyer and Huckleberry Finn

Did You Know?
The strongest earthquake in U.S. history was centered in New Madrid in 1811.

MONTANA

Origin of name: The Latin form of a Spanish word meaning "mountainous"

Entered union (rank): November 8, 1889 (41)

Motto: *Oro y plata* (Gold and silver)

Tree: ponderosa pine

Flower: bitterroot

Bird: western meadowlark

Other: animal: grizzly bear; stones: sapphire and agate

Song: "Montana"

Nickname: Treasure State

Residents: Montanan

Land area: 145,556 square miles (376,991 sq km)

Population (2005): 926,865

Home of: Grasshopper Glacier, named for the grasshoppers that can be seen frozen in ice

Did You Know?
Glacier National Park has 60 glaciers, 200 lakes and countless streams.

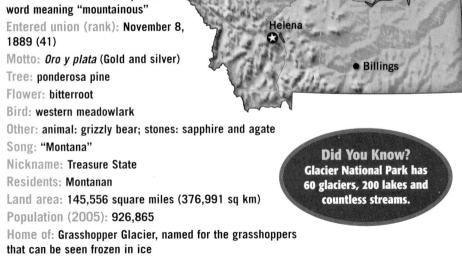

NEBRASKA

Origin of name: **From an Oto Indian word meaning "flat water"**

Omaha
Lincoln ✪

Entered union (rank): **March 1, 1867 (37)**
Motto: **Equality before the law**
Tree: **cottonwood**
Flower: **goldenrod**
Bird: **western meadowlark**
Other: **ballad: "A Place Like Nebraska";
soft drink: Kool-Aid**
Song: **"Beautiful Nebraska"**
Nicknames: **Cornhusker State and Beef State**
Residents: **Nebraskan**
Land area: **76,878 square miles (199,113 sq km)**
Population (2005): **1,747,214**
Home of: **The only roller-skating museum in the world, in Lincoln**

Did You Know?
A favorite summer drink, Kool-Aid, was invented in Hastings.

NEVADA

Origin of name: **From the Spanish, "snowcapped"**
Entered union (rank): **October 31, 1864 (36)**
Motto: **All for our country**
Trees: **single-leaf piñon and bristlecone pine**
Flower: **sagebrush**
Bird: **mountain bluebird**
Other: **metal: silver; reptile: desert tortoise**
Song: **"Home Means Nevada"**
Nicknames: **Sagebrush State, Silver State and Battle Born State**
Residents: **Nevadan, Nevadian**
Land area: **109,806 square miles (284,397 sq km)**
Population (2005): **2,334,771**
Home of: **The Devil's Hole pupfish, found only in Devil's Hole, an underground pool near Death Valley**

✪ Carson City
Las Vegas ——●

Did You Know?
Nevada is the driest state in the country, with about seven inches of rainfall each year.

United States

267

NEW HAMPSHIRE

★ CAPITAL: **CONCORD**
★ LARGEST CITY: **MANCHESTER**
★ ABBREVIATION: **N.H.**
★ POSTAL CODE: **NH**

Origin of name: **From the English county of Hampshire**
Entered union (rank): **June 21, 1788 (9)**
Motto: **Live free or die**

Tree: white birch
Flower: purple lilac
Bird: purple finch
Other: amphibian: spotted newt; sport: skiing
Songs: "Old New Hampshire" and "New Hampshire, My New Hampshire"
Nickname: Granite State
Residents: New Hampshirite
Land area: 8,969 square miles (23,231 sq km)
Population (2005): 1,299,500
Home of: Artificial rain, first used near Concord in 1947 to fight a forest fire

Concord
Manchester

Did You Know?
The world's highest wind speed, 231 m.p.h., was recorded on top of Mount Washington.

NEW JERSEY

★ CAPITAL: **TRENTON**
★ LARGEST CITY: **NEWARK**
★ ABBREVIATION: **N.J.**
★ POSTAL CODE: **NJ**

Origin of name: **From the Isle of Jersey in the English Channel**
Entered union (rank): **December 18, 1787 (3)**
Motto: **Liberty and prosperity**

Tree: red oak
Flower: purple violet
Bird: eastern goldfinch
Other: folk dance: square dance; shell: knobbed whelk
Song: "I'm from New Jersey"
Nickname: Garden State
Residents: New Jerseyite, New Jerseyan
Land area: 7,419 square miles (19,215 sq km)
Population (2005): 8,698,879
Home of: The world's first drive-in movie theater, built in 1933 near Camden

Newark
Trenton

Did You Know?
The street names in the game Monopoly were named after streets in Atlantic City.

NEW MEXICO

Origin of name: From Mexico

Entered union (rank): January 6, 1912 (47)

Motto: *Crescit eundo* (It grows as it goes)

Tree: piñon

Flower: yucca

Bird: roadrunner

Other: cookie: biscochito; vegetables: chilies and beans

Song: "O Fair New Mexico"

Nickname: Land of Enchantment

Residents: New Mexican

Land area: 121,365 square miles (314,334 sq km)

Population (2005): 1,903,289

Home of: Smokey Bear, a cub orphaned by fire in 1950, buried in Smokey Bear Historical State Park in 1976

Santa Fe
Albuquerque

Did You Know?
Each night thousands of bats swarm out of Carlsbad Caverns to eat insects.

NEW YORK

Origin of name: In honor of the Duke of York

Entered union (rank): July 26, 1788 (11)

Motto: *Excelsior* (Ever upward)

Tree: sugar maple

Flower: rose

Bird: bluebird

Other: animal: beaver; muffin: apple

Song: "I Love New York"

Nickname: Empire State

Residents: New Yorker

Land area: 47,224 square miles (122,310 sq km)

Population (2005): 19,227,088

Home of: The first presidential Inauguration. George Washington took the oath of office in New York City on April 30, 1789.

Albany

New York City

Did You Know?
New York City was one of the nation's first capitals. Congress met there from 1785 to 1790.

United States

269

NORTH CAROLINA

★ CAPITAL: **RALEIGH**
★ LARGEST CITY: **CHARLOTTE**
★ ABBREVIATION: **N.C.**
★ POSTAL CODE: **NC**

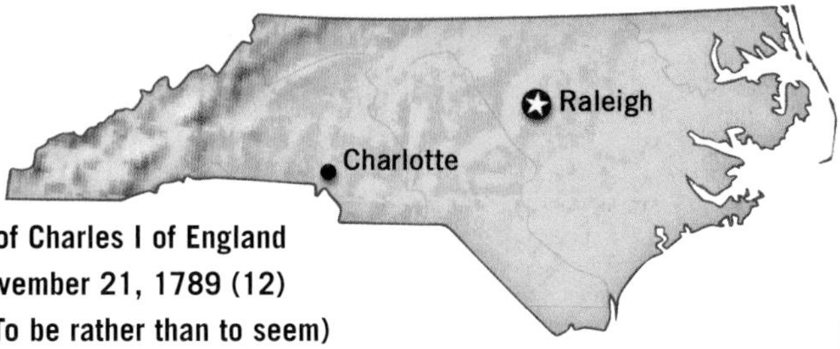

Origin of name: In honor of Charles I of England
Entered union (rank): November 21, 1789 (12)
Motto: *Esse quam videri* (To be rather than to seem)
Tree: pine
Flower: dogwood
Bird: cardinal
Other: dog: plott hound; historic boat: shad boat
Song: "The Old North State"
Nickname: Tar Heel State
Residents: North Carolinian
Land area: 48,718 square miles (126,180 sq km)
Population (2005): 8,541,221
Home of: Virginia Dare, the first English child born in America, on Roanoke Island around 1587

Did You Know?
Although the state was pro-Union and antislavery, it joined the Confederacy.

NORTH DAKOTA

★ CAPITAL: **BISMARCK**
★ LARGEST CITY: **FARGO**
★ ABBREVIATION: **N.D.**
★ POSTAL CODE: **ND**

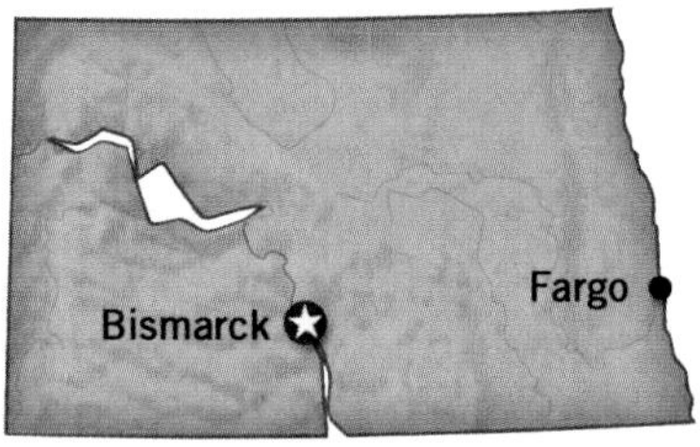

Origin of name: From the Sioux word, meaning "allies"
Entered union (rank): November 2, 1889 (39)
Motto: Liberty and union, now and forever: one and inseparable
Tree: American elm
Flower: wild prairie rose
Bird: western meadowlark
Other: equine: Nokota horse; grass: western wheatgrass
Song: "North Dakota Hymn"
Nicknames: Sioux State, Flickertail State, Peace Garden State and Rough Rider State
Residents: North Dakotan
Land area: 70,704 square miles (183,123 sq km)
Population (2005): 634,366
Home of: The "World's Largest Buffalo," a 26-foot-high, 60-ton concrete monument

Did You Know?
Farms cover more than 90% of North Dakota's land.

OHIO

Columbus

Origin of name: From an Iroquoian word meaning "great river"

Entered union (rank): March 1, 1803 (17)

Motto: With God all things are possible

Tree: buckeye

Flower: scarlet carnation

Bird: cardinal

Other: beverage: tomato juice; fossil: trilobite

Song: "Beautiful Ohio"

Nickname: Buckeye State

Residents: Ohioan

Land area: 40,953 square miles (106,067 sq km)

Population (2005): 11,459,011

Home of: The first electric traffic lights, invented and installed in Cleveland in 1914

Did You Know?
The Cincinnati Reds were the world's first professional baseball team.

OKLAHOMA

Oklahoma City

Origin of name: From two Choctaw Indian words meaning "red people"

Entered union (rank): November 16, 1907 (46)

Motto: *Labor omnia vincit* (Labor conquers all things)

Tree: redbud

Flower: mistletoe

Bird: scissor-tailed flycatcher

Other: furbearer: raccoon; waltz: "Oklahoma Wind"

Song: "Oklahoma!"

Nickname: Sooner State

Residents: Oklahoman

Land area: 68,679 square miles (177,880 sq km)

Population (2005): 3,523,553

Home of: The first parking meter, installed in Oklahoma City in 1935

Did You Know?
Oklahoma City's state capitol building is the only capitol in the world with an oil well (it's dry) under it.

United States

OREGON

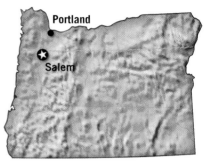

Portland

Salem

Origin of name: **Unknown**

Entered union (rank): **February 14, 1859 (33)**

Motto: *Alis volat propriis* **(She flies with her own wings)**

Tree: **Douglas fir**

Flower: **Oregon grape**

Bird: **western meadowlark**

Other: **fish: Chinook salmon; nut: hazelnut**

Song: **"Oregon, My Oregon"**

Nickname: **Beaver State**

Residents: **Oregonian**

Land area: **96,003 square miles (248,647 sq km)**

Population (2005): **3,594,586**

Home of: **The world's smallest park, totaling 452 square inches, created in Portland in 1948 for snail races**

Did You Know? Oregon's state flag is the only one with designs on both sides.

PENNSYLVANIA

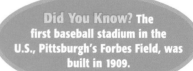

Harrisburg

Philadelphia

Origin of name: **In honor of Sir William Penn, father of state founder William Penn. It means "Penn's Woodland."**

Entered union (rank): **December 12, 1787 (2)**

Motto: **Virtue, liberty and independence**

Tree: **hemlock**

Flower: **mountain laurel**

Bird: **ruffed grouse**

Other: **dog: Great Dane; insect: firefly**

Song: **"Pennsylvania"**

Nickname: **Keystone State**

Residents: **Pennsylvanian**

Land area: **44,820 square miles (116,083 sq km)**

Population (2005): **12,406,292**

Home of: **The first magazine in America, the *American Magazine*, published in Philadelphia for three months in 1741**

Did You Know? The first baseball stadium in the U.S., Pittsburgh's Forbes Field, was built in 1909.

RHODE ISLAND

Origin of name: **From the Greek island of Rhodes**
Entered union (rank): **May 29, 1790 (13)**
Motto: **Hope**
Tree: **red maple**
Flower: **violet**
Bird: **Rhode Island Red hen**
Other: **shellfish: quahog; stone: cumberlandite**
Song: **"Rhode Island"**
Nickname: **Ocean State**
Residents: **Rhode Islander**
Land area: **1,045 square miles (2,706 sq km)**
Population (2005): **1,080,632**
Home of: **Rhode Island Red chickens, first bred in 1854; the start of poultry as a major American industry**

Providence

Did You Know?
Rhode Island is the smallest of the 50 U.S. states.

SOUTH CAROLINA

Origin of name: **In honor of Charles I of England**
Entered union (rank): **May 23, 1788 (8)**
Mottoes: *Animis opibusque parati* **(Prepared in mind and resources) and** *Dum spiro spero* **(While I breathe, I hope)**
Tree: **palmetto**
Flower: **yellow jessamine**
Bird: **Carolina wren**
Other: **hospitality beverage: tea; music: the spiritual**
Song: **"Carolina"**
Nickname: **Palmetto State**
Residents: **South Carolinian**
Land area: **30,111 square miles (77,988 sq km)**
Population (2005): **4,198,068**
Home of: **The first tea farm in the U.S., created in 1890 near Summerville**

Columbia

Did You Know?
South Carolina was the first state to secede from the Union. The Civil War started here.

United States

273

SOUTH DAKOTA

★ CAPITAL: **PIERRE**　　★ ABBREVIATION: **S.D.**
★ LARGEST CITY: **SIOUX FALLS**　　★ POSTAL CODE: **SD**

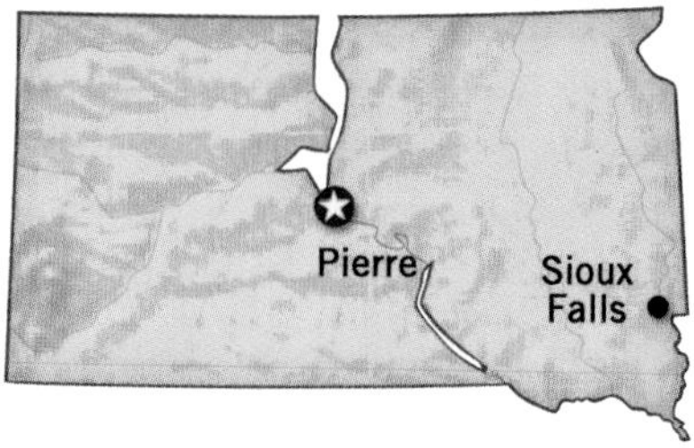

Origin of name: From the Sioux word, meaning "allies"

Entered union (rank): **November 2, 1889 (40)**

Motto: **Under God the people rule**

Tree: **black hills spruce**

Flower: **American pasqueflower**

Bird: **ring-necked pheasant**

Other: **dessert: kuchen; jewelry: Black Hills gold**

Song: **"Hail! South Dakota"**

Nicknames: **Mount Rushmore State and Coyote State**

Residents: **South Dakotan**

Land area: **75,898 square miles (196,575 sq km)**

Population (2005): **770,883**

Home of: **The world's largest natural indoor warm-water pool, Evans' Plunge, in Hot Springs**

Did You Know?
It took Gutzon Borglum 14 years to carve Mount Rushmore.

TENNESSEE

★ CAPITAL: **NASHVILLE**　　★ ABBREVIATION: **TENN.**
★ LARGEST CITY: **MEMPHIS**　　★ POSTAL CODE: **TN**

Origin of name: **Of Cherokee origin; the exact meaning is unknown**

Entered union (rank): **June 1, 1796 (16)**

Motto: **Agriculture and commerce**

Tree: **tulip poplar**

Flower: **iris**

Bird: **mockingbird**

Did You Know?
Nashville, site of the Grand Ole Opry, is considered the country-music capital of the world.

Other: **amphibian: Tennessee cave salamander; animal: raccoon**

Songs: **"Tennessee Waltz," "My Homeland, Tennessee," "When It's Iris Time in Tennessee" and "My Tennessee"**

Nickname: **Volunteer State**

Residents: **Tennessean, Tennesseean**

Land area: **41,220 square miles (106,759 sq km)**

Population (2005): **5,900,962**

Home of: **Graceland, the estate and gravesite of Elvis Presley**

TEXAS

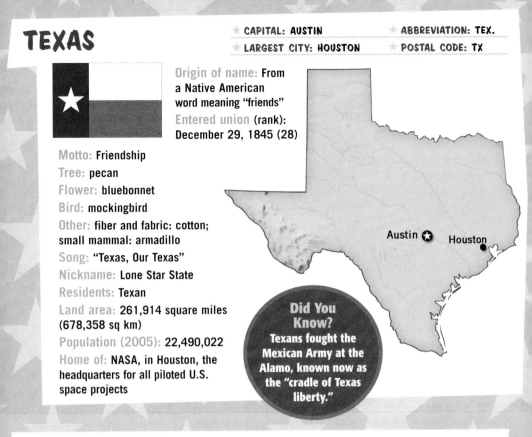

Origin of name: From a Native American word meaning "friends"

Entered union (rank): December 29, 1845 (28)

Motto: Friendship
Tree: pecan
Flower: bluebonnet
Bird: mockingbird
Other: fiber and fabric: cotton; small mammal: armadillo
Song: "Texas, Our Texas"
Nickname: Lone Star State
Residents: Texan
Land area: 261,914 square miles (678,358 sq km)
Population (2005): 22,490,022
Home of: NASA, in Houston, the headquarters for all piloted U.S. space projects

Did You Know?
Texans fought the Mexican Army at the Alamo, known now as the "cradle of Texas liberty."

UTAH

Salt Lake City

Origin of name: From the Ute tribe, meaning "people of the mountains"

Entered union (rank): January 4, 1896 (45)

Motto: Industry
Tree: blue spruce
Flower: sego lily
Bird: California gull
Other: cooking pot: Dutch oven; fruit: cherry
Song: "Utah, We Love Thee"
Nickname: Beehive State
Residents: Utahn, Utahan
Land area: 82,168 square miles (212,816 sq km)
Population (2005): 2,389,039
Home of: Rainbow Bridge, the largest natural stone bridge in the world, 290 feet high, 275 feet across

Did You Know?
Driving the "golden spike" at Promontory Point in 1869 completed the transcontinental railroad.

United States

275

VERMONT

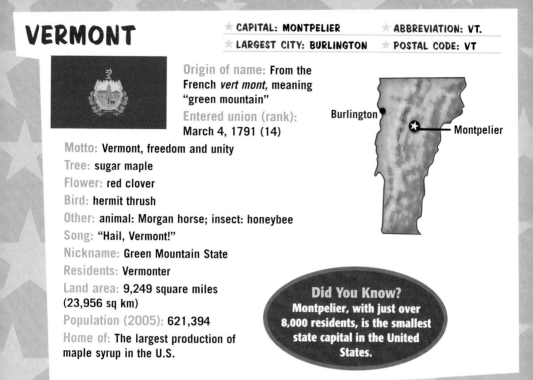

Origin of name: From the French *vert mont,* meaning "green mountain"

Entered union (rank): March 4, 1791 (14)

Motto: Vermont, freedom and unity

Tree: sugar maple

Flower: red clover

Bird: hermit thrush

Other: animal: Morgan horse; insect: honeybee

Song: "Hail, Vermont!"

Nickname: Green Mountain State

Residents: Vermonter

Land area: 9,249 square miles (23,956 sq km)

Population (2005): 621,394

Home of: The largest production of maple syrup in the U.S.

Did You Know?
Montpelier, with just over 8,000 residents, is the smallest state capital in the United States.

VIRGINIA

Origin of name: In honor of Elizabeth I, "Virgin Queen" of England

Entered union (rank): June 25, 1788 (10)

Motto: *Sic semper tyrannis* (Thus always to tyrants)

Tree: dogwood

Flower: American dogwood

Bird: cardinal

Other: dog: American foxhound; shell: oyster shell

Song: "Carry Me Back to Old Virginia"

Nicknames: The Old Dominion and Mother of Presidents

Residents: Virginian

Land area: 39,598 square miles (102,558 sq km)

Population (2005): 7,459,827

Home of: The only full-length statue of George Washington

Did You Know?
Jamestown was the first permanent English settlement in North America.

WASHINGTON

Origin of name:
In honor of George
Washington

Entered union (rank):
November 11, 1889 (42)

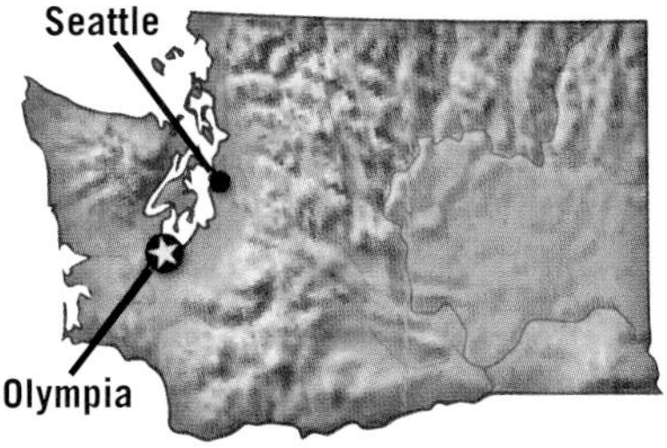

Motto: *Al-ki* (Indian word meaning "by and by")

Tree: western hemlock

Flower: coast rhododendron

Bird: willow goldfinch

Other: fossil: Columbian mammoth; fruit: apple

Song: "Washington, My Home"

Nickname: Evergreen State

Residents: Washingtonian

Land area: 66,582 square miles (17,447 sq km)

Population (2005): 6,203,788

Home of: The Lunar Rover, the vehicle used by
astronauts on the Moon in 1971. Boeing, in Seattle, makes
aircraft and spacecraft.

Seattle

Olympia

Did You Know?
The Grand Coulee
dam, on the Columbia
River, is the largest
concrete structure
in the U.S.

WEST VIRGINIA

Origin of name: In honor
of Elizabeth I, "Virgin Queen"
of England

Entered union (rank):
June 20, 1863 (35)

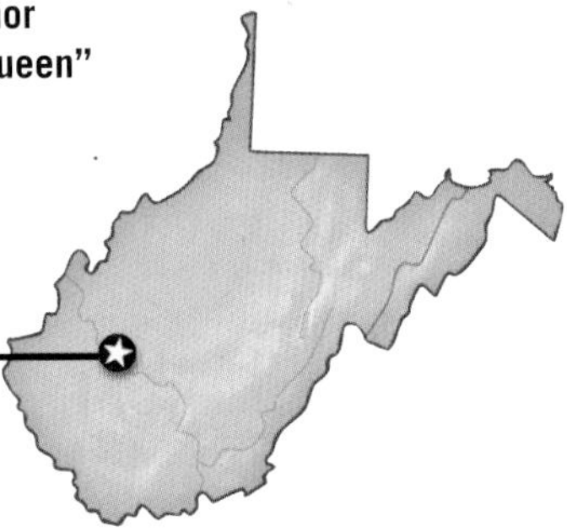

Motto: *Montani semper liberi*
(Mountaineers are always free)

Tree: sugar maple

Flower: rhododendron

Bird: cardinal

Other: animal: black bear; fruit: golden delicious apple

Songs: "West Virginia," "My Home Sweet Home,"
"The West Virginia Hills" and "This Is My West Virginia"

Nickname: Mountain State

Residents: West Virginian

Land area: 24,087 square miles (62,384 sq km)

Population (2005): 1,815,354

Home of: Marbles. Most of the country's glass marbles
are made around Parkersburg.

Charleston

Did You Know?
Mother's Day was first
celebrated in Grafton
in 1908.

United States

277

WISCONSIN

★ CAPITAL: **MADISON**
★ LARGEST CITY: **MILWAUKEE**
★ ABBREVIATION: **WIS.**
★ POSTAL CODE: **WI**

WISCONSIN
1848

Origin of name: French corruption of an Indian word whose meaning is disputed

Entered union (rank): May 29, 1848 (30)

Motto: Forward

Tree: sugar maple

Flower: wood violet

Bird: robin

Other: dance: polka; symbol of peace: mourning dove

Song: "On, Wisconsin"

Nickname: Badger State

Residents: Wisconsinite

Land area: 54,314 square miles (140,673 sq km)

Population (2005): 5,509,026

Home of: The typewriter, invented in Milwaukee in 1867

● Milwaukee
★ Madison

Did You Know?
Wisconsin produced a 17-ton cheddar cheese for the 1964 New York World's Fair.

WYOMING

★ CAPITAL: **CHEYENNE**
★ LARGEST CITY: **CHEYENNE**
★ ABBREVIATION: **WYO.**
★ POSTAL CODE: **WY**

Origin of name: From a Delaware Indian word meaning "mountains and valleys alternating"

Entered union (rank): July 10, 1890 (44)

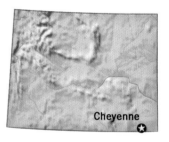

Cheyenne ★

Motto: Equal rights

Tree: cottonwood

Flower: Indian paintbrush

Bird: meadowlark

Other: dinosaur: *Triceratops*; gemstone: jade

Song: "Wyoming"

Nickname: Equality State

Residents: Wyomingite

Land area: 97,105 square miles (251,501 sq km)

Population (2005): 506,529

Home of: Independence Rock, a huge granite boulder that covers 27 acres and has the names of 5,000 early pioneers carved on it

Did You Know?
Wyoming, with just over 500,000 people, ranks 50th in state population.

WASHINGTON D.C.

The District of Columbia, which covers the same area as the city of Washington, is the capital of the United States. D.C. history began in 1790 when Congress took charge of organizing a new site for the capital. George Washington chose the spot, midway between the northern and southern states on the Potomac River. The seat of government was transferred from Philadelphia, Pennsylvania, to Washington, D.C., on December 1, 1800, and President John Adams became the first resident of the White House.

Motto: *Justitia omnibus* (Justice to all)

Flower: American Beauty rose

Tree: scarlet oak

Land area: 68.25 square miles (177 sq km)

Population (2005): 553,523

CAPITAL LANDMARKS

In addition to the White House, several architectural masterpieces and symbolic landmarks are found in our nation's capital. Here are some of them.

Capitol Building This is where Congress meets and conducts business.

Jefferson Memorial This memorial to Thomas Jefferson is modeled on the Roman Pantheon.

Lincoln Memorial Lincoln's Gettysburg Address is carved into the walls of the south chamber, and his famous Second Inaugural Address is on the north-chamber wall.

National Archives The records of the three branches of government, including the Declaration of Independence, are kept here.

Smithsonian Institution The Smithsonian is a network of 14 museums, art galleries and research centers.

Vietnam Veterans Memorial This V-shaped monument lists the names of the 58,000 veterans who died during the Vietnam War.

Washington Monument This monument to our first President stands just over 555 feet high. Stones from the 50 states and several foreign countries line the inside walls.

Vietnam Veterans Memorial

THE COMMONWEALTH OF PUERTO RICO

Puerto Rico is located in the Caribbean Sea, about 1,000 miles east-southeast of Miami, Florida. A U.S. possession since 1898, it consists of the island of Puerto Rico plus the adjacent islets of Vieques, Culebra and Mona.

San Juan, the capital of Puerto Rico

Capital: San Juan

Land area: 3,459 square miles (8,959 sq km)

Population estimate (2005): 3,894,855

Languages: Spanish and English

Motto: *Joannes Est Nomen Eius* (John is his name)

Tree: Silk-cotton

Flower: Puerto Rican hibiscus

Bird: Stripe-headed tanager English

National anthem: "La Borinqueña"

Did You Know?
The U.S. governs several other territories in addition to Puerto Rico. They include Guam, the Commonwealth of the Northern Mariana Islands, the U.S. Virgin Islands, American Samoa and Wake Island.

VOLUNTEERING

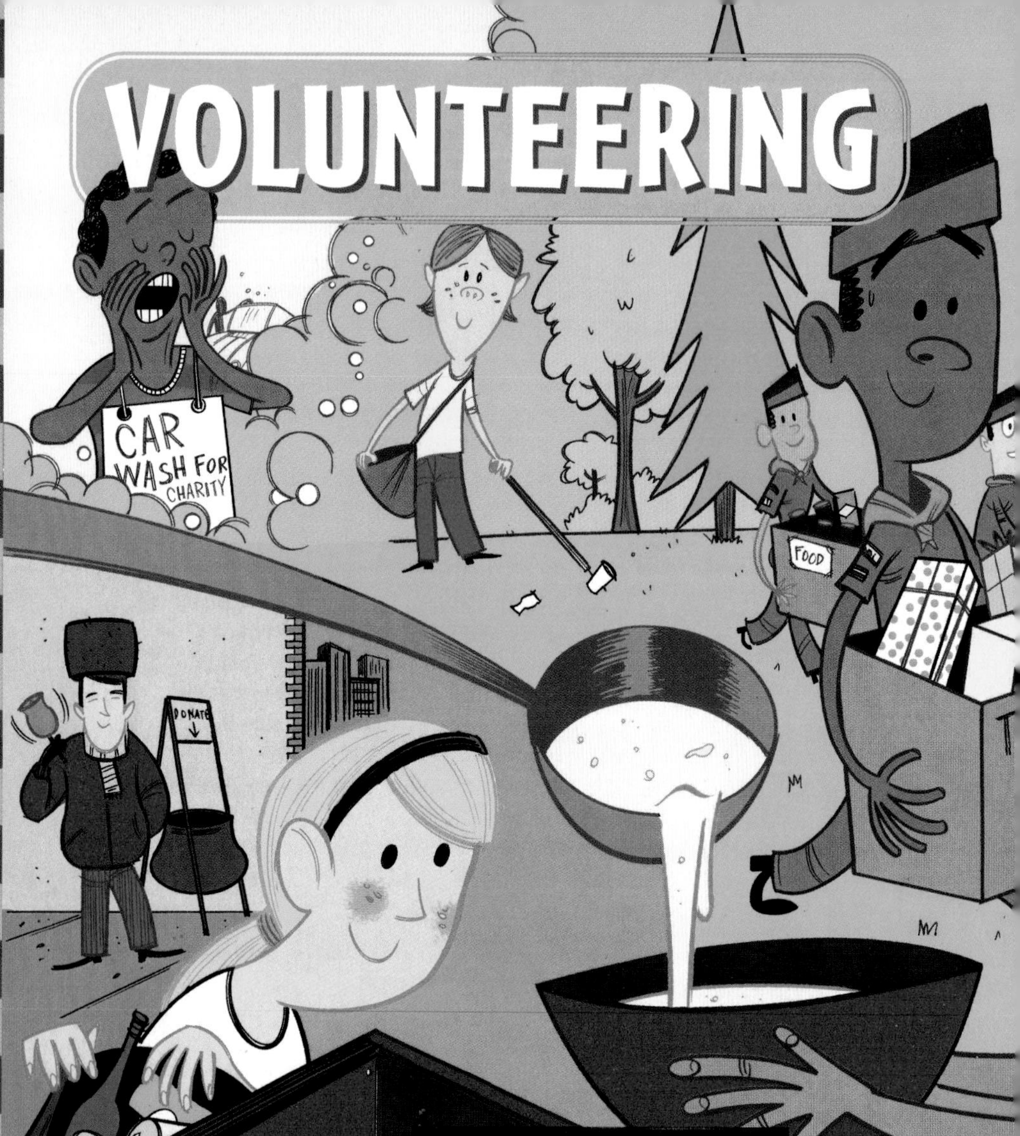

HELPING HANDS

About 29% of all Americans volunteer each year. They spend on average about 52 hours a year helping others. Here's a look at the most popular ways people volunteer.

Type of activity	% of population involved in activity
Educational or youth service	27%
Hospital or other health organization	7.5%
Civic, political, professional or international group	7%
Environmental or animal care	1.7%
Public safety	1.5%

Source: Bureau of Labor Statistics

Kids to the Rescue

*Everyone joins in to help
hurricane survivors*

Most of the United States was undamaged by Hurricane Katrina's path of destruction in 2005. Yet, the storm ripped through Americans' hearts. More than $1 billion in donations poured in to help the victims of Katrina. Here are some ways that kids have made a difference.

LEADERS OF THE PACK

When members of the Kantor family of Bethesda, Maryland, heard about kids uprooted by the storm, they had an idea: collect 1,000 backpacks full of school supplies and other useful stuff and send them to the kids who are sheltered in the Houston Astrodome. Their idea caught on like wildfire! More than 10,350 backpacks were sent out from their local Project Backpack headquarters alone. At least 35 new distribution points were set up in other cities, and backpacks went to relocated kids all over the nation.

LEMON AID

One of the classic ways that kids raise money is by opening a lemonade stand. Brianna Jones, 10, of Williamstown, Massachusetts, added a twist to that idea. She sold lemonade, baked goods—and tomatoes! "My classmate's mom brought tomatoes from her garden, and lots of people bought them," Brianna told TFK. In just four hours, Brianna made $1,625. "I didn't expect to raise that much," she said.

BREAK THE BANK!

Kids broke into countless piggy banks after Katrina hit. "We like to say that we are teaching the power of the penny," sixth-grade teacher Sherrie Jackson told TFK. Students at Meneley Elementary School, in Gardnerville, Nevada, found out that even small change adds up quickly.

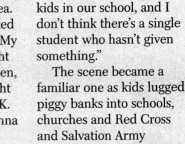

Californians Dana Slomiak and Hilary Chuh make a sale.

"We got $300 a week just in pennies, and our total is about $2,000," says Jackson. "There are 550 kids in our school, and I don't think there's a single student who hasn't given something."

The scene became a familiar one as kids lugged piggy banks into schools, churches and Red Cross and Salvation Army collection sites across the country. At the California State Fair, the biggest piggy bank in the world, which stands 14 feet tall, 21 feet long and 18 feet wide, took in more than $5,000 for Katrina survivors in the last five days of the fair.

*—By Claudia Atticot,
David Bjerklie and
Brenda Iasevoli*

The Kantor sisters (from left: Melissa, 11, Jenna, 8, and Jackie, 14) started Project Backpack in Bethesda, Maryland.

Call it drive-through generosity. In Mississippi, Roger Stancher and Samantha Jones collect coins from drivers.

Volunteering

PITCH IN

HERE ARE SOME TIPS TO GET YOU STARTED ON A SERVICE PROJECT.

- Identify a problem that exists in your community.
- Learn more about the problem, and think about ways to solve it.
- Set a goal for the project.
- Decide what supplies and help you'll need.
- Get your school involved! Encourage other students to help you with your project. Parents can also lend a helping hand.
- Have fun! Knowing that you are helping to make a difference should bring you enjoyment.

CAN'T DECIDE WHAT TO DO FOR A PROJECT? HERE ARE SOME IDEAS.

- Visit a local retirement or nursing home. Sing songs, recite poems or read to the residents.
- Donate old toys, clothing and toiletries to families in need.
- Have a bake sale. Choose an organization or a cause to support.
- Pick up papers, cans and litter.
- Help the hungry and the homeless. Cook or serve a meal at a shelter.
- Help people with special needs. Volunteer to help at a Special Olympics event. Bring books and toys to kids at local hospitals.
- Get involved in government. Find out what you can do to encourage people to register to vote. Identify a local problem, and write to officials with ideas for how to fix it.

FROM TFK MAGAZINE

Late for School?

In 2005, Kimani Ng'ang'a, 85, visited the United Nations in a school bus. He tried to get help for 100 million kids around the world who cannot afford to go to school. Ng'ang'a, of Kenya, Africa, is the world's oldest elementary-school student. He started classes in 2004 when Kenya began offering free public school. "You are never too old to learn," he said.

Americans to the Rescue

Americans often help when disasters strike in other countries. These are the foreign disasters that brought the biggest donations to the American Red Cross.

Disaster	Year	Amount donated
1. Asian tsunami	2004	$556 million
2. Hurricane Mitch	1998	$50 million
3. Wars in the Balkans	1999	$39 million
4. Famine in Africa	1985	$25 million
5. Mexican earthquake	1985	$20 million

Source: Center for Philanthropy at Indiana University

 Learn how to volunteer and make a difference at timeforkids.com/fixtheworld

HELP WANTED

These organizations give kids opportunities to make a difference.

American Society for the Prevention of Cruelty to Animals (ASPCA)
424 E. 92nd St.
New York, NY 10128
212-876-7700
www.aspca.org
Kids can hold fund raisers and collect blankets, towels and toys for animals in shelters.

Do Something
423 W. 55th St., 8th Floor
New York, NY 10019
212-523-1175
www.dosomething.org
Works with kids to identify important issues and create community projects

Family Cares
1400 I St., NW, Suite 800
Washington, D.C. 20005
800-865-8683
www.1-800-volunteer.org
Encourages families to work together to help those in need in their community

Habitat for Humanity
121 Habitat St.
Americus, GA 31709-3498
229-924-6935
www.habitat.org
Kids help build homes for people in need around the world.

Make-A-Wish Foundation
3550 N. Central Ave.
Suite 300
Phoenix, AZ 85012-2127
800-722-WISH (9474)
www.wish.org
Kids help raise money to grant the wishes of children with life-threatening illnesses.

National Park Service Jr. Ranger Programs
1849 C St., NW
Washington, D.C. 20240
202-208-6843
www.nps.gov/learn/juniorranger.htm
Kids can participate in Jr. Ranger programs to help protect our national parks.

Youth Volunteer Network
2000 M St., NW, Suite 500
Washington, D.C. 20036
415-346-4433
www.youthnoise.com
Voice an opinion on how to fight poverty in the U.S. or learn how to make a difference.

Special Olympics
1325 G St., NW, Suite 500
Washington, D.C. 20005
800-700-8585
www.specialolympics.org
Kids can volunteer to help raise money and run the events.

Toys For Tots
Marine Toys For Tots Foundation
P.O. Box 1947
Quantico, VA 22134
703-640-9433
www.toysfortots.org
Kids can donate holiday presents to other children.

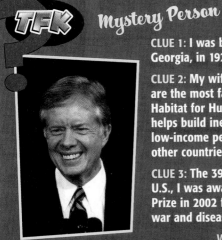

TFK Mystery Person

CLUE 1: I was born in Plains, Georgia, in 1924.

CLUE 2: My wife, Rosalynn, and I are the most famous volunteers for Habitat for Humanity, a group that helps build inexpensive homes for low-income people in the U.S. and other countries.

CLUE 3: The 39th President of the U.S., I was awarded the Nobel Peace Prize in 2002 for my efforts to end war and disease around the world.

WHO AM I?

(See Answer Key that begins on page 342.)

Homework Tip!

Don't try to do homework in the same room that other siblings are playing. They will distract you.

Volunteering

283

WEATHER

Highest Recorded Temperatures

PLACE	DATE	°F*	°C**
WORLD: El Azizia, Libya	Sept. 13, 1922	136	58
UNITED STATES: Death Valley, California	July 10, 1913	134	57

Lowest Recorded Temperatures

PLACE	DATE	°F*	°C**
WORLD: Vostok, Antarctica	July 21, 1983	−129	−8
UNITED STATES: Prospect Creek, Alaska	Jan. 23, 1971	−80	−62

* degrees Fahrenheit **degrees Celsius

The Heat Is On!

Welcome to life in the greenhouse

Traffic in Los Angeles, California, burns fossil fuels, clogs highways and pollutes the atmosphere.

Chinese factory workers ride home. China is growing and rapidly becoming a huge greenhouse-gas polluter.

Hurricanes Katrina, Rita and Wilma packed such a powerful punch that many people have wondered, "Is this just bad luck or is global warming to blame?" Warm ocean water, after all, is what fuels a hurricane's ferocious winds.

Climate scientists agree that our world is getting warmer. Nine of the 10 warmest years on record have been in the past decade. Scientists are convinced that this warming trend is being pushed by humans.

The atmosphere naturally traps heat from the Sun, much like a glass greenhouse warms the air inside. This "greenhouse effect" makes life possible on our planet.

But people are intensifying the natural greenhouse effect. Enormous amounts of polluting gases are produced when we burn fossil fuels such as coal and oil to produce power for our cities, factories and cars and to heat our homes.

By pumping more and more of these gases into the atmosphere, humans are turning up the thermostat. And the effects are clear, according to Kevin Trenberth of the National Center for Atmospheric Research: "We are already seeing fewer frost days, heavier rains and more droughts and heat waves."

The best chance to slow global warming is to reduce the amount of greenhouse gases that are put into the atmosphere. Most of the world's countries have signed a treaty called the Kyoto Protocol, which requires them to pledge to reduce their greenhouse emissions. But the U.S. has not. President George W. Bush has been sharply criticized for this, but he says it would be too costly for U.S. companies to meet the emission limits.

One thing is certain: Efforts to turn down the heat will have to involve the entire world if they are to succeed. "Climate change is truly a global issue," says Trenberth, "and one that may prove to be humanity's greatest challenge."

—By David Bjerklie

The Natural Greenhouse Effect

1. Sunlight hits the Earth, giving it warmth and energy.

2. Carbon dioxide (CO_2) in the atmosphere traps some of the heat, keeping the Earth warm.

SUNLIGHT

HEAT

Earth's Atmosphere

Pollution's Impact

3. As pollution increases, CO_2 and other heat-trapping gases build up. When too much heat is held in by the atmosphere, the Earth grows warmer.

HEAT

go — Learn about global warming at timeforkids.com/globalwarming

Weather

A hurricane seen from space.

Gathering Speed

Tropical wind systems are classified according to their wind speeds. The faster wind blows, the more destructive it gets. Here's a look at how hurricanes are classified.

Tropical Storm: Winds 40–73 miles per hour (m.p.h.)
Category 1: Winds 74–95 m.p.h.
Category 2: Winds 96–110 m.p.h.
Category 3: Winds 111–130 m.p.h.
Category 4: Winds 131–155 m.p.h.
Category 5: Winds greater than 155 m.p.h.

The National Hurricane Center

Fear Factor

Don't panic if forecasters call for a hurricane watch, but be prepared if they mention a hurricane warning.

HURRICANE WATCH A hurricane is possible within 36 hours. Stay tuned to the radio and television for more information. The Hurricane Center is tracking the storm and trying to predict where it may come ashore.

HURRICANE WARNING A hurricane is expected within 24 hours. You may be told to evacuate. You and your family should begin making preparations to clear out.

What's in a Name?

Because several hurricanes can occur at the same time, officials assign short, distinctive names to the storms to avoid confusion among weather stations, coastal bases and ships at sea. A storm is given a name once its winds reach an intensity of 40 m.p.h. These are the names that have been chosen by the National Hurricane Center for Atlantic storms in 2007 and 2008.

2007	2008
Andrea	Arthur
Barry	Bertha
Chantal	Cristobal
Dean	Dolly
Erin	Edouard
Felix	Fay
Gabrielle	Gustav
Humberto	Hanna
Ingrid	Ike
Jerry	Josephine
Karen	Kyle
Lorenzo	Laura
Melissa	Marco
Noel	Nana
Olga	Omar
Pablo	Paloma
Rebekah	Rene
Sebastien	Sally
Tanya	Teddy
Van	Vicky
Wendy	Wilfred

Did You Know?

The center of a hurricane, called the eye, is completely calm.

For the costliest hurricanes in U.S. history:
www.factmonster.com/costlyhurricanes

It's a Twister

A tornado is a dark, funnel-shaped cloud made up of violently churning winds that can reach speeds of up to 300 m.p.h. A tornado's width can measure from a few feet to a mile, and its track can extend from less than a mile to several hundred miles. Tornadoes generally travel in a northeast direction at speeds ranging from 20 to 60 m.p.h.

Tornadoes are most often caused by giant thunderstorms, called supercells. These highly powerful storms form when warm, moist air along the ground rushes upward, meeting cooler, drier air. As the rising warm air cools, the moisture it carries condenses, forming a massive thundercloud, sometimes growing to as much as 50,000 feet in height. Winds at different levels of the atmosphere feed the updraft and cause the formation of the tornado's characteristic funnel shape.

The Fujita scale classifies tornadoes according to the damage they cause. Almost half of all tornadoes fall into the F1, or "moderate damage" category. These tornadoes reach speeds of 73 to 112 m.p.h. and can overturn automobiles and uproot trees.

Only about 1% of tornadoes are classified as F5, causing "incredible damage." With wind speeds in excess of 261 m.p.h., these storms can hurl houses and cars far and wide.

Most tornadoes form in the central and southern United States, where warm, humid air from the Gulf of Mexico collides with cool, dry air from the Rockies and Canada. This area, called tornado alley, extends from the Rocky Mountains to the Appalachians, and from Iowa and Nebraska to the Gulf of Mexico. Tornadoes can also take place in other places throughout the United States, Europe, Asia and Australia.

Thunder and Lightning

When air rises and falls within a thunderstorm, positive and negative charges form in the storm cloud. The bottom of the thundercloud has a negative charge, and the top has a positive charge. A flash of lightning can happen inside a cloud, moving between the positively and negatively charged areas. Lightning also takes place when a charge becomes so strong that the air can't stop it from jumping from the cloud to the ground, which has a positive charge. The average flash of lightning could turn on a 100-watt light bulb for more than three months. The air near a lightning strike is five times hotter than the surface of the Sun. The intense heat causes the air to expand faster than the speed of sound, creating thunder.

What's the Weather?

TEMPERATURE

Air temperature is often measured by a mercury thermometer. When the temperature rises, the mercury expands and rises in the thermometer tube. When the temperature falls, the mercury contracts and falls.

In the U.S., the Fahrenheit scale is used most often. On this scale, 32° is the freezing point of water, and 212° is the boiling point.

The Celsius, or centigrade, scale is used by the World Meteorological Organization and most countries in the world. On this scale, 0° is freezing, and 100° is boiling.

To convert Fahrenheit to Celsius, subtract 32, multiply by 5, and divide the result by 9.

Example:
To convert 50°F to °C:
50 − 32 = 18;
18 x 5 = 90; 90 ÷ 9 = **10°C**

To convert Celsius to Fahrenheit, multiply by 9, divide by 5, and add 32.

Example:
To convert 10°C to °F:
10 x 9 = 90; 90 ÷ 5 = 18;
18 + 32 = **50°F**

CELSIUS	FAHRENHEIT
−50	−58
−40	−40
−30	−22
−20	−4
−10	14
0	32
5	41
10	50
15	59
20	68
25	77
30	86
35	95
40	104
45	113
50	122

Weather Words

Air pressure Air has weight. Air pressure is the weight of the air, or atmosphere, pushing down on Earth. The closer you are to sea level, the greater is the air pressure because there's increasingly more air above you. The higher you are, the lower is the air pressure. Barometers measure air pressure.

Blizzard A major snowstorm with strong winds of 35 m.p.h. or more

Clouds Little drops of water that hang in the atmosphere. The major types of clouds are: nimbostratus (thick clouds that create precipitation); cumulus (flat-bottomed, white, puffy); cumulonimbus (mountains of dark, heavy clouds); stratus (a low, gray blanket); and cirrus (thick, feathery).

Hail Pellets of ice and snow created within clouds that then fall to Earth. Hailstones can sometimes be quite large and can cause major damage.

Humidity The amount of water vapor in the air. Relative humidity is the amount of water in the air compared to the amount of water the air can hold at that temperature. When the relative humidity reaches 100%, the air has reached its dew point. Once the air reaches this point, water vapor turns back into water in the form of rain, snow, clouds or fog.

Hurricane Violent storms in the Atlantic Ocean with strong winds from 40 to 150 m.p.h.

They are called typhoons in the Pacific.

Sleet A mixture of falling rain and snow, or a mixture of rain and ice pellets

Water cycle The process of water changing from one state to another and water's movement from one place to another. For example, when it rains, water drops fall to Earth. This water evaporates from the surface of Earth and enters the atmosphere as water vapor, which condenses into droplets that form clouds. The droplets grow heavier as they combine and fall to Earth as rain.

Wind chill The wind-chill temperature indicates how cold people feel when the wind blows during cold weather. Wind makes the temperature feel much colder than the thermometer reading.

Greatest Snowfalls in North America			
DURATION	PLACE	DATE	INCHES
24 hours	Silver Lake, Colorado	April 14–15, 1921	76
1 month	Tamarack, California	January 1911	390
1 storm	Mt. Shasta Ski Bowl, California	February 13–19, 1959	189
1 season	Mt. Baker, Washington	1998–1999	1,140

Greatest Rainfalls in North America			
DURATION	PLACE	DATE	INCHES
1 minute	Unionville, Maryland	July 4, 1956	1.23
20 minutes	Curtea-de-Arges, Romania	July 7, 1889	8.1
12 hours	Grand Ilet, La Réunion	January 26, 1980	46
24 hours	Foc-Foc, La Réunion	January 7–8, 1966	72
12 months	Cherrapunji, India	August 1860– August 1861	1,042

Droughts

Droughts are unusually long periods of insufficient rainfall that can ruin crops and dry up water supplies.

One of the worst droughts in history occurred in Egypt from 1200 to 1202 B.C. Every year, the flooding of the Nile River left rich soil that the ancient Egyptians used to grow crops. But after a shortage of rain, the Nile didn't rise. People were unable to grow food and began to starve to death. The final death toll was 110,000, from starvation and disease.

Many states in the U.S. experienced drought in the 1930s. About 80% of the population was affected by drought. An enormous Dust Bowl covered about 50 million acres of the Great Plains. During 1934, dry areas stretched from New York to the coast of California.

Drought caused the Dust Bowl.

Avalanches

An avalanche is any fast movement of snow, ice, mud or rock down a mountainside or slope. Avalanches can reach speeds of more than 200 miles per hour. They are triggered by such events as earthquake tremors, human-made disturbances or excessive rainfall.

The worst snowslide in U.S. history occurred in 1910 in the Cascade Mountains in Wellington, Washington. Nearly 100 people were trapped when their train became snowbound. An avalanche then swept them to their deaths in a gorge 150 feet below the tracks.

The world's worst avalanche took place in Peru in 1962. About 4,000 people were killed when tons of ice and snow slid down Huascarán Peak in the Andes Mountains.

An avalanche in Peru killed thousands.

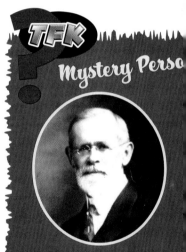

TFK

Mystery Perso

CLUE 1: **I was known as the father of the U.S. Weather Bureau.**

CLUE 2: **In 1868, I used weather observations from areas around Cincinnati to produce weather forecasts for the region. These were the nation's first official weather predictions.**

CLUE 3: **I created daily weather reports for regions across the nation. These predictions were so accurate, Mark Twain gave me the nickname Old Probabilities.**

WHO AM I?

(See Answer Key that begins on page 342.)

WORLD

Saving a Life

More than 1 billion people on our planet live in crushing poverty. They don't have enough food to eat and die from diseases that are prevented in wealthier nations. Helping those millions of families live longer, healthier lives is our generation's great challenge. Here are some health heroes who are trying to meet that challenge.

A Race to Save Lives

Andrea and Barry Coleman run Riders for Health, a charity that trains health workers in six African nations to drive and repair motorcycles. Riders is helping deliver lifesaving supplies to Africans living in hard-to-reach areas. Motorbikes "are made to deal with heat and dust," Barry told TIME. In Zimbabwe, deaths from malaria, a disease carried by mosquitoes, fell 20% after Riders began delivering mosquito nets.

He Put Grandmas to Work

Babies in the Asian country of Nepal were dying because of a lack of vitamin A in their diet. International-health specialist Ram Shrestha had an idea: enlist grandmothers to help. Today, there are about 49,000 grandmas distributing vitamin A pills to Nepalese children each year. Why does Shrestha do it? "As a Nepali, it was my duty," he told TIME.

Big Rewards for Growing Strong

Thanks to Vicky Alvarado, kids in Honduras are rewarded for growing well. Nearly 40% of Honduran kids under age 5 suffer from malnutrition. The problem is worst in poor villages. Alvarado, a teacher and nurse, began a national program to award pins to healthy kids. "The mothers can see the goal," Alvarado told TIME. In the Central American country, 2,000 villages have nutrition programs. Like the kids, that number keeps growing.

Growing Crops

Dr. Sonia Ehrlich Sachs, of the Earth Institute at Columbia University in New York City, has worked hard to improve the lives of poor people. The Earth Institute's team helped to provide fertilizers and better seeds to villagers in Sauri, Kenya, so villagers could grow more food crops to feed their hungry families. "In just one growing season," Sachs told TFK, "the villagers grew three times more corn and beans than they did before."

Can a Vaccine Prevent Malaria?

Deaths from malaria have doubled in the past decade in parts of Africa. But a doctor named Pedro Alonso offers hope to a poor, rural town in Mozambique. Alonso has been testing a vaccine to prevent malaria, and it seems to be working. In a test, the vaccine dramatically reduced the risk of getting the deadly disease in children younger than 2. "This is a breakthrough," Alonso told TIME. He hopes to have an approved vaccine by 2010.

World

Millions of Americans visit foreign countries for business and pleasure. Here are the five most popular destinations for Americans.

1. Mexico
2. Canada
3. United Kingdom
4. France
5. Italy

Source: U.S. Department of Commerce

Most Livable & Least Livable Countries

The United Nations's Human Development Index ranks nations according to their citizens' quality of life. The rankings are based on life expectancy, education and income.

Source: Human Development Report, 2005, United Nations

MOST LIVABLE	LEAST LIVABLE
1. Norway	1. Niger
2. Iceland	2. Sierra Leone
3. Australia	3. Burkina Faso
4. Luxembourg	4. Mali
5. Canada	5. Chad
6. Sweden	6. Guinea-Bissau
7. Switzerland	7. Central African Republic
8. Ireland	8. Ethiopia
9. Belgium	9. Burundi
10. United States	10. Mozambique

Did You Know?

In November 2005, Angela Merkel, head of Germany's Christian Democratic Party, became the Chancellor. She is the first woman and the first person from the former East Germany to lead the country.

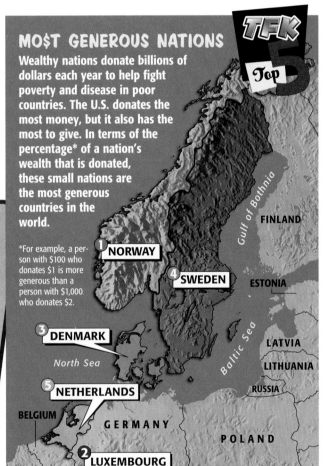

MO$T GENEROUS NATIONS

Wealthy nations donate billions of dollars each year to help fight poverty and disease in poor countries. The U.S. donates the most money, but it also has the most to give. In terms of the percentage* of a nation's wealth that is donated, these small nations are the most generous countries in the world.

*For example, a person with $100 who donates $1 is more generous than a person with $1,000 who donates $2.

1 NORWAY
2 LUXEMBOURG
3 DENMARK
4 SWEDEN
5 NETHERLANDS

FINLAND
Gulf of Bothnia
ESTONIA
LATVIA
LITHUANIA
RUSSIA
Baltic Sea
North Sea
BELGIUM
GERMANY
POLAND
FRANCE
CZECH REPUBLIC

THE WORLD'S NATIONS FROM A TO Z

On the following pages you will find information about the world's nations. Here's an example.

If you divide the population by the area, you can find out the population density—how many people there are per square mile.

This tells the main languages and the official languages (if any) spoken in a nation. In this case, most people in the nation speak Icelandic.

This is the type of money used in the nation.

This tells an interesting fact about the country.

ICELAND

Where? Europe
Capital: Reykjavik
Area: 39,768 sq mi (103,000 sq km)
Population estimate (2006): 296,737
Government: Constitutional republic
Language: Icelandic
Monetary unit: Icelandic króna
Life expectancy: 80.2
Literacy rate: 100%
Did You Know? Iceland boasts the world's oldest constitution, drafted around 930.

Life expectancy is the number of years a person can expect to live. It's affected by heredity, a person's health and nutrition, the healthcare and wealth of a nation and a person's occupation.

This tells the percentage of people who can read and write.

AFGHANISTAN

Where? Asia
Capital: Kabul
Area: 251,737 sq mi (647,500 sq km)
Population estimate (2006): 29,928,987
Government: Multiparty republic
Languages: Pushtu, Dari Persian, other Turkic and minor languages
Monetary unit: Afghani
Life expectancy: 42.5
Literacy rate: 36%
Did You Know? Islam is Afghanistan's official religion.

ALBANIA

Where? Europe
Capital: Tirana
Area: 11,100 sq mi (28,750 sq km)
Population estimate (2006): 3,563,112
Government: Emerging democracy
Languages: Albanian (Tosk is the official dialect), Greek
Monetary unit: Lek
Life expectancy: 77.1
Literacy rate: 87%
Did You Know? This former communist country is now a struggling democracy.

ALGERIA

Where? Africa
Capital: Algiers
Area: 919,590 sq mi (2,381,740 sq km)
Population estimate (2006): 32,531,853
Government: Republic
Languages: Arabic (official), French, Berber dialects
Monetary unit: Dinar
Life expectancy: 72.7
Literacy rate: 70%
Did You Know? The Sahara is a desert that covers about 85% of Algeria.

ANDORRA

Where? Europe
Capital: Andorra la Vella
Area: 181 sq mi (468 sq km)
Population estimate (2006): 70,549
Government: Parliamentary democracy
Languages: Catalán (official), French, Spanish
Monetary units: French franc and Spanish peseta
Life expectancy: 83.5
Literacy rate: 100%
Did You Know? This country has the world's highest life expectancy.

For tons of world statistics, go to:
www.factmonster.com/worldstats

World

ANGOLA

Where? Africa
Capital: Luanda
Area: 481,350 sq mi
(1,246,700 sq km)
Population estimate (2006):
11,190,786
Government: Republic
Languages: Bantu, Portuguese (official)
Monetary unit: Kwanza
Life expectancy: 36.8
Literacy rate: 42%
Did You Know? In 2002, Angola ended a decades-long civil war.

ANTIGUA AND BARBUDA

Where? North America
Capital: St. John's
Area: 171 sq mi
(443 sq km)
Population estimate (2006): 68,722
Government: Constitutional monarchy
Language: English
Monetary unit: East Caribbean dollar
Life expectancy: 71.6
Literacy rate: 89%
Did You Know? Christopher Columbus explored Antigua in 1493.

ARGENTINA

Where? South America
Capital: Buenos Aires
Area: 1,068,296 sq mi
(2,766,890 sq km)
Population estimate (2006): 39,537,943
Government: Republic
Languages: Spanish (official), English, Italian, German, French
Monetary unit: Peso
Life expectancy: 75.7
Literacy rate: 96%
Did You Know? Most Argentineans are of Spanish or Italian descent.

ARMENIA

Where? Asia
Capital: Yerevan
Area: 11,500 sq mi
(29,800 sq km)
Population estimate (2006): 2,982,904
Government: Republic
Language: Armenian
Monetary unit: Dram
Life expectancy: 71.2
Literacy rate: 99%
Did You Know? About 60% of the world's 8 million Armenians live outside Armenia.

AUSTRALIA

Where? Pacific Islands
Capital: Canberra
Area: 2,967,893 sq mi
(7,686,850 sq km)
Population estimate (2006): 20,090,437
Government: Democracy
Language: English
Monetary unit: Australian dollar
Life expectancy: 80.3
Literacy rate: 100%
Did You Know? Australia's Great Barrier Reef is the largest coral reef in the world.

AUSTRIA

Where? Europe
Capital: Vienna
Area: 32,375 sq mi
(83,850 sq km)
Population estimate (2006): 8,184,691
Government: Federal Republic
Language: German
Monetary unit: Euro (formerly schilling)
Life expectancy: 78.9
Literacy rate: 98%
Did You Know? Three-quarters of Austria is covered by the Alps.

AZERBAIJAN

Where? Asia
Capital: Baku
Area: 33,400 sq mi
(86,600 sq km)
Population estimate (2006): 7,911,974
Government: Republic
Languages: Azerbaijani Turkic, Russian, Armenian
Monetary unit: Manat
Life expectancy: 63.2
Literacy rate: 97%
Did You Know? Oil recently discovered in Azerbaijan may improve its economy.

BAHAMAS

Where? North America
Capital: Nassau
Area: 5,380 sq mi
(13,940 sq km)
Population estimate (2006): 301,790
Government: Parliamentary democracy
Language: English
Monetary unit: Bahamian dollar
Life expectancy: 65.6
Literacy rate: 96%
Did You Know? The Bahamas is made up of more than 700 islands.

BAHRAIN

Where? Asia
Capital: Manamah
Area: 257 sq mi
(665 sq km)
Population estimate (2006): 688,345
Government: Constitutional monarchy
Languages: Arabic (official), English, Farsi, Urdu
Monetary unit: Bahrain dinar
Life expectancy: 74
Literacy rate: 89%
Did You Know? Bahrain is an archipelago in the Persian Gulf.

BANGLADESH

Where? Asia
Capital: Dhaka
Area: 55,598 sq mi
(144,000 sq km)
Population estimate (2006):
144,319,628
Government: Parliamentary democracy
Languages: Bangla (official), English
Monetary unit: Taka
Life expectancy: 61.7
Literacy rate: 43%
Did You Know? Until 1971, Bangladesh was part of Pakistan.

BARBADOS

Where? North America
Capital: Bridgetown
Area: 166 sq mi
(431 sq km)
Population estimate (2006): 279,254
Government: Parliamentary democracy
Language: English
Monetary unit: Barbados dollar
Life expectancy: 71.6
Literacy rate: 97%
Did You Know? Barbados was a British colony before its independence in 1966.

BELARUS

Where? Europe
Capital: Minsk
Area: 80,154 sq mi
(207,600 sq km)
Population estimate (2006): 10,300,483
Government: Republic
Language: Belarussian
Monetary unit: Belarussian ruble
Life expectancy: 68.6
Literacy rate: 100%
Did You Know? Belarus was part of the Soviet Union until becoming independent in 1991.

BELGIUM

Where? Europe
Capital: Brussels
Area: 11,781 sq mi
(30,510 sq km)
Population estimate (2006): 10,364,388
Government: Constitutional monarchy
Languages: Dutch (Flemish), French,
German (all official)
Monetary unit: Euro (formerly Belgian franc)
Life expectancy: 78.4
Literacy rate: 98%
Did You Know? Nuclear power generates
more than 75% of Belgium's electricity.

BELIZE

Where? Central America
Capital: Belmopan
Area: 8,865 sq mi
(22,960 sq km)
Population estimate (2006): 279,457
Government: Parliamentary democracy
Languages: English (official), Creole,
Spanish, Garifuna, Mayan
Monetary unit: Belize dollar
Life expectancy: 67.4
Literacy rate: 94%
Did You Know? Belize is the only English-
speaking country in Central America.

BENIN

Where? Africa
Capital: Porto-Novo
Area: 43,483 sq mi
(112,620 sq km)
Population estimate (2006): 7,460,025
Government: Multiparty democracy
Languages: French (official), African
languages
Monetary unit: CFA franc
Life expectancy: 50.8
Literacy rate: 41%
Did You Know? Benin's pottery, masks
and bronze statues are world renowned.

BHUTAN

Where? Asia
Capital: Thimphu
Area: 18,147 sq mi
(47,000 sq km)
Population estimate (2006): 2,232,291
Government: Monarchy
Language: Dzongkha
Monetary unit: Ngultrum
Life expectancy: 54
Literacy rate: 42%
Did You Know? About 75% of
Bhutanese are Buddhists.

BOLIVIA

Where? South America
Capital: La Paz (seat of
government), Sucre
(legal capital)
Area: 424,162 sq mi (1,098,580 sq km)
Population estimate (2006): 8,857,870
Government: Republic
Languages: Spanish (official), Quechua,
Aymara, Guarani
Monetary unit: Boliviano
Life expectancy: 65.1
Literacy rate: 87%
Did You Know? Bolivia has had more than
190 revolutions and coups since 1825.

BOSNIA AND HERZEGOVINA

Where? Europe
Capital: Sarajevo
Area: 19,741 sq mi
(51,129 sq km)
Population estimate (2006): 4,025,476
Government: Emerging democracy
Languages: The language is called
Serbian, Croatian or Bosnian depending
on the speaker.
Monetary unit: Dinar
Life expectancy: 72.6
Literacy rate: 94.6%
Did You Know? This country was a part
of Yugoslavia until 1992.

BOTSWANA

Where? Africa
Capital: Gaborone
Area: 231,800 sq mi (600,370 sq km)
Population estimate (2006): 1,640,115
Government: Parliamentary republic
Languages: English (official), Setswana
Monetary unit: Pula
Life expectancy: 34.2
Literacy rate: 80%
Did You Know? The Kalahari is a desert located in this southern African country.

BRAZIL

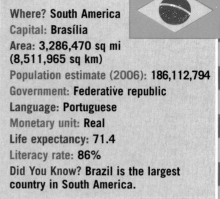

Where? South America
Capital: Brasília
Area: 3,286,470 sq mi (8,511,965 sq km)
Population estimate (2006): 186,112,794
Government: Federative republic
Language: Portuguese
Monetary unit: Real
Life expectancy: 71.4
Literacy rate: 86%
Did You Know? Brazil is the largest country in South America.

BRUNEI

Where? Asia
Capital: Bandar Seri Begawan
Area: 2,228 sq mi (5,770 sq km)
Population estimate (2006): 372,361
Government: Constitutional sultanate
Languages: Malay (official), Chinese, English
Monetary unit: Brunei dollar
Life expectancy: 74.5
Literacy rate: 92%
Did You Know? This tiny country is ruled by a sultan who is one of the richest men in the world.

BULGARIA

Where? Europe
Capital: Sofia
Area: 48,822 sq mi (110,910 sq km)
Population estimate (2006): 7,450,349
Government: Parliamentary democracy
Language: Bulgarian
Monetary unit: Lev
Life expectancy: 71.8
Literacy rate: 99%
Did You Know? Bulgaria was a communist country until 1991.

BURKINA FASO

Where? Africa
Capital: Ouagadougou
Area: 105,870 sq mi (274,200 sq km)
Population estimate (2006): 13,925,313
Government: Parliamentary republic
Languages: French (official), tribal languages
Monetary unit: CFA franc
Life expectancy: 44.2
Literacy rate: 27%
Did You Know? This country was formerly named Upper Volta.

BURUNDI

Where? Africa
Capital: Bujumbura
Area: 10,745 sq mi (27,830 sq km)
Population estimate (2006): 6,370,609
Government: Republic
Languages: Kirundi and French (both official), Swahili
Monetary unit: Burundi franc
Life expectancy: 43.4
Literacy rate: 52%
Did You Know? Burundi was once a German colony.

For a list of the rulers of the world:
www.factmonster.com/worldrulers

World

CAMBODIA

Where? Asia
Capital: Phnom Penh
Area: 69,900 sq mi
(181,040 sq km)
Population estimate (2006): 13,607,069
Government: Democracy under a
constitutional monarchy
Languages: Khmer (official), French, English
Monetary unit: Riel
Life expectancy: 58.4
Literacy rate: 70%
Did You Know? Cambodia's Angkor Wat
temple is one of the world's wonders.

CAMEROON

Where? Africa
Capital: Yaoundé
Area: 183,567 sq mi
(475,440 sq km)
Population estimate (2006): 16,380,005
Government: Unitary republic
Languages: French and English
(both official), African languages
Monetary unit: CFA franc
Life expectancy: 48
Literacy rate: 79%
Did You Know? Germany, France and
Britain once controlled Cameroon.

CANADA

Where? North America
Capital: Ottawa, Ontario
Area: 3,851,788 sq mi
(9,976,140 sq km)
Population estimate (2006): 32,805,041
Government: Parliamentary democracy
Languages: English and French
(both official)
Monetary unit: Canadian dollar
Life expectancy: 80
Literacy rate: 97%
Did You Know? Canada is the world's
second largest country.

CAPE VERDE

Where? Africa
Capital: Praia
Area: 1,557 sq mi
(4,033 sq km)
Population estimate (2006): 418,224
Government: Republic
Languages: Portuguese, Crioulo
Monetary unit: Cape Verdean escudo
Life expectancy: 70.1
Literacy rate: 77%
Did You Know? Off the northwest coast
of Africa, Cape Verde is made up of
ten islands and five islets.

CENTRAL AFRICAN REPUBLIC

Where? Africa
Capital: Bangui
Area: 240,534 sq mi
(622,984 sq km)
Population estimate (2006): 3,799,897
Government: Republic
Languages: French (official), Sangho,
Arabic, Hansa, Swahili
Monetary unit: CFA franc
Life expectancy: 41.4
Literacy rate: 51%
Did You Know? This country was called
the Central African Empire from 1976
to 1979.

CHAD

Where? Africa
Capital: N'Djamena
Area: 495,752 sq mi
(1,284,000 sq km)
Population estimate (2006): 9,826,419
Government: Republic
Languages: French (official), Sangho,
Arabic, Hansa, Swahili
Monetary unit: CFA franc
Life expectancy: 48.2
Literacy rate: 48%
Did You Know? The country is named for
its largest lake, Lake Chad.

CHILE

Where? South America
Capital: Santiago
Area: 292,258 sq mi
(756,950 sq km)
Population estimate (2006): 15,980,912
Government: Republic
Language: Spanish
Monetary unit: Peso
Life expectancy: 76.4
Literacy rate: 96%
Did You Know? Chile's Atacama Desert is the driest place on Earth.

CHINA

Where? Asia
Capital: Beijing
Area: 3,705,386 sq mi
(9,596,960 sq km)
Population estimate (2006): 1,306,313,812
Government: Communist state
Languages: Chinese (Mandarin), local dialects
Monetary unit: Yuan
Life expectancy: 72
Literacy rate: 86%
Did You Know? China is the most populous country in the world.

COLOMBIA

Where? South America
Capital: Bogotá
Area: 439,733 sq mi
(1,138,910 sq km)
Population estimate (2006):
42,954,279
Government: Republic
Language: Spanish
Monetary unit: Peso
Life expectancy: 71.4
Literacy rate: 93%
Did You Know? Coffee is Colombia's major crop.

COMOROS

Where? Africa
Capital: Moroni
Area: 838 sq mi
(2,170 sq km)
Population estimate (2006): 671,247
Government: Republic
Languages: French and Arabic (both official), Shaafi Islam (Swahili dialect), Malagasu
Monetary unit: CFA franc
Life expectancy: 61.6
Literacy rate: 57%
Did You Know? Comoros is made up of three tiny islands off the East African coast.

CONGO, DEMOCRATIC REPUBLIC OF THE

Where? Africa
Capital: Kinshasa
Area: 905,562 sq mi
(2,345,410 sq km)
Population estimate (2006): 60,085,004
Government: Dictatorship
Languages: French (official), Swahili, Lingala, Ishiluba, Kikongo, others
Monetary unit: Congolese franc
Life expectancy: 49.1
Literacy rate: 66%
Did You Know? This country was formerly named Zaïre.

CONGO, REPUBLIC OF THE

Where? Africa
Capital: Brazzaville
Area: 132,046 sq mi
(342,000 sq km)
Population estimate (2006): 3,039,126
Government: Dictatorship
Languages: French (official), Lingala, Kikongo, others
Monetary unit: CFA franc
Life expectancy: 49.5
Literacy rate: 84%
Did You Know? Petroleum production provides 90% of the country's revenues and exports.

COSTA RICA

Where? Central America
Capital: San José
Area: 19,730 sq mi
(51,100 sq km)
Population estimate (2006): 4,016,173
Government: Republic
Language: Spanish
Monetary unit: Colón
Life expectancy: 76.6
Literacy rate: 96%
Did You Know? This country's name means "rich coast."

CÔTE D'IVOIRE

Where? Africa
Capital: Yamoussoukro
Area: 124,502 sq mi
(322,460 sq km)
Population estimate (2006): 17,298,040
Government: Republic
Languages: French (official), African languages
Monetary unit: CFA franc
Life expectancy: 48.4
Literacy rate: 51%
Did You Know? More than 60 distinct tribes are represented in Côte d'Ivoire.

CROATIA

Where? Europe
Capital: Zagreb
Area: 21,829 sq mi
(56,538 sq km)
Population estimate (2006): 4,495,904
Government: Parliamentary democracy
Language: Croatian
Monetary unit: Kuna
Life expectancy: 74.1
Literacy rate: 99%
Did You Know? Croatia was part of Yugoslavia until declaring independence in 1991.

CUBA

Where? North America
Capital: Havana
Area: 42,803 sq mi
(110,860 sq km)
Population estimate (2006): 11,346,670
Government: Communist state
Language: Spanish
Monetary unit: Peso
Life expectancy: 77
Literacy rate: 97%
Did You Know? Fidel Castro has ruled Cuba since 1959.

CYPRUS

Where? Middle East
Capital: Nicosia
Area: 3,572 sq mi (9,250 sq km)
Population estimate (2006): 780,133
Government: Republic
Languages: Greek, Turkish
Monetary unit: Cypriot pound, Turkish lira
Life expectancy: 77.5
Literacy rate: 98%
Did You Know? This nation is divided by a long-standing conflict between its Greek and Turkish populations.

CZECH REPUBLIC

Where? Europe
Capital: Prague
Area: 30,450 sq mi
(78,866 sq km)
Population estimate (2006): 10,241,138
Government: Parliamentary democracy
Language: Czech
Monetary unit: Koruna
Life expectancy: 75.8
Literacy rate: 100%
Did You Know? Until 1993, the country was part of Czechoslovakia, which no longer exists.

DENMARK

Where? Europe
Capital: Copenhagen
Area: 16,639 sq mi
(43,094 sq km)
Population estimate (2006): 5,432,335
Government: Constitutional monarchy
Languages: Danish, Faeroese,
Greenlandic, German
Monetary unit: Krone
Life expectancy: 77.4
Literacy rate: 100%
Did You Know? One of Denmark's territories,
Greenland, is the world's largest island.

DJIBOUTI

Where? Africa
Capital: Djibouti
Area: 8,800 sq mi
(23,000 sq km)
Population estimate (2006): 476,703
Government: Republic
Languages: Arabic and French (both
official), Afar, Somali
Monetary unit: Djibouti franc
Life expectancy: 43.1
Literacy rate: 68%
Did You Know? Djibouti's capital is
one of Africa's major seaports.

DOMINICA

Where? North America
Capital: Roseau
Area: 290 sq mi
(750 sq km)
Population estimate (2006): 69,029
Government: Parliamentary democracy
Languages: English (official), French patois
Monetary unit: East Caribbean dollar
Life expectancy: 74.4
Literacy rate: 94%
Did You Know? This mountainous
Caribbean island nation was explored by
Columbus in 1493.

DOMINICAN REPUBLIC

Where? North America
Capital: Santo Domingo
Area: 18,815 sq mi
(48,730 sq km)
Population estimate (2006): 8,950,034
Government: Representative democracy
Languages: Spanish
Monetary unit: Peso
Life expectancy: 67.6
Literacy rate: 85%
Did You Know? This country and Haiti
make up the island of Hispaniola in the
Caribbean.

EAST TIMOR

Where? Asia
Capital: Dili
Area: 5,814 sq mi
(15,057 sq km)
Population estimate (2006): 1,040,880
Government: Republic
Languages: Tetum, Portuguese (official),
Bahasa Indonesia, English
Monetary unit: U.S. dollar
Life expectancy: 65.6
Literacy rate: 48%
Did You Know? East Timor is the world's
newest country, formed in 2002.

ECUADOR

Where? South America
Capital: Quito
Area: 109,483 sq mi
(283,560 sq km)
Population estimate (2006): 13,363,593
Government: Republic
Languages: Spanish (official), Quechua
Monetary unit: U.S. dollar
Life expectancy: 76
Literacy rate: 93%
Did You Know? The country takes its
name from the equator, which runs
through it.

World

EGYPT

Where? Africa
Capital: Cairo
Area: 386,660 sq mi
(1,001,450 sq km)
Population estimate (2006): 77,505,756
Government: Republic
Language: Arabic
Monetary unit: Egyptian pound
Life expectancy: 70.7
Literacy rate: 58%
Did You Know? Almost 95% of Egypt is desert.

EL SALVADOR

Where? Central America
Capital: San Salvador
Area: 8,124 sq mi
(21,040 sq km)
Population estimate (2006): 6,704,932
Government: Republic
Language: Spanish
Monetary unit: U.S. dollar
Life expectancy: 70.9
Literacy rate: 80%
Did You Know? El Salvador is the smallest country in Central America.

EQUATORIAL GUINEA

Where? Africa
Capital: Malabo
Area: 10,830 sq mi
(28,050 sq km)
Population estimate (2006): 535,881
Government: Republic
Languages: Spanish (official), French (second official), pidgin English, Fang, Bubi, Creole
Monetary unit: CFA franc
Life expectancy: 55.1
Literacy rate: 86%
Did You Know? This is Africa's only Spanish-speaking country.

ERITREA

Where? Africa
Capital: Asmara
Area: 46,842 sq mi
(121,320 sq km)
Population estimate (2006): 4,561,599
Government: Transitional
Languages: Afar, Bilen, Kunama, Nara, Arabic, Tobedawi, Saho, Tigre, Tigrinya
Monetary unit: Nakfa
Life expectancy: 52.7
Literacy rate: 59%
Did You Know? Once a part of Ethiopia, Eritrea became independent in 1993.

ESTONIA

Where? Europe
Capital: Tallinn
Area: 17,462 sq mi
(45,226 sq km)
Population estimate (2006): 1,332,893
Government: Parliamentary democracy
Languages: Estonian (official), Russian, Finnish, English
Monetary unit: Kroon
Life expectancy: 71.4
Literacy rate: 100%
Did You Know? Estonia is one of the three Baltic countries.

ETHIOPIA

Where? Africa
Capital: Addis Ababa
Area: 485,184 sq mi
(1,127,127 sq km)
Population estimate (2006): 73,053,286
Government: Federal republic
Languages: Amharic (official), English, Orominga, Tigrigna, others
Monetary unit: Birr
Life expectancy: 48.6
Literacy rate: 43%
Did You Know? Remains of the oldest-known human ancestors have been found in Ethiopia.

FIJI

Where? Oceania
Capital: Suva
Area: 7,054 sq mi
(18,270 sq km)
Population estimate (2006): 893,354
Government: Republic
Languages: Fijian, Hindustani, English (official)
Monetary unit: Fiji dollar
Life expectancy: 69.2
Literacy rate: 94%
Did You Know? Fiji is made up of 332 islands in the South Pacific.

FINLAND

Where? Europe
Capital: Helsinki
Area: 130,127 sq mi
(337,030 sq km)
Population estimate (2006): 5,223,442
Government: Republic
Languages: Finnish and Swedish (both official)
Monetary unit: Euro (formerly markka)
Life expectancy: 78.2
Literacy rate: 100%
Did You Know? Laplanders live in the north of Finland, above the Arctic Circle.

FRANCE

Where? Europe
Capital: Paris
Area: 211,208 sq mi
(547,030 sq km)
Population estimate (2006): 60,656,178
Government: Republic
Language: French
Monetary unit: Euro (formerly French franc)
Life expectancy: 79.4
Literacy rate: 99%
Did You Know? France is the world's top travel destination.

GABON

Where? Africa
Capital: Libreville
Area: 103,347 sq mi
(267,670 sq km)
Population estimate (2006): 1,389,201
Government: Republic
Languages: French (official), Fang, Myene, Bateke, Bapounou/Eschira, Bandjabi
Monetary unit: CFA franc
Life expectancy: 56.5
Literacy rate: 63%
Did You Know? Most of Gabon is covered by a dense tropical forest.

THE GAMBIA

Where? Africa
Capital: Banjul
Area: 4,363 sq mi
(11,300 sq km)
Population estimate (2006): 1,593,256
Government: Republic
Languages: English (official), native tongues
Monetary unit: Dalasi
Life expectancy: 54.8
Literacy rate: 40%
Did You Know? Gambia is Africa's smallest country.

GEORGIA

Where? Asia
Capital: T'bilisi
Area: 26,911 sq mi
(69,700 sq km)
Population estimate (2006): 4,677,401
Government: Republic
Languages: Georgian (official), Russian, Armenian, Azerbaijani
Monetary unit: Lari
Life expectancy: 75.6
Literacy rate: 99%
Did You Know? Georgia was part of the Soviet Union before its breakup in 1991.

GERMANY

Where? Europe
Capital: Berlin
Area: 137,846 sq mi
(357,021 sq km)
Population estimate (2006): 82,431,390
Government: Federal republic
Language: German
Monetary unit: Euro (formerly Deutsche mark)
Life expectancy: 78.5
Literacy rate: 99%
Did You Know? The country was divided into East and West Germany from 1949 to 1990.

GHANA

Where? Africa
Capital: Accra
Area: 92,456 sq mi
(239,460 sq km)
Population estimate (2006): 21,029,853
Government: Constitutional democracy
Languages: English (official), native tongues
Monetary unit: Cedi
Life expectancy: 56.3
Literacy rate: 75%
Did You Know? Ghana was formerly a British colony called the Gold Coast.

GREECE

Where? Europe
Capital: Athens
Area: 50,942 sq mi
(131,940 sq km)
Population estimate (2006): 10,668,354
Government: Parliamentary republic
Language: Greek
Monetary unit: Euro (formerly drachma)
Life expectancy: 78.9
Literacy rate: 98%
Did You Know? Greece is known for its magnificent ancient temples, particularly the world-renowned Parthenon.

GRENADA

Where? North America
Capital: Saint George's
Area: 133 sq mi
(344 sq km)
Population estimate (2006): 89,502
Government: Constitutional monarchy
Language: English
Monetary unit: East Caribbean dollar
Life expectancy: 64.5
Literacy rate: 90%
Did You Know? This Caribbean island was explored by Columbus in 1498.

GUATEMALA

Where? Central America
Capital: Guatemala City
Area: 42,042 sq mi
(108,890 sq km)
Population estimate (2006): 14,655,189
Government: Republic
Languages: Spanish (official), Indian languages
Monetary unit: Quetzal
Life expectancy: 65.2
Literacy rate: 71%
Did You Know? Most Guatemalans are of Mayan or Spanish descent.

GUINEA

Where? Africa
Capital: Conakry
Area: 94,925 sq mi
(245,860 sq km)
Population estimate (2006): 9,467,866
Government: Republic
Languages: French (official), native tongues
Monetary unit: Guinean franc
Life expectancy: 49.7
Literacy rate: 36%
Did You Know? Guinea's chief exports are agricultural products and minerals, especially bauxite.

GUINEA-BISSAU

Where? **Africa**
Capital: **Bissau**
Area: **13,946 sq mi (36,120 sq km)**
Population estimate (2006): **1,416,027**
Government: **Republic**
Languages: **Portuguese (official), African languages**
Monetary unit: **CFA franc**
Life expectancy: **47**
Literacy rate: **42%**
Did You Know? **This country was once a Portuguese colony.**

GUYANA

Where? **South America**
Capital: **Georgetown**
Area: **83,000 sq mi (214,970 sq km)**
Population estimate (2006): **765,283**
Government: **Republic**
Languages: **English (official), Amerindian dialects**
Monetary unit: **Guyana dollar**
Life expectancy: **65.1**
Literacy rate: **99%**
Did You Know? **Guyana's people are primarily of East Indian and African descent.**

HAITI

Where? **North America**
Capital: **Port-au-Prince**
Area: **10,714 sq mi (27,750 sq km)**
Population estimate (2006): **8,121,622**
Government: **Elected government**
Languages: **Creole and French (both official)**
Monetary unit: **Gourde**
Life expectancy: **52.6**
Literacy rate: **53%**
Did You Know? **This country and the Dominican Republic make up the island of Hispaniola in the Caribbean.**

HONDURAS

Where? **Central America**
Capital: **Tegucigalpa**
Area: **43,278 sq mi (112,090 sq km)**
Population estimate (2006): **6,975,204**
Government: **Republic**
Languages: **Spanish, Amerindian dialects**
Monetary unit: **Lempira**
Life expectancy: **66.2**
Literacy rate: **76%**
Did You Know? **About 80% of Honduras is mountainous.**

HUNGARY

Where? **Europe**
Capital: **Budapest**
Area: **35,919 sq mi (93,030 sq km)**
Population estimate (2006): **10,006,835**
Government: **Parliamentary democracy**
Language: **Magyar (Hungarian)**
Monetary unit: **Forint**
Life expectancy: **72.2**
Literacy rate: **99%**
Did You Know? **Magyar is the Hungarian name for Hungary's people.**

ICELAND

Where? **Europe**
Capital: **Reykjavik**
Area: **39,768 sq mi (103,000 sq km)**
Population estimate (2006): **296,737**
Government: **Constitutional republic**
Language: **Icelandic**
Monetary unit: **Icelandic krona**
Life expectancy: **80.2**
Literacy rate: **100%**
Did You Know? **Iceland boasts the world's oldest constitution, drafted around 930.**

INDIA

Where? Asia
Capital: New Delhi
Area: 1,269,338 sq mi
(3,287,590 sq km)
Population estimate (2006): 1,080,264,388
Government: Republic
Languages: Hindi (national), English;
24 major languages plus more than 1,600
dialects
Monetary unit: Rupee
Life expectancy: 64
Literacy rate: 60%
Did You Know? India is the world's
second most populous country.

INDONESIA

Where? Asia
Capital: Jakarta
Area: 741,096 sq mi
(1,919,440 sq km)
Population estimate (2006): 241,973,879
Government: Republic
Languages: Bahasa Indonesia (official),
Dutch, English; more than 500 languages
and dialects
Monetary unit: Rupiah
Life expectancy: 69.3
Literacy rate: 89%
Did You Know? Indonesia has the largest
number of active volcanoes in the world.

IRAN

Where? Middle East
Capital: Tehran
Area: 636,293 sq mi
(1,648,000 sq km)
Population estimate (2006): 68,017,860
Government: Theocratic republic
Languages: Farsi (Persian), Azari,
Kurdish, Arabic
Monetary unit: Rial
Life expectancy: 69.7
Literacy rate: 79%
Did You Know? Iran was once known
as Persia.

IRAQ

Where? Middle East
Capital: Baghdad
Area: 168,753 sq mi
(437,072 sq km)
Population estimate (2006): 26,074,906
Government: Transitional
Languages: Arabic, Kurdish
Monetary unit: Iraqi dinar
Life expectancy: 68.3
Literacy rate: 40%
Did You Know? The ancient civilization
of Mesopotamia was located in what is
today called Iraq.

IRELAND

Where? Europe
Capital: Dublin
Area: 27,136 sq mi
(70,280 sq km)
Population estimate (2006): 4,015,676
Government: Republic
Languages: English, Irish Gaelic
Monetary units: Euro (formerly Irish
pound, or punt)
Life expectancy: 77.4
Literacy rate: 98%
Did You Know? The name for Ireland in
Gaelic (the Irish language) is Eire.

ISRAEL

Where? Middle East
Capital: Jerusalem
Area: 8,020 sq mi
(20,770 sq km)
Population estimate (2006): 6,276,883
Government: Parliamentary democracy
Languages: Hebrew (official), Arabic,
English
Monetary unit: Shekel
Life expectancy: 79.2
Literacy rate: 95%
Did You Know? Modern Israel became
a country in 1948.

ITALY

Where? Europe
Capital: Rome
Area: 116,305 sq mi
(301,230 sq km)
Population estimate (2006): 58,103,033
Government: Republic
Language: Italian
Monetary unit: Euro (formerly lira)
Life expectancy: 79.5
Literacy rate: 99%
Did You Know? Italy is known for its magnificent art treasures and architecture.

JAMAICA

Where? North America
Capital: Kingston
Area: 4,244 sq mi
(10,991 sq km)
Population estimate (2006): 2,731,832
Government: Parliamentary democracy
Languages: English, patois English
Monetary unit: Jamaican dollar
Life expectancy: 76.1
Literacy rate: 88%
Did You Know? Jamaica once had a large slave population that worked on sugarcane plantations.

JAPAN

Where? Asia
Capital: Tokyo
Area: 145,882 sq mi
(377,835 sq km)
Population estimate (2006): 127,417,244
Government: Constitutional monarchy
Language: Japanese
Monetary unit: Yen
Life expectancy: 81
Literacy rate: 99%
Did You Know? The Japanese name for the country is Nippon.

JORDAN

Where? Middle East
Capital: Amman
Area: 34,445 sq mi
(89,213 sq km)
Population estimate (2006): 5,759,732
Government: Constitutional monarchy
Languages: Arabic (official), English
Monetary unit: Jordanian dinar
Life expectancy: 78.1
Literacy rate: 91%
Did You Know? Jordan is a kingdom ruled by the Hashemite dynasty.

KAZAKHSTAN

Where? Asia
Capital: Astana
Area: 1,049,150 sq mi
(2,717,300 sq km)
Population estimate (2006): 15,185,844
Government: Republic
Languages: Kazak (Qazaq) and Russian (both official)
Monetary unit: Tenge
Life expectancy: 66.1
Literacy rate: 98%
Did You Know? Oil was discovered in Kazakhstan in 2000. It was the largest oil find in 30 years.

KENYA

Where? Africa
Capital: Nairobi
Area: 224,960 sq mi
(582,650 sq km)
Population estimate (2006): 33,829,590
Government: Republic
Languages: English (official), Swahili, several others
Monetary unit: Kenyan shilling
Life expectancy: 47.2
Literacy rate: 85%
Did You Know? About 40 different ethnic groups live in Kenya.

KIRIBATI

Where? Pacific Islands
Capital: Tarawa
Area: 313 sq mi (811 sq km)
Population estimate (2006): 103,092
Government: Republic
Languages: English (official), I-Kiribati (Gilbertese)
Monetary unit: Australian dollar
Life expectancy: 61.3
Literacy rate: Not available

Did You Know? This nation is made up of three widely separated island groups in the South Pacific.

KOREA, NORTH

Where? Asia
Capital: Pyongyang
Area: 46,540 sq mi (120,540 sq km)
Population estimate (2006): 22,912,177
Government: Communist dictatorship
Language: Korean
Monetary unit: Won
Life expectancy: 71.1
Literacy rate: 99%

Did You Know? North Korea is one of the world's few communist countries.

KOREA, SOUTH

Where? Asia
Capital: Seoul
Area: 38,023 sq mi (98,480 sq km)
Population estimate (2006): 48,422,644
Government: Republic
Language: Korean
Monetary unit: Won
Life expectancy: 75.6
Literacy rate: 98%

Did You Know? About half of South Korea's religious people are Christian; the other half are Buddhist.

KUWAIT

Where? Middle East
Capital: Kuwait
Area: 6,880 sq mi (17,820 sq km)
Population estimate (2006): 2,335,648
Government: Constitutional monarchy
Languages: Arabic (official), English
Monetary unit: Kuwaiti dinar
Life expectancy: 76.8
Literacy rate: 84%

Did You Know? This small country has the fourth largest oil reserves in the world.

KYRGYZSTAN

Where? Asia
Capital: Bishkek
Area: 76,641 sq mi (198,500 sq km)
Population estimate (2006): 5,146,281
Government: Republic
Languages: Kyrgyz (official), Russian
Monetary unit: Som
Life expectancy: 67.8
Literacy rate: 97%

Did You Know? The Tien Shan mountain range covers about 95% of the country.

LAOS

Where? Asia
Capital: Vientiane
Area: 91,429 sq mi (236,800 sq km)
Population estimate (2006): 6,217,141
Government: Communist state
Languages: Lao (official), French, English
Monetary unit: Kip
Life expectancy: 54.7
Literacy rate: 53%

Did You Know? Laos is one of the 10 poorest countries in the world.

For a look at the most populous cities in the world:
www.factmonster.com/populouscities

LATVIA

Where? Europe
Capital: Riga
Area: 24,938 sq mi
(64,589 sq km)
Population estimate (2006): 2,290,237
Government: Parliamentary democracy
Language: Latvian
Monetary unit: Lats
Life expectancy: 70.9
Literacy rate: 100%
Did You Know? One of the three Baltic countries, Latvia is located in the far north of Europe.

LEBANON

Where? Middle East
Capital: Beirut
Area: 4,015 sq mi
(10,400 sq km)
Population estimate (2006): 3,826,018
Government: Republic
Languages: Arabic (official), French, English
Monetary unit: Lebanese pound
Life expectancy: 72.3
Literacy rate: 87%
Did You Know? About 60% of Lebanese are Muslim and 30% are Christian.

LESOTHO

Where? Africa
Capital: Maseru
Area: 11,720 sq mi
(30,350 sq km)
Population estimate (2006): 1,867,035
Government: Monarchy
Languages: English and Sesotho (both official), Zulu, Xhosa
Monetary unit: Loti
Life expectancy: 36.8
Literacy rate: 85%
Did You Know? This small African kingdom is surrounded on all sides by South Africa.

LIBERIA

Where? Africa
Capital: Monrovia
Area: 43,000 sq mi
(111,370 sq km)
Population estimate (2006): 3,482,211
Government: Republic
Languages: English (official), tribal dialects
Monetary unit: Liberian dollar
Life expectancy: 47.9
Literacy rate: 58%
Did You Know? Liberia was founded by freed American slaves in 1847.

LIBYA

Where? Africa
Capital: Tripoli
Area: 679,358 sq mi
(1,759,540 sq km)
Population estimate (2006): 5,765,563
Government: Military dictatorship
Languages: Arabic, Italian, English
Monetary unit: Libyan dinar
Life expectancy: 76.3
Literacy rate: 83%
Did You Know? The world's highest temperature ever recorded (136°F) was in Al Azizyah, Libya, in 1922.

LIECHTENSTEIN

Where? Europe
Capital: Vaduz
Area: 62 sq mi
(160 sq km)
Population estimate (2006): 33,717
Government: Constitutional monarchy
Languages: German (official), Alemannic dialect
Monetary unit: Swiss franc
Life expectancy: 79.4
Literacy rate: 100%
Did You Know? This tiny kingdom has been neutral in all of Europe's wars since 1868.

LITHUANIA

Where? Europe
Capital: Vilnius
Area: 25,174 sq mi
(65,200 sq km)
Population estimate (2006): 3,596,617
Government: Parliamentary democracy
Languages: Lithuanian (official), Polish, Russian
Monetary unit: Litas
Life expectancy: 73.5
Literacy rate: 100%
Did You Know? One of the three Baltic countries, Lithuania is located in northern Europe.

LUXEMBOURG

Where? Europe
Capital: Luxembourg
Area: 999 sq mi
(2,586 sq km)
Population estimate (2006): 468,571
Government: Constitutional monarchy
Languages: Luxembourgian, French, German
Monetary unit: Euro (formerly Luxembourg franc)
Life expectancy: 78.6
Literacy rate: 100%
Did You Know? This tiny kingdom is located in central Europe.

MACEDONIA

Where? Europe
Capital: Skopje
Area: 9,781 sq mi
(25,333 sq km)
Population estimate (2006): 2,045,262
Government: Emerging democracy
Languages: Macedonian, Albanian
Monetary unit: Denar
Life expectancy: 73.5
Literacy rate: Not available
Did You Know? Until Macedonia declared independence in 1991, it was part of Yugoslavia.

MADAGASCAR

Where? Africa
Capital: Antananarivo
Area: 226,660 sq mi
(587,040 sq km)
Population estimate (2006): 18,040,341
Government: Republic
Languages: Malagasy and French (both official)
Monetary unit: Malagasy franc
Life expectancy: 56.5
Literacy rate: 69%
Did You Know? Madagascar is the world's fourth largest island.

MALAWI

Where? Africa
Capital: Lilongwe
Area: 45,745 sq mi
(118,480 sq km)
Population estimate (2006): 12,158,924
Government: Multiparty democracy
Languages: English and Chichewa (both official)
Monetary unit: Kwacha
Life expectancy: 37.5
Literacy rate: 63%
Did You Know? About 20% of Malawi is made up of a large lake named Nyasa.

MALAYSIA

Where? Asia
Capital: Kuala Lumpur
Area: 127,316 sq mi
(329,750 sq km)
Population estimate (2006): 23,953,136
Government: Constitutional monarchy
Languages: Malay (official), Chinese, Tamil, English
Monetary unit: Ringgit
Life expectancy: 72
Literacy rate: 89%
Did You Know? Most of Malaysia is located in Southeast Asia; a smaller portion is located on the island of Borneo.

MALDIVES

Where? Asia
Capital: Male
Area: 116 sq mi
(300 sq km)
Population estimate (2006): 349,106
Government: Republic
Languages: Dhivehi (official), Arabic,
Hindi, English
Monetary unit: Maldivian rufiyaa
Life expectancy: 63.7
Literacy rate: 97%
Did You Know? This group of islands
lies off the southern coast of India.

MALI

Where? Africa
Capital: Bamako
Area: 478,764 sq mi
(1,240,000 sq km)
Population estimate (2006): 12,291,529
Government: Republic
Languages: French (official), African
languages
Monetary unit: CFA franc
Life expectancy: 45.3
Literacy rate: 46%
Did You Know? The fabled, ancient city
of Timbuktu is located in Mali.

MALTA

Where? Europe
Capital: Valletta
Area: 122 sq mi
(316 sq km)
Population estimate (2006): 398,534
Government: Republic
Languages: Maltese and English (both
official)
Monetary unit: Maltese lira
Life expectancy: 78.7
Literacy rate: 93%
Did You Know? The country is made up of
five small islands in the Mediterranean.

MARSHALL ISLANDS

Where? Pacific Islands
Capital: Majuro
Area: 70 sq mi
(181.3 sq km)
Population estimate (2006): 59,071
Government: Constitutional government
Languages: Marshallese and English
(both official)
Monetary unit: U.S. dollar
Life expectancy: 69.7
Literacy rate: 94%
Did You Know? The Marshall Islands
were once a dependency of the U.S.

MAURITANIA

Where? Africa
Capital: Nouakchott
Area: 397,953 sq mi
(1,030,700 sq km)
Population estimate (2006): 3,086,859
Government: Republic
Languages: Arabic (official), French
Monetary unit: Ouguiya
Life expectancy: 52.3
Literacy rate: 42%
Did You Know? This northern African
country is primarily desert.

MAURITIUS

Where? Africa
Capital: Port Louis
Area: 788 sq mi
(2,040 sq km)
Population estimate (2006): 1,230,602
Government: Parliamentary democracy
Languages: English (official), French,
Creole, Hindi, Urdu, Hakka, Bojpoori
Monetary unit: Mauritian rupee
Life expectancy: 72.1
Literacy rate: 86%
Did You Know? Most of this island's
population is of African or Indian descent.

MEXICO

Where? North America
Capital: Mexico City
Area: 761,600 sq mi
(1,972,550 sq km)
Population estimate (2006): 106,202,903
Government: Republic
Languages: Spanish, Indian languages
Monetary unit: Peso
Life expectancy: 74.9
Literacy rate: 92%
Did You Know? Teotihuacán (circa 300–900) was once the largest city in the Americas.

MICRONESIA

Where? Pacific Islands
Capital: Palikir
Area: 271 sq mi
(702 sq km)
Population estimate (2006): 108,105
Government: Constitutional government
Languages: English (official), native languages
Monetary unit: U.S. dollar
Life expectancy: 69.4
Literacy rate: 89%
Did You Know? Four different island groups make up this country.

MOLDOVA

Where? Europe
Capital: Chisinau
Area: 13,067 sq mi
(33,843 sq km)
Population estimate (2006): 4,455,421
Government: Republic
Languages: Moldovan (official), Russian, Gagauz
Monetary unit: Moldovan leu
Life expectancy: 65
Literacy rate: 99%
Did You Know? This eastern European country was once a part of the Soviet Union.

MONACO

Where? Europe
Capital: Monaco
Area: 0.75 sq mi
(1.95 sq km)
Population estimate (2006): 32,409
Government: Constitutional monarchy
Languages: French (official), English, Italian, Monégasque
Monetary unit: French franc
Life expectancy: 79.4
Literacy rate: 99%
Did You Know? Bordering France, this tiny nation is famous for its casinos.

MONGOLIA

Where? Asia
Capital: Ulaanbaatar
Area: 604,250 sq mi
(1,565,000 sq km)
Population estimate (2006): 2,791,272
Government: Parliamentary republic
Languages: Mongolian (official), Turkic, Russian, Chinese
Monetary unit: Tugrik
Life expectancy: 64.2
Literacy rate: 99%
Did You Know? Mongolia is Asia's most sparsely populated country.

MOROCCO

Where? Africa
Capital: Rabat
Area: 172,413 sq mi
(446,550 sq km)
Population estimate (2006): 32,725,847
Government: Constitutional monarchy
Languages: Arabic (official), French, Berber dialects, Spanish
Monetary unit: Dirham
Life expectancy: 70.3
Literacy rate: 52%
Did You Know? About 99% of Moroccans are of Arab-Berber descent.

MOZAMBIQUE

Where? Africa
Capital: Maputo
Area: 309,494 sq mi
(801,590 sq km)
Population estimate (2006): 19,406,703
Government: Republic
Languages: Portuguese (official), Bantu languages
Monetary unit: Metical
Life expectancy: 40.9
Literacy rate: 48%
Did You Know? In 1992, Mozambique endured a devastating drought.

MYANMAR (BURMA)

Where? Asia
Capital: Rangoon
Area: 261,969 sq mi
(678,500 sq km)
Population estimate (2006): 42,909,464
Government: Military regime
Languages: Burmese, minority languages
Monetary unit: Kyat
Life expectancy: 56
Literacy rate: 83%
Did You Know? In 1989, the government changed the name of Burma to Myanmar.

NAMIBIA

Where? Africa
Capital: Windhoek
Area: 318,694 sq mi
(825,418 sq km)
Population estimate (2006): 2,030,692
Government: Republic
Languages: Afrikaans, German, English (official), native languages
Monetary unit: Namibian dollar
Life expectancy: 44.8
Literacy rate: 84%
Did You Know? Namibia achieved independence from South Africa in 1990.

NAURU

Where? Pacific Islands
Capital: Yaren District (unofficial)
Area: 8.2 sq mi (21 sq km)
Population estimate (2006): 13,048
Government: Republic
Languages: Nauruan (official), English
Monetary unit: Australian dollar
Life expectancy: 62.3
Literacy rate: Not available
Did You Know? Nauru is the smallest island nation in the world.

NEPAL

Where? Asia
Capital: Kathmandu
Area: 54,363 sq mi
(140,800 sq km)
Population estimate (2006): 27,676,547
Government: Constitutional monarchy
Languages: Nepali (official), Newari, Bhutia, Maithali
Monetary unit: Nepalese rupee
Life expectancy: 59.4
Literacy rate: 45%
Did You Know? Mount Everest, on Nepal's border, is the world's highest mountain.

THE NETHERLANDS

Where? Europe
Capital: Amsterdam
Area: 16,036 sq mi
(41,532 sq km)
Population estimate (2006): 16,407,491
Government: Constitutional monarchy
Language: Dutch
Monetary unit: Euro (formerly guilder)
Life expectancy: 78.7
Literacy rate: 99%
Did You Know? About 40% of the Netherlands is land reclaimed from the sea.

NEW ZEALAND

Where? Pacific Islands
Capital: Wellington
Area: 103,737 sq mi (268,680 sq km)
Population estimate (2006): 4,035,461
Government: Parliamentary democracy
Languages: English (official), Maori
Monetary unit: New Zealand dollar
Life expectancy: 78.5
Literacy rate: 99%
Did You Know? The first people to inhabit New Zealand were the Maoris, who settled there about 1,200 years ago.

NICARAGUA

Where? Central America
Capital: Managua
Area: 49,998 sq mi (129,494 sq km)
Population estimate (2006): 5,465,100
Government: Republic
Language: Spanish
Monetary unit: Cordoba
Life expectancy: 70
Literacy rate: 68%
Did You Know? Nicaragua is the largest but most sparsely populated Central American country.

NIGER

Where? Africa
Capital: Niamey
Area: 489,189 sq mi (1,267,000 sq km)
Population estimate (2006): 11,665,937
Government: Republic
Languages: French (official), Hausa, Songhai, Arabic
Monetary unit: CFA franc
Life expectancy: 42.2
Literacy rate: 18%
Did You Know? Most of Niger is located in the Sahara.

NIGERIA

Where? Africa
Capital: Abuja
Area: 356,700 sq mi (923,770 sq km)
Population estimate (2006): 128,771,988
Government: Republic
Languages: English (official), Hausa, Yoruba, Ibo, more than 200 others
Monetary unit: Naira
Life expectancy: 46.5
Literacy rate: 68%
Did You Know? Nigeria is Africa's most populous country.

NORWAY

Where? Europe
Capital: Oslo
Area: 125,181 sq mi (324,220 sq km)
Population estimate (2006): 4,593,041
Government: Constitutional monarchy
Languages: Two official forms of Norwegian, Bokmål and Nynorsk
Monetary unit: Krone
Life expectancy: 79.2
Literacy rate: 100%
Did You Know? Norway extends farther north than any other European country.

OMAN

Where? Middle East
Capital: Muscat
Area: 82,030 sq mi (212,460 sq km)
Population estimate (2006): 3,001,583
Government: Monarchy
Languages: Arabic (official), English, Indian languages
Monetary unit: Omani rial
Life expectancy: 72.8
Literacy rate: 76%
Did You Know? Oman's major product is oil.

PAKISTAN

Where? Asia
Capital: Islamabad
Area: 310,400 sq mi
(803,940 sq km)
Population estimate (2006): 162,419,946
Government: Republic
Languages: Punjabi, Sindhi, Siraiki,
Pashtu, Urdu (official), others
Monetary unit: Pakistan rupee
Life expectancy: 62.6
Literacy rate: 46%
Did You Know? K2, the world's second
highest mountain, is in Pakistan.

PALAU

Where? Pacific Islands
Capital: Koror
Area: 177 sq mi (458 sq km)
Population estimate (2006): 20,303
Government: Constitutional government
Languages: Palauan, English (official)
Monetary unit: U.S. dollar
Life expectancy: 69.8
Literacy rate: 92%
Did You Know? Palau is made up of
200 islands.

PANAMA

Where? Central America
Capital: Panama City
Area: 30,193 sq mi
(78,200 sq km)
Population estimate (2006): 3,039,150
Government: Constitutional democracy
Languages: Spanish (official), English
Monetary unit: Balboa
Life expectancy: 72.1
Literacy rate: 93%
Did You Know? The Panama Canal links
the Atlantic and Pacific oceans and is
one of the world's most vital waterways.

PAPUA NEW GUINEA

Where? Pacific Islands
Capital: Port Moresby
Area: 178,703 sq mi
(462,840 sq km)
Population estimate (2006): 5,545,268
Government: Constitutional monarchy
Languages: English, Tok Pisin,
Hiri Motu, 717 native languages
Monetary unit: Kina
Life expectancy: 64.6
Literacy rate: 66%
Did You Know? More languages are
spoken in this country than in any other.

PARAGUAY

Where? South America
Capital: Asunción
Area: 157,046 sq mi
(406,750 sq km)
Population estimate (2006): 6,347,884
Government: Republic
Languages: Spanish (official), Guaraní
Monetary unit: Guaraní
Life expectancy: 74.6
Literacy rate: 94%
Did You Know? More than half of
Paraguay's workers are employed in
either agriculture or forestry.

PERU

Where? South America
Capital: Lima
Area: 496,223 sq mi
(1,285,220 sq km)
Population estimate (2006): 27,925,628
Government: Republic
Languages: Spanish and Quechua (both
official), Aymara, other native languages
Monetary unit: Nuevo sol
Life expectancy: 69.2
Literacy rate: 91%
Did You Know? Peru's Machu Picchu is
an incredible ancient Incan fortress in
the Andes mountains.

THE PHILIPPINES

Where? Asia
Capital: Manila
Area: 115,830 sq mi
(300,000 sq km)
Population estimate (2006): 87,857,473
Government: Republic
Languages: Filipino (based on Tagalog) and English (both official), regional languages
Monetary unit: Peso
Life expectancy: 69.6
Literacy rate: 96%
Did You Know? The country is made up of more than 7,000 tropical islands.

POLAND

Where? Europe
Capital: Warsaw
Area: 120,727 sq mi
(312,683 sq km)
Population estimate (2006): 38,635,144
Government: Republic
Language: Polish
Monetary unit: Zloty
Life expectancy: 74.2
Literacy rate: 100%
Did You Know? The Polish name for the country is Polska.

PORTUGAL

Where? Europe
Capital: Lisbon
Area: 35,672 sq mi
(92,391 sq km)
Population estimate (2006): 10,566,212
Government: Parliamentary democracy
Language: Portuguese
Monetary unit: Euro (formerly escudo)
Life expectancy: 77.3
Literacy rate: 93%
Did You Know? Many of the world's famous explorers were Portuguese, including Magellan and Vasco de Gama.

QATAR

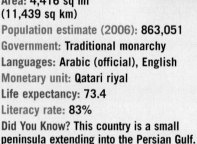

Where? Middle East
Capital: Doha
Area: 4,416 sq mi
(11,439 sq km)
Population estimate (2006): 863,051
Government: Traditional monarchy
Languages: Arabic (official), English
Monetary unit: Qatari riyal
Life expectancy: 73.4
Literacy rate: 83%
Did You Know? This country is a small peninsula extending into the Persian Gulf.

ROMANIA

Where? Europe
Capital: Bucharest
Area: 91,700 sq mi
(237,500 sq km)
Population estimate (2006): 22,329,977
Government: Republic
Languages: Romanian (official), Hungarian, German
Monetary unit: Leu
Life expectancy: 71.1
Literacy rate: 98%
Did You Know? Romania was once a Roman province known as Dacia.

RUSSIA

Where?
Europe and Asia
Capital: Moscow
Area: 6,592,735 sq mi
(17,075,200 sq km)
Population estimate (2006): 143,420,309
Government: Federation
Languages: Russian, others
Monetary unit: Ruble
Life expectancy: 66.8
Literacy rate: 100%
Did You Know? Russia is the world's largest country.

RWANDA

Where? Africa
Capital: Kigali
Area: 10,169 sq mi
(26,338 sq km)
Population estimate (2006): 8,440,820
Government: Republic
Languages: Kinyarwanda, French, English
(all official)
Monetary unit: Rwandan franc
Life expectancy: 46.6
Literacy rate: 70%
Did You Know? Ethnic violence killed about
800,000 Rwandans in 1994.

SAINT KITTS AND NEVIS

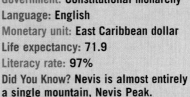

Where? North America
Capital: Basseterre
Area: 101 sq mi
(261 sq km)
Population estimate (2006): 38,958
Government: Constitutional monarchy
Language: English
Monetary unit: East Caribbean dollar
Life expectancy: 71.9
Literacy rate: 97%
Did You Know? Nevis is almost entirely
a single mountain, Nevis Peak.

SAINT LUCIA

Where? North America
Capital: Castries
Area: 239 sq mi
(620 sq km)
Population estimate (2006): 166,312
Government: Parliamentary democracy
Languages: English (official), patois
Monetary unit: East Caribbean dollar
Life expectancy: 73.3
Literacy rate: 67%
Did You Know? The major crop of this
Caribbean island is bananas.

SAINT VINCENT AND THE GRENADINES

Where? North America
Capital: Kingstown
Area: 150 sq mi
(389 sq km)
Population estimate (2006): 117,534
Government: Parliamentary democracy
Languages: English (official),
French patois
Monetary unit: East Caribbean dollar
Life expectancy: 73.3
Literacy rate: 96%
Did You Know? This country's highest
point is the active volcano Soufrière.

SAMOA

Where? Pacific Islands
Capital: Apia
Area: 1,104 sq mi
(2,860 sq km)
Population estimate (2006): 177,287
Government: Constitutional monarchy
Languages: Samoan, English
Monetary unit: Tala
Life expectancy: 70.4
Literacy rate: 100%
Did You Know? Samoa, now independent,
was once ruled by Germany and
New Zealand.

SAN MARINO

Where? Europe
Capital: San Marino
Area: 24 sq mi
(61 sq km)
Population estimate (2006): 28,880
Government: Republic
Language: Italian
Monetary unit: Italian lira
Life expectancy: 81.5
Literacy rate: 96%
Did You Know? Tiny San Marino is
part of the Italian peninsula.

For a list of kingdoms and monarchs of the world:
www.factmonster.com/monarchs

World

SÃO TOMÉ AND PRÍNCIPE

Where? Africa
Capital: São Tomé
Area: 386 sq mi (1,001 sq km)
Population estimate (2006): 187,410
Government: Republic
Language: Portuguese
Monetary unit: Dobra
Life expectancy: 66.6
Literacy rate: 79%
Did You Know? The recent discovery of oil may bring wealth to this poor nation.

SAUDI ARABIA

Where? Middle East
Capital: Riyadh
Area: 756,981 sq mi (1,960,582 sq km)
Population estimate (2006): 26,417,599
Government: Monarchy
Language: Arabic
Monetary unit: Riyal
Life expectancy: 75.2
Literacy rate: 79%
Did You Know? This country contains two of Islam's holiest cities, Mecca and Medina.

SENEGAL

Where? Africa
Capital: Dakar
Area: 75,749 sq mi (196,190 sq km)
Population estimate (2006): 11,126,832
Government: Republic
Languages: French (official), Wolof, Serer, other dialects
Monetary unit: CFA franc
Life expectancy: 56.6
Literacy rate: 40%
Did You Know? Senegal's capital, Dakar, is the westernmost point of Africa.

SERBIA AND MONTENEGRO

Where? Europe
Capital: Belgrade
Area: 39,517 sq mi (102,350 sq km)
Population estimate (2006): 10,829,175
Government: Republic
Languages: Serbian, Albanian
Monetary unit: Yugoslav new dinar
Life expectancy: 74.4
Literacy rate: 93%
Did You Know? In 2003, the country changed its name from Yugoslavia.

SEYCHELLES

Where? Africa
Capital: Victoria
Area: 176 sq mi (455 sq km)
Population estimate (2006): 81,188
Government: Republic
Languages: English and French (both official), Seselwa
Monetary unit: Seychelles rupee
Life expectancy: 71.5
Literacy rate: 58%
Did You Know? This island nation is located in the Indian Ocean.

SIERRA LEONE

Where? Africa
Capital: Freetown
Area: 27,699 sq mi (71,740 sq km)
Population estimate (2006): 6,017,643
Government: Constitutional democracy
Languages: English (official), Mende, Temne, Krio
Monetary unit: Leone
Life expectancy: 42.7
Literacy rate: 31%
Did You Know? This nation is one of the poorest countries in the world.

SINGAPORE

Where? Asia
Capital: Singapore
Area: 267 sq mi
(692.7 sq km)
Population estimate (2006): 4,425,720
Government: Parliamentary republic
Languages: Malay, Chinese (Mandarin), Tamil, English (all official)
Monetary unit: Singapore dollar
Life expectancy: 81.5
Literacy rate: 93%
Did You Know? Singapore is the second most densely populated country in the world.

SLOVAKIA

Where? Europe
Capital: Bratislava
Area: 18,859 sq mi
(48,845 sq km)
Population estimate (2006): 5,431,363
Government: Parliamentary democracy
Languages: Slovak (official), Hungarian
Monetary unit: Koruna
Life expectancy: 74.2
Literacy rate: Not available
Did You Know? Until 1993, the country was part of Czechoslovakia, which now no longer exists.

SLOVENIA

Where? Europe
Capital: Ljubljana
Area: 7,820 sq mi
(20,253 sq km)
Population estimate (2006): 2,011,070
Government: Parliamentary republic
Languages: Slovenian, Serbo-Croatian
Monetary unit: Slovenian tolar
Life expectancy: 75.9
Literacy rate: 100%
Did You Know? Slovenia was part of Yugoslavia until declaring independence in 1991.

SOLOMON ISLANDS

Where?
Pacific Islands
Capital: Honiara
Area: 10,985 sq mi
(28,450 sq km)
Population estimate (2006): 538,032
Government: Parliamentary democracy
Languages: English, Solomon pidgin, more than 60 Melanesian languages
Monetary unit: Solomon Islands dollar
Life expectancy: 72.4
Literacy rate: Not available
Did You Know? Experts think people have lived here since about 2000 B.C.

SOMALIA

Where? Africa
Capital: Mogadishu
Area: 246,199 sq mi
(637,657 sq km)
Population estimate (2006): 8,591,629
Government: Transitional government
Languages: Somali (official), Arabic, English, Italian
Monetary unit: Somali shilling
Life expectancy: 47.7
Literacy rate: 38%
Did You Know? Between January 1991 and August 2000, Somalia had no working government.

SOUTH AFRICA

Where? Africa
Capital (administrative):
Pretoria
Area: 471,008 sq mi (1,219,912 sq km)
Population estimate (2006): 44,344,136
Government: Republic
Languages: 11 official languages: Afrikaans, English, Ndebele, Pedi, Sotho, Swazi, Tsonga, Tswana, Venda, Xhosa, Zulu
Monetary unit: Rand
Life expectancy: 44.1
Literacy rate: 86%
Did You Know? South Africa is the world's largest producer of gold.

SPAIN

Where? Europe
Capital: Madrid
Area: 194,896 sq mi
(504,782 sq km)
Population estimate (2006): 40,341,462
Government: Parliamentary monarchy
Languages: Castilian Spanish (official), Catalan, Galician, Basque
Monetary unit: Euro (formerly peseta)
Life expectancy: 79.4
Literacy rate: 98%
Did You Know? Spain is the closest European country to Africa.

SRI LANKA

Where? Asia
Capital: Colombo
Area: 25,332 sq mi
(65,610 sq km)
Population estimate (2006): 20,064,776
Government: Republic
Languages: Sinhala (official), Tamil, English
Monetary unit: Sri Lankan rupee
Life expectancy: 72.9
Literacy rate: 92%
Did You Know? Sri Lanka was once called Ceylon.

SUDAN

Where? Africa
Capital: Khartoum
Area: 967,493 sq mi
(2,505,810 sq km)
Population estimate (2006): 40,187,486
Government: Authoritarian regime
Languages: Arabic (official), English, tribal dialects
Monetary unit: Sudanese dinar
Life expectancy: 58.1
Literacy rate: 61%
Did You Know? Sudan is Africa's largest country.

SURINAME

Where? South America
Capital: Paramaribo
Area: 63,039 sq mi
(163,270 sq km)
Population estimate (2006): 438,144
Government: Constitutional democracy
Languages: Dutch (official), Surinamese, English
Monetary unit: Suriname guilder
Life expectancy: 69.1
Literacy rate: 93%
Did You Know? Suriname is named after its earliest inhabitants, the Surinen Indians.

SWAZILAND

Where? Africa
Capital: Mbabane
Area: 6,704 sq mi
(17,360 sq km)
Population estimate (2006): 1,173,900
Government: Monarchy
Languages: Swazi (official), English
Monetary unit: Lilangeni
Life expectancy: 37.5
Literacy rate: 82%
Did You Know? The nation's King is one of the world's last absolute monarchs.

SWEDEN

Where? Europe
Capital: Stockholm
Area: 173,731 sq mi
(449,964 sq km)
Population estimate (2006): 9,001,774
Government: Constitutional monarchy
Language: Swedish
Monetary unit: Krona
Life expectancy: 80.3
Literacy rate: 99%
Did You Know? The Nobel Prizes (except the Peace Prize) are awarded each year in Sweden.

SWITZERLAND

Where? Europe
Capital: Bern
Area: 15,942 sq mi (41,290 sq km)
Population estimate (2006): 7,489,370
Government: Federal republic
Languages: German, French, Italian (all official), Romansch
Monetary unit: Swiss franc
Life expectancy: 80.3
Literacy rate: 99%
Did You Know? Switzerland, in central Europe, is the land of the Alps.

SYRIA

Where? Middle East
Capital: Damascus
Area: 71,498 sq mi (185,180 sq km)
Population estimate (2006): 18,448,752
Government: Republic
Languages: Arabic (official), French, English
Monetary unit: Syrian pound
Life expectancy: 69.7
Literacy rate: 77%
Did You Know? Damascus is considered the oldest capital city in the world.

TAIWAN

Where? Asia
Capital: Taipei
Area: 13,892 sq mi (35,980 sq km)
Population estimate (2006): 22,894,384
Government: Multiparty democracy
Language: Chinese (Mandarin)
Monetary unit: New Taiwan dollar
Life expectancy: 77.1
Literacy rate: 86%
Did You Know? The nation was once called Formosa. The name, meaning *the beautiful,* was given by Portuguese explorers.

TAJIKISTAN

Where? Asia
Capital: Dushanbe
Area: 55,251 sq mi (143,100 sq km)
Population estimate (2006): 7,163,506
Government: Republic
Language: Tajik
Monetary unit: Somoni
Life expectancy: 64.5
Literacy rate: 99%
Did You Know? Once part of the Soviet Union, its name means "land of the Tajiks."

TANZANIA

Where? Africa
Capital: Dar es Salaam
Area: 364,898 sq mi (945,087 sq km)
Population estimate (2006): 36,766,356
Government: Republic
Languages: Swahili and English (both official), local languages
Monetary unit: Tanzanian shilling
Life expectancy: 44.9
Literacy rate: 78%
Did You Know? Mount Kilimanjaro, in Tanzania, is the highest mountain in Africa.

THAILAND

Where? Asia
Capital: Bangkok
Area: 198,455 sq mi (514,000 sq km)
Population estimate (2006): 65,444,371
Government: Constitutional monarchy
Languages: Thai (Siamese), Chinese, English
Monetary unit: Baht
Life expectancy: 71.4
Literacy rate: 96%
Did You Know? Thailand was once known as Siam.

TOGO

Where? Africa
Capital: **Lomé**
Area: **21,925 sq mi
(56,790 sq km)**
Population estimate (2006): **5,681,519**
Government: **Republic**
Languages: **French (official), Éwé, Mina,
Kabyé, Cotocoli**
Monetary unit: **CFA franc**
Life expectancy: **53**
Literacy rate: **61%**
Did You Know? **The Danish, Germans,
British and French once ruled Togo.**

TONGA

**Where?
Pacific Islands**
Capital: **Nuku'alofa**
Area: **290 sq mi
(748 sq km)**
Population estimate (2006): **112,422**
Government: **Constitutional monarchy**
Languages: **Tongan, English**
Monetary unit: **Pa'anga**
Life expectancy: **69.2**
Literacy rate: **99%**
Did You Know? **Polynesians have lived
on Tonga for at least 3,000 years.**

TRINIDAD AND TOBAGO

Where? North America
Capital: **Port-of-Spain**
Area: **1,980 sq mi
(5,130 sq km)**
Population estimate (2006): **1,088,644**
Government: **Parliamentary democracy**
Languages: **English (official), Hindi,
French, Spanish**
Monetary unit: **Trinidad and Tobago
dollar**
Life expectancy: **69.3**
Literacy rate: **99%**
Did You Know? **Columbus explored
Trinidad in 1498.**

TUNISIA

Where? Africa
Capital: **Tunis**
Area: **63,170 sq mi
(163,610 sq km)**
Population estimate (2006): **10,074,951**
Government: **Republic**
Languages: **Arabic (official), French**
Monetary unit: **Tunisian dinar**
Life expectancy: **74.7**
Literacy rate: **74%**
Did You Know? **Bordering the
Mediterranean, Tunisia stretches south
into the Sahara.**

TURKEY

**Where?
Europe and Asia**
Capital: **Ankara**
Area: **301,388 sq mi (780,580 sq km)**
Population estimate (2006): **69,660,559**
Government: **Parliamentary democracy**
Language: **Turkish**
Monetary unit: **Turkish lira**
Life expectancy: **72.1**
Literacy rate: **87%**
Did You Know? **Turkey was once the
home of the Byzantine and the
Ottoman empires.**

TURKMENISTAN

Where? Asia
Capital: **Ashgabat**
Area: **188,455 sq mi
(488,100 sq km)**
Population estimate (2006): **4,952,081**
Government: **Republic**
Languages: **Turkmen, Russian, Uzbek**
Monetary unit: **Manat**
Life expectancy: **61.3**
Literacy rate: **98%**
Did You Know? **About nine-tenths of the
country is desert, mainly the Kara-Kum.**

TUVALU

Where? Pacific Islands
Capital: Funafuti
Area: 10 sq mi
(26 sq km)
Population estimate (2006): 11,636
Government: Constitutional monarchy
Languages: Tuvaluan, English
Monetary unit: Tuvaluan dollar
Life expectancy: 67.7
Literacy rate: Not available
Did You Know? Tuvalu was formerly named the Ellice Islands.

UGANDA

Where? Africa
Capital: Kampala
Area: 91,135 sq mi
(236,040 sq km)
Population estimate (2006): 27,269,482
Government: Republic
Languages: English (official), Swahili, Luganda, Ateso, Luo
Monetary unit: Ugandan shilling
Life expectancy: 50.4
Literacy rate: 70%
Did You Know? Uganda's brutal former dictator, Idi Amin, died in 2003.

UKRAINE

Where? Europe
Capital: Kyiv (Kiev)
Area: 233,089 sq mi
(603,700 sq km)
Population estimate (2006): 47,425,336
Government: Republic
Language: Ukrainian
Monetary unit: Hryvnia
Life expectancy: 66.7
Literacy rate: 100%
Did You Know? In 1986, a reactor blew at Chernobyl, causing the worst nuclear power accident in history.

UNITED ARAB EMIRATES

Where? Middle East
Capital: Abu Dhabi
Area: 32,000 sq mi
(82,880 sq km)
Population estimate (2006): 2,563,212
Government: Federation
Languages: Arabic (official), English
Monetary unit: U.A.E. dirham
Life expectancy: 75
Literacy rate: 78%
Did You Know? This country is made up of seven Gulf states.

UNITED KINGDOM

Where? Europe
Capital: London
Area: 94,525 sq mi
(244,820 sq km)
Population estimate (2006): 60,441,457
Government: Constitutional monarchy
Languages: English, Welsh, Scots, Gaelic
Monetary unit: British pound
Life expectancy: 78.3
Literacy rate: 99%
Did You Know? The United Kingdom is made up of England, Wales, Scotland and Northern Ireland.

UNITED STATES

Where? North America
Capital: Washington, D.C.
Area: 3,717,792 sq mi
(9,629,091 sq km)
Population estimate (2006): 295,734,134
Government: Republic
Languages: English, Spanish (spoken by a sizable minority)
Monetary unit: U.S. dollar
Life expectancy: 77.4
Literacy rate: 97%
Did You Know? The U.S. is the world's third largest country and the world's third most populous country.

URUGUAY

Where? South America
Capital: Montevideo
Area: 68,040 sq mi
(176,220 sq km)
Population estimate (2006): 3,415,920
Government: Republic
Language: Spanish
Monetary unit: Peso
Life expectancy: 75.9
Literacy rate: 98%
Did You Know? The first inhabitants
of Uruguay were a people called
the Charrúas.

UZBEKISTAN

Where? Asia
Capital: Tashkent
Area: 172,741 sq mi
(447,400 sq km)
Population estimate (2006): 26,851,195
Government: Republic
Languages: Uzbek, Russian, Tajik
Monetary unit: Uzbekistani som
Life expectancy: 64.1
Literacy rate: 99%
Did You Know? In 2001, Uzbekistan gave
the U.S. a base to fight the Taliban and
al-Qaeda in Afghanistan.

VANUATU

Where? Pacific Islands
Capital: Port Vila
Area: 5,700 sq mi
(14,760 sq km)
Population estimate (2006): 205,754
Government: Republic
Languages: English and French (both
official), Bislama
Monetary unit: Vatu
Life expectancy: 62.1
Literacy rate: 53%
Did You Know? Vanuatu is an
archipelago of 83 islands.

VATICAN CITY (HOLY SEE)

Where? Europe
Capital: none
Area: 0.17 sq mi
(0.44 sq km)
Population estimate (2006): 890
Government: Ecclesiastical
Languages: Latin, Italian
Monetary unit: Italian lira
Life expectancy: 77.5
Literacy rate: 100%
Did You Know? This nation is the
world's smallest country.

VENEZUELA

Where? South America
Capital: Caracas
Area: 352,143 sq mi
(912,050 sq km)
Population estimate (2006): 25,375,281
Government: Republic
Languages: Spanish (official), native
languages
Monetary unit: Bolivar
Life expectancy: 74.1
Literacy rate: 93%
Did You Know? Venezuela's Angel Falls
is the world's highest waterfall.

VIETNAM

Where? Asia
Capital: Hanoi
Area: 127,243 sq mi
(329,560 sq km)
Population estimate (2006): 83,535,576
Government: Communist state
Languages: Vietnamese (official),
French, English, Khmer, Chinese
Monetary unit: Dong
Life expectancy: 70.4
Literacy rate: 94%
Did You Know? The country was divided
into North and South Vietnam in 1954,
and reunified in 1976.

YEMEN

Where? Middle East
Capital: Sanaa
Area: 203,850 sq mi (527,970 sq km)
Population estimate (2006): 20,727,063
Government: Republic
Language: Arabic
Monetary unit: Rial
Life expectancy: 61.4
Literacy rate: 50%
Did You Know? In 1990, North and South Yemen joined to form the Republic of Yemen.

ZAMBIA

Where? Africa
Capital: Lusaka
Area: 290,584 sq mi (752,610 sq km)
Population estimate (2006): 11,261,795
Government: Republic
Languages: English (official), local dialects
Monetary unit: Kwacha
Life expectancy: 39.4
Literacy rate: 81%
Did You Know? Zambia changed its name from Northern Rhodesia after it gained independence in 1964.

ZIMBABWE

Where? Africa
Capital: Harare
Area: 150,803 sq mi (390,580 sq km)
Population estimate (2006): 12,746,990
Government: Parliamentary democracy
Languages: English (official), Ndebele, Shona
Monetary unit: Zimbabwean dollar
Life expectancy: 37.8
Literacy rate: 91%
Did You Know? Before gaining independence in 1965, this country was called Rhodesia.

The Security Council can send U.N. troops to help settle disputes.

The United Nations

The **United Nations (U.N.)** was created after World War II to provide a meeting place to help develop good relations between countries, promote peace and security around the world and encourage international cooperation in solving problems.

The major organizations of the U.N. are the Secretariat, the Security Council and the General Assembly.

The **Secretariat** is the management center of U.N. operations and is headed by the Secretary-General, who is the director of the U.N.

The **Security Council** is responsible for making and keeping international peace. Its main purpose is to prevent war by settling disputes between nations. The Security Council has 15 members. There are five permanent members: the U.S., the Russian Federation, Britain, France and China. There are also 10 temporary members that serve two-year terms.

The **General Assembly** is the world's forum for discussing matters that affect world peace and security and for making recommendations concerning both. The U.N. has no power of its own to enforce decisions. Including the 51 original member nations, it is made up of a total of 191 countries.

World

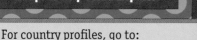
For country profiles, go to:
www.factmonster.com/countries

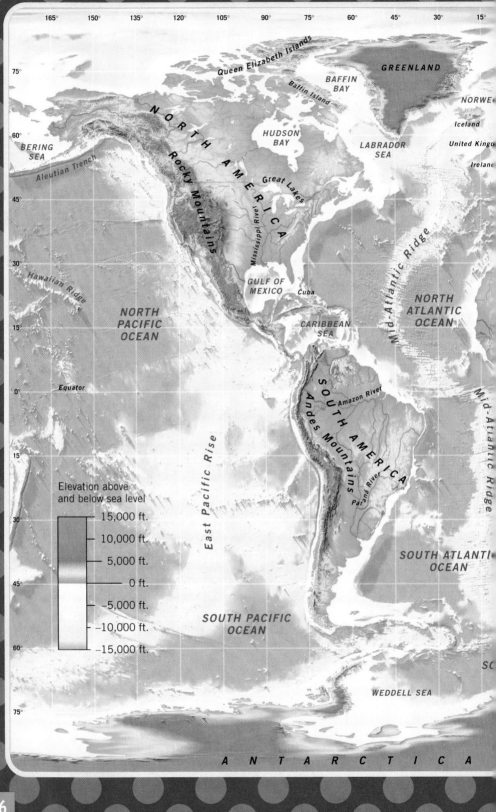

165° 150° 135° 120° 105° 90° 75° 60° 45° 30° 15°

Queen Elizabeth Islands

GREENLAND

BAFFIN BAY

Baffin Island

75°

NORWE

Iceland

HUDSON BAY

N O R T H   A M E R I C A

LABRADOR SEA

United Kingo

60°

BERING SEA

Irelan

Aleutian Trench

Rocky Mountains

45°

Great Lakes

Mississippi River

Mid-Atlantic Ridge

30°

Hawaiian Ridge

GULF OF MEXICO

Cuba

NORTH ATLANTIC OCEAN

NORTH PACIFIC OCEAN

CARIBBEAN SEA

15°

Equator

0°

S O U T H   A M E R I C A

Amazon River

Mid-Atlantic Ridge

East Pacific Rise

Andes Mountains

15°

Elevation above and below sea level

Paraná River

15,000 ft.

30°

10,000 ft.

5,000 ft.

SOUTH ATLANTI OCEAN

0 ft.

45°

−5,000 ft.

−10,000 ft.

SOUTH PACIFIC OCEAN

−15,000 ft.

SC

60°

WEDDELL SEA

75°

A N T A R C T I C A

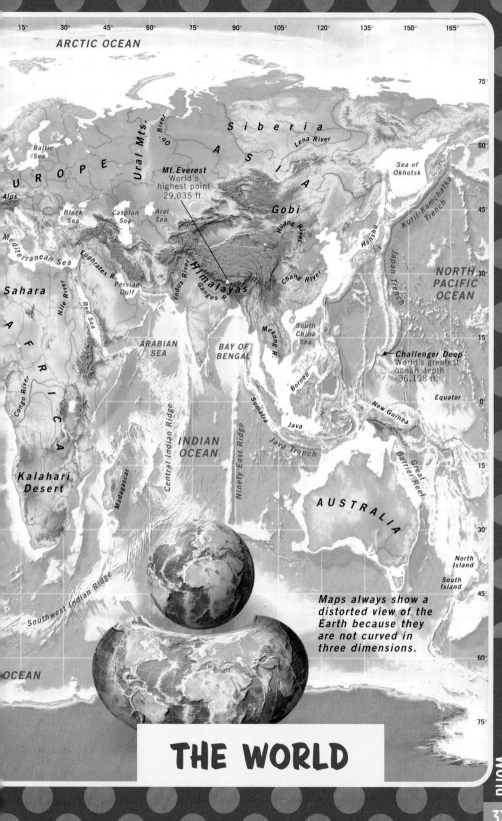

THE WORLD

15° 30° 45° 60° 75° 90° 105° 120° 135° 150° 165°

75°

S i b e r i a

E U R O P E

A S I A

Ural Mts.

Lena River

Sea of
Okhotsk

60°

Baltic
Sea

90 River

Mt. Everest
World's
highest point
29,035 ft.

Gobi

Kuril-Kamchatka
Trench

45°

Alps

Black
Sea

Caspian
Sea

Aral
Sea

Huang River

Honshu

Mediterranean Sea

Euphrates R.

Persian
Gulf

Indus River

Himalayas

Chang River

Japan Trench

NORTH
PACIFIC
OCEAN

30°

Sahara

Nile River

Red Sea

Ganges R.

15°

A F R I C A

Congo River

ARABIAN
SEA

BAY OF
BENGAL

Mekong R.

South
China
Sea

Challenger Deep
World's greatest
ocean depth
36,198 ft.

Borneo

Equator

0°

Central Indian Ridge

INDIAN
OCEAN

Sumatra

New Guinea

Kalahari
Desert

Madagascar

Ninety East Ridge

Java

Java Trench

Great
Barrier Reef

15°

AUSTRALIA

30°

Southwest Indian Ridge

North
Island

45°

South
Island

Maps always show a
distorted view of the
Earth because they
are not curved in
three dimensions.

60°

OCEAN

75°

THE WORLD

AFRICA

INDIAN OCEAN

Antananarivo
MADAGASCAR

Moroni
COMOROS

Dar es Salaam
Zanzibar
Mombasa

TANZANIA
Lake Nyasa
Lake Tanganyika
Kigoma

RWANDA
BURUNDI
Bujumbura
Bukavu

MALAWI
Lilongwe
Blantyre

MOZAMBIQUE
Cidade de Nacala
Beira
Maputo

Mozambique Channel

ZIMBABWE
Harare

Durban

SWAZILAND
Mbabane
Pretoria
Johannesburg
Maseru
LESOTHO

ZAMBIA
Lusaka
Lubumbashi
Kitwe
Kananga

BOTSWANA
Gaborone

SOUTH AFRICA
Port Elizabeth

DEMOCRATIC REPUBLIC OF THE CONGO
Kinshasa

ANGOLA
Lubango
Namibe

NAMIBIA
Windhoek
Walvis Bay

Cape Town

Brazzaville
Pointe-Noire
Luanda

(EQUATORIAL GUINEA)

ATLANTIC OCEAN

0 mi.   500 mi.   1,000 mi.
0 km   500 km   1,000 km

ASIA AND THE MIDDLE EAST

UNITED KINGDOM
NETHERLANDS
BELGIUM
LUXEMBOURG
FRANCE
SWITZERLAND
AUSTRIA
SLOVENIA
ITALY
CROATIA
BOSNIA AND
HERZEGOVINA
YUGOSLAVIA
ALBANIA
MACEDONIA
GREECE

DENMARK
GERMANY
CZECH
REPUBLIC
SLOVAKIA
HUNGARY
ROMANIA
BULGARIA

NORWAY
SWEDEN
FINLAND

RUSSIA
ESTONIA
LATVIA
LITHUANIA
POLAND
BELARUS
UKRAINE
MOLDOVA

RUSSIA

Khanty-Mansiysk
Yakaterinburg
Chelyabinsk
Magnitogorsk
Imeni Gastello
Omsk
Novosibirsk
Astana
Qaraghandy
(Karaganda)
To
Ke

LIBYA

Mediterranean
Sea

Istanbul
Izmir
Ankara
TURKEY
Adana
Nicosia
CYPRUS
Aleppo
Beirut
LEBANON
ISRAEL
Damascus
SYRIA
Tel Aviv
Jerusalem
Amman
JORDAN
Tabuk

Black
Sea
GEORGIA
T'bilisi
ARMENIA
Yerevan
AZERBAIJAN
Mosul
Irbil
Tabriz
Kirkuk
Baghdad
Kermanshah
IRAQ

Caspian
Sea
Baku

Aral
Sea
Nukus
TURKMENISTAN
Ashgabat

UZBEKISTAN
Tashkent
Samarkand
Fergana
Dushanbe
TAJIKISTAN

Bishkek
Almaty
KYRGYZSTAN

KAZAKHSTAN
Tyuratam

Tehran
Esfahan
Mashhad
Herat

Claimed
by India
Kabul
Islamabad
Srinagar
AFGHANISTAN

EGYPT

AFRICA

SUDAN

Red
Sea
Jiddah
Mecca
Abha
ERITREA
Sanaa
Taizz
Aden
DJIBOUTI

Al Basrah
Kuwait
KUWAIT

Persian
Gulf
Manama
BAHRAIN
Riyadh
Doha
Abu Dhabi
QATAR

SAUDI ARABIA

Shiraz
IRAN
Kerman

Quetta
Multan
Faisalabad
PAKISTAN
Delhi

Karachi

Muscat
OMAN

Arabian Sea

YEMEN
Al Makalla
UNITED ARAB
EMIRATES

NEPAL
Kanpur
Kathm

INDIA
Nagpur
Hyderabad
Mumbai
(Bombay)
Pune

ETHIOPIA

UGANDA
KENYA
SOMALIA

0 mi.   500 mi.   1,000 mi.

0 km   500 km   1,000 km

INDIAN OCEAN

Bangalore
Cochin
Madurai
Chennai
(Madras)
Jaffna

Bay
Beng

Colombo
SRI LAN

ARCTIC OCEAN

Bering Sea

Cherskiy

Tiksi

Verkhoyansk

RUSSIA

Magadan

Kamchatka Peninsula

Yakutsk

Petropavlovsk-Kamchatskiy

S I B E R I A

Sea of Okhotsk

'sk

asnoyarsk

znetsk

Khabarovsk

Irkutsk

Sakhalin

Harbin

Sapporo

Ulaanbaatar

Changchun

Vladivostok

MONGOLIA

Gobi

Shenyang

JAPAN

Jinxi

N. KOREA

Hohhot

Beijing

P'yongyang

Tokyo

Tianjin

Seoul

Nagoya

Taiyuan

Jinan

Taegu

Kyoto

Osaka

Pusan

Kobe

PACIFIC OCEAN

Lanzhou

S. KOREA

Hiroshima

Qingdao

Fukuoka

Xi'an

CHINA

Nagasaki

Hefei

Shanghai

Chengdu

Wuhan

Chongqing

asa

Naha

phu

HUTAN

Fuzhou

Taipei

ANGLADESH

Xiamen

Dhaka

Liuzhou

TAIWAN

Chittagong

Nanning

Guangzhou

Kao-hsiung

YANMAR (BURMA)

Mandalay

Hanoi

Macao

Hong Kong

Chiang Mai

LAOS

Luzon

Rangoon

Vientiane

Baguio

Quezon City

Da Nang

THAILAND

Manila

Bangkok

VIETNAM

PHILIPPINES

CAMBODIA

Cebu

Phnom Penh

Ho Chi Minh City

Phuket

Songkhla

Davao

Borneo

World

331

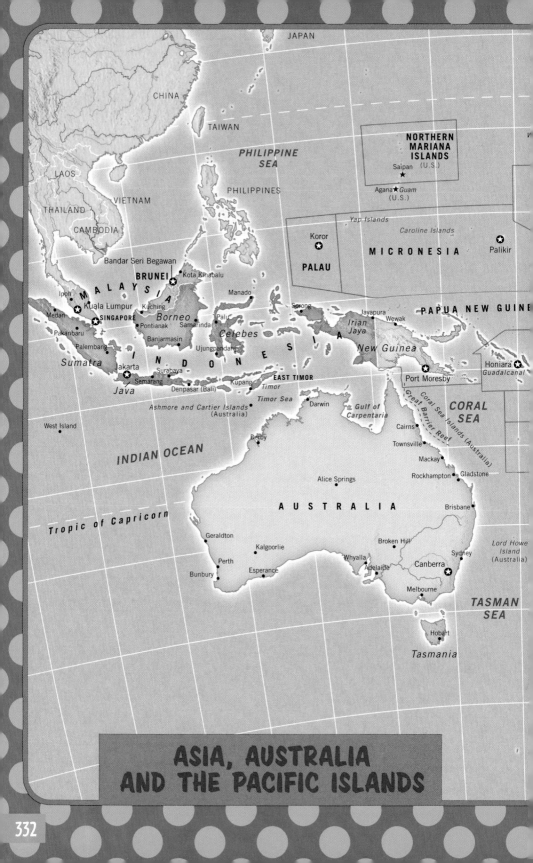

JAPAN

CHINA

TAIWAN

LAOS

THAILAND

VIETNAM

CAMBODIA

PHILIPPINES

PHILIPPINE
SEA

NORTHERN
MARIANA
ISLANDS

Saipan ★
(U.S.)

Agana ★ *Guam*
(U.S.)

Yap Islands

Caroline Islands

Koror ✪

PALAU

MICRONESIA

Palikir ✪

Bandar Seri Begawan

BRUNEI

Ipoh

M A L A Y S I A

Kuala Lumpur

Kuching

SINGAPORE

Medan

Pakanbaru

Palembang

Sumatra

Kota Kinabalu

Borneo

Pontianak

Samarinda

Banjarmasin

Manado

Palu

Celebes

Ujungpandang

Sorong

Jayapura

Wewak

*Irian
Jaya*

PAPUA NEW GUINEA

New Guinea

Honiara ✪
Guadalcanal

Jakarta

I N D O N E S I A

Semarang

Surabaya

Java

Denpasar (Bali)

Kupang

EAST TIMOR

Timor

Port Moresby

Timor Sea

Ashmore and Cartier Islands
(Australia)

Darwin

*Gulf of
Carpentaria*

Coral Sea Islands (Australia)

Great Barrier Reef

CORAL
SEA

West Island

INDIAN OCEAN

Derby

Cairns

Townsville

Mackay

Rockhampton

Gladstone

Alice Springs

A U S T R A L I A

Brisbane

Tropic of Capricorn

Geraldton

Kalgoorlie

Broken Hill

*Lord Howe
Island*
(Australia)

Perth

Whyalla

Sydney

Bunbury

Esperance

Adelaide

Canberra

Melbourne

TASMAN
SEA

Hobart

Tasmania

ASIA, AUSTRALIA
AND THE PACIFIC ISLANDS

Tropic of Cancer

Johnston Atoll (U.S.) •

Honolulu •
Hilo •
Hawaii
(U.S.)

ARSHALL ISLANDS

✪
Majuro

PACIFIC OCEAN

Kingman Reef (U.S.)
Palmyra Atoll (U.S.)

Tarawa
✪

Howland Island (U.S.) •
• Baker Island (U.S.)

Gilbert
Islands

K I R I B A T I

Jarvis
Island •
(U.S.)

Line Islands

Equator

Phoenix Islands

OLOMON
SLANDS

Funafuti
✪

TUVALU

TOKELAU (N.Z.)

Mata-Utu

SAMOA

**WALLIS AND
FUTURA**
(FR.) ★

Apia ★

Pago
Pago

COOK ISLANDS
(N.Z.)

Marquesas
Islands

VANUATU

**AMERICAN
SAMOA**

★
Port Vila

✪ Suva

TONGA

Alofi
★

Papeete •
Society
Islands
• Tahiti

Tuamotu Archipelago

umea

FIJI

Nuku'alofa
✪

NIUE
(N.Z.)

Avarua
★

FRENCH POLYNESIA (France)

**NEW
CALEDONIA**
(France)

Kermadec Islands
(N.Z.)

Adamstown
★

orfolk Island
on
lia)

International Date Line

**PITCAIRN
ISLANDS**
(U.K.)

NEW ZEALAND

Auckland •

• Hastings
✪ Wellington
• Christchurch   Chatham Islands

• Dunedin
vercargill •

Stewart Island

0 mi.   500 mi.   1,000 mi.

0 km   1,000 km

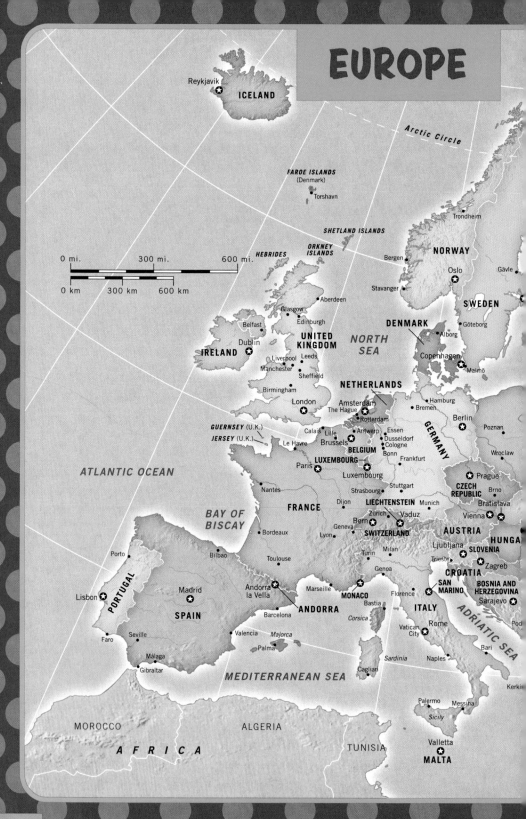

EUROPE

Arctic Circle

Reykjavik ✪ **ICELAND**

FAROE ISLANDS
(Denmark)

● Torshavn

Trondheim ●

SHETLAND ISLANDS

ORKNEY ISLANDS

Bergen ● **NORWAY**

Oslo ✪

Gävle ●

HEBRIDES

Aberdeen ●

Stavanger ● **SWEDEN**

Göteborg ●

Glasgow ●
Edinburgh ●

DENMARK

Ålborg ●

Belfast ●

UNITED KINGDOM

Leeds ●

NORTH SEA

Copenhagen ✪

Malmö ●

IRELAND

Dublin ✪

Liverpool ●
Manchester ●

Sheffield ●

Hamburg ●

Berlin ✪

Birmingham ●

London ✪

NETHERLANDS

Amsterdam ✪
The Hague ●
Rotterdam ●

Bremen ●

GERMANY

Poznań ●

GUERNSEY (U.K.)

JERSEY (U.K.)

Calais ● Lille ●
Antwerp ●

Essen ●
Düsseldorf ●
Cologne ●

Wrocław ●

Le Havre ●

Brussels ✪

Bonn ●

Frankfurt ●

ATLANTIC OCEAN

Paris ✪

BELGIUM

LUXEMBOURG

Luxembourg ✪

Prague ✪

CZECH REPUBLIC

Brno ●

Nantes ●

Strasbourg ●

Stuttgart ●

Bratislava ●

FRANCE

Dijon ●

LIECHTENSTEIN

Munich ●

Vienna ✪

BAY OF BISCAY

Geneva ●

Zurich ●
Bern ✪

Vaduz ✪

AUSTRIA

HUNGA

Bordeaux ●

Lyon ●

SWITZERLAND

Ljubljana ✪ **SLOVENIA**

Porto ●

Bilbao ●

Turin ●

Milan ●

Trieste ●

Zagreb ✪

Toulouse ●

Genoa ●

CROATIA

Madrid ✪

Andorra la Vella ✪

Marseille ●

MONACO

Florence ●

SAN MARINO ✪

BOSNIA AND HERZEGOVINA

Lisbon ✪

PORTUGAL

ANDORRA

Bastia ●

ITALY

Sarajevo ●

Barcelona ●

Corsica

Vatican City ✪

Rome ✪

Po●

SPAIN

Valencia ●

Majorca

ADRIATIC SEA

Faro ●

Seville ●

Palma ●

Naples ●

Bari ●

Málaga ●

Sardinia

Cagliari ●

Gibraltar ●

MEDITERRANEAN SEA

Kerki●

Palermo ●

Messina ●

MOROCCO

ALGERIA

Sicily

Valletta ✪

MALTA

A F R I C A

TUNISIA

0 mi.   300 mi.   600 mi.

0 km   300 km   600 km

Murmansk

Oulu

FINLAND

mpere

Helsinki

ESTONIA

Tallinn

LATVIA

a

UANIA

Vilnius

BELARUS

Minsk

Brest

Homyel'

L'viv

Derazhnya

UKRAINE

Kiev

Kharkiv

Voroshilovgrad

Gorlovka

Makeyevka

Zhdanov

Rostov

Chisinau

Iasi

Odessa

Mykolavia

Kerch'

MOLDOVA

Simferopol'

ROMANIA

Sevastopol'

Craiova

Bucharest

Constanta

GRO

Sofia

Varna

BULGARIA

je

BLACK SEA

DONIA

aloniki

Istanbul

Volos

T U R K E Y

CE

Izmir

Athens

Crete

CYPRUS

SYRIA

LEBANON

IRAQ

IRAN

Arkhangel'sk

Pechora

ASIA

R U S S I A

Izhevsk

Nizhniy Novgorod

Kazan

Moscow

Samara

Smolensk

Lipetsk

Saratov

Voronezh

KAZAKHSTAN

Volgograd

Groznyy

St. Petersburg

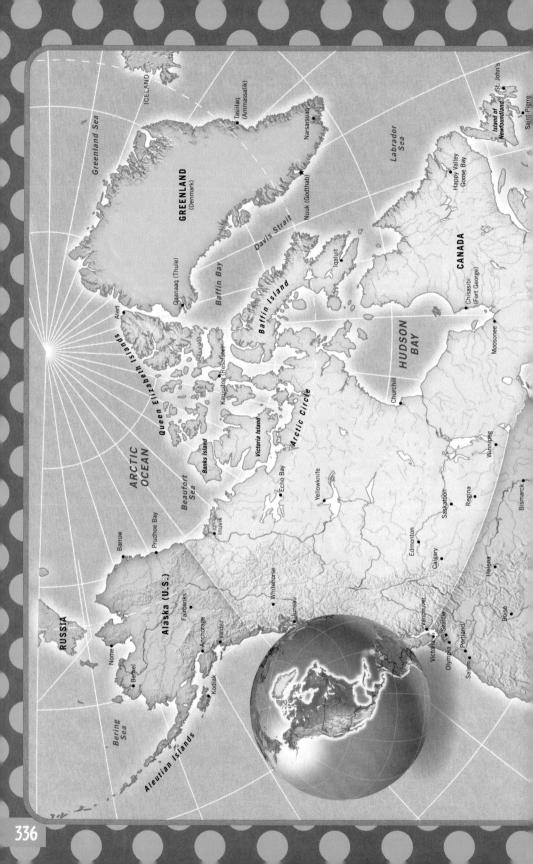

ICELAND

Greenland Sea

Tasiilaq
(Ammassalik)

Narsarsuaq

GREENLAND
(Denmark)

*Labrador
Sea*

Happy Valley
Goose Bay

*Island of
Newfoundland*

St. John's

Saint-Pierre

Qaanaaq (Thule)

Davis Strait

Nuuk (Godthab)

Iqaluit

CANADA

Alert

Baffin Bay

Chisasibi
(Fort George)

Queen Elizabeth Islands

Baffin Island

**HUDSON
BAY**

Moosonee

Kugaaruk (Resolute)

Churchill

**ARCTIC
OCEAN**

Winnipeg

Victoria Island

Arctic Circle

Banks Island

Echo Bay

Yellowknife

Saskatoon

Bismarck

Regina

*Beaufort
Sea*

Barrow

Prudhoe Bay

Edmonton

Helena

Inuvik

Calgary

RUSSIA

Nome

Alaska (U.S.)

Fairbanks

Whitehorse

Boise

Bethel

Anchorage

Valdez

Juneau

Vancouver

Seattle

Victoria

Olympia

Portland

Kodiak

Salem

*Bering
Sea*

Aleutian Islands

NORTH AMERICA AND CENTRAL AMERICA

UNITED STATES

ATLANTIC OCEAN

BERMUDA (U.K.)
★ Hamilton

BAHAMAS
Nassau ★
Freeport

TURKS AND CAICOS ISLANDS (U.K.)
Grand Turk ★

VIRGIN ISLANDS (U.S., U.K.)

SAINT MAARTEN/ SAINT MARTIN (Neth. Antilles)/(Guad.)

SAINT BARTHÉLEMY (Guad.)

ANGUILLA (U.K.)

ANTIGUA AND BARBUDA

DOMINICA

SAINT KITTS AND NEVIS
GUADELOUPE (Fr.)
MONTSERRAT (U.K.)
MARTINIQUE (Fr.)
SAINT LUCIA
BARBADOS
SAINT VINCENT AND THE GRENADINES
GRENADA

TRINIDAD AND TOBAGO

DOMINICAN REPUBLIC
PUERTO RICO (U.S.)
San Juan ★
Santiago ★
Santo Domingo ★

HAITI
Port-au-Prince ★

CUBA
Havana ★
Camagüey
Guantánamo
Montego Bay

JAMAICA
Kingston ★

CAYMAN ISLANDS (U.K.)
George Town ★

NETHERLANDS ANTILLES (Neth.)
ARUBA (Neth.)

CARIBBEAN SEA

VENEZUELA

GUYANA

COLOMBIA

Concord
Augusta
Boston
Albany
Providence
Hartford
New York
Buffalo
Harrisburg
Philadelphia
Cleveland
Pittsburgh
Dover
Baltimore
Washington, DC
Cincinnati
Norfolk
Frankfort
Richmond
Nashville
Raleigh
Columbia
Atlanta
Savannah
Montgomery
Tallahassee
Jacksonville
Charleston
Birmingham

Milwaukee
Detroit
Toledo
Chicago
Madison
Springfield
Indianapolis
Louisville
Saint Louis
Memphis
Jackson
Little Rock
Baton Rouge
New Orleans

Des Moines
Omaha
Lincoln
Topeka
Kansas City
Jefferson City

Denver
Santa Fe
Oklahoma City
Dallas
Austin
Houston
San Antonio

Phoenix
El Paso
Ciudad Juárez

Los Angeles
San Diego
Tijuana

Hermosillo

La Paz

Mazatlán

Puerto Vallarta

Guadalajara
León
Acapulco
Oaxaca
Puebla
Mexico City ★
Veracruz
Tampico
Monterrey

MEXICO

Mérida
Cancún

GULF OF MEXICO

Gulf of California

Tropic of Cancer

PACIFIC OCEAN

BELIZE
Belmopan ★
Belize City

GUATEMALA
Guatemala City ★

HONDURAS
Tegucigalpa ★

EL SALVADOR
San Salvador ★

NICARAGUA
Managua ★

COSTA RICA
San José ★

PANAMA
Panama City ★

Miami

Scale:
0 mi. 500 mi. 1,000 mi.
0 km 500 km 1,000 km

World

337

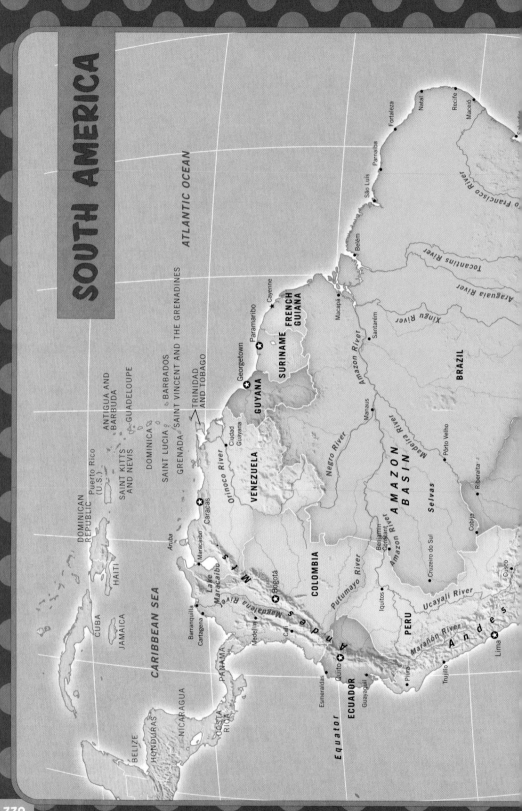

SOUTH AMERICA

ATLANTIC OCEAN

CARIBBEAN SEA

BELIZE
HONDURAS
NICARAGUA
COSTA RICA
PANAMA

CUBA
JAMAICA
HAITI
DOMINICAN REPUBLIC
Puerto Rico (U.S.)

ANTIGUA AND BARBUDA
GUADELOUPE
DOMINICA
SAINT KITTS AND NEVIS
SAINT LUCIA
BARBADOS
GRENADA
SAINT VINCENT AND THE GRENADINES
TRINIDAD AND TOBAGO

Aruba

Barranquilla
Cartagena
Maracaibo
Lake Maracaibo
Medellín
Cali
Bogotá ☆
Caracas ☆
Ciudad Guayana
Orinoco River

VENEZUELA
COLOMBIA

GUYANA
Georgetown ☆
Paramaribo ☆
SURINAME
FRENCH GUIANA
Cayenne ★

Negro River
Amazon River
Manaus
Macapá
Belém
Santarém
Xingu River
Tocantins River
Araguaia River
São Francisco River

Esmeraldas
Quito ☆
Guayaquil
ECUADOR
Equator

Putumayo River
Iquitos
Piura
Trujillo
PERU
Lima ☆
Cusco
Ucayali River
Marañón River
Madeira River
Benjamin Constant
Amazon River
Cruzeiro do Sul
Pôrto Velho
Riberalta
Cobija

AMAZON BASIN
Selvas

BRAZIL

Andes

Natal
Recife
Maceió
Fortaleza
Parnaíba
São Luís

338

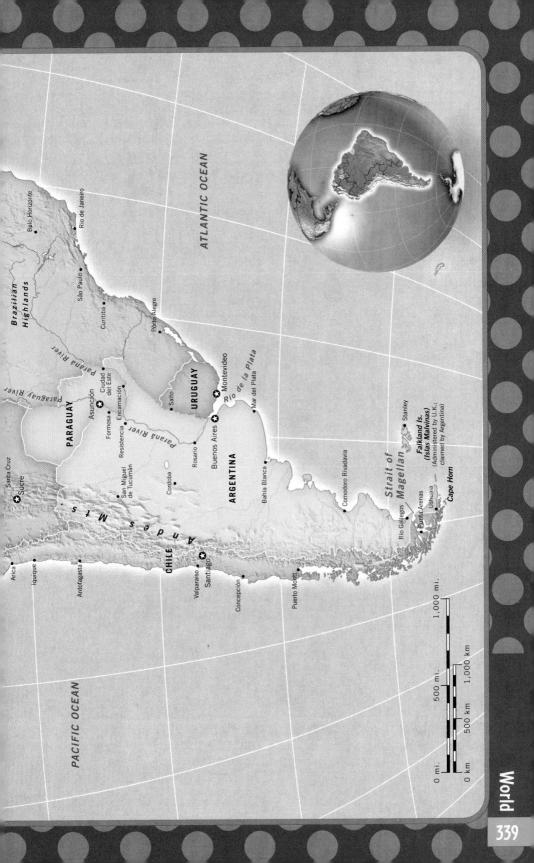

PACIFIC OCEAN

ATLANTIC OCEAN

Brazilian
Highlands

Belo Horizonte
Rio de Janeiro
São Paulo
Curitiba
Pôrto Alegre

Paraná River

PARAGUAY
Asunción
Ciudad del Este
Encarnación
Formosa
Salto
Resistencia
Paraná River
Paraguay River

Santa Cruz
Sucre

URUGUAY
Montevideo
Río de la Plata
Mar del Plata
Rosario
Buenos Aires

San Miguel
de Tucumán
Córdoba

ARGENTINA

Bahía Blanca

Andes Mts.

Arica
Iquique
Antofagasta

CHILE

Valparaíso
Santiago
Concepción

Puerto Montt

Comodoro Rivadavia

Strait of
Magellan

Río Gallegos
Punta Arenas
Ushuaia

Stanley

Falkland Is.
(Islas Malvinas)
(Administered by U.K.;
claimed by Argentina)

Cape Horn

0 mi.   500 mi.   1,000 mi.

0 km   500 km   1,000 km

0 km   500 km   1,000 km

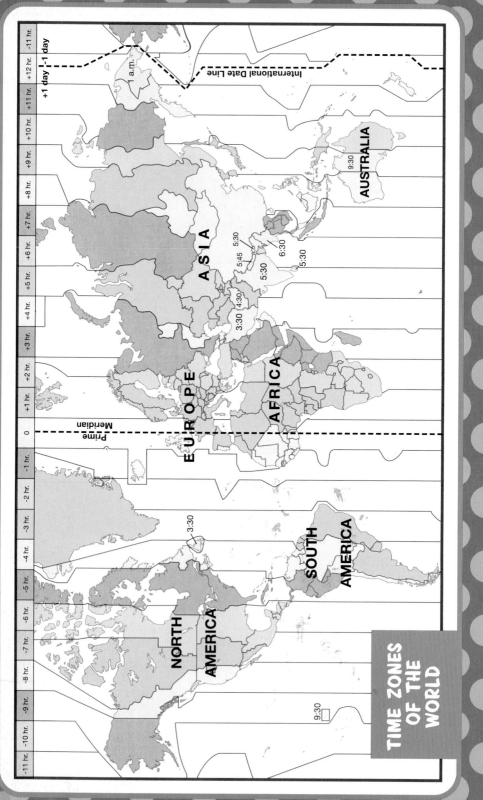

TIME ZONES
OF THE
WORLD

World Population Milestones

1 billion in 1804	
2 billion in 1927	**123 years later**
3 billion in 1960	**33 years later**
4 billion in 1974	**14 years later**
5 billion in 1987	**13 years later**
6 billion in 1999	**12 years later**

Source: United Nations Population Division

Did You Know?

Benjamin Franklin was the first U.S. diplomat. He was called upon in 1776 to help get France to support American independence. In 1778 he became ambassador to France. In 1783, Franklin, along with John Jay and John Adams, negotiated a peace treaty with Great Britain called the Treaty of Paris.

Facts to Consider

- Only 82 countries, representing 57% of the world's population, are fully democratic.
- Just 125 countries, with 62% of the world's population, have a free or partly free press.
- Of the world's estimated 854 million adults who can't read, 544 million are women.

TFK
Puzzles & Games — Alpha-Bout

In Spain and Mexico, bullfighting is a popular sport. The person who fights the bull is called a matador. What's a matador's favorite sport? Unscramble each word below, then read down the shaded column for the punchline. Ole!

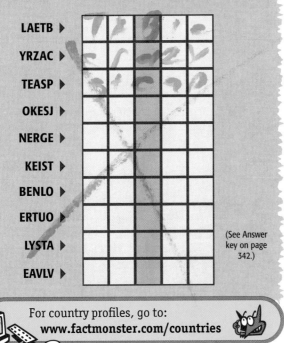

LAETB ▶

YRZAC ▶

TEASP ▶

OKESJ ▶

NERGE ▶

KEIST ▶

BENLO ▶

ERTUO ▶

LYSTA ▶

EAVLV ▶

(See Answer key on page 342.)

TFK
Mystery Person

CLUE 1: I am a lawyer, a politician and a human-rights activist. I was born in Ireland in 1944.

CLUE 2: In 1990, I became the first woman President of Ireland. At the time, I was one of only three female heads of state in the world.

CLUE 3: I served as the President of Ireland for almost seven years. I stepped down to work for the United Nations.

WHO AM I?

(See Answer Key that begins on page 342.)

For country profiles, go to:
www.factmonster.com/countries

World

ANIMALS

Page 29 **Mystery Person:** John J. Audubon

ART

Page 33 **Mystery Person:** Frida Kahlo

BOOKS

Page 38 Anagram Anxiety: A. *Treasure Island*, B. *Little Women*, C. *Robinson Crusoe*, D. *Stuart Little*, E. *Huckleberry Finn*

Page 39 **Mystery Person:** Shel Silverstein

BUILDINGS & LANDMARKS

Page 43 High, There: B. Eiffel Tower (1,056 feet, counting the antenna), D. St. Louis Gateway Arch (630 feet), F. Washington Monument (555 feet), C. Great Pyramid of Cheops (450 feet), A. Clock Tower of Big Ben (316 feet), E. Statue of Liberty (305 feet, including pedestal)

CALENDARS & HOLIDAYS

Page 48 A Kooky Classroom:

Page 51 **Mystery Person:** Virginia O'Hanlon

COMPUTERS & THE INTERNET

Page 57 Quality Control: 1. C, 2. B, 3. D, 4. C
Page 57 **Mystery Person:** Charles Babbage

DINOSAURS

Page 61 **Mystery Persons:** Jack Horner

ENVIRONMENT & ENERGY

Page 71 **Mystery Person:** Wangari Maathai

FOOD

Page 75 **Mystery Person:** Emeril Lagasse

GEOGRAPHY

Page 83 The Magnificent Seven: 1. Europe, 2. Africa, 3. Australia, 4. Asia, 5. South America, 6. Antarctica, 7. North America

Page 83 **Mystery Person:** Thor Heyerdahl

GOVERNMENT

Page 94 **Mystery Person:** Frances Perkins
Page 95 Supreme Challenge:

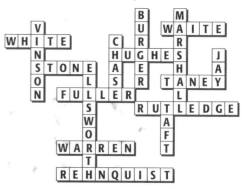

Page 95 Presidential Succession: Carlos Gutierrez, Secretary of Commerce; Elaine Chao, Secretary of Labor

HEALTH & BODY

Page 105 **Mystery Person:** Dorothea Dix

HISTORY

Page 107 Who Said That?: 1. Martin Luther King, 2. Michael Jordan, 3. Ella Fitzgerald, 4. Langston Hughes, 5. Shirley Chisholm

HOMEWORK HELPER
Page 137 **Mystery Person:** Mary Titcomb

INVENTIONS & TECHNOLOGY
Page 143 **Mystery Person:** Garrett Morgan

KIDS OF THE WORLD
Page 147 **Mystery Person:** Flavia Bujor

LANGUAGE
Page 151 Making Change: HARD, LARD, LORD, LORE, SORE, SORT, SOFT
Page 153 **Mystery Person:** J.R.R. Tolkien

MATH
Page 162 Roman Numerals: King Louis the Fourteenth; the building's year is 1871.
Page 165 Sum It Up:

Page 165 **Mystery Person:** Lewis Carroll

MONEY
Page 175 Showing Their Age: B. Michelin Man (1898), A. Morton Salt Girl (1914), D. Jolly Green Giant (1926), E. Miss Chiquita (1944), C. Poppin' Fresh (1965)

MOVIES & TV
Page 179 Lines to Remember: 1. E, 2. F, 3. J, 4. I, 5. H, 6. A, 7. B, 8. D, 9. G, 10. C
Page 181 **Mystery Person:** Sidney Poitier

MUSIC
Page 185 **Mystery Person:** Louis Armstrong

PRESIDENTS
Page 199 **Mystery Person:** Harry S. Truman

SPACE
Page 223 Space Race: 1. b, 2. a, 3. b, 4. b, 5. b, 6. a, 7. b, 8. b, 9. a, 10 b
Page 223 **Mystery Person:** Galileo Galilei

SPORTS
Page 237 **Mystery Person:** Satchel Paige

TRANSPORTATION
Page 241 **Mystery Person:** Rudolf Diesel

UNITED STATES
Page 246 Road Trip:

VOLUNTEERING
Page 283 **Mystery Person:** Jimmy Carter

WEATHER
Page 289 **Mystery Person:** Cleveland Abbe

WORLD
Page 341 Alpha-Bout: Basketbull
Page 341 **Mystery Person:** Mary Robinson

INNER FRONT COVER
On the Grid-dle: Meet you at the corner

INNER BACK COVER
State the facts: North Dakota

military
  branches of, 171
  country budgets, 171
  honoring, 170
Milky Way, 215
Milosevic, Slobodan, 113
minerals, 213
Minerva (Athena), 187
Mineta, Norman, 87
Minnesota, 265
Minotaur, 189
Miranda v. Arizona, 88
mission blue butterfly, 20
Mississippi, 265
Missouri, 266
Moldova, 312
mollusks, 23
moment magnitude, 78
Monaco, 312
Monet, Claude, 32
money, 172–175
  corporate revenues, 172
  currency, 174, 175
  jobs for kids, 175
  peer-to-peer marketing, 173
  richest Americans, 175
Mongolia, 312
monkeys, capuchin, 24
Monopoly (game), 268
Monroe, James, 114, 191
Monroe Doctrine, 114, 191
Monsters, Inc., 178
Montagnier, Luc, 208
Montana, 266
months, 50
mood words, 121
Moon, 215, 222, 277
Morman Church, 200
Morocco, 312
Morris, Desmond, 30
Morton, Levi P., 194
Moseley, Henry, 210
Moses, 108
mosquitoes, 25
Mother's Day, 48, 277
motorcycles, 239, 291
mountain biome, 71
Mount Everest, 81
Mount Fai Shan, 202
Mount Rushmore, 274
Mount Saint Helens, 77
Mount Washington, 2681
movies, 176–179
  Academy Awards, 179
  costs to make, 178
  DVDs, 180
  memorable lines, 179

most-rented videos, 180
top animated films, 178
top kids' movies, 179
Walt Disney, 177
Mozambique, 313
Muhammad, 109, 203
Muharram, 201
multiplication table, 160
muscle cells, 102
muscles, 102
muscular system, 104
music, 182–185
  album sales, 184
  dancers, 185
  instruments, 184
  songs most downloaded, 182
  songs most played on radio,
    182
  types of, 183
Muslims. *See* Islam
Myanmar (Burma), 313
MyPyramid, 98
mythology, 186–189
  Aztec, 188
  Egyptian, 188
  Greek, 186–187, 189
  Norse, 188
  Roman, 186–187
myths, 38

N

Nagasaki, 112
names
  common first names, 246
  of hurricanes, 286
  of pets, 28
Namibia, 313
narrative essays, 119
NASA, 222, 275
NASCAR, 236
National Archives, 279
National Association for the
    Advancement of Colored
    People (NAACP), 112
National Basketball Association
    (NBA), 227
National Football League (NFL),
    228
national forests, 69
National Hockey League, 231
national parks, 248–249
National Park Service Jr. Ranger
    Programs, 283
nations
  listing, 293–325
  most and least livable, 292

most popular U.S.
    destinations, 292
Nauru, 313
Navy, U.S., 171
Nebraska, 267
Nepal, 291, 313
Nephthys, 188
Neptune (planet), 218
Neptune (Poseidon), 187
nerve cells, 102
nerves, 105
nervous system, 105
Netherlands, 292, 313
    North Sea protection works, 43
neutrons, 210
Nevada, 267
Nevelson, Louise, 32
Newbery Medal, 39
New Deal, 116
New England Patriots, 228
New Hampshire, 268
New Jersey, 268
New Mexico, 269
New Orleans, 12, 262
Newton, Sir Isaac, 155
New Year's Day, 46
New York, 269
New York City, 269
New Zealand, 314
Nextel Cup Series, 236
NFL Pro Bowl, 228
Nicaragua, 314
Nichols, Wallace J., 19
Nicholson, Jim, 87
Niger, 314
Nigeria, 314
Nile River, 81, 289
Nixon, Richard M., 117, 170, 196
nonfiction, 38
Norse gods and goddesses, 188
North America, 80
    map, 326
North Atlantic Treaty Organization
    (NATO), 112
North Carolina, 270
North Dakota, 270
northern spotted owl, 20
North Pole, 83, 112
North Sea protection works, 43
Norton, Gale, 87
Norway, 292, 314
note taking, 130
nuclear energy, 64
nuclear-power-plant accidents, 67
numbers
  cardinal, 161
  decimals, 158, 159

Project Backpack, 281
Protestantism, 111, 200, 202
protons, 210
pseudonyms, 153
publishing process, 36
Pueblo culture, 110
Puerto Rico, Commonwealth of, 279
Purim, 201
pyramids, Egypt, 42
Pythagoras, 155

Q
Qatar, 316

R
Ra, 188
rabbits, 29
raccoon, 70
Race to Save the Lord God Bird, The (Hoose), 39
racial segregation, 106–107, 116
racing, 236
raffia palm, 212
Rahman, Abd al-, 109
railroad
    trains, 239, 241
    transcontinental, 115, 275
rain, artificial, 268
Rainbow Bridge, 275
rainfall, 289
rain forest, 71
Raksha Bandhan, 49
Ramadan, 201
rap music, 183
Rapunzel Unbraided, 177
Raschka, Chris, 39
reading, by boys and girls, 37
Reagan, Ronald W., 197, 199
recycling, 68, 69
red blood cells, 102
Red Cross, donations to, 282
red-winged blackbird, 23
Reid, Harry, 86
reincarnation, 203
religion, 200–203
    holidays, 201
    separation of church and state, 201
    in the U.S., 200
    in the world, 200, 202–203
Rembrandt, 32
Renaissance, 110
renewable energy resources, 63, 64

Renoir, Pierre-August, 33
reptiles, 22
    as pets, 28
Republican Party, 92
research
    on Internet, 55
    for oral reports, 125
    for research papers, 128
research papers, 128–129
respiratory system, 105
revolutions, of planets, 215
Rhode Island, 273
Rhode Island Red chickens, 273
Rice, Condoleezza, 87
Richter scale, 78
Riders for Health, 291
Ring of Fire, 77
roadside attractions, 251
Roberts, John, 11, 88
robots, 138, 142
Rockefeller, Nelson A., 196
rock music, 183
rocks, 213, 265
Roentgen, Wilhelm, 208
Roe River, 81
roller skates, 139
Roman Catholic Church, 110, 202
Roman Empire, 109
Romania, 316
Roman mythology, 186–187
Roman numerals, 162
Rome
    Colosseum, 44
    history, 109
    Pantheon, 44
    Vatican, 45
Roosevelt, Franklin D., 112, 116, 195
Roosevelt, Theodore, 194
Rosh Hashanah, 201
rotifers, 23
rounding numbers, 158
roundworms, 23
Routh, Brandon, 17
Rowling, J.K., 35
Rubens, Peter Paul, 33
Rumsfeld, Donald, 87
Rurik, Prince, 109
Russia, 316
    children in, 145
    history, 109, 113
    space program, 112, 222
Russian Revolution, 112
Russo-Japanese War, 112
Rutkowski, Howard, 30
Rwanda, 317
Ryder Cup, 232

S
Sachar, Louis, 15,
Sachs, Sonia Ehrlich, 291
Sacramento Monarchs, 227
Sacred Mosque, 202
safety, online, 52, 53
Sahara desert, 81
Saint Kitts and Nevis, 317
Saint Lucia, 317
St. Patrick, 109
St. Patrick's Day, 47
Saint Vincent and the Grenadines, 317
Samoa, 317
San Antonio Spurs, 227
San Diego Zoo, 26
sandwiches, 75
San Francisco 49ers, 228
San Marino, 317
São Tomé and Príncipe, 318
Saturn (planet), 13, 217
Saudi Arabia, 318
Scalia, Antonin, 8
Shavuot, 201
school lunches, 73
Schumacher, Michael, 236
Schwa Was Here, The (Shusterman), 39
science, 204–213
    cladistics, 209
    cloning, 205
    discoveries, 208
    elements, 210–211
    loopy liquids, 209
    prehistoric periods, 206
    questions and answers, 207
    rocks, 213
science fiction, 38
Scieszka, Jon, 37
seahorses, 25
searching, Internet, 55
Sears Tower, 40, 41, 260
seasons, 51
sea turtles, 19, 20
secondary sources, 129
Secretariat, United Nations, 325
Security Council, United Nations, 325
sedimentary rocks, 213
seeing-eye dogs, 24
segmented worms, 23
Seismosaurus, 59, 61
Senate, 86
Senegal, 318

CREDITS

Courtesy Purdue University. 140: (clockwise from top left) Corbis/PunchStock; Stockdisc/PunchStock; Designpics.com/PunchStock;·Bettmann/Corbis. 141: Photodisc/PunchStock; Brand X Pictures/PunchStock (2). 142: (clockwise from top left) ©2000 Peter Menzel/ Robosapiens/www.menzelphoto.com; Erika Sugita/Reuters/Corbis; Ralph Crane/Time-Life Pictures/Getty Images. 143: AP Photo; Big Cheese Photo/PunchStock.

Kids of the World: 144: Royalty-Free/Hollingsworth Studios/PunchStock. 145: Paul A. Souders/Corbis; Royalty-Free/Hollingsworth Studios/PunchStock. 146: Royalty-Free/Hollingsworth Studios/PunchStock; Helen King/Corbis. 147: Ritu Upadhyay; Ed Bailey/AP Photo.

Language: 149: Courtesy Merriam-Webster, Inc. 151: Mark Wilson/Getty Images/NewsCom. 152: Photo Disc. 153: Hulton-Getty Archive/NewsCom.

Math: 162: Tibor Bognar/Corbis; Angelo Hornak/Corbis. 165: Bettmann/Corbis.

Military & War: 166: North Wind Picture Archives. 167: The Granger Collection; North Wind Picture Archives. 168: Bettmann/Corbis. 169: Time-Life Pictures/Getty Images; Marco Di Lauro/Getty Images/NewsCom. 170: (top to bottom) Bettmann/Corbis; Shawn Thew/AFP/NewsCom; Mansell/Time-Life Pictures/Getty Images; Royalty-Free/Corbis. 171: ©Purestock/SuperStock/NewsCom; Adam Butler/AP Photo; Catherine Karnow/Corbis.

Money: 173: Dan Bality/Reuters. 174: The U.S. Mint; istock (3). 175: Morton Salt; Michelin Group; Chiquita Brands; General Mills (2).

Mythology: 186: The Granger Collection. 187: Mary Evans Picture Library (3); The Granger Collection (Artemis). 188: The Granger Collection (2). 189: The Granger Collection; Mary Evans Picture Library (2).

Movies & TV: 177: (clockwise from top left) Walt Disney Co.; ©Disney Enterprises, Inc. (4). Walt Disney Productions. 178: KRT/NewsCom; Sony Pictures/Zuma Press/NewsCom; Bryan Smith/Zuma Press/NewsCom. 179: Photofest (2). 180: KRT/NewsCom; Touchstone Pictures/Zuma Press/NewsCom. 181: Fox/AdMedia/NewsCom; Lisa O'Connor/Zuma Press/NewsCom; Douglas Kirkland/Corbis.

Music: 183: Trevor Kent/INFGoff.com/NewsCom; Kristin Callahan/Ace Pictures/NewsCom. 184: Photodisc (4). 185: (clockwise from top) AP Photo; Kathy Willins/AP Photo; Toronto Star/Zuma Press/NewsCom; Tsuni/Gamma Presse/NewsCom.

Presidents: 190: Scripps Howard Photo Service/NewsCom. 191: Scripps Howard Photo Service/NewsCom; Picture History/NewsCom; Picture History/NewsCom; Scripps Howard Photo Service/NewsCom; Picture History/Picture History/NewsCom. 192: Picture History/NewsCom (6). 193: Picture History/NewsCom; Anthony Berger/Picture History/NewsCom; Picture History NewsCom (4). 194: Picture History/NewsCom (6). 195: Picture History/NewsCom (5); Ewing Galloway/Index Stock Imagery/NewsCom. 196: Toronto Star/Zuma Press/NewsCom; Library of Congress; JFK Collection/Zuma Press/NewsCom; Ewing Galloway/Index Stock Imagery/NewsCom; Al Stephenson/Zuma Press/NewsCom; Jerzy Dabrowski/Zuma Press/NewsCom. 197: Scripps Howard Photo Service/NewsCom; Courtesy Reagan Library/Zuma Press/NewsCom; White House/Photographer Showcase/NewsCom; Ron Sachs/Photographer Showcase/NewsCom; Eric Draper/Photographer Showcase/NewsCom. 198: National Gallery of Art, Washington, D.C./Erich Lessing/Art Resource, N.Y. 199: Toronto Star/Zuma Press/NewsCom.

Religion: 201: Harry Cubluck/AP Photo; Joe Reedle/Getty Images. 202: (background) Shigemi Numazawa/Atlas Photo Bank/Photo Researchers, Inc.; David H. Wells/Corbis; Stockdisc/PunchStock; Photodisc/PunchStock. 203: Kazuyoshi Nomachi/Corbis; Paul Seheult/Eye Ubiquitous/Corbis; Image Source/PunchStock.

Science: 205: Ann Young-Joon/AP Photo; Reuters; Texas A & M University/Reuters. 207: Paul A. Souders/Corbis; Dynamic Graphics/PunchStock. 208: The Granger Collection (2); Brown Brothers. 212: Frans Lanting/Minden Pictures; Patti Murray/Earth Scenes. 213: (clockwise from left) C.C. Lockwood/Earth Scenes; Breck

P. Kent/Earth Scenes; Lowell Georgia/Corbis; Kaj R. Svensson/Photo Researchers, Inc.

Space: 215: (clockwise from top) Illustration by Rick Nease; Shigemi Numazawa/Atlas Photo Bank/Photo Researchers, Inc.; Stephen & Donna O'Meara/Photo Researchers, Inc. 216: (background) Chris Bjornberg/Photo Researchers, Inc.; Detlev Van Ravenswaay/Photo Researchers, Inc. (2); Mike Agliolo/Photo Researchers, Inc. 217: Science Source/Photo Researchers, Inc; Chris Bjornberg/Photo Researchers, Inc. (2). 218: Detlev Van Ravenswaay/Photo Researchers, Inc. (2); STScl/NASA/Photo Researchers, Inc. 219: Reuters; AFP/Getty Images. 222: (clockwise from top left) AP Photo; NASA TV/AP Photo; NASA/AP Photo; WGBH-TV/AP Photo; Chris Butler/Photo Researchers, Inc. 223: Mark Garlick/Photo Researcher, Inc.; The Granger Collection; John Chumack/Photo Researchers, Inc.

Sports: 225: Dennis Macdonald/PhotoEdit; Robert A. Davis. 226: (clockwise from top left) Mark J. Terrill/AP Photo; James A. Finley/AP Photo; Carolyn Kaster/AP Photo; Ray Stubblebine/Corbis. 227: David Zalubowski/AP Photo; Rich Pedroncelli/AP Photo; Paul Vathis/AP Photo. 228: (from top) AP Photo; Elise Amendola/AP Photo; Focus on Sports/Getty Images. 229: (from top) AJ Mast/icon SMI/NewsCom; Harry Cabluck/AP Photo; Kvork Djansezian/AP Photo. 230: Thomas Kienzie/AP Photo. 231: George Bridges/KRT/NewsCom; AP Photo. 232: Peter Cosgrove/AP Photo; Peter Dejong/AP Photo. 233: (clockwise from top) George Tiedemann/Zuma Press/NewsCom; David Gray/Reuters/NewsCom; Joe Mahoney/Scripps Howard Photo Source/NewsCom. 234: Susan Walsh/AP Photo; Rob Tringall/Sports Chrome/NewsCom. 235: Kevork Djansezian/AP Photo; Mark Baker/AP Photo. 236: (clockwise from top left) Sam Sharp/Corbis; Kendall Newberry/AP Photo; Brent Smith/Reuters/Corbis. 237: (clockwise from left) David Gray/Reuters/NewsCom; Phil Coale/AP Photo; AP Photo.

Transportation: 238: Jeff Kowalsky/AFP/NewsCom; Carl De Souza/AFP/NewsCom. 239: Kieran Doherty/Reuters/NewsCom. 240: AP Photo; Kevin Fleming/Corbis; Topical Press Agency/Getty Hulton Archive/NewsCom. 241: Issei Kato/Reuters/NewsCom; Topical Press Agency/Getty Images/NewsCom; Culver Pictures; David Dees.

United States: 243: (fireworks) Keith Manis/Fortune; Guy Calaf/World Picture News/Life Magazine (5). 244: The Granger Collection; Photodisc/PunchStock. 247: Peter Turnley/Corbis; Keith Levit/Index Stock Imagery/NewsCom. 248: (clockwise from top left) Stephen Frink/Corbis; National Park Service; Frans Lanting/Corbis. 249: (from top) Kurt Markus/LIFE Magazine; Picture History/NewsCom; Index Stock Imagery/NewsCom. 250: Patty DiRienzo/Silver Image; PR News Foto/NewsCom. 251: RoadsideAmerica.com; Kevin Fleming/Corbis; William Thomas Cain/Getty/NewsCom. 279: Wolfgang Kaehler/Corbis; Nik Wheeler/Corbis.

Volunteering: 281: Jason Redmond/Ventura County Star; Danuta Otfinowski; Damon Higgins/Palm Beach Post/Zuma Press. 282: Stan Honda/AFP/Getty Images. 283: Arthur Grace/Zuma Press/NewsCom.

Weather: 285: Joseph Sohm/Corbis; Natalie Behring/Onasia.com; Chart by Trevor Johnston. 286: Photodisc/PunchStock; Andy Newman/AP Photo. 287: Corbis/PunchStock; Comstock Image/PunchStock. 287: UpperCut Images/PunchStock. 289: (clockwise from top left) Upper Cut Images/PunchStock; Comstock Images/PunchStock; no credit; Bettmann/Corbis; The Granger Collection.

World: 291: Graham Trott; Brooks Kraft/Corbis; Courtesy Sonia Ehrlich Sachs, Earth Institute at Columbia University, N.Y.C.; Andrew Kaufman/Contact; Peter Van Agtmael/Polaris. 341: Jean-Marc/Reuters.

ILLUSTRATIONS Timothy Barnes: 225. Daryll Collins: 1, 8, 18, 37, 46, 54, 66, 72, 84, 100, 118, 120, 130, 134, 148, 155, 176, 179, 186, 187, 204, 212, 224, 230, 239, 242, 245, 288, 290. Felipe Galindo: 36, 60, 68. Mike Gorman: 24, 33, 34, 38, 43, 50, 57, 58, 62, 74, 76, 94, 96, 101, 103, 122, 123, 150, 154, 172, 180, 200, 210, 213, 214, 280, 282. Brad Holland: 102. David Klug: 173. Dean Macadam: 53, 101. Jane Sanders: 68 (2), 78 (map). Michael Sloan: 48. Steve Wacksman: 2, 30, 40, 52, 72, 91, 99, 106, 119 (icons through 137), 138, 143, 144, 151, 158, 166, 166 (icon through 169), 175, 181, 182, 190, 206, 209, 220-221, 238, 246, 284, 292.

Credits

359

TIME FOR KIDS online

Check out timeforkids.com, your online news, homework helper and exploration destination!

Look for news, polls, interactive features and games.

Go Around the World with Time For Kids and learn about different cultures, languages and more.

Search the best kid-recommended websites to help you with your homework.

Use our step-by-step guides, idea organizers, checklists and more to help you write winning nonfiction papers.

Millions of kids each week go to FactMonster.com for tons of facts, puzzles and games, cool featur and homework help!

Get the facts on animals, the planets, presidents, movies and more.

Tips and ideas for creating a spectacular science project.

How smart are you? Take a quiz on flags, ice cream, Harry Potter or Lemony Snicket.

Your opinion counts! Vote in our fun polls and se what other kids think.